unquiet dreams

mark del franco

ACE BOOKS, NEW YORK

THE BERKLEY PUBLISHING GROUP
Published by the Penguin Group
Penguin Group (USA) Inc.
375 Hudson Street, New York, New York 10014, USA
Penguin Group (Canada), 90 Eglinton Avenue East, Suite 700, Toronto, Ontario M4P 2Y3, Canada
(a division of Pearson Penguin Canada Inc.)
Penguin Books Ltd., 80 Strand, London WC2R 0RL, England
Penguin Group Ireland, 25 St. Stephen's Green, Dublin 2, Ireland (a division of Penguin Books Ltd.)
Penguin Group (Australia), 250 Camberwell Road, Camberwell, Victoria 3124, Australia
(a division of Pearson Australia Group Pty. Ltd.)
Penguin Books India Pvt. Ltd., 11 Community Centre, Panchsheel Park, New Delhi—110 017, India
Penguin Group (NZ), 67 Apollo Drive, Rosedale, North Shore 0632, New Zealand
(a division of Pearson New Zealand Ltd.)
Penguin Books (South Africa) (Pty.) Ltd., 24 Sturdee Avenue, Rosebank, Johannesburg 2196,
South Africa

Penguin Books Ltd., Registered Offices: 80 Strand, London WC2R 0RL, England

This is a work of fiction. Names, characters, places, and incidents either are the product of the author's imagination or are used fictitiously, and any resemblance to actual persons, living or dead, business establishments, events, or locales is entirely coincidental. The publisher does not have any control over and does not assume any responsibility for author or third-party websites or their content.

UNQUIET DREAMS

An Ace Book / published by arrangement with the author

PRINTING HISTORY
Ace mass-market edition / February 2008

Copyright © 2008 by Mark Del Franco.
Cover art by Jaime DeJesus.
Cover design by Judith Lagerman.
Interior text design by Tiffany Estreicher.

ISBN: 978-0-441-01569-6

ACE
Ace Books are published by The Berkley Publishing Group,
a division of Penguin Group (USA) Inc.,
375 Hudson Street, New York, New York 10014.
ACE and the "A" design are trademarks belonging to Penguin Group (USA) Inc.

PRINTED IN THE UNITED STATES OF AMERICA

10 9 8 7 6 5 4 3 2 1

To my sister Michele, who is brave and strong.
And to my partner, Jack Custy, who isn't fazed anymore
when I ask where my guillotine is.

acknowledgments

Many culprits contributed their time, energy, and ideas to make this book the best it can be. Front and center are Anne Sowards, my editor, whose enthusiasm and insight know no bounds; my kickin' agent, Rachel Vater, who knows her stuff and gives excellent feedback and support; Cameron Dufty, Ace editorial assistant, who keeps the wheels turning; Sara and Bob Schwager, copyeditors extraordinaire, who have to deal with strange new words and the hyphens that love them (or not); and, of course, all the folks at Ace Books.

Publishing my first novel has given me the pleasure of meeting many new people, notably Melissa Marr and Jeaniene Frost, sage advisors and wicked friends, and the friends and colleagues from the LiveJournal online community of Fangs_Fur_Fey. It's been inspiring seeing their works and getting to know them as well as all the readers who took the time to come to a signing, drop a note, write a review, and pass the word. Many, many thanks to all of you.

Big thanks to my sisters and parents, who are secretly publicity machines in their spare time.

Special thanks to Kelley Horton for her emergency photography and friendship with that guy who used to work down the hall.

And lastly but not leastly, thanks to Francine Woodbury,

who had the pleasure of telling me when the manuscript went Horribly, Horribly Wrong, prompting me to revise it in record time. This book literally would not exist if not for her astute, yet evil, eye.

And whispering in their ears
Give them unquiet dreams

—W. B. Yeats

1

No good phone calls come at seven o'clock in the morning. Strike that. No good phone calls from Detective Leonard Murdock come at seven o'clock in the morning. Actually, strike that, too. No good phone calls from Detective Leonard Murdock come at seven o'clock in the morning unless you count the fact that it means I might have a paying job. Of course, it also means someone is dead, too, but that's where the "no good" part comes in.

That's how I make my living now. Waiting for the phone to ring. Hoping a crime has been committed. Ideally, one that Murdock needs a little fey expertise on. Some people make the mistake of thinking I used to be a high-powered druid working the crime unit for the Fey Guild. The only "used-to-be" part of that is working for the Guild. I'm still Connor Grey, druid. Just because I've lost most of my abilities doesn't mean I am not what I am. To be fey, to be a member of a species that can manipulate what is superstitiously called magic, is not just a job description. It's a state of being.

And my current state of being was in the backseat of a

cab wishing I had a cup of coffee. Murdock had given me an address in the deep end of the Weird. The Weird is not the nicest neighborhood in Boston. It's certainly not the safest. But it's where the fey live when they have nowhere else to go. There's a comfort in that, a community of sorts, that out-siders don't understand. Especially when so many people end up dead here.

The cab pulled off Old Northern Avenue onto a narrow lane that ran between two burnt-out warehouses. A block away, the lane ended at a desolate field with a small group of people wandering about, which, given the early hour, could only be my destination. I paid the driver, got out, and shiv-ered. It was cold—too cold for early October and much colder than when I got in the cab just a few blocks away. I looked up at the sky and sensed more than saw a faint white haze in the air that was by no means natural.

The early morning sun cast a surreal light, bleaching col-ors like a faded photograph. At the curb, a police car with its blue lights flashing enhanced the effect with a silvery sheen. Across the field from where I stood, the officers' uniforms looked almost black and the medical examiner's coat a stark white. I recognized Murdock immediately by his long trench coat even though it appeared pale beige instead of its normal camel color. The field looked ashen.

I stepped across the remains of a sidewalk and walked to-ward them. It had rained like hell the night before, and while the field should have been muddy, it was now an uneven sur-face of frozen ruts. I made my way to the center of activity, a body in dark clothing lying on the ground.

Murdock didn't see me until I was standing next to him. "Bit nippy," I said.

He didn't startle, but smiled slightly as he cupped his hands over his mouth and blew into them. "That's part of why I called you."

I nodded. As a human, Murdock has no fey abilities, but he's worked the Weird long enough to know when some-thing is, well, weird. He's good at what he does, and part of what makes him good is that he knows when to ask for help. It's a lesson I'm still learning.

I bunched my own cold hands into the pockets of my leather jacket. It didn't occur to me when I left the apartment that I'd need gloves in early October. "What do you have?"

He gestured at the obvious body. "Tell me why I called you."

I stepped away from him, then between another officer and the medical examiner. On first glance at the body, my chest tightened. "Dammit, Murdock, you could have warned me it was a kid."

"Late teens, we're guessing. Haven't checked for ID yet," he said.

The cop standing next to me nodded without saying anything. When you're with law enforcement, you see a lot of things you'd rather not. Dead kids are the worst. The younger they are, the worse it is. Even if this guy—this boy—turned out to be eighteen or nineteen, he still had a helluva lot of life to miss out on. And his parents, if he had them, were still going to be heartbroken. Telling the parents is the second-worst thing about it.

I put that aside for now and took in the scene. Lying faceup was a white male with dark brown hair, obviously young, with a pained grimace locked on his face. His head angled up too sharply to one side, which probably meant a broken neck. His arms and legs splayed out haphazardly. One foot had an orange Nike sneaker, the other just a plain white sock. He wore two hooded black sweatshirts, generic-looking jeans, and a bright yellow bandana on his head. The bandana was wrapped so that knotted ends stuck out from his temples. At a guess, I'd go with gangbanger. So far, unremarkable.

I swept my eyes up and down the body again. His clothes were frozen. That meant he was out in the rain long enough to get soaked before the air got cold enough to freeze him. And the mud around him. He was embedded in it, sunk a good two or three inches into the ground.

I scanned the periphery of the body and gazed outward in concentric circles as I turned. "He ended up here before the mud froze, but there're no footprints and no indication he was dragged. No sign of a struggle."

"Bingo," said Murdock. "Tossed or dropped?"

Now I saw why Murdock had called me. The kid was too far from the edge of the field to have landed in this spot on his own. Either someone with tremendous strength had tossed him in or someone who could fly had dropped him. A fairy dropping him was an obvious possibility. I estimated the shortest distance to the street at fifty feet, well within the range of strength for a troll or even a dwarf. It could have also been an Unseelie, one of the shunned fey that don't fit easily into any species category. We didn't see a lot of those in Boston, but it was too early to rule out them out.

"I'd go for dropped," I said. "There's no slippage in the mud. He looks like he came straight down. I suppose if he were flung the right way from the street, he wouldn't slide, but dropped is the easier explanation."

Murdock nodded as though he had come to the same conclusion. "Naturally, that leads to 'why?' "

I shrugged. "I don't know, Murdock. Look at the gear he's wearing. I think you're looking at a gang fight."

He tilted his head to the side as he continued looking at the body. "No physical signs of struggle, no visible bruises. We might find something when he's stripped, but why would a fey bother with him?"

"Fey gangs are out there, too, Murdock. The xenos figure out how to hold their own against the fey ones. You know that," I said. "And the human ones have been known to hire freelancers for a little revenge. I'd check that angle."

He didn't look convinced, but that's Murdock's nature. He wouldn't be happy until he nailed it down precisely. I know he has more than a few files of unsolved cases that he uses for bedtime reading. He's the type.

"Can you sense anything off him?" Murdock asked.

At one time, I had the ability to manipulate essence on a

high level. I was growing, maturing into my skills to the point where I thought I might end up being one of the most powerful druids alive. It sounds vain and ambitious, which is why I would never have admitted the thought aloud to anyone. I had attracted the attention of some very powerful people, who took me under their wings, some of them literally. The more I learned, the more I saw that I hadn't peaked yet.

But I fell. More like, "was knocked on my ass." Hot on the trail of a miscreant terrorist elf named Bergin Vize, I had cornered him in a power plant. Just when I thought I could take him out, Something Happened. No one knows quite sure what, but it involved a lot of essence, a Teutonic ring of power, and a smidge of nuclear energy. I don't remember anything after catching up to him. I woke up dead inside, with no real ability anymore, a mysterious mass in my head that feels like molten knives stabbing my brain whenever I try to manipulate essence. It gives me a really, really bad headache.

Now I have just a few abilities, none of which is extraordinary for someone of my kind. Human normals can replicate most of what I can do with the right accessories. Except for one thing, which is literally sense essence. For some reason, that skill remains strong. It might be because it's a biological function. Receptors in my nose and eyes are what make it work. Most fey have the ability to some extent, but not as strongly as druids. Researchers have been studying the phenomenon for decades with no real understanding.

So, it was time for my parlor trick. "Can I have everyone step away from the body a moment?" I said.

Since working with Murdock, I was beginning to recognize more of the local force. In turn, they were getting used to me being around to help. The officers and medical examiner shuffled back to allow me a clear space.

I crouched over the victim, trying not to think about how young he was. Sometimes when you see dead bodies, you can tell if they knew what was coming. This kid did. He died scared. I shook the thought away and inhaled. The boy had been dead awhile. Between the cold and the rain, most of the essence he had recently come in contact with had faded. What hit me immediately was troll. Trolls have a strong essence that lingers. They also stink. That lingers, too. The next strongest essence was human, but not the victim's. He had been with another human for an extended period before he died. To complicate matters, I picked up traces of two different elves and a fairy, all weak enough that I could not place the actual clans.

I told Murdock what I had found. "Our victim keeps very strange company."

"Well, it is the Weird," he said.

I stood up. "True. But you don't get elves and fairies hanging out together much. And everyone is creeped out by trolls."

"That's Guild talk, Connor. Politics don't mean shit down here."

He had a point. Publicly, the Guild was all about fey crime investigation first, politics second. Operatively, it's the other way around. It makes a show of unity between the fey races—druids and fairies, elves and dwarves all one big happy family. But underneath lies chronic suspicion of each other's motives. It's been going on for over a century. The Celtic and Teutonic races had a little war that got out of hand, and somehow it caused the event known as Convergence. Modern reality found itself merged with parts of Faerie that it thought were just myth and legend. And the fight continues, sometimes physically, but mostly in boardrooms now.

Me, I couldn't care less about Faerie. I was born here. I have no nostalgia for a place I've never known. While leaders of both sides talk about return, I'll take this reality, thank you. Besides, I've asked people who would know, and there's no Guinness in Faerie, so it couldn't be that great.

"You're right. But it still complicates things. He came in contact with two of the races that could have dropped him here. If I thought about it, I could probably come up with a way for an elf to do it, too. They're pretty strong," I said.

Murdock shrugged. "Hence, the job. We have some leads now. And unless this kid ends up being the son of the president of the United States, you know the Guild is not going to take the case. So it's mine. Ours, if you want in."

I didn't have to think about it. I hate unsolved kid murders, human or fey. "I'm in."

He turned his face to the sky. "What about this cold? It's only around here."

I had a little mind hiccup. Seeing Murdock check out the sky had me thinking for a moment that he could see the residual essence I was seeing, which wasn't possible for a human. Then I realized he was just doing what everyone does when they talk about the weather; they look up.

I scanned the strip of sky above us. The haze of essence covered the entire block we were on. "I'm curious about that myself. There's a residual haze of essence up there. Let's check it out."

I walked across the field, with Murdock a step behind me. We crossed the street to an abandoned warehouse. Grabbing the end of a fire-escape ladder, I gave it a hard tug. It clattered down to within a few feet of the pavement. I gave the metal rungs a good shake to make sure they'd stay attached. Even as I did it, I tried to understand my logic. Why would potentially pulling a fire escape down on top of me be somehow safer than having the fire escape collapse under me? Fortunately, it held.

We jogged the six flights without speaking, our breaths streaking warm plumes into the cold air. Murdock and I work out often together. The fire escape was like doing the StairMaster, only colder. At the top, we used a vertical ladder to the roof. Actually, the remains of the roof. Most of it had fallen in, creating an open crater of space with a lovely view of the rubble-strewn top floor.

The rising sun hit us full in the face, and I felt a surge of essence from Murdock. Even as I turned to look at him, it faded. As a human normal, Murdock's essence should register on the low end of the scale. A few months earlier, he had helped me accidentally save the world and caught a nasty blast from an insane fairy. Or elf. It's hard to describe. Anyway, since then his essence has been mucked up.

Everyone's essence is unique, like fingerprints, and the different species of fey resonate differently. Murdock's essence fluctuates throughout the day from normal to damn strong. What makes that odd is that usually only the fey have strong essence. Elves and fairies. Trolls and dwarves. Druids and the like. Yet, Murdock always feels human. He says he doesn't feel any different except for an occasional adrenaline surge. He's on outpatient from Avalon Memorial Hospital now. I'm no healer, but I have a sneaky suspicion they're as baffled as I am.

Above us, a streak of white haze marked a trail of essence. That's where the cold was coming from. Weather manipulation was probably as old as Faerie itself. Keeping crops growing, protecting livestock, and clearing or clouding the skies for a battle were keen motivation for developing the ability. Boosting existing conditions was simple; changing clear skies to rain was complex. The end result depends on the manipulator's level of skill and ability.

The after-effect of this particular manipulation was pedestrian in results but grand in execution. The ambient air temperature had been lowered below freezing, something that was fairly easy to do in early October near the open ocean because the air was already cold and changeable. The level of ability applied, however, was impressive. The haze was easily two or three blocks wide, nearly three-quarters of a mile long, and sufficiently long lasting to freeze water. That took Power of the serious kind.

The northern edge of the haze, not far from where we stood near Old Northern Avenue, had begun to break up, indicating the effect was not being maintained. As it snaked southward, its density increased. At the far southern end, it appeared uniform. That told me that the spell had been initiated nearby and sent southward—first effects were the first to fade. Even as I watched, the spell eroded away from us.

"I doubt this is related, Murdock," I said. "It's a pretty powerful spell and looks like it had a defined purpose. I think the kid just happened to die here. Whoever has the ability to make this level of cold happen probably has more creative ways to kill someone and hide the body."

"And the powerful don't really care what happens down here beneath them," said Murdock.

I didn't respond. I didn't need to. That statement summarized an entire conversation for Murdock and me. He's been on the police force a long time, long enough to get out of the Weird. I ended up living in it when I lost everything else, and it opened my eyes. No one cares about the Weird, at least no one official. Sure, around election time politicians will give a nice little speech about making the place better and cleaning out the riffraff. The only problem with that is most people outside the Weird consider everyone in it to be that riffraff. Murdock and I know better. Lots of good people live down here, people who fell through the cracks of everywhere else. And, yeah, some of them are a little shady. But most of them are only trying to get by. They don't deserve to be ignored. A few nasties poke their heads up every once in a while. When they do, they find Murdock waiting to smack them down again. And if they're fey, I get to help.

"So, what do you know about gangs?" I asked.

Murdock shrugged. "Just the majors. The Sapiens. The TruKnights. HiFlys. A couple of others. I know mostly snitches. I don't keep close track of the rivalries unless it's related to a case I'm on. I've got good ties with the gang unit, though. I'll check to see if yellow and black is a known xeno."

Xeno was the current catchy moniker for humans, mostly teenagers and early twentysomethings, who don't like the fey and form a nice little social club whose entertainment involves harassment and, all too often, violence against the fey. The phrase itself doesn't make sense unless you knew it

was evolved from "xenophobic gangs." Don't get me wrong—
there are plenty of fey gangs, too, that technically meet the
definition of xenophobic. But they are seen as the minority,
and so their antagonists earned the xenophobic badge first.

I looked down at the field, then the surrounding area. "Do
you know whose turf it is? Nothing's here but empty buildings."

I waited while Murdock flipped through his mental files.
"Not sure. I don't think anybody's. It's elves to the south.
Human and fairies along Oh No. I think this is a no-
man's-land." Oh No was the local nickname for Old Northern Avenue. You hear the phrase used with everything from
fear to laughter.

"If a gangbanger dies in an empty field and no one is
around to hear it, is he a gangsta?" I said. Murdock didn't
laugh. I wasn't really trying to be funny.

Murdock blew into his hands again. "I still don't like this
cold. You know I like to rule out anomalies at crime scenes
only for good reason. You're more likely to find out what it
was for."

"Sure," I said. I had contacts that Murdock couldn't necessarily cultivate. For one thing, I was fey. While it doesn't
always produce cooperation and honesty among the fey, simple psychology still applies. Like groups are more willing to
extend trust to one of their own. I also lived right in the
Weird, and people can tell. Places generate their own essence
imprints, and if you stay in them long enough, you pick it up,
too. Murdock smells like South Boston, not the Weird. That's
not a criticism. It's like recognizing someone's accent. Whatever attributes you assign to that is your own prejudice.

The sun rose higher, and the temperature went up a little.
The erosion of the weather spell seemed to increase. Interesting. That meant sunlight was meant to dissipate it. Whatever it was for, was for last night only.

"Looks like it's going to be a nice day," I said.

Murdock's two-way radio squawked, then emitted a string

of gibberish that pretended to be a woman speaking. Murdock cocked his head and lowered the volume. How cops understood those things was beyond me.

Murdock's eyes flicked up to my face. "We've got another body."

2

I moved several newspapers off Murdock's passenger seat and got in his car. The man is fastidious about his personal appearance but has slob tendencies that manifest themselves in any vehicle he happens to drive. When the heat came on, I detected the faint whiff of chicken wings.

"Where are we going?" I asked.

"Down Harbor Street," he said.

"Harbor? You got pulled off a murder scene for a dead body in the Tangle?"

He nodded. "Code came in possible high profile. We need to get in and assess before the Guild shows up."

If the Weird is the ass end of Boston neighborhoods, the Tangle is the ass end of the Weird. The place gets its name from the chaotic network of streets that twist around each other, a confusing interplay of real and not-so-real lanes and buildings. To explain Boston's oddly laid-out streets, an urban legend claims they're paved over cow paths. In the Tangle, the cows apparently were drunk as hell.

Even I admit that it's a rough place. It's no wonder the place makes the news. Drugs and the more esoteric types of body trades are the primary commercial ventures. Gangs rule the streets. Spellcasters openly offer their services for questionable enterprises. An inordinate number of people go missing, or at least were often last seen alive there.

If the Guild tends to ignore the happenings in the Weird, it positively pretends the Tangle doesn't even exist. While I'm no longer the Guild's biggest fan, they do have a point. Lots of people wish the Tangle didn't exist. But it does, so there's no excuse to let what goes on there, go on. And, naturally, the Guild only gets involved if someone important gets caught up.

We pulled onto Harbor Street, not technically the Tangle, but close enough. Murdock just parked in the middle of the street. Police privilege. He wasn't the first. Two squad cars were already on scene, and an officer was frantically unraveling crime scene tape in a wide arc in front of a building thirty feet away. He looked pale, a little green around the gills even.

We stepped out of the car into more cold. I looked up and saw the southern edge of the weather spell ripple and shift as the last of it evaporated in the morning sun. We walked toward the cordoned-off storefront, two large plate-glass windows with slogans like HELP US, HELP YOU and WE RISE ONLY TOGETHER. A multihued sign above the door said UNITY.

The signs reminded me that not everyone was willing to abandon the Weird. Just like I had come to care about the people down here, others did, too. Along with the sinners, a few hardy saints marched down here, struggling to make a difference. Some of them try to persuade people off the paths they have chosen. Some just hand out bandages to get someone through the day. At best, they make tiny dents. At worst, they get themselves caught up in the shifting alliances. I figured that's what we were probably walking into now, someone who had poked their nose in a little too deep.

We ducked the tape, and the smell hit me immediately. "Damn, Murdock, I can sense a lot of blood from here. It's an elf."

Two more officers stood just inside the door. One of them seemed to be concentrating on keeping his jaw clamped shut. The other one nodded at us. "Hope you haven't had breakfast."

Not a good sign. The police see a lot, especially in rougher neighborhoods. They deal with most of it with gallows humor. When they openly acknowledge the severity of a murder scene, it is definitely not a good sign.

"That bad?" asked Murdock.

"Worse," said the officer. He pointed inside. "Nine-one-one call came from a phone in the front room. Door was unlocked when we got here. No one here but the victim."

Murdock nodded. It is a time-honored tradition to remain anonymous in the Weird. Murdock gave me a quick look and stepped inside. I followed, already tamping down my senses to deaden the scent of blood.

The front room spanned the width of the building and ran back about thirty feet. Several groupings of cast-off furniture filled the near section, behind those was a Ping-Pong table, and behind that were three old metal desks. The walls were painted a jarringly vibrant shade of yellow and covered with posters proclaiming the virtues of friendship, cooperation, and racial harmony. The cynic in me couldn't help snorting. Not that it wasn't all well-intentioned. But this close to the Tangle, it smacked of naïveté.

Two archways stood on opposite sides of the back wall. "The left side," I said to Murdock. The stench was unavoidable.

Murdock went first. He stopped in the archway, blocking my view. "Sweet mother of God," he whispered. He turned away from the door with his eyes closed. I was not going to like it. I stepped into the archway and froze.

Half of my brain began objectively assessing what I was seeing. The other half was screaming. The room was long and narrow, no windows, with a closed door at the rear. A desk had been flipped forward to my right. Everything that had been on it had scattered to the floor. Four of the five chairs in the room were either upturned or broken. The fifth was embedded in the back wall. Every conceivable surface was sprayed with blood. Floors. Walls. Ceiling. At my feet lay a left hand with the lower half of a forearm attached. I could see a right arm under one of the chairs. I assumed a separate bloody mangle near the desk was the lower extremities. Gobbets of body organs appeared to be smeared everywhere. To the right and about eight feet up, a head peered out of a bloody crater in the wall. The face had been flattened. Other than my ability to sense its essence, the only remaining clue to race of the individual was a long, pointed ear that was sticking straight out in the wrong direction.

I closed my eyes. I could hear Murdock breathing through his mouth. If I was going to help, I had to use my nose. The scent of blood overwhelmed, the elf essence coating everything. Two things jumped out at me, though. At least one troll had spent a lot of time in the room, and I could sense a second. I moved forward a little.

"Don't touch anything," Murdock said. I nodded. Contaminating a crime scene like this would not be looked on tolerantly by anyone.

I could sense fear. The feeling is more intuitive than technical. I'm not a dog. But sometimes strong emotion seems to color how essence feels to me, like salt or pepper on a steak. The odd thing was, I wasn't sensing the fear from the elf, which suggested to me that whatever happened to him was unexpected. He literally hadn't seen it coming. But fear permeated the place, a fear intense enough to announce the presence of at least one human normal. That's the one thing you can always sense from a human.

I turned away from the carnage. "We should get in that back room."

Murdock led the way back to the front door. "How long ago did this call go out on the wire?" he asked the same officer by the door.

He looked at his watch. "Probably ten minutes or so."

Murdock looked at me. "We don't have much time. Let's

go." We broke into a jog out the door, ducked under the tape again, and made our way to a narrow back alley. For this part of the neighborhood, the alley was surprisingly clean. Probably some do-gooder project. The back door to the building was the self-closing type, but wasn't quite closed. Murdock pulled out his gun.

I don't carry a gun. Never did. Once I didn't need to with all the other abilities I had. Now I avoid them because the metal content messes up whatever little ability I do have. I flattened myself against the wall behind Murdock. He stretched forward and tugged quickly at the door handle, simultaneously pulling back into firing stance. The door swung open, briefly revealed a darkened room, then began to close. Murdock grabbed it before it could lock. He scuttled across the face of the door, pulling it open as he moved to the opposite side. No sounds came out. No gunfire, which was good, and no explosive shot of essence, which was even better. Neither of us was equipped to deal with that. I ducked my head into the opening and back.

"Empty," I mouthed to him.

Gun forward, Murdock leaped into the room to the opposite side again. I could picture him inside, the two of us pressed against the wall between us. I waited a long two seconds, listening. "Clear," he called out.

I walked in to find Murdock holstering his gun. He kept the holster open.

The back room was mainly storage, some stacked chairs and folding tables, boxes and filing cabinets, and some standard office equipment: a fax machine, a photocopier, and some kind of large-size printer. Faint levels of essence from all species permeated the space, in tribute to the apparent ethic of the place. Given that, the strong register of troll and human stood out. The troll was definitely the same one I had sensed in the office space. The human was strong enough to be identifiable, but with the mess in the other room, I couldn't tell if the fear I had felt there was from the same person.

"I'd say someone hid in here while the action in the other

room went on. When everything went down, they ran out the back door," said Murdock.

Made sense to me. It would explain why the inside door was closed and the back door was open. Someone was in too much of hurry to worry about securing the door.

Murdock's two-way squawked. It was only one word, so I understood it. "Company."

Murdock looked around. "Did you touch anything?"

"Okay, second time you've done that. I'm not an amateur," I said.

"Sorry. Guild's here. Let's go." He had the good sense to look chagrined. I let it pass, because at the least it showed why I liked working with him. Murdock paid attention to details. We backed out of the room and left the door exactly how we found it. As we walked back up the building, I paused. More troll essence. It led off to the right, into the Tangle. It didn't surprise me. If I were a troll and needed to blend in with the scenery fast, that's where I'd go.

When we reached the front of the building, the activity level had increased dramatically in a short period of time. Two more police cars, an EMT van, the medical examiner's car, a Boston morgue wagon and a Guild one, and a black town car now cluttered the street. The interesting action was occurring at the front door, where several people were arguing.

As we arrived, the officer we had left at the door was blocking the entrance, preventing people from getting inside, including one very attractive and angry fairy. The officer looked relieved when he saw us. "Here he is now, ma'am. Lieutenant Detective Murdock is ranking officer. Sir, this is Community Liaison Officer macNeve."

"We've met," said Murdock.

Keeva macNeve spun on her heel to face us in full intimidation mode. She had her wings unveiled and shot a little essence into them to make the silvery gossamer flicker yellow and white. All five-foot-eight of her projected anger and authority. I love Keeva in a lather. She's very good at it. She even somehow gets her mop of red hair to undulate. And to her credit, it works most of the time to get her what she wants.

"You two. I should have guessed," she said.

"Hi, Keeva," I said. "You're up early. New job keeping you on your toes?" Keeva and I used to work together at the Guild. When I say "work together," I mean we worked in the same general geographic area trying not to pummel each other as we solved cases. That's just as much a comment on my behavior as on hers. She recently got promoted to Community Liaison Officer for Community Affairs due to a rather sudden vacancy. It's a polite title. Internally at the Guild, the job is really Chief of Investigations.

"We have a major situation here, Connor. This is a Guild case."

"We were just securing the scene," said Murdock.

"Did you touch anything?" Keeva asked him. I resisted the urge to smirk.

Murdock smiled tightly. "No, ma'am. Would you like to fill us in?"

"No," she said. She turned back to the officer. "Move." He looked at Murdock, who nodded. Bowing politely, he stepped aside, and Keeva strode through the door, followed by a rather sallow-skinned druid that I guessed was the Guild coroner.

"Left-hand door," I called out. Through the plate glass, we watched them cross the room and walk directly to the archway. The coroner backed out immediately, even more sickly colored if that were possible, and bolted through the front door. He made sounds behind his vehicle that we all tried to ignore out of professional courtesy as well as our own need not to join him. I could only guess he hadn't been on the job very long. After several moments, Keeva reappeared and paused at the archway as she obviously pulled herself together. She lifted her head and came outside.

"You could have warned me," she said. I have to give her credit; she still looked more angry than ill.

I feigned innocence. "You seemed in a rush."

"My people will be here momentarily. You need to pull everyone out," Keeva said. The coroner returned from behind the car with his kit over his shoulder.

For someone just arriving, she seemed too much in a hurry to get rid of us. "Who do you think the victim is, Keeva?"

She gave me a long tense look, then relaxed. "You'll know soon enough. It's Alvud Kruge."

That gave me a "whoa" moment. If someone told me I would find an elf with international diplomatic ties smeared across the back room of a storefront on the edge of the Tangle, I wouldn't have believed it if I hadn't seen it. My gaze went up to the sign above the storefront. Unity. Of course, he would be here. Alvud Kruge has been an advocate for peace for decades, often at odds with his own people in the Teutonic Consortium back in Germany. Had been. He'd even been on the board of directors at the Boston Guildhouse, something that also didn't endear him to his compatriots.

Murdock rubbed his eyes. "God, I've had better mornings."

"How did you know it was him?" I asked.

Keeva gazed at me without speaking for a long moment. I've known her a long time. That look means either she's weighing how much she wants to share or how much she's going to lie. "Kruge was a Guild director. His addresses get flagged for security. You know that, Connor."

That was true. Guild members have a lot of enemies for one reason or another. The higher up in the food chain you go, the more people you have waiting to knock you down. Above all else, the Guildhouse protects its own. Even though they had the ill grace to kick me out when I was down, they still provided me a fair amount of security. Nothing flashy, but enough to let me sleep at night in my own bed in my own apartment without worrying about spells in the dark. As head of the crime unit, Keeva was at the top of the contact list for anything associated with Guild execs. So she went for the plausible. Nothing I could call her on. Yet. But that hesitation before answering intrigued me. As usual with her, more than the obvious was probably going on. I decided to play on her side for the moment.

"Someone used a weather spell last night. It extended almost from this exact location back up to Oh No," I said.

Keeva looked up at the sky. The sun was fully up, and any trace of the essence haze I had seen earlier was gone.

"I thought the cold might be related. Did you notice anything else?" She even sounded like she was treating me like a colleague. While she's not given to admitting inadequacies, Keeva knows that druids have higher sensitivity to more types of essence than fairies, even a member of the Danann clan like her. Dananns may be some of the most powerful beings on the planet, but they still can't find a dwarf in a tunnel without a flashlight.

It was an easy thing to share for now. Her druid coroner would tell her the same thing later anyway. "Some conflicting troll and human essence in the back room and the alley. I'm getting multispecies hits everywhere. No one I recognized."

"That's it?"

"That's it."

Her eyes narrowed. "How did you get here so fast? It may be early for me, but I know damn well you don't usually roll out of bed until noon."

"Murdock called me in on another murder nearby when this call came in," I said.

"It's a kid. Looks like a fairy might have dropped him," Murdock said.

Keeva nodded absently as she examined the front door. She might have heard Murdock, she might not have. Boston P.D. calls were not that interesting to her or the Guild. She reached out and held the doorknob. It's a little Danann trick. What they cannot always perceive with their eyes and nose, they can sometimes do by touch. She moved her hand to the doorjamb, then back to the knob. Her brow creased.

"Are you getting something?" I asked.

She looked up. "Hmm? I'll read your report when it gets

sent over, Detective. If you're only at 'might-have-dropped,' it doesn't sound like something the Guild needs to take. Kruge's going to suck up a lot of resources."

Murdock and I exchanged knowing looks. No surprises. Even if the Weird wasn't involved, Kruge would have taken precedence. It's the way of the world. His death was going to make international headlines. The kid up the street might make a quick mention on the early news, but after that it would be twenty-four-hour Kruge.

I could hear a low-level hum that was beginning to build. I knew that sound. Keeva and I both looked up, but no one else did yet. They'd catch it in a moment. The hum turned into a whirring noise, and six fairies came into view above us. A Guild security unit. Gods, I miss showing up with them. All tricked out in black leather, chrome helmets, and white energy pulsating in their wings. People get out of the way when they show up. Even cops. Like the cops standing next to us who sidled down to the sidewalk. It only takes "accidentally" getting hit once with a little essence bolt to get the message that you don't mess with them. They landed in a loose circle around me, Keeva, and Murdock. I could feel Murdock give off one of his odd essence surges.

"It's fine, guys," Keeva said to them. "They were just leaving." She looked at me with a cocked eyebrow.

I smiled. "It was nice seeing you, too, Keeva."

"We both have work to do, Connor," she said and walked back into the building.

The security unit stepped in a little closer. "Relax. We're going," I said.

Now came the pissing-game part. They blocked our way to the car, but without even asking Murdock, I knew we were not going to walk around them. With a reasonable look on my face, I stepped up on them and gestured politely with my hands that we wanted to pass. They in turn did not respond immediately to make us think they weren't going to move. Then two of them stepped apart with barely enough room to walk between them. Murdock and I made sure to rub our shoulders against them as we passed through the gap. We didn't look back as we went to the car, but as we got in, we almost simultaneously stared back at them. I wasn't surprised to see all six turned in our direction. Murdock started up the car and slowly drove forward. He reached the crime scene tape and drove through it. The entire time we all stared at each other, which was more difficult for Murdock and me since we couldn't make eye contact through those chrome helmets. This is how grown men maintain their dignity without breaking noses. It's silly and important, and most women never understand it. We turned onto Summer Street and headed back to Old Northern.

"I hate those guys," Murdock said.

"Yeah, I wish I had them as my crew, too," I said.

Murdock allowed himself a smile. "She's got her hands full with that. It looks interesting, but it's going to end up all press conferences."

That's Murdock right there. He's a smart guy who wants to stay a cop. Not a police officer. Not a department flunky. A cop. Cops enforce the law and solve crimes. Everything else is bull to guys like him.

I like the attitude, but I have to confess to a certain ambivalence. Most of us get into law enforcement because we want to make the world a better place. I could have gone the scholar route and run with the Druidic College crowd. Or the diplomatic route and gone to work for the Seelie Court. But I chose the Ward Guild because it gets to do stuff that produces results you can see. And, I have to admit, you sometimes get your picture in the paper. I miss the glory. I've been too busy working on purging my old arrogance to give up my vanity.

We pulled up at the first murder scene. The body had been removed, and the medical examiner had left. Just a couple of beat officers were wandering the field taking notes. Murdock turned the car around and drove up to the Avenue.

"Looks like I've got paperwork to start. What angle do you want to take?" Murdock asked.

I considered for a moment. We really didn't have much to

go on. Multiple unknown essences and a possible gang connection. "I think I'll start with the gang angle, see if anyone knew of anything going down last night."

He nodded. "I'll set you up with some profile. I'm going to try and ID the kid and work his associates, check a few sources."

Murdock turned down Sleeper Street. I was glad I didn't have to ask him outright for a ride. Cabs don't like to pick people up down near the Tangle, and even if I expensed it, the fare would cut into my meager cash flow until the reimbursement check came in. Boston P.D. accounting is wicked slow.

I got out of the car. "I'll call you if I think of anything."

"Yep," Murdock said and pulled away. He never says good-bye, not even on the phone.

I let myself into my building and felt the security spell as I passed inside. It's one of the disability benefits from the Guild. Since I lost my abilities in the line of duty, they at least had the decency to provide some protections. Small compensation for kicking me out of my job, but at least I have some chance against some idiot who might come looking for revenge. I can open or close the door with a vocal command, even seal it, if I feel I'm in danger. I haven't had to activate it, which is fortunate, and, frankly, I would use it only if truly necessary. The Guild would have to come and reset it on-site and that would be a little humiliating. There's my vanity again.

I entered my two-room apartment and surveyed the mess. I sleep in the living room because I like using the bedroom as an office. An unmade, slept-in futon with a view of the kitchen can be depressing, but it's mine. The clock on the counter blinked 11:14 A.M. Not even noon, and I had had to look at two dead bodies. That's my surreal life in the Weird. For the start of the mundane part of my day, I made some desperately needed coffee.

3

Coffee is not something that keeps me awake. It just keeps me alive. Whenever I end up working on a case with Murdock, it seems I never get enough sleep. After a short nap, I sat in my study, staring out the window at the planes taking off from the airport. I had dreamed of wandering lost through a field of bones.

For the past few months, I had been having prescient dreams. Lots of fey do, but I never did until recently. They're not visual in the sense of watching a movie. They involve personal metaphors, and you have to figure out your own. I'm not very good at understanding them, mainly because the ability seems weak. When you're fey and live in the world where Freud existed, it's even more difficult to decide if a field of bones is a symbol of a dead kid in a vacant lot or the ruins of a battlefield. And, of course, spicy food gives me nightmares, but I love pepperoni.

After another fortifying cup of coffee, I threw on the trusty leather jacket and went out to make rounds. The neighborhood was in day mode, tired faces running the usual errands. I caught snippets of conversation here and there as I paused at corners or lingered near storefront windows. By far, the major topic was the death of Alvud Kruge. Whether or not Keeva wanted to keep his name quiet for a while, it didn't matter down in the Weird. Everyone knew someone who knew someone who knew Kruge. No one mentioned the dead kid.

I made way back to the field off Old Northern. The cops had gone, leaving behind nothing but footprints and fluttering crime scene tape that, first, would keep no one out and, secondly, was pointless. The afternoon sun had melted the frozen ground into a muddy slop. Any evidence that had been missed this morning was likely sunken in the muck, leaving any hope of trace evidence gone for good.

I strolled the perimeter of the field, trying to get a sense of the scene. As I had noted earlier, not a single building on the block appeared occupied, at least not legally. Most of them had the standard complement of broken windows and boarded-up doors. Some foot traffic had been through since the cops left. I could sense fey, mostly dwarves. Nothing unusual. No mysterious figures lurking in doorways. No black-cloaked man rushing away. No woman with big dark sunglasses leaving a single rose. Just one very pink, excited-looking flit descending toward me.

"Here you are!" he said.

"Hey, Joe." Joe's an old friend. Real old, as in been around since I was born. His real name is Stinkwort, which he doesn't like to use for obvious reasons. As one of the diminutive fairies known as flits, he has enough hassle over his size and his pink wings. When you're a foot tall, you manage what you can.

"I've been looking for you everywhere! Have you heard? Alvud Kruge is dead!" He soared around me, his eyes lit with excitement.

"I know. I saw."

"You did? I heard he was exploded. Was he exploded? Was it gross?"

I nodded. "That's a fair description, and, yes, it was gross. How did you find out?"

He did a back loop right in front of me. "Oh, some flits got in before the Guild put up an essence barrier. No one can get in now. I just keep bouncing back." He paused in a hover and leaned in confidentially. "They're getting good at that. I'm going back tonight to find a work-around."

For want of a better word, flits can teleport. They have their own word for it, but it's in Cornish and doesn't flow off the tongue easily. It translates roughly as "I am here, and I want to go there in the time of the now" or something close to that. Ergo, teleport. How they do it is another matter and a mystery. Of all the fey that came through from Faerie after Convergence, the flits have apparently remained as they always were—secretive, happy, and a little crazy. They have little interest, no pun intended, in furthering scientific investigation as to how they exist.

"Sounds a little disrespectful, Joe."

He shook his head. "Nah. The body will be gone. I just want to annoy those Guild goons by getting past them."

I smiled. Flits are not the most welcome fey at the Guild, mostly because they don't respond well to the organizational structure. They have their own loyalties. Besides, they're easily distracted, which makes them lousy employees.

"I'm working on a case, Joe. A human kid died in this field last night."

Joe frowned as he looked at the muddy expanse. He fluttered away, hovered right over the spot where the body was, then returned to hang in the air in front of me. "He was dead when he got here."

That took me by surprise. "How do you know that?"

"There's no echo. When he left the world, he left his shout somewhere else."

This was news to me. "I don't understand."

He, of course, looked at me like I'm an idiot. "His shout. His last shout. Everyone shouts when they leave, and it echoes for a while. There's no echo here."

That's flits for you. Know one your entire life, and he'll surprise you with an ability you had no idea he had. It made a sort of logical sense. I knew flits could hear when someone died. I've been in Joe's presence when another flit died nearby. He knew what happened immediately. So did every flit in the vicinity. I didn't know about the echo, though.

"He had a broken neck. I thought he might have died from being dropped."

Joe pulled his chin in, a look of doubt on his face. "You think a fairy killed him?" Despite what he has experienced over a very long lifetime, Joe refuses to believe that a fairy—no matter what clan—could possibly have done something wrong. When proved otherwise, he invariably chalks it up to aberrant behavior that couldn't possibly happen again. It's amusingly prideful.

I glanced around the area. "It would fit with how we found the body. Can you do me a favor? The kid was missing a shoe. Can you check the area from above and look for an orange Nike?"

"Sure," he said. He flew straight up and turned in a slow circle. After another moment, he came back down. "What's an orange Nike?" he asked.

"A running shoe, Joe. Soft leather, rubber sole."

He nodded vigorously. "Oh, right. Heard about those."

I shook my head and smiled as he popped back up and circled the field. No sooner did he sail out of sight over a building than three dwarves appeared at the end of the block opposite me. As they surveyed the scene, they stopped when they saw me and stared. I had a feeling I knew what was coming. They all wore the same black hoodies with yellow bandanas. They swaggered their way around the mud toward me.

"Got a problem?" said the one on the left. The other two hung back a little.

"We've all got problems," I said, keeping my voice neutral. When you are alone in a desolate area, and three people wearing the same outfits come up to you, you don't do two things: act scared or give attitude. The first is like tuna to a cat. The second is like a mouse. Unless, of course, they're all wearing orange. Then, they're probably just the late shift getting out of Dunkin' Donuts.

"I don't think you belong here," he said. He didn't change his voice. Given the way he was scoping me out, I guessed he was trying to figure if I was human or druid or glamoured. Dwarves don't sense essence very well unless it's pretty strong. Given my current disabled state, I doubt I gave off much of a druid aura at all. If trouble started, a human would be easy for them to handle; a lone druid would be manageable, even if he was in better shape than me; someone glamoured would be a wild card. It could be a fairy or an elf or some other powerful fey that might have an unpleasant reason for hiding his identity by appearing to be something else. Regardless, being on the receiving end of a dwarf fist is unpleasant for any of them.

"Sometimes I think I don't belong anywhere," I said in my best world-weary, leather-jacket-cool tone. It plays well in the Weird.

He moved a step closer. "I'm talking right here, right now." Evidently, he had decided I was tuna.

"A kid died here last night. I'm working the case."

Magic words. Of course, I didn't actually say I was Guild or Boston P.D., but implying was enough. All three of them shifted their postures, not in relief, but with an air of nonchalance meant to convey they weren't doing anything less legal than strolling down the sidewalk. In the Weird, people with badges are treated cautiously because they're rarely friends.

"Know anything about that?" I asked into the silence.

Head shaking all around.

"He was wearing a black hoodie and a yellow bandana. Sound familiar?"

Again, more head shaking, with some shoulder shrugging thrown in. From three guys wearing black hoodies and yellow bandanas.

I slipped my hands in my pockets and looked around like I was appraising the real estate. "I heard this territory's up for grabs."

"You heard wrong," said the first dwarf. The other two gave me hard, tough-guy stares.

"So, if I thought someone killed this kid in some kind of turf dispute, I'd be wrong?"

"There's no dispute. This is Moke's."

I nodded as if in agreement. "I think I need to talk to Moke."

The dwarf shrugged. "Maybe he'll hear about that. He's pretty busy, though."

I smiled. "If you run into him, tell him Connor Grey said hello."

The dwarf spun on his heel. "We got better things to do," he said over his shoulder as he walked away. The other two gave me one last look and followed him. I decided not to try to keep them talking when they clearly didn't want to.

I didn't know of any dwarves named Moke. And I didn't know if that was a good thing or a bad one. I didn't go down this end of the Avenue much, and gangs are diligently territorial. My end of the neighborhood tended to have a lot of human and fairy groups hanging out. They didn't get on much with dwarves, so this Moke probably stayed on his end.

As I suspected, the whole thing was looking like a gang dispute. It was hard not to be a little disappointed. Gang murders meant not much work. The likelihood of members discussing the situation with the police was small. And the perpetrator probably had more to fear from his rivals than the law. It looked like I would get maybe one or two days' pay out of it before Murdock had to move on to other things. The case would probably remain unsolved with a gang reprisal that I would never know about.

For the second time in a half hour, something came flying down at me. I realized with horror that it was a winged Nike in all its pink and orange glory. As it got closer, Joe's head appeared over the laces. He was actually sitting inside it.

"Why didn't you say it was a sneaker? I know what a sneaker is," he said.

"Joe, I said 'find it' not 'take it.' You've just contaminated evidence in a murder case." For the record, it's hard to look angry at someone sitting in a running shoe floating in the air.

He pulled a long face. "I'll put it back then. You could have been clearer."

"Where was it?"

"On a roof four or five buildings over that way," he said. As he pointed, he almost lost the shoe. I resisted the urge to grab it.

"Please, put it back *exactly* where it was and in the same position. I'll meet you there. Wait for me in front of the right building so I can find it."

"What if someone sees me?" he said.

"That's the least of my concerns right now, Joe. No one's going to see you if you don't want them to." Most flits are shy to the point of reclusiveness. They've set themselves up for a vicious circle, though. They're shy because their size often gives them unwanted attention, but because they're rarely seen, they attract even more attention when they do appear. It wasn't so bad in the Weird, since fey of different sizes were hardly unusual. Joe's usually not so sensitive to it, but I could tell I upset him. He'll get over it because he understands enough about my job to know he screwed up.

He turned the shoe and flew off. Skipping the shortcut through the mud, I made my way around the field to the next street over. More empty buildings, though a few of these looked like they might be inhabited. Rough curtains hung in warehouse windows, and sometimes people even showed their faces through sooty glass. This end of the Avenue was not known for entertainment. It was close to the Tangle, which meant trouble, so only the truly desperate lived here or, ironically, the kind of people that the desperate feared.

At the top of a building stoop, I found Joe standing defiantly in full view of the street. I knew he'd get over it.

"Sorry," he said as I walked up the steps.

"Yeah, I know. I didn't mean to yell. Can I get up to the roof from here?"

He nodded. "It's empty as far as I can tell. Smells bad, too, and not in a good way."

I pursed my lips, then decided not to ask for a clarification of that last part. We entered the building through a smashed-open door. Joe hovered over my right shoulder as we ascended the stairs. He was right. The place stank, bodily secretions being the main culprit. The sagging staircase rose dimly before me and would have had the same gray, dingy look should sunlight ever penetrate. Spray-painted graffiti was most evident the first two flights, in several languages and three alphabets, but dwindled as we went upward. The smell faded, too, but that was probably due more to open windows allowing wind through than any diminishment of the source.

The stairs topped out at the roof through a small, doorless penthouse enclosure. The sun blinded me briefly after the dark interior of the building. I examined the roof surface before stepping out. In this part of town, rotting roofs come with the package. This one looked more solid than most. Others had been there before, demonstrated by three mismatched lawn chairs, a wooden telephone cable spool set on its side as a table, and enough empty bottles and cans to open a recycling center.

"Where is it?" I asked.

Joe put on a mock-curious face. "What? You mean that strange orange Nike shoe sneaker over there by the washing machine that I've never seen before in my life?"

I can't stay angry at Joe for long. Annoyed yes, but it's not in his nature to provoke me, and he always feels bad when he does. "That would be the one," I said.

I walked over to the incongruity that was a washing machine on a roof. Whenever I see something like that, I wonder about the motivation of the people who put it there, why it occurred to them to lug something so heavy to such an odd place. The Nike lay on its side near it. I could only sense Joe's essence at the spot, so that was a good sign that no else had been there. It helped confirm my suspicion that the kid lost it in the air.

"Well, at least your essence fades quickly. No one will find it if they look." Flit essence can be elusive. Flits being so small, their essence fades almost instantly under most conditions.

I scanned the nearby buildings. We were about a quarter mile away from the field where the kid had ended up. I couldn't see any sight lines that might produce witnesses, just other roofs that no one would likely be on in the rain and cold of the previous night. Off to the south, someone floated up into view. Even at this distance, I could see a slight distortion in the air that indicated wings. The sun glinted off something metallic. The chrome helmet of a Guild security guard. He drifted back down.

I brought my attention back to the running shoe. Having been out in the rain, it had no more essence on it than the kid's other clothing. I squatted down to look more closely. A few dark spots flecked the visible side.

"Joe, after you picked this up, did it touch the ground again or did anything drip on it?"

Stinkwort pulled his head out of the washing machine. "No. I picked it up by the laces and put it back *exactly* how I found it."

I leaned as close as I could get my nose to the Nike without falling over. When you work for the Guild, no one blinks an eye at what a druid might do to sense essence. When you're all alone on a roof with nothing to identify you as an investigator, you look like a guy with a shoe fetish. I hoped no one could see me. I waited for any essence to assert itself. After a long moment, just the slightest hint whispered up to me, so faint I was worried I might be imagining it. Elf essence. Only one thing would retain any indication of essence after that much rain. Blood.

I looked back toward the Tangle, then turned to sight the line to the field. The shoe was almost on a straight line between Kruge's storefront and the dead kid. Could be a coincidence. Or could be this wasn't just a gang feud.

"Did anyone see you, Joe?"

His eyes narrowed at me. "Just some dwarves."

"Black hoodies? Yellow bandanas?"

He nodded. "I don't want to ask. Why?"

I shrugged. "Just curious. There's some elf blood on the shoe."

He gave me an exasperated look. "Just some elf blood, he says. Like one of the most famous elves in the city didn't just get exploded up the street on the same night. Like, oh, did you happen to see a gang of marauding dwarves, he says. Nothing to worry about, Joe. Nope, nope, nothing at all."

"You're letting your imagination run away with you, Joe," I said. "I'm sure it's just coincidental."

"Just because it's a coincidence, doesn't mean I can't get killed because I touched some smelly Ikey."

"Calm down, Joe. And it's a Nike. And it doesn't smell. It's brand-new."

"Except for the elf blood," he said.

I tried to give him a reasonable look. "It's just a little. Hardly any. I can't even tell if it's Alvud Kruge's."

He rolled his eyes. "I feel so reassured."

"Look, Joe, it's a gang feud, pure and simple. He could have picked up the elf blood anywhere. He had an odd mix of essence on him, so there's no telling where he got it. Murdock and I are running the gang angle, and once he gets some gang names to contact, this will be all over. No one even knows you were involved."

He looked at me unconvinced. "You forget the marauding dwarves."

"They weren't marauding, and unless dwarves can suddenly fly, there's no reason for them to connect you to a shoe on a roof they couldn't even see."

He nodded. A sly look came over his face. "I bet you want to know about gangs."

"That's the plan."

He smiled knowingly. "I know someone who can help you. Knows all the gangs from here to Southie. Want me to set up a meeting?"

Joe is not a poker player. Every once in a while, he gets it in his head that I'm lonely. So he finds some poor soul that he thinks is just perfect for me. The problem is, most of the time "just perfect" to Joe means "odd person I met that no one else will go out with." All evidence to the contrary, I tend to be a little more discriminating. "I don't need a date, Joe."

"No! Honor spit! I really know someone who knows gangs and would be juiced to talk to you."

"Okay, set it up, then. I'll bring Murdock."

He hesitated for a moment, which made me think he might be fibbing about a date. "Okay. That's okay. Just don't say Murdock's a cop. He might not be happy about that."

"Fine," I said. I pulled out my cell phone and called Murdock. He was not going to like how I was about to complicate the case.

4

In spite of being amused by Stinkwort's paranoia, I was getting uncomfortable standing in front of the building waiting for Murdock. Clearly, word had spread about our presence on the street. An assortment of people found time to stroll by with no apparent errand in mind. A few peered at us curiously, as if a stranger hanging out in front of an abandoned building was surprising in this part of town. To a certain extent, it probably was. Around that part of the neighborhood, strangers didn't like to attract too much attention unless they were trying to send a message. I hoped ours said keep away until the cops show up.

Most people looked at us suspiciously, though. Joe's marauding dwarves showed themselves down at the one corner. They numbered six now. One more, and they'd be a cliché.

Murdock's voice mail had picked up when I called, and he hadn't called back yet. He usually called me back right away, but it had been almost twenty minutes. I didn't want to leave a message about the running shoe at the station house without talking to him, though. It was his case, and he should be on-site when a unit came to pick up the evidence.

Joe fidgeted about the stoop. "Do I have to stay? The windows across the street have eyes in them, and they're not an even number."

"Yes, we have to see if Murdock wants to arrest you."

"What?" he shrieked. Several heads turned in an avid hope that some action was about to happen. We disappointed them.

"Just kidding, Joe. We do need to tell him what happened. It's up to him what he wants to report."

"Well, I wish he'd hurry up. I'm bored."

I just nodded. I was used to Joe's definition of interesting. It had no logic to it, so I gave up trying to understand it years ago. I have seen him stare at a patch of grass for hours with an avidity I couldn't fathom. And yet, here we were in one of the more sketchy parts of the Weird with a veritable parade of fey folk slinking by, and he was bored.

I idly wondered if the Tangle were a taste of what Faerie was like, if the old country still existed. Few humans lived down this end of the neighborhood. Humans did live in Faerie, but none seemed to have come through the Convergence. The concentration of fey folk had to have been high in Faerie, by definition. With all that power, all that essence manipulation, it's no surprise that legends portray the place as dangerous and precarious. Even in the short time we stood on the sidewalk, I could feel little spell pings tossed our way. I could no longer actively discern their exact nature, but having been in places like this before my accident, I could guess.

Some people were probably checking to see if we were glamoured, most likely me. Flits don't lend themselves to glamouring. They're too small to pretend to be something else. Occasionally, they might glamour themselves as small animals or even plants, but it was much easier for them so use their own essence to fade from sight if they were trying to blend into their surroundings. Besides, they don't really like using essence outside themselves, which is what a glamour is—essence concentrated in something like a necklace or a stone or a ring that operates almost independently of the user.

Sometimes glamours are harmless, like enhancing one's appearance. Everyone has something they wish they could change about themselves, and some people prefer glamours to a nip and tuck. Even that has its limits, though. More than a few people have gone home with a hot babe only to discover later they were with a woman in the geriatric league. Sometimes they are used for privacy, like when someone just wants to just go about their business without having to interact with people they know. Sometimes they're meant to deceive, which I admit has come in handy with investigative work on occasion.

Ultimately, glamours are lies. They go to the crux of relationships. If you can't trust what you're seeing, then maybe you can't trust that person at all. And that's why I kept getting pinged. When you live in a dangerous neighborhood, you want to know who is who and how much to be on guard around them.

Beside me, Joe made a growling sound. A moment later, he threw a broadcast sending. *We don't have drugs!*

I chuckled. Half of the people who went by were using sendings to ask us for drugs. Certain sciences call it telepathy, but conceptually sendings are different. You impress auditory thoughts on essence and direct them where you want them to go. That's a fey ability up and down. You get used to the little whispers in your mind, unless, of course, you're annoyed because you're bored.

Joe flinched. "Ow! Did you feel that?"

"Yeah."

"Idiots," he muttered.

A short spasm in my head told me that someone had cast a spell nearby. Since my accident, some spells feel like a nail in my brain. I haven't tracked the types that have the most effect to detect a pattern, but scrying definitely tops the list. Someone starts trying to predict the future, and it's migraine hell. Whatever spell just went off wasn't scrying, but the fact

that Joe felt it as pain meant it was hard and crude in execution, the equivalent of someone blowing a whistle in your
ear. It usually indicated someone who had little training or
was in a big hurry.

I looked at my watch. A half hour had gone by since I
called Murdock. He tended not to call me only when he was
either in a meeting or on radio silence. Then and during the
occasional private recreational activity. It was a little early in
the day as far as the latter, even for him, and he still called
me if he were not too, let's say, intimately distracted. It an-
noys the hell out of his dates.

A waft of something acrid tickled my nose. "You smell
that, Joe?"

"That burning smell? I thought it was just part of the natural aroma of the street."

Others had picked up the scent. Heads turned, craning to
look up at the buildings, consternation fixed on faces. I did it
myself, but couldn't see anything. The wind shifted, and the
odor increased. A huge gust of wind came up, and a cloud of
thick black smoke engulfed us from the doorway behind us.
Tears burned in my eyes as I stumbled down the steps to the
sidewalk. The wind shifted again, and I was able to see
again. Joe popped into view directly in front of me. He must
have winked out as soon as he sensed the smoke coming.

I wiped my eyes and turned around. Smoke spewed from
the upper stories of the building. Along the cornice, I could
see flames. "Dammit! Joe, the shoe! Get the shoe!"

He vanished, then reappeared immediately. "Okay, just to
be clear this time, you want me to pick it up and bring it
here, right?"

"Yes. Go! Go!"

I swore under my breath as he vanished again. It was the
spell. Someone had been watching, someone who actually
had a reason to watch us. Given the time delay, I'd go the
minion route. Someone reported back to someone, and that
someone ordered up a fire spell. I spun around to the street.
In the gathering crowd, I could see the six dwarves that had

lingered up the street. That didn't mean there hadn't been one I missed. Hell, they could have just used a cell phone.

I stalked across the street toward them. It's a measure of how my face must have looked, because the small crowd parted as I came up on the curb. I went up to the first dwarf, the same one whom I had spoken to earlier, and poked him on the shoulder. "Who'd you call? Moke?"

At the mention of Moke, several onlookers moved farther back. A couple even turned heel and walked away. The dwarf looked down at his shoulder, then back at me. "Nobody."

I poked him again. "Was it Moke?"

He grabbed my forearm with a hand like a vise grip, and my body shields activated. They're not much good anymore, just enough to blunt the force of a blow, but I would still feel it. In my anger, I'd forgotten. You don't poke a dwarf if you can't follow through with a fight.

"I said nobody." He flung me away from him, and I sprawled into the street. As I got to my feet, he moved toward me. Before he reached me, a blur of pink light flashed between us, and he stopped.

Joe hovered in front of the dwarf. In one hand, the charred remains of the Nike dangled. In the other, the sharp white flame of his sword pointed directly at the dwarf's nose.

"Got a problem, shorty?" Joe asked. He grinned, a tough, cold line across his face. Joe has a repertoire of grins. This one was for sending chills down the spine, and it works like you wouldn't believe. The dwarf didn't move and didn't take his eyes off the blade. To the casual observer, it doesn't look like much, just a few inches of narrow white light with flickers of blue flame surrounding it. But anyone who has ever faced a flit with a blade knows better. It's sharp as a thought and burns with essence.

"Let it go, Banjo. We've got company," said one of the other dwarves.

Banjo shifted his gaze to Joe's face, then mine. He stepped back. A siren cut through the sounds the burning building was making. I felt more than saw a car pull up behind us quickly and stop.

"We got better things to do," Banjo said. He walked off, with his cadre of boys fast on his heels. Joe hovered after them a bit just to make sure they didn't change their minds.

"Everything okay here?"

I turned to see Murdock leaning against his car. A collection of tough-looking elves and fairies wearing red and black leather posed on the other side of the car, an amusing visual effect he had no idea was going on. "Yeah, just a little arson and a smidge of street fighting."

Murdock smiled and nodded up the street at Joe. "He's better than a Doberman."

I nodded, rubbing my shoulder. "Yeah, and more fun to drink with."

A deep horn blast announced the arrival of a fire truck. Murdock looked up at the burning building. "I'm going to guess that has something to do with the evidence you mentioned."

"Yeah. Did."

Joe took that moment to return. He smiled—much more pleasantly—and handed me a smoldering lump of rubber and canvas. "I'm not bored anymore."

I took the shoe by its laces and held it out to Murdock. "This is the kid's. It had some elf blood on it, but it's gone now obviously."

Murdock leaned in his car window to retrieve an evidence bag. Murdock held the bag open, and I dropped in the shoe. He zipped the bag closed and held it up, waiting for the smoldering to die off for lack of air.

"Elf blood," he said. He looked at me with a knowing smirk. "Why do I not like the implications of that?"

"Because you know I think it was Kruge's, even though I couldn't definitively sense it, and now I can't prove it. And because you don't like coincidences any more than I do, we're going to have to figure out how the cases are connected without missing other evidence in case they're not."

He pursed his lips, nodding. "Yep."

That's why I like working with Murdock. No bickering without a good reason. Oh, sure, we disagree, sometimes a lot. We debate, though, not argue, and usually end up at a place we're both comfortable with. Just like he knew where my thinking was heading, I knew he wasn't going to discourage me until he thought the trail was dead cold.

"This is the first time I touched it," Joe blurted.

Murdock looked at Joe, then me. "Oh?"

I shook my head in amused exasperation. "He sat in it." I told Murdock what happened. No surprise, he shrugged.

"Doesn't matter now. The bigger question is when you were spotted."

Two cop cars appeared on either end of the block. Another fire truck pulled up, followed by an ambulance van. "Um, Murdock, shouldn't you be doing something?"

He craned his neck over the roof of his car. "Yeah. Get in. If we don't leave now, they'll box us in."

"Leave? Don't you have to police something?"

He walked around his car and got in. "Homicide, Connor. Is there anyone in the building?"

I looked at Joe. "Nope," said Joe.

"Then get in before my clothes start smelling like smoke."

"I'm going to watch the fire," said Joe.

"Suit yourself. Let me know about your gang contact," I said. I don't think he heard me, though. He was already drifting higher up for a better view. I tossed some juice bottles off the passenger seat and got in. Murdock backed all the way up the street to the corner and bounced the car around. He coasted over to Summer Street and made his way back toward downtown.

"What took you so long?" I asked.

"Doctor's appointment. New healer."

"What did he say?"

"He says what they all say. He can't find anything wrong with me except my essence is suped-up. I told him I'm fine, it's only the fey who seem to think I'm not."

I nodded. "It's not that there's anything wrong with you, Murdock. Remember that kid, Shay? How I kept telling you he had an oddly strong essence for a human? He still felt like a human normal to me. You feel like a fey human, if there's such a thing. You feel like what I bet a human from Faerie would feel like. It's never been seen post-Convergence, and they don't understand it."

As he stopped for a red light, he gave me a sideways glance and smiled. "Sounds familiar."

"Touché," I said. At Avalon Memorial, they didn't understand my condition either. "Who's the doctor?"

He accelerated with the light change. "I don't think he's a doctor, actually. He said he was a medic. Do the fey have army medics?"

I laughed. "That's his title. *Midach*. He must be old school. You should ask Gillen Yor his name. He'll know."

"Why so interested?"

"Beyond the obvious that I hope you're okay, if he can figure out what's going on with you, maybe he can figure out what's going on with me. We sort of have opposite problems. The source might be the same."

"I knew this would end up being about you," he said.

I felt anger rise. "I said I hoped you're okay, didn't I? Don't you think I feel enough guilt about it?"

As usual, Murdock put me right in my place. He laughed. "I'm joking, ya fool. I knew it would irritate you. It's not your fault I have some freaky essence now, just like if you got shot on another case, it wouldn't be my fault. Unless, of course, I shot you. By accident, I mean. Let it go, Connor. I'm fine."

"Jerk," I said. I slouched deeper in my seat. He was right, of course. But I had put a lot of people in danger on that case, especially him. I had involved him—a human normal—in a situation where ability was being manipulated on an enormous scale. It could have killed him. It almost did. I'm still not sure if it was ego or error. Either way, I didn't like doubting myself. I'm not used to it. I didn't say anything more. I know what it feels like to have something wrong that no one knows how to fix.

"Anyway, we ID'd the kid," Murdock said. "Dennis Farnsworth. Sixteen years old. Some petty shoplifting charges. All dropped. No big trouble."

I knew it. Sixteen. "Until now."

"Until now," Murdock repeated.

"Any family?"

He nodded. "Mother. Two sisters. They live on D Street." He turned onto D Street.

My stomach gave a slight clench. I knew what was coming. "Have they been notified?"

"Yeah. We get the easy part. All we have to do is question her while she's in shock."

I hate talking to parents about their dead kids. You knock on a door. It opens. They take one look at you with your solemn face, and they know. They always know. You don't even have to be wearing a uniform. They can smell cop a mile a way. Doesn't matter what rung of the social ladder they're on. They know a cop who has that look isn't stopping by for the Auxiliary Association's annual donation drive. The last thing they want to talk about is how maybe their kid was not hanging with the right crowd.

Sunset was coming on, the sky turning a deep purple. The streetlights hadn't kicked on yet, but already house lights burned more visibly, the taillights of cars standing out a little more. You travel far enough down D Street, you get out of the Weird and into South Boston. If you don't travel that far, you end up in the twilight zone between the two neighborhoods. Not dangerous with a capital "D," but barely safe with a small "s."

It was easy to spot where the Farnsworths lived. The triple-decker wooden townhouse shone with light. One lone news van from the local cable station had parked not too far away. I could lay odds I knew where the network stations were. Murdock parked by a fire hydrant.

We walked up the sidewalk to the house, nodded to the

beat officer who was keeping an eye on things, and mounted the porch steps. Several kids stared at us, an unusual mix of fey and human, street kids, with hard stares and harder lives. No gang colors that I could see.

We went through the open door into the house, the heat of many people wafting over us. To the right, a staircase led to the upper apartments. The Farnsworth place was on the first floor, another open door that met the entryway on the landing.

Murdock stepped in first, pausing to take in the scene. Over his shoulder I could see people clustered in a modest living room. On the couch a red-eyed woman sat, stout, thin, dyed blond hair clipped to one side with a child's red barrette. She had her arm wrapped around a small girl, who half lay in her lap, maybe seven years old, with solemn eyes roaming the room. Another young girl, a few years older, sat on her other side, her face pressed against her mother's shoulders, eyes as red as the woman's.

"Mrs. Farnsworth?" Murdock spoke softly.

The woman lifted her head in our direction without speaking.

"Mrs. Farnsworth, I'm Detective Leonard Murdock. I'm very sorry for your loss today."

She didn't so much nod as rock back and forth slightly. "Thank you."

"Is there somewhere we can talk?"

Another woman crossed the room, sat on the couch, and with gentle hands took the younger child into her own lap. Mrs. Farnsworth squeezed her other daughter's hand and stood. Without speaking, she led us through a crowded hallway lined with more people. Their conversations fell away as we passed, their faces tracking with questions.

We entered a back bedroom, obviously her room, crowded with a bedroom set too large for the space. Everything was neat and orderly, the faint odor of dime-store rose water in the air. She sat on the bed.

"Mrs. Farnsworth, when was the last time you spoke to Dennis?"

"Last night before I went to work. He was supposed to be watching his sisters. Molly said he went out about eleven o'clock and made her swear not to tell. He said he'd be back in an hour."

"Did he seem different? Preoccupied? Worried?"

She shook her head. "He seemed fine. Happy. It was just a regular day."

"Do you know if he was in any kind of trouble?" Murdock asked.

She shook her head again. "Not that I knew. He's that age when it isn't cool to confide in his mother."

"What about his father?"

Her voice and face went flat. "Gone. Ten years."

"What about friends? A lot of kids on the porch."

She shrugged. "I don't know his friends anymore. I work two jobs. Denny was quiet. He was trying to stay out of trouble."

"Was it working?" I asked. Murdock shot me a look, but I ignored him.

"I don't know," she said in a tiny voice.

I crouched down so that she could look down at me. "I'm sorry, Mrs. Farnsworth, I didn't introduce myself. I'm Connor Grey. I'm helping to investigate any unique aspects to this . . . situation. Do you know why Dennis was on Summer Street?"

She shrugged. "He hung around up the Weird. Found some group that he liked."

"A gang?"

Finally, she stirred out of her lethargy. "He is not in a gang! Denny hated gangs. That's how he got in trouble—some gang trying to recruit him. His high school counselor got him involved in a community group."

I liked and didn't like where this was going. "Unity?"

She nodded. "That's it. He seemed to like it there. His grades went up."

"Did Dennis know Alvud Kruge?"

Her eyes searched the carpet. "He talked about Mr. K. all the time. He liked him."

"Do you know what happened to Alvud Kruge today?"

She closed her eyes. "Yes. My son couldn't have done something like that."

"I'm sorry, I didn't mean to imply that."

"Mrs. Farnsworth, did Dennis confide in anyone?" Murdock asked.

Her face hardened a bit as she looked at him. "He had a girlfriend. Crystal. Crystal Finch."

"Do you have an address or phone number?"

"No. Somewhere on E Street. He ended the relationship."

"Why's that?" Murdock asked.

"Because I asked him to. That girl was bad news. Bad family. Trouble."

"Is there anyone you can think of that might have wanted to cause Dennis harm?"

She exhaled sharply through her nose. "Look where we live. I work two jobs, and this is the best I can do. No one needs a reason to harm you around here. And I can't think of a single reason why someone would . . . why someone would . . ." She teared up. "No, I don't know." The tears began to spill.

"Mrs. Farnsworth . . ." Murdock began.

She bunched a tissue under her nose. "I want my girls. Please, get my girls. I don't want to talk anymore."

Murdock pulled a business card out of his pocket. "Okay. Here, please call me if you think of anything. I'll call on you tomorrow to see if you need anything."

She took the card wordlessly, not looking at it. I stood and backed out of the room with Murdock. He turned back a moment. "If I may ask one more question, Mrs. Farnsworth, did Denny have a pair of orange Nikes?"

She shook her head. "No. He had white sneakers. I don't know what kind."

"Thank you," Murdock said. We made our way back through the apartment. Murdock paused by the couch and squatted in front of the older girl. "Are you Molly?" She nodded.

"Did Denny say where he was going last night?"

She stared at Murdock with wide, solemn eyes. "No. He said he had something important to do."

"Did he say what?"

Molly glanced at the woman cradling her sister. She leaned close to Murdock. "No, but he went with Crystal," she whispered. "I saw her up the street. Don't tell Mum or she'll be mad."

Murdock smiled to reassure her. "I won't. Your mum's asking for you and your sister."

We left the apartment. The porch was decidedly emptier than when we had arrived. The fey kids were gone. Of the ones left, Murdock started asking about their relationship to Dennis. I stepped down to the sidewalk. He was just covering the bases. I was willing to bet that the kids who really knew Denny Farnsworth had left when they saw us. Tough kids don't talk to cops if they can avoid it.

I wandered back to Murdock's car. As I leaned against the fender, I noticed a woman a couple of houses down. If the height of her skirt were any indication, she had not taken into account the coming night chill. And if the flash of her sequin top was any indication, she had wandered into the wrong end of the neighborhood. She wasn't watching the street, though. She watched the Farnsworth house, craning her neck every time a girl stepped onto the porch. Just the girls. A gut-level intuition kicked in.

I strolled over. As I got closer, I could see the heavy makeup, the overdyed hair. She had that look that said early thirties, trying to cover up enough wear and tear for someone in her forties desperately hoping she looked in her twenties. It probably worked later in the evening.

Without looking at me, she said, "Not now, hon. I got business."

"Mrs. Finch?" I said.

Her head whipped around fast on that. She eyed me up and down, then turned back to watch the house. "Not hardly."

"Looking for Crystal?"

She bit her lower lip and looked at me sideways. "You know where she's at?"

"That answers my next question. She's not here, Mrs. Finch. I got the feeling inside she wouldn't be welcome."

She flipped her hair and stared directly at me know. Cool, hard eyes, not the type I would find comforting if I were looking for a little short-term company. "Ain't no Mrs. Finch. That was Crystal's daddy's name. You a cop?"

"Not really. But I'd still like to talk to Crystal."

"Oh, you'd 'like to talk to Crystal,' " she mimicked. "Get in line, buddy. I haven't seen her in three days. When I heard about Denny, I thought I might get her here."

I glanced up at the house. Murdock had made his way onto the steps and was talking to the last couple of kids remaining. "You don't seem very upset."

She shrugged. "Not my kid. Shit happens."

"What can you tell me about Crystal?"

She narrowed her eyes. "Crystal? How about she's an ungrateful little bitch who owes me seventy-five bucks, and if she don't turn up real soon, she can just stay wherever she's landed. How's that?"

"Very maternal," I said.

She curled her upper lip. "Go to hell, Mr. Not-really-a-cop. You see Crystal, you tell her I want my cash." She walked away, her high heels boring holes into the sidewalk. I watched her go and thought you don't have to be fey to land on the wrong side of the street around here.

I went back to Murdock's car to wait for him. Night descended on the city, a darker night than usual. Death may be the great equalizer, but the Weird is a close second. That two people died there, one so prominent, the other so not, demonstrates it. The fact that they had a connection to each other shows how the high and low can both find the same knock on the door.

5

A high-pitched ringing jolted me out of sleep. I knew that sound and dreaded it every time I heard it. One of my protection wards had gone off. I slid out of bed into my jeans in one smooth motion. In less than two seconds, I was across the room and standing to the side of the door with a classic Louisville slugger in my hand. The bat had two functions: it was charged with a deflector spell that would activate if someone threw essence at me, and it hurt like hell if I whomped someone with it. In either case, the idea was to give me some breathing space to call for help if I needed it.

Several wards protect my apartment. Some of them are passive—they act like barriers against charged essence. Some are reactive—like those that test for an individual's essence to determine whether that person is someone I trust. That's how people like Murdock and Joe can come and go without freaking out the wards. And some are active, doing a regular scan for any unusual activity. None of them will completely protect me. That's where the signal wards come in. They're scattered around the building and keyed to my essence. I touch one, and an emergency signal shoots to the Guild. Only I know where they all are. They are my fail-safe, presuming I live long enough for help to arrive.

My apartment is on a dead-end hallway, so anyone making the turn at the top of the stairs has only my place to go to. The alarm that had gone off was a simple proximity alert at the end of the outside hall. It's a silent alarm—only I can hear it in my head. I felt another alarm go off, the one within five feet of the door, followed immediately by a banging.

"UBS," a voice called out.

I relaxed, but only a little. It wouldn't be the first time someone pretended to be a delivery service before they turned all assassin on you.

"Got any ID?" I called back. I did not move to look through the peephole. That would be expected. Whoever was on the other side of the door would know where I was standing at that moment and could take it as an opportunity to, oh, blow a hole in my head.

"Hello?" the voice said with an edge of annoyance.

I gave a quick look through the peep. He looked like a brownie—tawny skin, curly hair, button nose. The essence trickling through the door verified it as well. And he had the standard brown UBS uniform with the yellow shield sewn into the pocket, though that could have been filched.

Brownies aren't the most powerful of the fairies. They didn't have enough essence to make much of a living charging wards or serving as useful bodyguards. They are good at helping with simple tasks that people hate doing, like housecleaning. A lot of brownies actually did market themselves as housekeepers. The one drawback is their tendency to take insult over the slightest matters. At which point, they mutate into boggarts and become obsessed with vindication. Where they could be quite shy and pleasant as brownies, their boggart aspect is relentlessly annoying. Some bright guy turned that into an advantage by starting the United Brownie Service, one of the most reliable delivery services in the world. When UBS comes calling, you either answer or risk being stalked by an angry boggart.

"How'd you get in the building?" I asked.

"The door was open. Look, I'm double-parked. I've got a letter for Connor Grey. Are you him?"

"Just leave it," I said.

"I need a signature." Definitely annoyed now. I gave another look-see. His eyes were bulging a little. If I teased him out a bit more, he'd go boggie. I once knew a guy in a divorce case who lived on the run for three months with a screaming, maniacal boggart chasing him down with a subpoena. Not pretty.

I decided to risk it and open the door. You can't live your life assuming every nutty fairy at your door wants to kill you. The brownie gave me a grudging, almost relieved, smile. I doubt they like going boggart any more than someone likes being on the receiving end of it. Going boggie is a mania and has got to be exhausting.

"Are you Connor Grey?" he asked.

"Yes."

"I need to see your ID." I didn't argue. It would just make him upset, so I pulled out my wallet.

He nodded and made a notation on his clipboard. "An emergency meeting of the Guild board of directors has been called for tomorrow."

I leaned against the doorjamb. "And that concerns me because . . . ?"

He looked down at his clipboard. "You are the druid Connor Grey, right?"

"Yeah, but . . ."

"So I have you listed as Lady Briallen ab Gwyll's alternate. She's out of town."

I cocked an eyebrow. "You're kidding."

He gave me an annoyed look and held his clipboard up. There it was, an official notice from Guildmaster Manus ap

Eagan for a board of directors' meeting tomorrow. Sure enough, there I was, listed as Briallen's alternate.

"Sign here," the brownie said, pointing. I chuckled and signed. The brownie handed me an envelope and snatched the clipboard back. "Thanks."

"Please shut the front door for me."

"Sure!" He gave me a ridiculous smile. I could not fathom being that happy doing errands. They prefer their brownie aspect over the boggart. By their very nature, they can swing between the two in moments, so having the opportunity to be helpful to me probably took the edge off his initial annoyance with me.

Briallen was an old friend and mentor. She had been on the Boston Guildhouse board of directors since its founding. I knew she was traveling in the Far East over the summer on some obscure educational junket that I could never quite clarify no matter how often I asked. I remember a discussion with her years ago about listing me as a temporary alternate director. I couldn't believe she had never changed it, especially after the events of the last two years. It wasn't like her to overlook something like that. On the other hand, what would be like her, though, is to remember exactly that and purposely not change it. For all her professions of being a scholar, which she is, she's not above a little politicking here and there.

Since the accident that left me ability-impaired, I had effectively been banned from the Guildhouse. The envelope contained a copy of the meeting notice and a Guildhouse building pass. Normally, I couldn't get in the front door of the Guildhouse without an escort, and here I was being invited to a governing board meeting. I couldn't wait to see the look on Keeva's face.

I could guess what the meeting was about. Alvud Kruge had been a board member. While the Guildhouse board had become more and more ineffectual over the years, fractured as it was by partisanship, with any luck it should be able to muster a coherent statement of condolences.

Now that I had the keys to the palace, I thought I'd drop in and surprise a couple of people. It would give me a chance to fill Keeva in on what had happened with the running shoe evidence and see what leads she was following for Kruge. If she would tell me. I never knew with her.

I spent the rest of the morning doing what I could to research gangs off the Internet. Not much help, really. Mostly newspaper articles talking about gangs on the Web. I did find a couple of local sites on the Weird, but they just referenced the usual suspects in the neighborhood in an odd travel guide style.

By early afternoon, I stood in the wide foyer of Boston's Ward Guildhouse. To the left, applicants snaked through a queue, a litany of the fey world's woes etched on their faces. This is how the fey deals with the world: A bad thing happens; you can't solve it yourself; you go to the Guildhouse and fill out an application for assistance; then you go home and never hear from them again unless you're really wealthy, really powerful, or really, really in trouble. In other words, most people don't get their fey problems resolved.

I didn't have to go through the rigmarole since I had a bona fide building pass. Which meant I could go through the much shorter queue to the right. It didn't mean all that much. I still didn't get to use the private employee entrance without a live employee with me. I used to. And I used to feel so cool doing it. That's the problem with being arrogant. Lame-ass things make you feel cool. But since I don't have much of anything to be arrogant about anymore, it's all about my lack of patience.

The elf at the desk checked my driver's license against the pass. Not a flicker of recognition passed over her face. So much for past glories. She returned the license and pass with a little clip I'd seen people use to hang their passes on their jackets. I slipped it into my pocket and strolled through security to the elevator lobby, checking myself out in the mirrored hallway.

As much as I despise the Guild these days, the Guild-house itself is still a fascinating place. As the local Boston headquarters for the fey world, all manner of folk work in the building. You get a heady mix of politics and scholarship and even some danger. No one leaves their animosities at the door. Old grievances play themselves out through misplaced memos or nuanced wordplay or meeting roulette. Despite its egalitarian philosophy, it's still a Seelie Court animal, though. The Celts hold sway. Sure they let in the elves and dwarves, but most of them get relegated to minor diplomatic meetings or, if they are actually employed by the Guild, rarely progress beyond midlevel positions. It's the same story on the other side of town at the Teutonic Consulate, only in reverse. One day the fairies and the elves will settle their disputes and immediately start arguing over whose building to use for a unified fey world.

The elevator descended so slowly it felt like it wasn't moving at all. The numbers lit up, flashed past the lobby and down. The third subbasement light flashed on, and the doors opened to the sound of blaring heavy-metal guitar. I walked down the long, vaulted corridor, idly running my finger along the bricks. Halfway to an opened door, thick oak on iron hinges, the music cut off, and I could here the unmistakable laugh of Meryl Dian.

"Stop making that face. I'm telling you that's Grieg's 54-3," she said.

"Then why not listen to the Grieg?" A deep, male voice replied. As Meryl laughed again, I froze in midstep. I hadn't heard that voice in a long time.

"This *is* listening to Grieg, only fresher," she said.

I started walking again and stopped at the open door.

"I like the stale version," said the man in her guest chair. He cocked his head back to look at me, then stood with a fluid, casual movement that belied his age.

Nigel Martin stood a little shorter than me, thin, his mostly silvered, wavy brown hair thrust back from his hairline to graze the top of his collar. He had that solid presence of someone sure of himself, gained from years of experience, which in his case was at least a century. His eyes were at once youthful and deep, and green like a sea storm. He wore regular street clothes—simple brown chinos, a white button-down with a hound's-tooth jacket. He could usually be mistaken for a stuffy professor at an Ivy League school.

Meryl gave me a broad smile. "Hey! Who let you in?"

"Hello, Nigel," I said, looking at him. I could feel how uncertain the smile was on my face as I extended my hand and almost breathed in relief when he clasped it.

"Connor. Meryl tells me you've been doing well."

I looked at her quickly. She remained seated, leaning back in her chair behind her desk piled high with the usual assortment of papers. Her eyes shifted back and forth between Nigel and me, a curious, observant look on her face.

"Yes, thanks. I didn't know you were back," I said.

He smiled a careful, warm smile. "I've been busy." He tilted his head toward Meryl. "Ms. Dian, it was a pleasure as always, but I must go." He turned back to me. "Don't be late tomorrow, Connor." He stepped forward, and I backed awkwardly into the hallway to let him pass.

"I won't," I said.

"'Bye, Nigel," Meryl called out, the enthusiasm trailing out of her voice.

I watched him walk the length of the corridor in his signature steady stride that showed of many foot journeys. He reached the elevator and hit the button. The doors opened, and he stepped inside. Not once did he glance back at me, even when he pressed the inside panel. The doors closed on his back.

I looked at Meryl. She wore one of her customary black outfits, a lace top with a formless V-neck sweater. She had decided to let her hair grow longer this year, almost shoulder-length. Today it was blond with magenta bangs. I thought it was cute, though I wouldn't admit it and deny myself the chance to rib her about it.

She furrowed a brow. "That was strange. Was that strange?"

I dropped myself into the vacated guest chair. "That was strange."

"What did you do?"

"Nothing," I said, frowning. It hit me immediately. Nigel was pissed because I had done nothing. Here I was, two years after my accident, and I had not made any effort to deal with it until recently. Nigel is, maybe "was" now, my mentor. I had been his prize pupil. Briallen verch Gwyll ab Gwyll had initiated me into the mysteries throughout most of my teen years. When I hit a strapping eighteen years old, she turned me over to Nigel.

Nigel wasn't in the States when I had my accident. He didn't come back either. I didn't take it personally. He often disappeared for months at a time. It didn't occur to me, though, that this had been the longest stretch of time between our meetings. "When did he come back?"

Meryl closed one eye as she thought. "July."

"Three months! And you didn't tell me?"

She looked annoyed. "I wasn't aware I was your social secretary. Besides, I assumed you knew."

"And yet you never mentioned him."

She gave me a level stare. "Uh, excuse me, neither did he, and it's not my job to keep you up-to-date on my social life."

I playfully curled my lip at her. "Fine, fine. I'm just annoyed. I can't believe he didn't call."

"If I remember correctly, a lot of people don't call you," she said sweetly.

"Ha-ha. Guess why I'm here."

She rolled her eyes. "You need something."

"Funny." I smiled and held up the building pass. "I'm attending a Guildhouse board meeting tomorrow as Briallen's alternate."

She chuckled and shook her head. "Priceless. The place really is going to hell."

"Go ahead, keep that up, and I won't invite you for coffee," I said.

She leaned back in her chair. "I hear you got tossed from the Kruge investigation."

I love the Guild. Like all organizations with secrets, it's a huge rumor mill. "I didn't get tossed because I was never on it. I just happened to get to the crime scene before Keeva, and she pulled rank."

Meryl nodded. "I heard she wasn't too happy about it. She's been desperately trying to impress Manny. It's driving him crazy."

"Manny? Since when do you call Manus ap Eagan 'Manny'?"

"We're old friends. He wasn't always Guildmaster, you know."

That gave me pause. Manus ap Eagan had been Guildmaster almost my entire life. I searched Meryl's face for some hint of her age, but she looked no older than late twenties, early thirties. I didn't sense any glamour about her either. It was even possible she was over fifty. Druids and druidesses live extremely long lives, and our physical appearance changes very slowly compared to human normals. I was almost forty years old, but looked and felt like a human normal in my twenties. I could tell she knew what I was thinking by the smirk on her face. Questioning her would be useless.

I smirked. "My, my. Guildmaster Eagan. Nigel Martin. Pretty impressive company you're keeping these days."

Her eyes went wide. She leaned forward and grabbed her phone. "Shoot! That reminds me. I was supposed to call Maeve back."

"What!"

She punched in a phone number. "She called during *Buffy*. I almost forgot."

My jaw dropped. "The High Queen of Tara called, and you let the machine pick up because you were watching *Buffy*?!"

She held her hand over the receiver and pitched her

voice low. "It was the 'Dark Willow' one. I don't have it on DVD."

We stared at each other. The corner of her mouth twitched, then she broke into a grin.

"You're a jerk," I said.

She laughed and hung up the phone. "Way too easy, Grey. So tell me about Kruge."

I filled her in on what I knew, including Dennis Farnsworth. ". . . and I think this gangbanger might be related," I finished.

She tilted her head in thought. "I guess it's possible in a 'golly gee I hope I can figure out how to get involved with the most important murder case in the world' kind of way."

"I can never thank you enough for your support," I said.

"I think the dwarves are your best bet. They're very territorial, especially down that end of the Weird."

"Yeah, I agree. I was wondering if . . ."

". . . I could do you a favor," she said with an smug, matter-of-fact tone.

I glowered at her. "Yes. Any chance you can score me some gang files?"

She laughed. "I'll see what I can dig up."

"So, how long have you known Nigel Martin?" I asked.

She sighed. "I thought you let that go too quickly."

I threw my hands in the air in feigned innocence. "What? I'm having a casual conversation about a mutual friend."

She cocked her head again. "There's really not much to tell. As far as I know, he showed up at the Guildhouse sometime in July—and no, don't ask me, I am not going to check the ID scanner logs for the precise date. He came to my office one day to ask me about Scandinavian relics. He comes by every couple of weeks to see what I find. We shoot the shit. End of story."

"What do you talk about?"

"I don't know. At first it was just business. Lately it's been music. He has the most archaic taste. I've been trying to convince him that the best thing to happen to Faerie music was Convergence."

I arched an eyebrow. "You were in Faerie?"

She laughed. "Goat's blood, Grey. I hope this isn't an example of the investigative skills your reputation claims."

"Where were you born?" is a game the fey like to play. The fey that came from Faerie were known as the Old Ones: Maeve, the High Queen at Tara; Donor Elfenkonig, the self-styled Elven King; Briallen, though she won't discuss it; Gillen Yor, High Healer at Avalon Memorial. Certainly, Nigel Martin, but he'd never said anything about it, and no one seems to remember him from there. Lots of others.

Some people believe the Old Ones, the ones directly from Faerie, are more powerful and adept at manipulating essence than their offspring. True or not, most people believe it, so to impress people, more fey than possible claim to have been born in Faerie. While druids and druidesses hold their age extremely well, I doubted Meryl could be that old.

"What kind of relics?" I asked.

She shrugged. "Rune stakes, mostly."

Rune stakes. Nigel certainly knew enough about Celtic rune stakes. He'd taught me everything I know about them. You get a stick, you scratch some ogham on it, you poke it somewhere. They were like stone wards, only much more precise since you can get pretty detailed with them. Scandinavian rune stakes used old Teutonic runes. So, that meant elf research most likely. Nigel is a political animal as well as a powerful druid. Know your enemy are the watchwords for both.

"Anything interesting?"

She toyed with a strand of her hair. "Sure. Tribal territory markers and a couple of evil eye type of things. I'm definitely going to try one of the evil eye things. I'm infested with Christian missionaries lately."

"So, let's go for coffee, and you can tell me all about it."

She shook her head. "Can't. I've got stuff I have to take care of."

"Maybe I could come by your place later. You could make dinner. Food's the fastest way to a man's heart, you know."

She cocked her head to the side. "Really? I thought it was the fourth intercostal space between the ribs."

I shook my head, looking at the ceiling. I pulled myself up out of the chair. "Fine. I'll just have to catch you when you don't have 'stuff.' "

She quirked an eyebrow up. "I've got lots of stuff."

"Okay! Okay! I'm leaving!" I said.

"Give my regards to Manny," she called as I walked out. I gave her the finger and smiled at the sound of her laugh all the way to the elevator.

The previous spring, I had stopped a madman from destroying reality and gotten my ass kicked. Between the strain of fighting powerful entities and the physical battering I took in the process, I'd almost died again. Meryl had stopped in often at the hospital to see me. Of course, she made a point of reminding me that she had healing abilities and always asked about my health, my treatment, and my essence. When I was discharged and went home, we developed an avid email correspondence. Which led to drinking together. Which led to the occasional lunch or dinner.

I didn't know what was going on with her. I liked being around her. I liked getting to know her. I liked that she gave me shit at every opportunity. Normally, I don't start getting those feelings until after I've slept with someone and, even then, not usually. This was different. I hadn't even had a good fevered dream about her, never mind gotten her naked. And it gave me an odd pleasure that if she knew that, she would act all annoyed and dismissive.

I hit the UP button. Due to the odd nature of the Guildhouse, with its towers and arches and spires, the doors opened on the fifteenth or the eighteenth floor, depending on how you counted. In any case, it was the Community Liaison Department, my old haunt where Keeva macNeve now held sway.

Since my accident helped boot me out of the Guild, I had been back only a few times and even then, insultingly, under escort. As I stood in the hall, knowing that Keeva had her job only because I saved her ass on her last major assignment, it finally struck home that I was never going to be back at the Guild as an investigator. The only place to do that was where I was standing, and there was no way in hell I could stomach Keeva as my boss.

The floor was surprisingly quiet. As I looked in at empty office after office, the only person I saw I didn't know. He didn't look up as I passed. I was about to turn around, when I found myself outside my old office. I didn't need a psychology course to get why I had ended up in front of the closed door. Seeing the empty nameplate next to it, I entertained the momentary thought that perhaps they were holding it for me even after all this time.

I pushed the door open and laughed. My desk was still there. My bookshelves. The floor lamp that I banged into every time I pushed my desk chair back. My desk chair was there, too. The credenza that I special ordered out of spite when accounting was giving me a hard time about my budget overruns. And every single flat surface was stacked with boxes. My office had become a storage room for old case files. So much for preserving the memory of me.

In another time, I would have nurtured a furious bitterness. Seeing that office, though, I really did have to laugh. What else could I do? The Wheel turns as It will, one of my favorite mentors likes to say. Who am I to rage against It?

I walked up to the window. At least the view had not changed and was still worth every penny. Boston Common at any time of year looks amazing. The oldest public park in the United States, and a fairy hill sits smack-dab in the middle of it. What's not to love?

I glanced down. Tucked between a chimney pot and the bottom of a flying buttress, a small cyclopean gargoyle squatted, a horn coming out of his forehead and his oversize genitalia proudly displayed. He's never told me his name, so

I keep calling him Virgil. He shows up at unexpected times and places. Gargoyles have a knack for omen and given that he could only be seen from this angle, I was willing to bet he knew I would decide to visit my old office. I waited to see if he would say anything. He rarely does, and after a few minutes, he still hadn't spoken. I knew I would spend the rest of the day, if not longer, wondering if his presence alone was supposed to indicate something.

"Are you lost?"

I turned at the sound of Keeva's voice. The Guildhouse has dampening wards everywhere, so I didn't sense her behind me. "No, just needed some paper clips."

She leaned against the door, her de rigueur black jumpsuit fitting snugly over a body that was made for things to fit snugly over. Keeva is without a doubt attractive and knows it. At the same time, she has that look, slightly bitter, like she's sure any moment she's going to smell something bad. It knocks her down the hotness scale in my book. Today, though, she just looked stressed, even pale. "How did you get in?"

I perched myself on the corner of the desk. *My* desk. "You wouldn't believe me if I told you." I had a perfectly legitimate reason to be in the building, but she didn't have to know that.

"Look, Connor. I'm busy. I am in no mood to talk about your visa."

I nodded. My visa. In all the action of the last twenty-four hours, I had actually not thought about it, which is amazing considering how obsessed with it I've been. I've been trying to go to Germany to track down the elf who almost killed me two years ago and again indirectly this past spring. I'm hoping for a little payback. Somehow I've been mysteriously put on the German no-entry list and can only get past it with a diplomatic visa, which only the Guild can provide. I guess I didn't have to put "want to kill someone in the Black Forest" on my application for them to figure out why I wanted to go.

"Come on, Keeva. Bergin Vize is running free. He obviously has some powerful connections there, or I wouldn't need the visa. Someone has to bring him in, and I think I deserve to be the one to do it."

She shook her head. "Connor, you ran around all summer telling anyone within earshot that you wanted to kill Bergin Vize. You know the Guild can't endorse that. Do not think for one moment I am distracted enough by Kruge's murder to sign off on a visa."

I shrugged. She wasn't willing to the first six times I asked. I didn't think she would be this time either. "You don't look so good."

She nodded instead of taking offense. "I haven't had much sleep in the last three days. Eorla Kruge has decided to bury her husband here, and I have two diplomatic delegations to coordinate in addition to the investigation."

"How is the Kruge investigation?"

She pursed her lips, crossed her arms, and looked down at her toes. "It's complicated. Troll essence everywhere, more than one, but the MO is all wrong. We're thinking some kind of rogue. Maybe the cleaning woman Kruge employed. Her name's Croda. She hasn't been seen since the murder. She has known drug gang connections, and Kruge was doing everything he could to take down the gangs."

"A troll cleaning lady? Isn't that an oxymoron?"

Keeva looked up, unamused. "Is there something you came up here for besides bothering me?"

"Actually, no. Do the names Dennis Farnsworth or Crystal Finch mean anything to you?"

She nodded. "Farnsworth is the kid that got killed the same night as Kruge. Murdock's report got passed to me this morning."

That surprised me. I keep forgetting how efficient Murdock can be. "You got the report? So the Guild's taking the case?"

She shrugged. "No. I got the report because Murdock thinks the Guild should take it. In fact, I have an entire Murdock file. He thinks all his cases are fey-related. He's worse than you are."

"Keeva, the kid had Kruge's blood on him. How can you ignore that?"

She gave me that long look again. "Correct me if I'm misquoting, but I believe the report says 'due to concurrent circumstances, elf blood evidence on running shoe may be related to Kruge case.' Also correct me if I'm misremembering, but I believe this blood evidence has also been destroyed. Is that what you're claiming I'm ignoring? Even if the kid was there, he's dead, so he's no help. I'm not seeing anything on the police report to follow up on. Is there something you know that's not in the report?"

"The kid was wearing gang gear. You have to look at that angle, too."

She nodded. "Kruge was a gang mediator. Practically everyone related to his outreach office has some gang history. He wasn't killed by some street kid, Connor. It was someone fey and someone powerful. If I start assuming every gang member is Kruge's killer, I'd be hauling in a third of the population from your end of town. If the kid's death becomes relevant, I might take the case. Right now, he's just collateral damage. I'll feed Murdock any info that might close what is, and remains, his case."

Keeva's focus on fey-only crimes was exactly what frustrated me about the Guild these days. She didn't even want to entertain the notion that a dead human kid was something to be upset about. "But . . ."

Annoyance crossed her face. "But, nothing, Connor. Look, whoever killed Kruge would have no problem killing Farnsworth. Why would he bother going through the effort of flying him almost a mile away and dropping him? It doesn't make sense. I think the kid saw what happened, ran, and got caught in his own little problems. I'll tell you this if only to get you out of my hair: I have another report on my desk. A gang fight happened two days ago involving elves. Your kid was wearing the colors of one of the gangs. You want to find a motive for your case, it's right there. Instead of trying to tell me how to do my job, why don't you go tell Murdock to do his and talk to the Boston gang unit."

I could tell by the self-satisfied smirk on Keeva's face that I did a bad job of hiding my surprise. I couldn't believe Murdock didn't tell me about the gang fight. It didn't change my gut feeling, but it certainly didn't help me get Keeva interested in the case.

"Can I see the file?"

"Ask Murdock. You have to leave now." Her voice was neutral. She wasn't just being obstinate this time. I knew the drill. She probably had every power player in the city breathing down her neck. Instead of pushing her buttons some more, I decided to enjoy her discomfort vicariously for now.

"Okay. Let me know if I can help," I said.

Nigel Martin appeared at the door. "Here you are," he said to Keeva.

She smiled at him. "Sorry, Nigel. Look who I bumped into."

He smiled thinly. "Connor."

"Twice in one day, Nigel. Almost like old times." I couldn't resist injecting a little sarcasm into my voice.

"Much has happened since then," he said.

"Maybe we can have dinner. Catch up," I said.

He glanced at Keeva. "Other things are more pressing at the moment. Perhaps another time."

I tried to appear unperturbed. "What brings you back to Boston?"

"Research," he said.

I waited a beat for him to ask me what I was doing. Then another beat. And another. "I'm working cases for the Boston P.D.," I finally said.

"Yes, I had heard that. I'm sorry, Connor, but we don't have time to socialize right now. Keeva and I have work to do," he said.

I tried to mask my embarrassment with a neutral face. I doubt I did it very well. Not in front of two people who knew me well enough to know the difference between my neutral face and my upset-but-hiding-it face. Nigel knew damn well how I would react to what he said. Sure enough, Keeva now had on her I'm-pretending-not-to-be-enjoying-this face.

"Sure, no problem. I just stopped by to say hello," I said.

Keeva stepped back to let me pass by the two of them as I went into the hallway. I continued walking without saying anything. As I was about to turn the corner to the elevator, she called my name. I looked back. They continued walking away from me as she spoke over her shoulder.

"Just so you know, I'm not going to screw up the Kruge investigation to spite you. If anything pans out on Farnsworth, let me know."

I smiled and nodded once. She turned and walked in the other direction. I knew she wouldn't screw up the investigation to spite me. If I found any key evidence, she would take credit for solving the case to spite me.

6

I could hear the phone ringing when I was in the shower, as phones tend to do at inconvenient times. I let the machine pick up. Unlike a lot of people, I don't leap out dripping wet to answer the phone. I don't always remember to check the answering machine because it's more or less my junk phone number. Anyone who really knows me and needs to reach me has my cell or knows someone who does. The apartment phone was for strangers and bill collectors, who apparently share it freely. Besides, I don't have caller ID on that line, and I like to choose whom I talk to when I'm wet and naked.

I hit the answering machine replay as I got dressed. "Hello, Mr. Grey. My name's Janey Likesmith. I work at the OCME. I have some information about a case you're involved in. I . . . um . . . I don't always get my messages, so please stop by the office so we can talk. I don't want to sound melodramatic, but the value of this may not last. I can explain in person. Thank you."

The OCME is the Office of the City Medical Examiner. At the moment, the only person I knew there was Dennis Farnsworth. Murdock, of course, knew the staff, but how anyone knew me was intriguing. I had to laugh about this Janey Likesmith not getting phone messages. The OCME had been in a slide downward for so long, the fact that the lights were on was a minor miracle. Asking for a decent receptionist was probably out of the question.

At the end of my street, a bitter wind swept up the channel and welcomed me to the outside world. Boston sits on a harbor, of course, and the Charles River frames it to the north, making the city an island of cold misery in the winter. Even in October, wind chills off the water pull the temperatures down in the freezing zone, and when you live in the Weird, you have no choice for decent transportation except your feet. There's a bus line that does run down Old Northern, but it doesn't take anyone where they want to go. I made my way over the Northern Avenue bridge with shoulders hunched against the wind, my ears freezing. While I'm not particularly vain about my hair, the least I figure I could save people is the spectacle of hat head. So, my ears freeze. I crossed into the financial district and hopped a bus to the South End.

The bus trundled down Washington Street, weaving in and out of the steel girders of the abandoned elevated subway. It's a strip of perpetual twilight, the el blocking out the sun during the day, sooty arc lights casting dim illumination at night. I hate buses. They're slow, irregular, and rank. It's hard to feel the least bit important if you have to ride a bus. It practically proclaims to the world you can't afford a car or cab fare. The subway is at least a convenience. A bus, though, a bus says sit in traffic, in discomfort, until you're late as hell. Fortunately, I didn't have an appointment.

Boston's South End is not South Boston. Newcomers make the mistake all the time. The South End is next to Southie, but it's a whole other world. Where Southie always maintains its identity as a middle-class Irish enclave, the South End is more like an eccentric sister that likes to change her image as often as possible. Sitting at the crossroads of other neighborhoods, it has an eclectic vibe of old

Irish, Lebanese, Asian, African-American, Hispanic, gay men and lesbians, rich and poor, college students, artists who can't be bothered with New York, and, yeah, a lot of fey. It has always been a neighborhood in flux, always interesting, and politically powerless. So, it ends up with a lot of city agencies like free clinics and welfare offices that other areas try their damnedest to keep out. And the OCME. No one ever wants to live next to the city morgue.

The bus left me in a cloud of blue exhaust, and I walked the final two blocks to the OCME. The place looks and feels tired, as though all the human tragedy that revolves through its doors has taken its toll on the building. I pushed through the scarred Plexiglas doors and found the reception desk. Of the four desks behind the main counter, an older woman occupied one and the others were empty. She did not look up.

"Excuse me?" I said. She still did not look, but held up her index finger as she continued reading something.

I felt a tingle of unexpected essence behind me and turned. A dark elf walked purposefully toward me, gave one glance at me, and placed some folders on the counter. As she perused her files, I couldn't imagine what she was doing at the OCME. Dark elves are rare in Boston, never mind working for human normals. They preferred keeping the peace in the southern parts of the country, particularly Atlanta and Birmingham,.

One of the better things about Convergence was the dark elves. They didn't much care for oppression of people based on skin color, something they found utterly ridiculous conceptually. If there was one thing the Alf and Swart elves agreed on, it was that they were elves first. Elves knew racism, but skin color alone wasn't something to base it on. Swarts had swiftly become involved in politics and pushed through the Civil Rights Act of 1934. I guess Congress didn't have much hope of defying a bunch of people who could chant their asses to hell and back.

The woman behind the counter still had her hand up. "Excuse me, I'm looking for Janey Likesmith," I said. Without moving anything else, the woman dropped her index finger forward and pointed.

"I'm Janey," the dark elf said, smiling as she extended her hand. She had deep brown skin and warm cocoa-colored eyes. Nutmeg brown hair swept over her delicate ear points and stopped abruptly at the nape of her neck. "You must be Mr. Grey."

"Connor. How'd you know?"

She leaned against the counter. "No one comes here looking for me unless I call them. Do you have a few minutes to look at something?"

"That's why I'm here," I said, smiling back so it wouldn't sound like sarcasm.

With an almost childlike excitement, she gathered her folders and led me across the hall to a stairwell. She wore chunky shoes that echoed loudly as she descended the steps. "I found something unusual in the Farnsworth case. I called you when I saw you were consulting with Detective Murdock. The Boston P.D. won't know what to do with it. No one here would get the ramifications." She paused at the basement door, concern troubling her face. "He won't mind, will he? That I called you and not him?"

"No, that's why he calls me, too."

She relaxed. "Oh, good. This way, please." She opened the door to another, dimmer hallway, and we were in the morgue area.

"Likesmith isn't a fey name," I said.

She threw me a smile. "It's Dokkheim, actually. I used to say to humans that where I come from it's 'like Smith.' So I changed it. The irony is now I have to explain it to the fey all the time."

She led me to a small lab with two tables, one empty, the other strewn with instruments, and walls lined with drawers. Without hesitation, she opened a particular drawer and pulled out several large envelopes and plastic bags. I recognized the Farnsworth boy's clothing in one of the larger ones. She laid them out on the table with care, immediately marking the tracking sheets to indicate the date and time she removed the items and put my name down as well. She lifted an envelope, removed a glass box about four inches square, and placed it on the table.

"You made a ward box?" I said.

She nodded. "As a precaution. I found these stamps in the lining of Dennis Farnsworth's hoodie."

Disappointment crawled across my mind. I'd seen stamps like this before. Kids licked them to get high. Farnsworth had drugs on him. The kid was running drugs while wearing Moke's gang colors.

I leaned closer. Five square stamps wrapped in individual plastic sleeves sat in the box. Each one was pale yellow with the ogham rune for oak on it. Janey opened the box, and I immediately felt the essence wafting off the stamps. With a small tweezers she removed one and placed it on a tray.

"You can feel the essence, can't you?" she said.

I shrugged. "Lots of drugs in the Weird have essence."

She nodded and used a second tweezers to remove the stamp from the sleeve. "Come closer, but don't touch it. I think dermal contact might cause absorption."

I stood closer to her and saw immediately what she meant. I could feel a rhythmic pulse of essence, and I felt attuned to it. "Oak," I said.

She smiled. "I thought you'd recognize it. My people are a woodland clan. We're both people of the Oak."

I didn't see the need to argue. All fey have affinities for working with certain types of essence. Druids primarily fall in the earth category, adept at working with plant life, particularly trees and particularly oak. It's why we like to use staffs and wands. Elves can chant essence out of most anything, but I didn't know that much about their affinities. That they even had them didn't surprise me.

"So, we have an essence-based drug derived from oak. I'm still not seeing anything odd."

"I worked with it for a while before I noticed. Feel it again," she said.

I concentrated on the stamp, felt the flow, could almost taste it on my tongue. A moment later, my brain felt like someone was squeezing it, and my shields slammed on so fast that I jerked back with grunt. The feeling stopped abruptly, and I opened my eyes. Janey had slipped the stamp back in the sleeve and put it back in the box.

She had concern on her face, confused, but real. "Are you okay?"

"Now I know why you put the ward field on it. It felt like something was trying to stab me in the head." I did a mental check on myself, but didn't notice any lingering effects.

She leaned against the table with crossed arms. "How odd. That's not what happened to me. There were six of these. I used one for testing and didn't think much about the essence coming off it until I realized I was just staring out the window." She gestured up at the small, grilled window. Not much to see but the fender of a car.

"Then someone came in and asked me to pick up coffee for the office, and I went. It wasn't until I was in line at Starbucks that I got annoyed. I usually get annoyed immediately when I get asked to be a gofer."

I pursed my lips. "So, there's a suggestive in it."

She nodded. "That's a pretty impressive feat to pull off in such a small item. I think more testing should be done, but we don't have the equipment here."

I looked around Janey's processing room. The OCME hardly had the trappings for a fey researcher. Hell, it hardly met the minimum requirements for a forensics lab. And yet here was a dark elf, an apparently intelligent individual, working for them. "Why are you here?"

She smiled. "You mean 'why am I not at the Guild?' Everyone asks eventually. The Guild did ask me to join. So did the Consortium. They get enough people to do what I do. At the OCME, I get to do whatever I want because human normals don't know how to sort through fey material. In a nutshell, I'm here because it helps a lot more than there."

"Sounds noble," I said. Lots of people turned down employment with the Guild, most of them for political or career reasons.

She shrugged and laughed. "Not really. My parents are what some people derisively call assimilationists. They think we're stuck here and are okay with it."

"And like parent, like daughter?"

Again, she shrugged. "I'm here-born, Mr. Grey. This is the only world I know. Faerie may be where my roots are, but it might as well be Antarctica as far as I'm concerned. It sounds very alien and beautiful, but not someplace I have the urge to live."

"Why didn't you call the Guild for help?"

She gave me a knowing look. "Because if the Guild cared, this boy wouldn't be here in the first place. This is a human murder case, Mr. Grey. At best, it would land in the research labs, not the crime unit."

"Could you do the tests with the right equipment?"

She shrugged. "Sure, but it's not likely on our budget."

I smiled. "Got a piece of paper?"

When Janey brought her hand out of the pocket of her smock, she held a spiral pad with a pen stuck in it. I like someone always ready to take notes. I wrote down Meryl's name and number and handed the pad back.

"Meryl's a friend. If she can, she'll get you to the right equipment."

Janey's ears flexed back in surprise. "Oh, I wasn't asking for that. I just thought you should know about it . . ."

"It's fine," I interrupted. "I wouldn't have offered if I didn't think it would help the case. And trust me, if Meryl has a problem with this, she'll let the both of us know."

She put the envelopes back in their respective drawers and led the way to the hall. We mounted the steps to the lobby.

"Thanks for calling me, Janey. I mean that. It's looking more and more like the kid was a drug runner, and things caught up with him."

She reached out a hand, and we shook. "I can't thank

you enough, Mr. Grey. I'll call Ms. Dian as soon as I get downstairs. It was a pleasure meeting you."

"My friends call me Connor."

"I'll take that as a compliment." She smiled and returned through the lobby to the flight of stairs down.

As I stepped out into the chill of the afternoon, I pulled my collar up around my neck. Farnsworth was running drugs. Murdock's theory was looking more likely than mine at this point. The kid was dead either way. I just wish once in a while I would find myself investigating an accidental death.

As I approached the corner, I found a pleasant surprise. A Lincoln Town Car sat idling at the curb. A brownie leaned against the front fender, a long, tawny sheepskin coat muffling her body, set off by red boots, red gloves, and a red chauffeur cap. She huddled herself against the cold and bounced on her heels when she saw me.

I felt a wave of pleasure. "Tibs!"

"I thought you'd never come out of there!" she called.

She waited until I was almost upon her, then took two steps and wrapped me in a hug, pressing a warm kiss on my lips. Her eyes glittered with affection as she stepped back. Tibbet was an old, sweet friend, a brownie by nature, but all woman. We met years ago at the Guild when I first joined. I was just coming into my own, and Tibs and I moved in the same party circles for a while. To call our affair romantic would be an exaggeration, but it was definitely mutual and fun. The fey have fewer hang-ups about sex than human normals. We don't stress about falling into bed unless a reason intrudes. Whenever Tibs and I weren't seeing other people, we were quite comfortable spending time together. We had a mutually satisfying thing for a while that ended as casually and friendly as it began.

She ruffled my hair. "Still handsome, I see."

I tugged her nut-brown ponytail. "Still gorgeous, I see."

She nodded at the car. "Hop in. The Old Man wants to see you."

I slid into the passenger seat of the stifling hot car.

"I will never get used to the winters here," Tibbet said as she settled into the driver's seat.

"It's hardly winter, Tibs."

She chuckled. "I lived in the Land of Summer, remember? I don't even like cold rain." She pulled into traffic and headed west.

"How'd you know I was here?"

"The Old Man told me. He said it's a sad place I wouldn't like, and he was right. I could feel it standing outside."

"It is, but it's also a helpful place, sometimes a hopeful one," I said. And it is. No one wants to end up in the OCME. But, if someone does, at least they try to figure out what happened to you. They don't always do it right, and they don't always get it right. But they always try. It's one of those places that you wonder how people can choose to work there. Then you meet them and understand.

"How's he doing?" I said.

Tibbet didn't answer for a long moment. Guildmaster Manus ap Eagan has been ill for almost a year. Fairies getting sick is rare, Danann fairies even rarer. It does happen, though.

"Not good," she said. "He gets weaker all the time. He hardly ever leaves the house." Her voice almost cracked. Tibbet has been with the Guildmaster since before Convergence. She's not quite a secretary, not quite a messenger or driver. *Aide-de-camp* comes to mind. Like all brownies, she's fiercely loyal to her chosen task, and after so much time, there's an understandable emotional connection. I placed my hand on the back of her neck and gave it a slight squeeze.

She smiled. "What about you?"

"The same," I said. "I've been exercising, but my abilities are still dead." I never like to talk about my condition. You can only tell people "no change" so many times. Doing ritual sun salutations at dawn has strengthened my essence, but at best it's made what little I can do work better. I haven't regained any more abilities.

Tibbet guided the car through the chaos of Kenmore Square, a confusing knot of five major roads pretending to be a traffic exchange. Boston streets are infamous for confusing the unwary visitor. Signage is poor, the squares are anything but, and the layout philosophy seems to be "try not to kill anybody." Tibbet's a pro, though, and we made it through with minimal terror or terrorizing. She took Brookline Avenue out of the city.

It is the nature of large cities to consume the smaller towns around them, usually for economic advantage. Boston acquired several towns, but not Brookline, which didn't see any advantage to joining a city of lower-class immigrants. To this day, it remains a place of privilege, one of the richest in the country, where anyone with enough money can find a place, even the fey. Manus ap Eagan had lived there for over half a century.

Tibbet took me into the exclusive Chestnut Hill neighborhood, location of some of the most expensive homes in the States. The landscaping is perfect, the acreage per house substantial, and not a stickball game to be seen. It's another world entirely from where I grew up in the rough and tumble South Boston. It's the kind of place where you keep expecting people to whisper for fear of disturbing deep, moneyed thoughts.

The Eagan estate began with a wrought-iron gate that opened without any prompting as we approached. Tibbet didn't use a remote. Likely, the whole place was warded to allow certain people to come and go and most people to not. The driveway wound in a stately curve lined with cedars that stood guarded reserve over the passing car. When the view opened up, you could see what some might call a house, while most everyone else would call it a heaping estate manor.

Tibbet pulled up to the enormous front doors, and we got out. Above the doors, a stained-glass panel depicted a man in a resplendent chair leaning back with his feet on the lap of a beautiful woman. As Tibbet held the door for me, I nodded upward. "Did you pose for that?"

She grinned. "Not likely."

The entry hall to the Guildmaster's house rose a full two stories and could hold a small army. Every year Eagan holds a kick-ass Winter Solstice party in the space. If you count the bathroom, it's the second room in the house I've been in. At the east wall, in the curve of a freestanding staircase, stood a rearing Asian elephant, the stuffed relic of a more unenlightened time.

In the middle of the west wall a massive fireplace stood. Above the mantel hung a larger-than-life portrait of High Queen Maeve of Tara, her deep black eyes staring out of a pale face, a cold majestic beauty. Maeve had posed for John Singer Sargent on her one and only visit to Boston almost a century ago. He had captured her perfectly. She looked like someone had just told her she couldn't have Europe for dessert.

At the back end of the hall, French doors gave onto a rolling lawn of brown grass. At the bottom of the lawn, topiary boxwoods had been torn ragged by the wind. The skeletal frame of a greenhouse sat in the white afternoon light.

"He's out back. He says the moisture makes him feel better," Tibbet said. She led me to the French doors and held one open for me.

"You're not coming?"

She shook her head. "I'll give you a ride back."

I walked down a brick path to the greenhouse. Its entrance worked like an air lock. Stepping through the inside door, humid air swept over me. Dense foliage smelled of decay, and I could hear low voices. Thick leaves dripped with water. I removed my jacket. I followed a sodden path through overgrown plants wilting with the heat. Long, spindly fronds left wet streaks on my arms. At the base of my skull, I felt a buzz like sleeping bees; the greenhouse had protection wards on it.

In the center of the greenhouse was a clearing. A maroon Persian rug had been rolled out. Ancient wing chairs sat with their backs to me and faced a graying wicker chair. The

Guildmaster leaned out from one of the chairs and looked in my direction, then struggled up on his feet. "Here he is," he said.

"You should sit," said whoever was sitting in the opposite wing chair. I couldn't sense who or what he was with all the wards in the place.

The Guildmaster answered him with a dismissive wave of his hand. He stood tall, with the stiff posture of someone in pain. His hawk nose stood out sharply between dark eyes nestled in sockets hollow from too much weight loss too fast. Gray-streaked dark hair hung lankly to his shoulders. The disturbing part, though, was the limp flutter of his wings, dim and lifeless against the backdrop all the fecund plant life. "Hello, Connor, I'm glad you could make it."

As if I would have refused the invitation. "It's good to see you again, sir."

He waved an open palm toward the wicker chair. "Sit, please."

As I made my way around the armchairs, I found myself face-to-face with High Druid Gerin Cuthbern. I did an excellent job of not rocking back on my heels. As a former Guild agent, I routinely worked with the upper echelons of society. Cuthbern, on the other hand, was upper echelon to the upper echelons. As High Druid of the Bosnemeton, he led all the druids and druidesses of the Grove for New England. His word was law. We did nothing without his say-so.

As soon as I realized it was him, I stopped, crossed my hands across my chest, and bowed slightly at the waist. "High Druid, it is an honor."

The old man nodded his shaggy mane of white hair. He had that solemn look important people get when they deign to notice the peasants. Gnarled hands loosely held an oak staff against his chest. Truth to tell, while I respect Gerin, I thought he was a bit of a prig. He was an Old One, to be sure, but one that sometimes didn't get that the old ways were gone.

"I remember you from your training, Connor. Such a shame what's become of you," he said.

It was hard not taking offense. I had heard Gerin make such blunt statements to others in open meetings of the Grove. Tact wasn't his strong point. Power was. I draped my jacket over the chair and sat. The wicker had the soft give of too much dampness. Eagan settled himself back into his armchair.

"One more Guild director and we'd have a quorum," Eagan said.

Gerin frowned "Not funny, Manus."

Eagan rolled his eyes and leaned toward me. "He's been like this all afternoon. He can't understand how a sick old fairy can tire of talking politics."

"And yet, he's well enough to meet with underlings. No offense, Connor," said Gerin.

"None taken, sir" I said. My ass.

Manus wagged a finger at me exaggeratedly. "Gerin's here as a Guild director, Connor. No 'sir-ring' to the High Druid allowed." The smile of a man used to having his way. I decided the best response was to smile myself.

A sudden cough racked Eagan. He took several moments to get under control. Gerin instinctively placed his hand on his back, but didn't do anything else as far as I could tell. Eagan wiped his hand across his forehead.

"A drink," he said, gasping.

Gerin sighed and pointed to a sago palm. "He hides whiskey in there from his brownie."

I got up and stepped to the large frond plant. Rummaging in the stalks, I found a flask, which I handed to Eagan. Gerin had the stern lecturing look I hated as a kid. Dananns had a wicked propensity for alcoholism. I didn't know whether Eagan had a problem or not, but Gerin's reference to Tibs as "his brownie" made me want to break out the booze just to annoy him.

Eagan chuckled through a swig. "It's medicinal."

Gerin just shook his head.

Eagan directed his gaze at me. "I need to ask you a favor. Ryan macGoren had some dealing with Alvud Kruge. I want to know what it was."

Ryan macGoren, the golden boy of the Danann fairy social set. Handsome, powerful, rich, and a Guild director on top of it all. The whole package for the right woman. A couple of years ago, I probably would have been hanging out with him. Now, his type annoyed me. Did not see this coming. "Why don't you just ask him?" I asked.

Eagan leaned toward me for emphasis. "Because I need him as an ally right now, and the question coming from me might be considered insulting under the circumstances."

I could see his point. Asking a supporter about his relationship with a savagely murdered colleague might put a damper on a friendship. At the same time, the Danann clan of fairies has its share of internecine politics. MacGoren was powerful in his own right, and given that he was made a director at the Guild in a relatively short time, he had powerful friends that Eagan might not like. "Why me?" I said.

Eagan glanced at Gerin. "You have a certain reputation that could be used to advantage."

"I think this is ill-advised, Manus," said Gerin.

"I know you do. But you can't ask either without risking insulting him."

"It could appear I'm interfering in the Kruge investigation," I said.

Eagan smiled slyly. "You've dealt with Keeva macNeve before."

Gerin shifted in his seat. He had managed to spend the entire conversation not acknowledging me. "Manus, Connor is powerless. As strong a fey as Alvud Kruge was, he died horribly. If this inquiry gets tangled in the murder case, Connor will have no chance if he stumbles across the murderer."

I didn't know whether to be touched that Gerin cared or insulted that he didn't think I could handle the situation. That he likely was right was beside the point. Either way, his attitude annoyed me.

Eagan took a swig from the flask and grimaced. "He did a fair job of surviving Castle Island last spring."

Gerin snorted. "I've read those reports, Manus. He's lucky he's not dead. He's lucky we're not all dead."

Eagan gave Gerin a wolfish grin. "I like luck."

"I'll do it," I said.

Gerin frowned and sat back in the chair. He rubbed his staff as if he were agitated. "You know his coming here was observed. Everything you do is observed. People will ask questions."

Eagan raised an eyebrow at me. "Ah, yes, well, how's Tibbet, Connor?"

I chuckled. He may be ill, but he was sharp. An old flame taking me to the big house while the master was ill was not the worst cover I'd ever heard. "I hope she's at least driving me home afterward."

"Of course," said Eagan.

"I still object to this, Manus. He has no abilities. He has no Guild authority . . ."

Eagan held up a hand. "He has a Guild director's ID."

"Purely by chance. Let's not let Briallen's propensity for not following the rules cause us to break rules ourselves. If I may say so, you seemed fixated on macGoren. I don't know that I'm comfortable with one of my people being pulled into your personal politics."

"It's not that personal, Gerin. These questions need to be asked. Normally, I would ask Keeva macNeve to look into this, but it would not be appropriate in this case. I want an objective ally here."

Gerin did look at me then. I felt an odd probing sensation, though whether he was actually trying to do something to me or it was his innate force of will I could not tell. "If I recall, allies do not fare well with this man," he said.

I wish I could say I was insulted, but I really shouldn't be. I knew I'd left a few pissed off people in my wake at the Guild. It's why no one comes around anymore now that I'd lost my abilities. They were willing to put up with me when it might help their careers. Now, I'm yesterday's news. I didn't need to be reminded of that, though.

Eagan looked at me a long time before he spoke. "People expect unpopular people to ask unpopular questions, Gerin. They often don't think beyond the annoyance of the questions and forget to wonder about the reasons behind them. It's an advantage. I think Connor will know what to do to protect himself."

I hoped I did. "I can take care of myself."

Gerin shook his head and sighed. "If your course is set, then it must play itself out."

"Yes, it must. Tibbet is waiting outside, Connor. It was a pleasure talking to you," Eagan said by way of dismissal.

It didn't seem like I had been very much a part of the conversation. I stood and picked up my jacket. As I shook Eagan's hand, it felt cold and damp. I turned to Gerin and bowed again. Apparently, the High Druid didn't think much of me. I tried not to look as humiliated as I felt.

"I'll let you know what I find," I said and walked out. As I stepped into the cold October air, Tibbet waited in the car near the back of the greenhouse. Eagan must have done a sending to let her know the meeting was ending. I jumped in to get out of the cold.

"You don't look happy," she said as she pulled around the house.

"It's nothing. I just feel like a mouse that's been tossed between two cats."

She chuckled. "Those two can do that to you. Do you want me to drop you anyplace special?"

"Home. Home would feel special right now."

She rubbed my thigh. "Oh, dear. It must have been bad. Just ignore them, Connor. That's what I do. They play too many games between them."

"Sage advice."

We indulged in catch-up conversation through the rest of the drive. She had not really been doing much since Eagan fell ill. That was fine. Other than almost dying and saving the world last spring, things had pretty much settled down to boredom for me, too.

When she arrived at my building, Tibbet put the car in park and slid across the seat. She wrapped her arms around me and hugged. I let my nose nestle in her hair. One of the things I love about Tibs is her scent. She always smells like warmth and comfort.

"Everything works out eventually," she said.

"Thanks."

She pulled back, a playful smile on her lips. "Do you want me to come up?"

"You don't have to do that, Tibs."

She eyed me with the hint of confusion. "I know that."

By that, I guessed she didn't realize Eagan had asked her to pick me up to cover our meeting. I should have realized. If she knew, Tibbet would have told me immediately when I got in the car at the OCME. "I'm sorry, Tibs. Bad timing. I didn't mean anything by that."

She ruffled my hair. "No harm. Take care of yourself, handsome."

I tugged her hair. "You, too, gorgeous."

Once inside my apartment, I went straight to the computer. During a case, I keep meticulous files. I logged the information from my visit with Janey Likesmith, cross-referencing it to Moke's drug-running gang. I leaned back, the desk chair letting out a squeal I never remembered to oil. Farnsworth had been running drugs. Which meant he was probably a gang hit. Which meant we were likely never going to find the perpetrator.

I sighed and started a file on Ryan macGoren. After watching any connection between Farnsworth and the Kruge murder evaporate, Eagan had handed me a back door into the murder investigation. No one could blame me for looking into Kruge as part of researching macGoren.

I paused and considered. Pride was rearing its head again. I missed the Guild. Not the political crap Eagan and Gerin were pulling me into, but the chance to work on big cases. It's where I belonged. I could feel that in my bones. But as Gerin had made abundantly clear, I wasn't in the big leagues anymore. I could get hurt. I pushed the thought roughly aside. I didn't care. If I had to risk my life to prove them wrong, I didn't have a problem with that. Because if I wasn't willing to risk everything, Gerin was right that I had no abilities. At all.

7

I took a run to the deli to pick up some dinner. When I got back to my apartment, a little mote of light spiraled above the futon. Judging by how dim and fading it was, the glow bee probably had been chasing me down all day. When I approached it, it put a burst of speed toward me and tapped my forehead, vanishing.

Midnight. Yggy's. The low energy of the glow bee made Joe's voice sound faint. You don't understand a glow bee like a sending; you actually hear it. People impress messages on them with their own essences. When it lands on you, the essence releases the message. It's quick, though. Try and put too much information into a glow bee, and it takes a while to sort out. On the other hand, too cryptic a message, and you find yourself scratching your head anyway. Joe and I had been exchanging them since I was a kid, before I was able to do a true sending. Now that I can't do decent sendings anymore, we're back to glow bees.

Yggy's. Interesting location. About the midpoint of the Avenue just beyond what passes for retail shops but before the commercial warehouses begin. Not the worst place in the

Weird, but starting to venture into that territory. It was a crossroads bar, one of those places where an elf can sit down with a fairy and either have a civil conversation or end up rolling around on the floor. I had almost forgotten Joe was setting up a meeting with his gang connection, and Yggy's would be the perfect place for it. The bar's one rule was no essence fighting.

Murdock didn't pick up when I tried his cell. He hadn't checked in at all, which was unusual, so I was relieved when he called me from his car just before midnight. Yggy's would be a good place for him to check out, learn more about how the fey can sit down and have a drink without all the race drama.

I was happy when Murdock called me from downstairs. It was getting chilly at night, and I didn't want to have to walk in the cold down to the bar. I tossed some newspapers from the passenger seat of his car into the back, where they landed, not accidentally, on a romance novel. Murdock has a secret passion for them. You might call it a secret, searing passion of towering desire. With flowing hair, ripped abs, and corsets. I tease him about it. He doesn't read the good kind. Every once in a while, I find a paperback lying around my apartment that he's left in a subtle effort to get me interested. I have read a couple, well researched, well written, but in the end, not so much my thing. Murdock thinks I'm single because I don't get romance. I point out he never goes out with someone more than twice.

"Okay, gang fight. Two nights ago. What happened and when were you going to tell me?" I said, as he pulled an illegal U-turn and drove the wrong way up Sleeper Street to the Avenue.

He threw me a look that was at once surprised and annoyed. "What's with the attitude? I was just going to bring it up."

"I heard about it from Keeva, who took much joy in my lack of knowledge, thank you. Why didn't you mention it the other day?"

He frowned. "I don't know. I must have been distracted by the fire. Nothing much to tell. A face-off between the TruKnights and the Tunnel Rats."

I grabbed the dash as he took the corner a little too fast. "Okay. TruKnights I know are elf and fairy kids. That makes the Tunnel Rats our dwarf boys?"

He nodded. "Don't know much about the dwarves. Keep to themselves mostly. You saw the colors: black hoodies and yellow bandanas. They claim a small area south of where the Farnsworth kid was found."

"Still leaving the question of why a human kid was wearing the colors of a dwarf gang," I said.

He nodded. "Except for the dead kid, all the members are dwarves as far as we know. The report didn't have much detail about why the fight happened. The TruKnights claim turf just east, so based on what you picked up from the Tunnel Rats you met, it was probably turf related. Two elves ended up in the hospital pretty cut up."

Dead kid. Murdock can do that, just refer to him as a dead kid. He's much better at emotional detachment than I am, at least when he's working. It's a cop thing, to an extent. He's seen more murders than I have, so he's got an extra layer of protection against the horror of it. Not jaded so much as resigned.

We left the working lights of the Avenue behind and entered a more desolate stretch of road that led to the warehouse district. Murdock pulled the car to the mostly empty curb. It wasn't an area where you left an unattended car parked for long. We got out and walked toward the harbor.

"I'm still convinced the blood on the kid's shoe was Kruge's," I said.

Murdock gave me a lopsided smile. "Of course you are."

Joe chose that moment to appear. Murdock is getting better at not being startled by a flit popping into view without warning, but you can still see the surprise on his face when it happens. He has to work on that if he ever wants to do undercover work with the fey.

Joe swirled around us, clearly pleased. "Right on time, guys. I just checked and our guy's inside. Let's go, let's go."

"What's the rush, Joe?" I asked.

I didn't get an answer, or, rather, I didn't get an answer from Joe. Yggy's is on the dead-end side of Congress Street north of the Avenue. A few people milled around the black-stained door with a "Y" painted in the middle. No one reputable. We were eyed with wary curiosity, but no one bothered us. The door slammed outward, followed by an airborne body that landed firmly in the gutter. Murdock and I exchanged glances.

Stinkwort laughed nervously. "I guess he decided to meet us outside!"

At that same moment, we were close enough for me to sense the guy's essence. I stopped short and glared at Joe. I didn't need an introduction, and I didn't need the guy to roll faceup for me to recognize him. Murdock paused a step ahead of me, turning back with a questioning look on his face.

Stinkwort zoomed ahead. "Cal! How are you doing, bud?"

Cal opened one eye and smiled. "Hey, Joe, what do you know?"

Joe crossed his arms, sat down on Cal's chest, and looked up with a self-satisfied, I-dare-you-to-get-mad-at-me smile.

"Hi, Cal," I said.

When he realized it was me, he opened his other eye in surprise. "Well, well, what do you know, little bro?"

I didn't hide the displeasure I felt. "Leo Murdock, meet Callin Grey. My brother."

Naturally, Murdock was surprised as hell. "You have a brother?"

Cal reached up a big, meaty hand. "Pleased to meet you, Leo."

Murdock shook and found himself pulling Cal off the ground while Joe fluttered up. "Same to you. And it's Murdock."

Cal stood a good five inches taller than either of us. We look nothing alike. He takes after our father—broad shouldered, barrel-chested, rough-cut facial features—but has our mother's coloring—ash-blond hair, light brown eyes that can appear yellow. He has an infectious smile that belies an unpredictable temper. Which is how he ends up in gutters a lot.

Joe clapped his hands. "Drinks are on me!"

"My favorite words," said Cal. He reached for the door handle to Yggy's.

"Didn't you just get thrown out?" I said.

He gave a sheepish smile. "Nah, not really. Just a prelim." He sauntered inside with Joe on his shoulder.

"You don't look happy," said Murdock.

"More ambivalent. Let's see where this goes," I said.

I opened the door, and Murdock passed inside. No one really stood as bouncer at Yggy's. It was the kind of the place that if you needed to rely on a bouncer to get you out of trouble, you didn't belong there in the first place. When the management wanted someone removed, the bartender usually asked one of the meaner, drunker customers to take care of it for a free round. There were always takers.

Immediately inside the door stood a coat check that no one ever used, but the coat-check girls, usually elves, always got tipped for their outfits, or suggestions thereof. After a short hallway, a large square bar area filled the front of the place. Stools surrounded it on all sides and could easily seat a few dozen people. Beyond that was a dance floor that was primarily an excuse to place wooden barrels to lean on when the bar was full. And beyond that was a pool table. For the right price, pool wasn't the only action the felt saw.

Cal waved to a sallow-looking fairy with shaggy black hair sprouting from various points on his skin. Not all the Celtic fairies are from the pretty Dananns clans. The fairy frowned and gave him the finger.

"My table's back here," Cal said over the low din. Yggy's is bar-loud, not club-loud. You can carry on a decent conversation without having to raise your voice too much over competing conversations and the new-wave-retro harp and fiddle classics on the sound system. Not far from the pool table, we slid around a battle-scarred table with four chairs in the style every New Englander knows as colonial. Joe flipped over the empty black plastic ashtray and used that as a seat. Cal waved four fingers at a waitress, who nodded and disappeared toward the bar.

Cal smiled down at Joe. "Someone said he had someone I needed to meet. Someone implied it was a date."

Joe put on an innocent look. "I never said date. Why does everyone think I want to set them up on dates?"

"Maybe because strange women end up with our phone numbers?" I said.

"Not true!" he said. He winked at Murdock. "It's not always women."

Murdock shot me a sly glance. Joe thinks I don't date enough and believes if he throws enough variety at me, someone will stick. Murdock can't understand how anyone can be without the company of women for more than a week. Since I don't rise to their baiting, they keep wondering if my interests lie outside the assumed. Of course, not rising to their baiting also means they keep baiting. I think we all enjoy it.

"How ya been, bro?" Cal asked. I hated the "bro." Even though Cal always used it, it felt like an affectation. The constant reminder of our relationship was a constant reminder that we were hardly buddies. When I lost my abilities two years back, Cal managed to show up at Avalon Memorial a week later, mildly sober, with enough contrition for the delay to indicate he meant it. It still irked me that he took so long. Our parents called the day I woke up, and they were in Ireland.

"Okay. Not much change. You?"

The waitress returned and dropped three tumblers of whiskey in front of us and a smaller one for Joe. We tapped glasses. While the three of us sipped, Murdock placed his back on the table. He wasn't on duty, but I could tell by the way his eyes kept shifting to the crowd, it was not the kind of place he liked to drink in.

"I'm okay," Cal said. "Been doing a little of this, a little of that."

We always started this way. Wary. Not going too deep.

"Heard from Mom and Dad?" I asked. Safe, yet unsafe, territory.

He shook his head. "You know them. They'll remember us eventually."

I didn't respond. Like all siblings, Cal and I have very different relationships with our parents. Cal sees their lack of contact as indifference. I see it as two people who get incredibly caught up in each other and their own lives. They care. Cal never realizes they call him more than me. But then, they worry about him more. If and when they return from meddling in Celtic politics, Cal will complain they won't leave him alone, and I will pretend I don't like their attention.

No one spoke for a long minute, while Joe hummed to himself watching us. I've got to give it to the little guy. He never quite gives up on getting the two of us back together.

"So, Joe's led me to believe you travel in interesting circles these days," I said.

Cal sipped his drink again, eyeing Joe. "Does he, now? Perhaps Joe might be more careful what he says where."

Joe barked like a dog at Cal. It's one of his nervous tics when someone throws a dig at him that lands. "I didn't say anything about your buried treasure, secret harem, or wine cellar. I just told him you might know about gang stuff down by the Tangle."

From the look on Cal's face, I think he would have preferred Joe told us about women or money. I already knew about the booze. Cal downed his whiskey and nodded at the waitress. Not a good sign.

"Why would I talk about something I know nothing about with a cop?" asked Cal.

Murdock's mouth went to a tight, straight line. Murdock

hated being made as the law. Of course, Cal wasn't stupid. Wearing a trench coat and tie in Yggy's and not drinking a free shot were dead giveaways. I felt Murdock's essence spike, and I could tell Cal felt it, too. He gave me a look that told me he found it odd. The waitress dropped him another drink on her way by.

"We're just looking for background, Cal," I said.

"Still don't know why you're talking to me."

I sighed. Every time Cal and I encounter each other, the animosity starts. It goes back a long way. We're never at outright war with each other, but there are too many issues between us for outright peace. "Look, Joe brought us to you. If you can't help, fine. I'm not looking to cause you trouble."

"Calm down, Con." He nodded at Murdock. "You trust him?"

"With my life. I can't say the same for him. I almost got him killed on our last case together."

Murdock chuckled. His essence settled down, more human normal.

Cal leaned forward, not looking me in the eye. "What do you want to know?"

"What about the Tunnel Rats?" Murdock asked.

Cal shrugged. "Enforcers mostly. T-Rats don't usually start something, but they've been known to end things pretty quick."

Murdock leaned forward, too. "My info is they're all dwarves, but we've got a dead human kid wearing their colors. Would they have killed him for wearing their colors?"

Cal shook his head, examining the swirling amber liquid in his glass. "No, they're not that sick-petty. They might rough someone up for it, but it'd be odd for them to go that far." He paused. "Oh, wait—did the kid have knots in his bandana?"

We both nodded. "That's why. The kid had something he didn't want his gang identified with, but the T-Rats wanted done. So, they let him wear their colors. Knots in a bandana are a heads-up that the kid isn't a T-Rat but has their protection."

"Sounds dangerous. If someone wanted to kill a Tunnel Rat, why would they care if someone was pretending to be one?"

Cal smiled. " 'Cause they don't know if they're bringing double hell down on themselves. Someone might not be afraid of the T-Rats but scared spitless of an associate. Kill the associate, get the T-Rats *and* the associate's gang in on your fight uninvited."

"What can you tell us about this dwarf named Moke who runs the gang?" I asked.

Caught mid-drink, Cal almost choked on his laugh. "Moke's no dwarf. He's a nasty-ass troll straight from the Kingland. The only thing the T-Rats are afraid of is their own boss eating them." He laughed and shook his head. "Moke a dwarf. That's the funniest thing I've heard in a while."

I tried not to feel the heat in my face. Cal likes to know better than his little brother. Even after all these years, he could take something I was naturally ignorant of and make me feel stupid ignorant. "Why would dwarves answer to a troll?"

" 'Cause he pays good money. Like I said, the T-Rats are hired fists. You run enough drugs down here, you need some strong-arm behind you. They are easy to buy."

"Drugs? What kind?" asked Murdock.

Cal paused before answering. Murdock and I had seen that look before, the shuffling of the mental index cards deciding what to discuss and what to pass over. It did not make me happy that my brother had to play that game with us. I had to wonder how he had been spending his time these days.

"Fey stuff," Cal said finally. "Small junk, mostly euphorics. Keeps him flush. The kind of stuff human kids go for instead of the hard stuff."

"Like weed," I said.

" 'Xactly. Lots of cash in it. Small bills. Easy. A lot of competition, though."

"Two nights ago there was a fight with the TruKnights," said Murdock.

Cal's eyes shot around the room as he hunched forward at the table. "Very nasty. The 'Knights are fairies and elves. The one thing they agree on is they're better than everyone else."

"Well, two elves ended up in the hospital. Would they have killed the kid to retaliate?" Murdock asked.

Cal shrugged. "Might've. The 'Knights aren't afraid of anybody. I hear Moke's poking at C-Note, and C-Note's not happy."

"C-Note?" Murdock said.

Cal got that look on his face again. He finished his drink and waved his hand in a circle over the table. The waitresses immediately came with a new round for everyone, including Murdock, who hadn't touched his first.

"Let me get someone over here, see if he's willing to talk," said Cal. I felt him shoot a sending into the room.

Joe turned his head in the direction the sending went, then grinned. "I thought so," he said.

A tall, thin man stumbled into a group of people near the pool table. He straightened up, flipping a head of curly red hair back, and bowed an apology. He continued toward us. I couldn't help smiling as I recognized his essence. He dropped himself down in the empty chair and slumped.

"Well, well, well, the Grey boys together again. What's it been, twenty years?" He had a grin that could only be described as jovial.

"Not quite that long, Clure," I said. The Clure was an old buddy, a drinking one by definition. The Cluries are a clan of hard-drinking fairies, the friends of bars everywhere. The Clure was both name and title, though he didn't insist on the "the" when you spoke directly to him. He led his local kin group, which basically meant he either started the party or knew where one was. We had gone on plenty of tears when Cal and I were in our twenties and not quite so at odds. "Clure, this is Murdock. Murdock, Clure."

Clure extended his hand. "Felicitations, Officer."

Murdock got annoyed again. He had to either drop the attitude or the clothes if he wanted to blend in. "Pleased to meet you," he said.

Joe was lying flat on the ashtray now. Alcohol did funny things to him. He hung his head upside down off the side of the ashtray and smiled. *"Fatla genes, Cluricane?"* he said in Cornish.

The Clure smiled down at him. "Just fine, my little pysky friend."

Cal pushed one of Murdock's glasses across the table, and the Clure downed it with relish. "We were just discussing C-Note," he said.

The Clure let out a whoop that made several heads turn. "Talk of the town, that one. That troll's making trouble for everyone, including himself."

Another troll. Interesting. Trolls are disagreeable and contrary by nature. Given their nocturnal habits, they tended to have friends in low places. For that matter, they were the low places.

"C-Note runs the Tangle," Cal said with a low voice.

"And he's trying to run a lot more," the Clure added.

"He runs the TruKnights," said Cal.

"What happened to Gandri?" said Murdock. The TruKnights were high profile enough that most cops knew some, and everyone knew their leader. Former leader, apparently.

"C-Note took him out without blinking a yellow eye," said the Clure. "The TruKnights didn't protest. They respect power. Are you drinking that?" He pointed to Murdock's other drink. Murdock pushed it toward him. At the same time, I felt the Clure broadcast a sending for a table round.

Joe took that moment to flutter up and drift away toward the pool table. Nothing bores him faster than talking about things he isn't the slightest bit interested in. Getting me and Cal together apparently was the only thing he wanted to accomplish, and that was done.

"What's this got to do with Moke?" I asked.

"So, you heard about that, huh?" said the Clure. "C-Note's looking to expand, and he stepped up on Moke in his own turf. Moke had to smack that back. He sent the T-Rats in for a good show. He's also got the T-Rats hassling C-Note's runners."

"What's the run?" asked Murdock.

"A few guns, not many. Not C-Note's style. Or the Weird's for that matter. C-Note's pushing some drugs Moke's not happy about."

Cal slowly swirled the dregs of his drink. "Float," he said.

The Clure nodded. "Yeah, Float. The kids love to dance with it," said Clure. The waitress dropped a new round on the table. Clure raised a glass. "I prefer the gift of the gods!" He downed the shot and pulled Murdock's over without asking.

"I've never heard of Float," Murdock said, voicing my own question.

Cal cleared his throat. He swayed in his chair. He'd killed three shots in less than a half hour and had a fourth in front of him. I doubted those were the first of the evening. "You will. It's C-Note's stuff. Makes you feel happy mellow high, like you're in a cloud. Strong shit. He's practically giving it away to seed demand. He's turning kids into evangelists. When they're not raving about Float, they're raving about C-Note."

"So, what, Moke's looking for a cut?" I asked.

The Clure shook his head. "Not with this stuff. C-Note's controlling distribution. Rumor has it he's even manufacturing the stuff. Moke's more worried about his own operations going under."

Murdock looked at me. "So C-Note's provoking Moke. Moke gives back. Turf battles. The Farnsworth kid got caught in the middle."

"But why was he in the middle? What would Unity be doing that Kruge didn't want anyone to know?" I asked.

Murdock shot me a warning glance. "That's just speculation." I let it drop. Cal might trust Murdock on my word, but for Murdock, Cal and the Clure were too unknown for him to discuss cases in front of them.

The Clure stepped right up to it, though. "Kruge! Poor guy. Wouldn't know fun if it bit him in the ass. He was C-Note's thorn. Kept trying to mess up his drug running."

Murdock played with an empty glass. "We're not looking at that. I'm looking into the kid. The Guild's taking care of Kruge."

As the Clure shrugged indifferently, his eyes hesitated a second at something over my shoulder. I turned a casual look. Things seemed normal for Yggy's, maybe a few more elves at the main bar than usual, but nothing I thought odd. When I brought my attention back to the table, I caught Cal and the Clure exchanging glances.

"Anything else I can help you with, Officer?" the Clure asked.

Murdock shook his head. I had a million questions, but I could tell Murdock wanted to drop it. I was willing to let it go. I could always hook up with the Clure later.

The Clure pushed back his chair, stood, and bowed. "Gentlemen, enjoy the show." He sauntered off into the crowd. I noticed the first person he went to was another Clurie. Once you realize who they are, they're easy to spot. They all look like brothers. Happy drunk ones.

And speaking of which, mine was hunched over, pondering his drink.

"You okay, Cal?" I asked. It was always a loaded question. Depending on his mood, Cal would either take it as criticism of his drinking or inappropriately personal. And still I ask it. We both have bad habits.

He frowned and grunted. Murdock gave me a look that said he was done. He began to get up.

"You know who this guy is you're hanging around with, Murdock?" Cal said.

I compressed my lips. Cal was prone to listing a litany of my sins.

"A little bit," said Murdock, lightly with a smile. He's been around drunks enough not to take them seriously. "He's a pretty good guy, I think."

Cal fixed a watery stare at Murdock. "He's a liar."

"Cal . . ." I said.

He brought a wavering finger up to his lips. "Shhhh, little bro."

"I have to be somewhere, Cal," said Murdock. It was a nice try, but Cal wasn't buying.

Cal waved him back into his seat. "Not yet. Not yet. I have to tell you about my little bro." He took another sip of his drink, while Murdock gave me a sympathetic shrug. "When we were little, I found the box. Remember that, little bro?"

"Murdock doesn't need to hear this, Cal." Old aggravation settled over me. No matter how many years went by, the same damn story had to come up.

"Course he does." He looked at Murdock again. "When we were little, I found the box. Now the box, Murdock, is a rite of passage for druids. I'm not going to tell you how they hide it because it's a big druid secret, and I'd have to kill you or fry your brain or something, but I found it like I was supposed to, and I couldn't get the damned thing open." He wobbled his head at me. "Now this little guy, he comes in and sees me with the box. Remember that, little bro?"

I started getting that sick feeling in my stomach I get whenever the box comes up. "Yeah, Cal, I remember."

He nodded, looking back in his drink. "Yeah, he remembers. He comes in pretty as you please and flips the box open."

Murdock looked interested yet puzzled, and I couldn't blame him.

"So I took the key out and brought it to our da," he continued. "And Da said, where did you get this? And I said, I opened the box. And Da said, no you didn't. And I said, sure I did, ask Connor, he was right there. And Da went to Connor and said tell me who opened the box. And Connor said, well, you tell him, Connor, tell him what you said."

I refused to play this game. I just stared at Callin, wishing it never happened.

He shook his head. "Fine, don't say." He looked at Murdock. "He said, Callin did, sir. And Da said, are you sure? And you know what my little brother said?" A big grin split his face. "He said, yes, 'cause my big brother's going to be the greatest druid ever."

Callin slapped the table with a laugh, then downed his drink. He smiled from me to Murdock to me again. He reached over and pawed the side of my head. "He's a liar, Murdock, but he always tells good ones."

We sat in uncomfortable silence. I hated when Cal brought it up. Something broke inside him that day. Our da was disappointed in his lie. Cal idolized our da, and the disappointment crushed him. What made it worse was that Da blamed Cal for my lie because Cal knew I'd back him up. Cal never could get past the fact that I had been forgiven the lie because of my loyalty, and he had not because of his pride. Things only got worse as my abilities proved much stronger than his. It's one of those moments in life you wish you could take back. Too many times, when I've had my own share of what Cal was drinking, I thought about that day and whether things would have turned out differently if I told the truth, whether Cal would have. But we'll never know.

A commotion at the bar blessedly broke the moment. We all turned to see an elf pushing a dwarf repeatedly in the shoulder. Another elf took that as his cue to start in on a druid standing next to him. Both elves wore red leather jackets with black bars running down the sleeves. TruKnights colors. I scanned the bar and saw more of them, even a couple of fairies, and all of them hassling someone.

"I don't think you want to be here anymore, Murdock," I said quietly.

He looked away from the bar and did the same scan. Cops don't run, but they're not stupid either. His hand instinctively went for his radio. He was stopped by the hard, firm grip of my brother's hand.

"Don't," said Cal, quiet and tense. I looked at him. The drunk telling stories suddenly looked suspiciously sober. Murdock started going for his gun.

"Wait, Leo," I whispered sharply. I hardly ever call him by his first name, and it had the effect I hoped it would. He paused. Cal nodded back to the bar, and we turned.

The Clure stood swaying before the elf. "Gentlemen, what seems to be the trouble?"

"Take a walk, Clure, this isn't your business," the elf said.

The Clure leaned past the elf and picked up a full beer glass from the bar. He tilted his head back and drank in one gulp. "Ah, my friend, but you've made it my business. You're breaking Yggy's rules. Keep it personal. Take the gang stuff outside."

"Those aren't our rules," said the elf.

The Clure smiled deeply as the bar became quiet. It was then that I realized that stationed in every nook and cranny of Yggy's were a helluva lot more Cluries than I had first thought. "I don't tell people rules they already know, my friend. I just remind people that neutral ground is Cluries ground, the rest is up to them."

"TruKnights make their own rules, Clure. Mind your step, or we'll mind it for you," said the elf.

"Wrong!" The Clure cried with delight, his smile going wider. The elf did not see it coming. The beer glass came flying around with a roundhouse punch that threw him against the wall. In moments, every Clurie was in a frenzy.

Cal jumped up. "Nice seeing you, bro," he tossed at me before he ran off into the fray.

"In the mood for some fun?" I asked Murdock. A chair whizzed over our table, and we ducked.

He laughed. "Nah, let's go."

By the time we made it halfway to the door, the place was a full-scale riot. Most of the tussle consisted of Cluries and TruKnights, but a few opportunists were getting their jabs in. My shields activated automatically, feeble and weak. They wouldn't keep a bottle from beaning me, but at least it wouldn't knock me out. Someone grabbed my shoulder and spun me around. Before I had a chance to react, a fist flew past me and into the face of the elf holding me. He sank to his knees, a deadweight.

"Nice reflexes," I said.

"Don't mention it," said Murdock. His essence surged around him, bright and clear. I'd never seen such a thing in a human normal. His eyes had a glint in them that made me nervous. He barreled his way through the bar, pushing bodies left and right with no effort whatsoever. I followed in his wake, too stunned to say anything. We stumbled out the door in a crush of several other people, half of them laughing and the other half swearing.

Joe popped into the air over us. "See, I knew you guys would have fun together!"

"Yeah, thanks, Joe," I said. I twisted to check if my jacket got ripped. It looked okay. Murdock flexed his hand open and shut a few times.

"Let's go before the beat cops show up," he said.

We walked up the alley, occasionally dodging someone running. "Oh, it's Yggy's. No one calls the cops unless someone gets killed," I said.

"And then I'd have to stay," he said. Good point.

We jumped into his car. Joe lingered above the sidewalk. "That's it? You're leaving?"

"It was work, Joe, not social," I said.

He looked over his shoulder, disappointed.

"Go on, if you want, Joe. Tell Cal . . . tell him it was good seeing him."

He smiled. "See you!" He blipped out.

Murdock pulled into traffic. "That was interesting."

"Yeah, we need to find this Moke," I said.

"I meant that you have a brother."

"We don't hang much. Long history," I said.

"I didn't get the whole box thing," said Murdock.

I didn't say anything for a moment. Druid rituals are secret, like Cal said. Some of those secrets make sense because they're about manipulating essence. Some of them are just the bonding of members of closed societies, and druids are all about bonding. Some things, though, are open secrets.

"It's the first step on the druidic path," I said, deciding I could tell Murdock what every potential druid learns on the playground. "Our abilities manifest around puberty, and the first sign is when a kid can see through the glamour hiding a box left where he might find it. If they can open the box, they're ready to start training. Inside is a key. We take the key to an adult druid we respect, and he arranges our testing and training."

"So Cal wasn't ready, and you were," said Murdock.

I nodded. "I idolized Cal as a kid. He's three years older than me. Back then, I didn't understand the significance of seeing the box at such a young age. It meant I was powerful—more powerful than Cal. I shouldn't have been able to see the box for a few more years. Cal was embarrassed he got caught in the lie. Then he was angry that not only had I manifested my abilities early, his didn't show up until almost two years later than most druid kids do. By that time, I was finished with my first-level training and had attracted a lot of attention that he thought I didn't deserve. Somehow, he got in his head that what happened to him is all my fault. It's kind of screwed up our relationship ever since."

Murdock nodded. He comes from a big family, four boys and two girls, so he knows the whole sibling rap in spades. Deep down, Cal and I know we can always rely on each other, but the competitive thing still gets in the way.

Murdock pulled onto Sleeper Street and stopped in front of my building. "So what's the key open?"

I gave him a small shrug. "It's symbolic. It's the key to knowledge, which guides our nature and leads us to truth. Knowledge, Nature, Truth. If High Druid Gerin Cuthbern had a podium, it'd be on a seal above it."

Murdock shook his head. "You know, we puny humans just enroll in prep school."

I laughed. "So, we look for Moke next?" I said, getting back to the point of the evening.

"Sure. If he's that big a deal, someone in the g-unit will know where to find him."

I got out of the car, candy wrappers and receipts chasing after my feet. "Call me."

"Duck next time," he said and pulled away.

I let myself in and walked up the stairs. Sleep would not be a problem after the whiskey shots and adrenaline rush of the fight. I tossed my jacket on the armchair in my living room, kicked off the boots, shucked the jeans, and dropped myself on the unmade futon. I stared at the ceiling, thinking about gangs and bar fights. And Cal. Between the drinking and the life he leads, he never seems to get anywhere. The old guilt creeps in whenever I see him because I can't help but wonder if I hadn't been as good as I was, would he have ever lost his self-confidence? I sighed. Everyone makes their own road, but it didn't make me feel any better.

We all have our doubts, but we, or at least I, try not to cause them for other people. Unless it was Keeva, in which case, I still needed more to convince her I was right. I rolled restlessly onto my stomach, thinking about how some dumb kid found death on his own road. And given where my own road seemed to be going, what my destination would end up being.

8

The Internet is an addictive beast, a trail of crumbs leading not home but deeper into the forest. It's much like the druidic path in that respect. You start off with a purpose, and if you stay focused, you achieve your reward. But if you are distracted or dazzled along the way, you find yourself on untrodden routes to nowhere of interest except to yourself.

I managed to research a fair amount on macGoren before venturing off into the wilds of the Web. He hadn't been in the States very long by fey standards, but he certainly had been active. In less than ten years, he had acquired sizable tracts of real estate around the city. His appointment to the Guild board seemed to be the culmination of some very well placed connections, both human and fey, as well as a driving ambition to lead. Not all that unusual for a Danann fairy. Being born and raised in a monarchial society tends to have some obvious nurture ramifications.

Despite his lack of disclosure, I didn't have to think too hard about Manus ap Eagan's desire for knowledge about macGoren. While it might be easy to say the Guild runs power plays, it's more true that power plays run the Guild.

Information always, under all circumstances, is key to how you play, and macGoren was a new player with little local history to discern motives and abilities. Eagan wanted an ally on the board. That he be a willing one or a blackmailed one was a footnote.

As far as I could tell, macGoren was not worth the worry. Yet, anyway. He seemed to be playing a straightforward Danann game: show up with shiny wings, woo the right fey, and toss the right amount of money at human normals. If I had to guess, he could be a contender for Eagan someday, but that day was still far off. Eagan's own machinations had a half-century head start.

The latest potential rung in macGoren's climb was a development company known as Seacorp. MacGoren had collected a group of local wheeler-dealers to spearhead economic projects for the city, and some had gotten it into their heads that some nice big buildings on the harbor would be just the ticket. That the site happened to be the Tangle was a minor impediment if the attendance at investor presentations was any indication. When people talked about cleaning up the city, the Weird was the first place to be mentioned, and most had the Tangle in mind. MacGoren was just playing local politics.

MacGoren's latest kick seemed to be to run dinner galas as charity fundraisers. In reality, they're promo and networking events designed to attract investors for Seacorp. Normally, you need an invitation to one of these things, but I'd gone to enough of them in the past to know how to bluff my way in. MacGoren had one of his parties scheduled for this evening, and I intended to be an unexpected guest.

But first, I checked my watch to be sure I would be at the Guildhouse in time for the directors' meeting. No sense irritating the movers and shakers when I was just getting in on a technicality. Besides, I do not have a reputation for being punctual, so showing up ready and on time would throw anyone who expected less.

I admit I fussed about dressing, finally deciding that going upscale might benefit me in the long run with the board. Deep purple and black vertically striped dress shirt in silk, black medium-weight wool pants, no pleats. Black dress boots. Two-button jacket. The October sun was warm enough that I didn't have to hide it all under a coat. It might have been two seasons old from when I had the money to burn, but it was all classic enough that not everyone would know.

I actually arrived early, did the same security dance from the previous day, and slipped into an elevator with almost a half hour to spare. The executive offices of the Guildhouse sit one flight up from my old office. Like any top management office suite, the rarefied and static atmosphere allows corporate leadership to function in unnatural silence. At this level, the floors were circular, and I padded around the thickly carpeted curve of the hallway to the boardroom in the center. The Guildhouse décor amplifies the dull sensation with its vaulted stone ceilings and its sound-deadening ancient tapestries hung along the corridors. All contrived, of course. The building went up in the sixties, so the choice of stone was intended to evoke history and grandeur. So it was easy to hear the angry voices before I even reached the door. Despite being early, I had managed to arrive late for an argument.

On one side of the boardroom table, Gerin Cuthbern gripped his staff with a gnarled hand. As High Druid of the Bosnemeton, he automatically had a seat on the Guildhouse board. Pinpoints of white light flickered in his eyes, something I had seen occasionally and was always glad that they weren't directed at me. Which, apparently, did not seem to prevent a tall elven woman from getting right up in his face.

"I will not stand for it, Gerin," the woman said.

Nigel Martin stood at the far end of the room, a cell phone pressed to his ear. He seemed to be paying more attention to his caller than the argument, which I knew was unlikely. Nigel never missed a thing.

"The Guild does have rules. I'm sure the Consortium can

appreciate that," Gerin said. His voice dripped with reasonableness, which I'm sure was not the main topic of conversation.

Opposite them, Ryan macGoren lounged idly against the wall, with his arms crossed and a bemused expression on his face. I recognized him immediately from my research, the wavy blond hair, aquiline features, and rippling wings in full display. Danann fairies in general are not prone to modesty, and he was no exception. You could feel the air of privilege about him.

"Do not even think it. You know Alvud never anticipated this," the elven woman said.

Not wanting to step into the argument, I sidled along the table and stood next to macGoren. He caught my eye and smirked. Without moving his body, the fairy slipped a languid hand out from the crook of his arm and offered it to me. "Ryan macGoren. Pleased to meet you finally." He spoke in full voice, as if the argument wasn't happening five feet away.

I shook his hand, wondering about the "finally" part of his hello. "Connor Grey."

He shifted his attention back to the woman and smiled. "The grieving widow," he stage-whispered.

Eorla Kruge—the Marchgrafin, if I remembered her Teutonic monarchial title correctly—certainly was a fine-looking woman. She wore her ebony hair in a silvered mesh, and her large, almond-shaped eyes held an intelligence that only the Old Ones have, eyes that have seen much in years human normals cannot even conceive. She wore a body-hugging dark green velvet business suit embroidered with silver and black leaves. Rings glittered on her hands, some plain bands of silver or gold, and others of emeralds and black sapphires. She resonated Power like a fuel cell. And she was pissed as hell.

"Eorla, you know the seat isn't hereditary. The Guild is an elective body," said Gerin.

The argument fell into place for me instantly. Eorla wanted to sit on the board. I couldn't blame her. I had wanted to do the same. Usually, someone has to die before any real turnover happens. Of course, if she thought that like I did, I'm sure she wasn't hoping it would be her husband.

"This is ridiculous, Gerin. You know you can't have a Guild board without Teutonic representation. How is that going to appear?" Eorla said.

"It will appear as the charter intends. We elect someone. We have other members that can represent your interests for now," he said.

She thrust her finger at him. "Who haven't even shown up for this meeting, and that is beside the point. Alvud and I have worked years for fey unity, and part of that is showing the world the fey can work together. You can't do that without an elf visibly active on the board."

Gerin had not changed his expression since I walked in, like he was patiently waiting for Eorla simply to agree with him. "And where are the dwarf directors and the representative for the solitary fey, Eorla? Manus invited them. I find it interesting that your allies choose this time to embarrass the board. How is that unity, Eorla?"

She pulled her hand back as if to strike him, then caught herself. "Do not dare to mock me, Gerin. You know this board needs the leadership I can provide."

Nigel closed his cell and strolled over. "I think we've covered this point several times now. Can we bring a more civil tone to the discussion?"

Eorla whirled on him. "Civil? Don't think I didn't hear every word Manus ap Eagan said to you. You tell him that 'the elf bitch' will be sitting at this table whether he likes it or not."

Nigel put on his placating face, which I had seen work in more than one situation where he wanted to get his way. "The Guildmaster is not feeling well, Eorla. He spoke out of turn. I will speak to him about that, but right now we need to remember why we are here."

Eorla wasn't buying it. She drew herself up and threw back her head. "I know exactly why I am here, Nigel. If this vote goes through, I will bring Maeve into it."

Nigel narrowed his eyes. "That's a sharp and narrow bridge to walk, Eorla. Don't depend on the High Queen to bow to your wishes again."

Eorla moved a threatening step closer to him. "So that's what this is about, is it? You and Gerin are angry that I persuaded Maeve to compromise at the Fey Summit last spring? I wasn't the only voice against you, Nigel, and some of them were Danann."

Here was the Guild dance of words and political revenge in full flower. As a member of the royal family, Eorla had high rank in the Teutonic Consortium. Last spring, the Seelie Court and the Consortium had held a Fey Summit to try to resolve their differences. On the surface it was about whether the fey should work together to figure out how to return to Faerie. In reality, it was military strategizing. Many Celtic fey—Nigel among them—wanted to increase the fairy warriors guarding the demilitarized zone outside the Consortium territory in Germany. Eorla brokered a deal with Maeve that if she didn't send the warriors, she'd convince the Elven King to back off his expansion threats. The Seelie Court is packed with Danann fairies who agree with her. So far, it's worked. The scuttlebutt is that Nigel didn't think it was a good idea. But then, Nigel has never trusted the Consortium.

Nigel smiled at her. "And while Maeve compromised, a Consortium operative staged a terrorist attack not four miles from here. Despite her actions afterward, Maeve's reputation was damaged among her own people. Do not think she will risk more for these compromises of yours."

Eorla's eyes shone as rage flowed off her in waves. If I hadn't been in a room with some of the most powerful fey in Boston, I would have been looking for the exit. As it was, my head started ringing with all the ambient essence. My sensing ability even kicked in a little.

When she spoke, Eorla had dropped her voice to a cutting edge. "That is a dangerous lie, Nigel Martin. That terrorist was not a Consortium operative. If you tell that tale to smear my people, you will get more than you bargain for."

He raised his eyebrows. "Is that a threat?"

She smiled at him. "I was counseling kings and queens long before you were even born, Nigel. I don't need to threaten. You may have Maeve's ear on occasion, but so do I. Do not forget that the treaty made at Tara is only a start. But I have something you don't: Donor Elfenkonig's ear, too. You may think this Guildhouse is not important enough for me to use that influence, but you would be wrong, Nigel."

"Please, Eorla, I am only asking that we follow the rule of law," Gerin said.

She turned her head toward him. "Where was your precious rule of law when my husband was murdered, Gerin? You couldn't even provide him with proper security. There is rot in this city, and the Guild must root it out instead of playing these druid games."

Nigel folded his hands in front of himself. "We will take your concerns under advisement, Eorla. But now, this meeting, for directors only, must commence."

She stared at Nigel for a long moment. With exacting slowness, she pivoted to Gerin, gave him an eyeful, and strode to the door. She paused. "There are those among the fey who prefer this constant strife. I do not. Continue down this path of division, gentlemen, and you will answer to me."

MacGoren made sure to wait long enough for her to be gone before he applauded.

Gerin sighed heavily, lowering himself into a chair. "She will be a problem."

MacGoren scoffed. "Oh, let her have the damned seat. It's not like we allow the Teuts any real power."

Several eyes shifted toward me, and away. Nigel cleared his throat. "Yes, well, I wouldn't put it that way, Ryan. Perhaps we should table the motion. We do not need to rush the decision."

Gerin leaned forward. "What better time to speak to Kruge's ideals than now, when attention is focused here? We have a quorum, let's install someone with whom we can work, Eorla's wishes be damned. She'll tire and go back home soon enough without Alvud here."

"Grey's only an acting director," said macGoren.

Gerin waved him off. "Alternates can vote on any matter."

"Except directorships," I said. Gerin shot me a look that would have curdled cat's milk. I shrugged. "What? I looked it up when Briallen made me her alternate."

Nigel smiled. "Interesting. Even when she isn't present, Briallen manages to insert herself. No matter, I cannot vote for Manus in any case."

Gerin thrust himself up from his chair. "You planned this, Nigel, to make me the fool."

"My dear Gerin, weren't you just talking about rules?" He said it pleasantly, but only a fool wouldn't hear the bite in Nigel's voice.

"I will speak to Manus about this, Nigel. This is an opportunity squandered," Gerin said. He leaned on his staff and left the room.

Nigel followed after more slowly, glancing at me as he neared the door. "How accidentally useful you can be, Connor," he said as he left.

I could feel heat in my face. He knew damned well he could have said that in a sending. Disappointment in me was one thing, but publicly embarrassing me in front of mac-Goren was purposeful. I needed to clear the air with him.

Ryan regarded me, his great wings undulating around him, shots of gold glimmering among the veining. Powerful. One of the more powerful Dananns I had met in a long, long time. "A druid with no ability trips up the plans of the Guild. The Wheel turns most peculiarly."

I gave macGoren a half smile. I was just a pawn in this little board game, and he had to know it. Nigel knew Gerin needed a quorum to vote for a new director, and he knew damned well I couldn't vote as an alternate. He must have let

Gerin think he was getting what he wanted—a Guild board packed with Celtic fey—only to pull the rug out from under him at the last minute. Games. Always games.

"That was a short meeting," I said.

MacGoren rolled his eyes with a bored look. "It was supposed to be to agree on a condolence statement to the Consortium. Gerin and Eorla decided to turn it into a snit just before you arrived."

I pulled a chair out and sat. "Is it always this pleasant?" I asked.

Ryan laughed. "This had to be the most pointless meeting yet, which is saying a lot. You were a nice surprise. Briallen seems to have thrown you into the pit. She must not like you. Evil, evil woman." He broke into a wide grin in case I wasn't getting the message he was joking.

"I'm sure she never expected me to need to fill in," I said.

He pursed his lips with a smirk. "Hmmm. Briallen sees much and tells little."

"Why the big deal about Eorla?" I asked. "Her husband was a director here, and she's no slouch from what I hear."

"Nigel despises Eorla. Gerin is not impressed with anyone who isn't a druid."

"Ryan?" a voice said behind me. Keeva stood in the doorway. A curious look traveled across her face as she took in the scene of me sitting in the boardroom, talking with mac-Goren.

"Ah, there you are. I told you the meeting was going to be short," he said. He walked over to her, slipped his arm around her waist, and kissed her quickly on the temple. I sighed mentally. Any hope that macGoren and I would become friendly went out the window. Now I knew why Manus asked me to investigate him instead of going to Keeva.

"I believe you know Keeva?" he said.

I looked at her over his shoulder. "Of course. We used to be partners."

Ryan macGoren smiled at her. "It's great working with her."

"I remember it well," I said. You could have frozen water with the smile Keeva gave me.

"You shouldn't be wandering around the building, Connor," she said.

"I told you, sweet, we were just finishing up the board meeting. That's why I called for you," said macGoren.

Keeva looked from me to macGoren. "He was at the board meeting?"

I couldn't resist a smug look. "I'm an acting director, Keeva. Let me know if I can help you with anything," I said.

The entire day had been worth it for the expression that came over her face. Keeva and I had an unspoken competition, one that hadn't died even when I was booted from the Guild. I have to confess a certain pleasure that she was apparently only dating a director while I had a pass that said I was one. It felt petty, yet satisfying.

She pointedly looked away from me. "I can't leave right now, Ryan. I have a few more things to do before tonight."

He casually ran his hand down her arm, clasping her hand and kissing it. "Of course, my dear, duty calls. If you need to meet me at the gala later, that's fine." At that, Keeva regained her usual composure.

MacGoren leaned toward me conspiratorially. "We'll be back here, Grey. They will want to continue their game. The fun will start if the dwarf director shows up. The best part is watching them fight over the director for the solitary fey. Everyone hates her, but they want her vote."

I sighed. "That's the problem with this place. Too many sides."

He laughed again. That laugh was getting irritating. "I always pick the same side, Grey. My own." With a brief nod, he escorted Keeva out.

I made my own way to the elevator. I just wanted out. Off the floor. Out of the Guildhouse. When I was with the Guild—playing the game, tracking the players, manipulating the nuances of relationships—it all made sense. It even felt important. I even liked it. But now, sitting in that boardroom had felt like running into a discarded lover. I could not for the life of me understand the appeal. I could say power. That certainly motivated me. But that meeting seemed a lot more about spite and petty vindictiveness. If only it all meant something real, and things would change for the better. But they wouldn't. No matter who got a seat at that particular table, it's always the same show, different channel.

I found it all sad, though. A man dies and his colleagues— even his wife—start to squabble over his corpse. Not pretty, but very Guild. I'm sure there had been a fight over who got my stapler after they kicked me out of my office. I noticed it was missing.

Now I had my own little games to figure out. Nigel's behavior irritated and confused me. I had trusted him with my life, yet now I wondered if that had been misplaced. My lack of ability did not matter to Briallen. She could have changed her designation of alternate anytime in the last two years, but she didn't. She could have done it because she saw this coming or because she thought I would regain my abilities. Either way, it showed she still had confidence in me. And she was trying to help me heal. Nigel had not approached me in the entire time since my accident, and he now brushed me off as if I were some novice trying to get his attention.

Then there was Ryan macGoren. Between the company he was keeping and his overfriendliness, he had to have some agenda. If he were with Keeva, she had to have mentioned me to him. And yet he tried hard to ingratiate himself with me when I knew damned well she probably had little nice to say about me.

I kicked myself for annoying Gerin Cuthbern. The High Druid of Boston was not someone to be trifled with, and I had managed to block his plans. Eorla would have found the legal loophole against him eventually, but by then Gerin would have had the upper hand if she had to come out swinging against an installed director.

I laughed. All these years, I had wanted inside that boardroom. In less than twenty minutes, I had managed to irritate one director, get insulted by another, be ignored by a third, and be befriended by one I wouldn't trust out of my sight. Whatever possessed me to want a piece of that action stumped me now. With any luck, I wouldn't have to deal with any of them again.

But I knew my luck.

9

I took the elevator down to the subbasement to see Meryl before heading over to macGoren's gala. She hadn't called in a couple of days, and I didn't know if that was a good thing or a bad thing. Of course, I hadn't called her either. When the doors opened, she was standing in front of them.

"I had a dream you were eating bones," she said.

I smiled. "Hi."

"Hi," she said. She joined me on the elevator and hit the button for the next subbasement level up.

"That's it?" I said.

She nodded. "Yep."

Meryl has a dreaming ability, and a strong one at that. Mine is embryonic by comparison. She also has a geas on her to tell people when she has a dream involving them. Geasa are fickle. They're obligatory restrictions or rules someone has to follow. No one likes having them, but everyone likes to be in a position to give one. The good thing is, it takes a certain amount of ability or authority to make them stick because they tend to be caught up in fate. If it doesn't suit the Wheel of the World, it's not going to make any difference.

Most people don't reveal their geasa because others can manipulate them. Say you aren't allowed to cross a bridge or something dire will happen. If someone knew that, likely they'd put something on the other side of a bridge to keep it away from you. They can be that petty.

"Was I making soup?" I asked.

"Nope. Just eating bones," she said. The doors opened onto the level where the Guildhouse had several research labs. It smells of chemicals and herbs and burnt things. The people that work there often smell the same. Meryl wasn't prone to escorting me around the Guildhouse. So, the fact that she had brought me to the research labs probably meant one thing.

"Ah, Janey Likesmith called you," I said.

I stepped out, but Meryl didn't. She just pointed. "Third door on the left."

"You're not coming?"

"Nope." She had a cold, neutral face.

I paused in the hallway. "Are you angry about something," I said.

She held the elevator and seemed to be trying to choose her words. "For future reference, do not give out my phone number without asking, do not put me on the spot by volunteering my services, and do not assume I am your secretary on call to arrange lab time. Got it?"

I cringed. "I'm sorry. I wasn't thinking."

"Quelle surprise," she said and released the door.

Ouch. It had seemed like such a logical thing at the time. Now I knew why she hadn't called. I'd have to think of something to make it up to her that didn't involve getting myself arrested.

I hit the third lab down the hall to find Janey hunched over a ward box. "How's it going?" I asked.

She looked up sternly, and I steeled myself for another lecture for something I hadn't thought about, but she relaxed as soon as she saw me. "Oh, hi, Connor! Thanks so much for this."

"Don't thank me, thank Meryl," I said.

Janey nodded. "I got the feeling she wasn't too happy about my being here."

I leaned against the door. "Not you. Me. I should have asked before I gave you her number."

Janey arched an eyebrow. "Ah. Yes. I can see how that might annoy someone."

The lab Janey occupied was deeper underground than her space at the OCME, but looked brighter and more professional. Her wooden worktable held several standard microscopes as well as odd stone-and-glass contraptions designed to work with essence. The funny part is the common equipment was contained in warding fields. In a fey lab, metals screw up the work because it causes warping of essence. The more sophisticated tools require essence to make them work and a delicate touch to keep that essence from interfering with whatever is being studied. "So, has this helped?" I asked.

Janey smiled broadly. "Definitely. I haven't had tools like this since college. I felt rusty coming in here, but I've found some interesting things for you."

Leaning across the table, she pulled a stone object closer. It looked much like an old-fashioned celestrial globe, only with several lenses attached and a small tray in the middle. On the tray, I recognized one of the drug stamps Dennis Farnsworth had been carrying. Janey maneuvered some levers, then stepped back for me. As I leaned in to look, the damned little thing on the tray gave me a sharp pain just like the other one had at the OCME. I looked through a series of stacked lenses and was greeted by what I expected, a lot of cells jammed together. "I don't really know what I'm looking at."

"Live cells," Janey said.

"Okay, I can see some movement if that's what you mean," I said.

"For one thing, I would think the cells should be dead by now. There's an essence on the stamps keeping them alive."

I pulled myself away from the lens. "Why would some-one go to that much trouble?"

She pursed her lips. "Potency, I would guess. I managed to pull the essence protection off and examine the cell essence directly. I have to say, it makes me uncomfortable. The cells have no cell wall, like animal cells, but contain chloroplasts and a large vacuole—sort of a water sac that plant cells have. I don't think these cells should exist. I think this is from some kind of animal/plant hybrid."

Other than the creep factor, the ramifications were not going anywhere fast for me. "Well, from the strong essence, the plant part is oak. Can you tell what kind of animal?"

She shook her head. "I'm baffled. There's an essence catalog next door that I tried cross-referencing with, but nothing comes up. I think you're looking at a rare solitary fairy or elf species. It's related to the oak family, but I don't know how. For want of a better word, Connor, I'd almost say we're looking at blood cells of some kind."

"Well, that's gross and different," I said.

"It's also where the compulsion is coming from. There seems to be yet a third essence mixed in it via spell transfer. Whenever I try to separate it out, the cell structure collapses and fades. As an educated guess, I'd say the spell enhances the compulsion ability inherent in the cells. I'm trying to conserve a sample. I've never seen anything like it."

I sighed and leaned against the table. "Well, I guess this confirms that the kid was involved in drug running, which is what Murdock suspected all along. If you can afford the time, I'd appreciate it if you could keep working on it."

She retrieved the sample and put it in a glass warding box. "Oh, sure. I'm a little slow on my end of things at the lab, so I can slip a few hours in here and there." She lifted the ward box and peered at the stamp. "What do you think the 'F' stands for?"

"It's a 'D.' It's ogham for oak," I said.

She wrinkled her nose. "No, it's not. It's the futhark."

Without getting any closer than necessary, I could see my

mistake. The ogham for oak is a line with two short strokes coming off it. Given the essence, I just assumed it was a "D" for "dair," the Celtic word for oak. Looking again, though, Janey was right. The two short strokes were slanted, not straight. It was an "F" rune, not ogham, the first letter of the futhark, the Germanic lettering system.

Realization struck me. "You're right. It stands for 'Float.' It's new. You'll probably be seeing more of it."

She considered it for a moment. "It's always something new. Does this help your case?"

"Yes and no, to be honest. It connects a few dots but makes the picture more tangled," I said.

She nodded. "I'm intrigued by the binding spell on it. There's something elven about it, but I can't place it."

I pushed myself away from the table. "You'll let me know if you come up with anything?"

"Of course. And thanks again," she said.

"Please, please, please, thank Meryl. And don't tell her I asked you to," I said.

She gave me a knowing smile. "Ah, that's the way of it."

"What?"

She shook her head. "Nothing. I'll tell her."

Despite the bright sun, a cool breeze caught at me when I left the building. October in Boston can be balmy or freezing. I bunched my hands in my jacket as I walked back to the Weird.

Dennis Farnsworth had been running drugs. I rolled the words around in my head, letting myself get comfortable with them. It's not the way I hoped he went, but there it was. Fair enough. I could live with that. Lots of kids think it's a way to make a little cash and get out of a rough neighborhood. They don't get that it just sucks them in deeper. It's not the best idea, but I've been living down in the Weird long enough to understand that the bad ideas are sometimes the only ones.

I could walk away from the case, let Murdock close the file, and move on. No one would question us. Just another dumb kid in a string of dead kids. People don't expect gang hits to get solved. The only people who care are the families and the gangs. The only time it gets bigger than that, when some politician or preacher or chanter starts up on gangs, is when someone squeaky-clean dies by accident. The scholar on his way home from Boston Latin High who gets caught in the cross fire of a drive-by or some office worker on a subway platform who accidentally gets bumped in front of a train during a brawl. Then it's news, and justice gets talked about. But Dennis Farnsworth died near the worst part of the worst neighborhood in Boston. And now the weather.

But I had loose ends. Dennis Farnsworth had been wearing the colors of a gang led by Moke. Moke had a turf rival in C-Note. C-Note was running a new drug called Float. Why would Dennis have been wearing one gang's colors and running another gang's drugs?

I pulled out my cell and called a number I didn't call that often. To my surprise, it still worked.

"Hey, little bro," Callin said.

"Hey. How'd you make out last night?"

"Not bad. Yggy's is neutral again. I appreciate the brotherly concern."

I ignored the sarcasm. "Listen, I was wondering if you can tell me where to find the gentleman responsible for that." Given that someone had been right on my heels when I found the Nike, I decided to be cautious with what I said.

"Maybe. I know a place he shows up sometimes."

"Where can I meet you?"

"Can't. I'm in the middle of something. I'll send Joe when I know something."

I felt oddly let down. "Okay. Great. And, um, Cal?"

"Yeah?"

"I am glad you're okay."

There was a short silence. "Thanks, man." He disconnected. I tried not to dwell on Callin. Most times, I can put him out of my mind. I didn't even know where he lived at the moment, but he obviously spent a lot of time down in the

Weird. I could try and take comfort in the fact that the Clure still hung around with him. The Cluries weren't so bad, more amoral than anything else. Fun as hell. Small comfort, but a comfort nonetheless.

I was still playing the connections around in my head a few hours later as I stood outside the Rowes Wharf Hotel. MacGoren's comment earlier to Keeva about a gala prompted the memory of having seen Seacorp's promotional schedule on their Web site. The latest dog and pony show for their waterfront project was scheduled at the hotel tonight. Given that Keeva was going to attend, I thought I'd kill two birds with one stone and try to get an update from her on the Kruge investigation as well as see what else I could learn about macGoren's business.

With a mixture of envy and annoyance, I watched many of the city's high-powered fey—the beautiful ones that the press called *flitterati*—entering the lobby. At one time, I mingled with these people, drank with them, ate with them, and slept with more than a few. Now, on the rare occasions I run into them, they get that faraway look in their eyes as though they cannot place where they know me from. The price of falling from on high is the angels tend to look busy when you drop by to say hello.

I slipped past security with laughable ease. Tricking myself out in a long leather coat and lots of black just sealed the deal. Picking the right entry point, in my case a city employee, strutting like a privileged fey, and I was sipping mediocre champagne before my presence even registered with anyone.

Since the Seacorp project involved hard-core real estate, major property owners circled around each other. MacGoren, of course, several high-ranking Consortium elves, and more dwarves than I had seen together in a long time. If memory served me correctly, and as a druid it usually did, dwarves didn't own much land near the Tangle, but they had to be concerned about their own nearby investments.

Seeing all these dwarves made me think of Moke. Murdock

had left me a message that he had some information and would fill me in later. Later was starting to look pretty late. I probably should have asked Cal about Moke, too, but that would have been pushing my luck with him. It didn't take much for us to trigger silence between us, and me looking like I was just hanging around him for information would probably piss him off again.

Waiters circulated with drinks and hors d'oeuvres, paying particular attention to the various city officials. If macGoren wanted the project to move forward, he had to make the mayor and local reps happy.

I mingled with a crowd perusing placards off the lobby. Maps and projections of potential development ranked down a long hallway that led to a banquet room. I did not see anything that I had not already researched, although the fact that all the land under consideration had not been secured seemed to be conspicuously absent.

As I studied a color-coded map of the piers on the south end of the Weird, I felt an essence coalesce behind me like a spear.

"Interested in investing?" Keeva asked.

I turned and smiled. She was in full impress mode, a lovely deep blue wool skirt, leaf-patterned blouse, and ivory-colored brocade vest setting off her flowing red hair. The small necklace she wore cast a glamour that made her seem to move in a haze of soft light. "You could say I've invested in the Weird for some time."

She rolled her eyes toward the ceiling. "Ah, yes. The Weird. Of course you'd go there."

"That's what the point of all this is, isn't it? Getting rid of the Weird?"

She shrugged. "Yes, Connor, that is the point. Does the city, any city for that matter, really need a neighborhood called the Weird?"

I pursed my lips. "I would think the people who live there think so."

She gave me an exaggerated bored look. "Why are you

here, Connor? Can I have at least a little time off from aggra-vations?"

"Old friends, you might say. Why are you here? Playing hostess?"

She shook her head. "Not really. I've been so busy, this is the first night in a week Ryan and I have been able to see each other."

"And you love a big party," I said.

She toasted the air with her glass. "And I love a big party."

"So, you two an item?"

"You could say that." She smiled smugly, the kind of smile that dared me to think their relationship was anything less than pure attraction. I'm sure that was there. I'm also sure that each had a private little pros and cons sheet on the other.

"How's the Kruge investigation?"

She checked our surroundings before responding. Even when she did, she pitched her voice for my ears only. "Still haven't found the troll Croda. She's the only connection to Kruge we have that we haven't been able to clear. Why, do you know something?"

I shook my head. Keeva had a habit of not asking for help. She had to be coming up really dry to ask me outright if I had heard anything.

I gestured with my glass. "And here's the man of the hour."

MacGoren moved in behind Keeva, wrapping his arm around her waist. Even to my doubting eye, the smile she gave him looked genuine. He tapped my glass, showing a wide smile. "Hello, Grey. Are you intercepting Briallen's so-cial invitations, too?"

I did my best to smile at his joke that I was sure was an unspoken dig. "Something like that. Nice turnout."

He glanced around him, assessing the gathering. "We'll see later in the evening. I'm gauging interest."

I looked at the map. "Looks like you're pretty interested. Don't you own most of this land?"

He nodded several times, his eyes roaming the maps as though he were confirming that all his properties had been noted. "You know your neighborhood well. There are some major pieces that need to be picked up to move forward, but, yes, a lot is mine."

I already knew that. An interesting bit of coincidence was that Dennis Farnsworth had been found on macGoren property. "A murder victim was found on some of that land."

MacGoren turned his smile into a pensive look. "Yes, I heard. It's sad when young people get caught up with drugs."

I kept my face and voice nonchalant. Janey Likesmith would file her research with the Farnsworth file, but it was too early for Keeva to have received it, never mind mention it to macGoren. "Who said anything about drugs?"

The smile quirked back on his face. "I just assumed. You know that neighborhood."

"Yes. I live there." Running down macGoren's holdings the previous night, I found two large parcels that were divided by a sliver of land he did not own. I brushed my fingers on the map. "Isn't this area where Alvud Kruge had his office?"

The smile hadn't left his face. "Alvud was interested in the project, if that's what you're asking."

I pursed my lips. "Alvud," not "Kruge." A little more familiarity there than I would have thought. "Interesting," I said. "A man with a reputation for social change was interested in destroying the neighborhood he was trying to save?"

I caught a chink in the smile. "Improving is the word, Grey."

I raised an eyebrow. "Kruge was going to sell?"

MacGoren shrugged. "We talked about it. Alvud was not one to stand in the way of progress."

I glanced back at the maps. "Well, he's not standing in anyone's way now."

MacGoren threw his head back and laughed. "Now there's black humor. Good thing I was with Keeva the night he died, or I'd be worried."

I locked eyes with Keeva, and she stiffened in mac-Goren's arms. She caught it, too. "I'd rather not talk about work," she said.

"I'm sorry, I didn't realize we were working, Keeva," I said.

She extricated herself from macGoren's embrace and took his hand. "We should be mingling."

MacGoren looked curiously at us both. "Yes, well, good to see you again, Grey."

I bowed my head. "And you."

I watched them walk away. She had just told me she hadn't been with macGoren in a week, and yet he lied and said they were together the night Kruge died. I half expected Keeva to turn back, give me a look that said she recognized that. But she didn't. I decided to give her the benefit of the doubt, for now. I had a feeling that macGoren was in for some interesting pillow talk tonight.

I wandered through the reception, eavesdropping where and when I could. It's remarkable what people will say loudly to each other in a noisy hallway as if no one else could hear their gossip. I was disappointed, though. No real gems came up, certainly nothing more interesting than my own conversation with macGoren. I had his connection to Kruge that Eagan was looking for, but it didn't look all that interesting yet. I didn't believe for a moment Kruge was interested in selling to him.

Alvud Kruge was the major topic of conversation. I didn't think anyone would mention Dennis Farnsworth, and I wasn't disappointed in that regard. Most of the people there had given to Kruge's causes at one time or another. They were the type. They just didn't seem to understand that his causes were about people like Farnsworth. Throw a little money around and hope it solves a problem. Kruge did more. He got his hands dirty on the street.

As I watched macGoren work the crowd with Keeva at his side, I had to wonder what dirtied his hands. Seacorp was a big project. He stood to make millions. What he probably didn't know was that the Weird was as much a concept as a place. He could bulldoze it, but these people would just move elsewhere. And they would remember what he had done. There's payback in that eventually. Especially if the foundations are laid on pain and rejection.

10

I had a nice surprise outside the hotel. Murdock was waiting for me in his car, parked in the fire lane outside the hotel. I had left him a voice mail telling him where I was going, but I didn't actually ask for a ride. For a change. Maybe he's getting to the point where he just assumes that. At least he hasn't bitten my head off about it like I'm sure someone else would.

One of my goals in life was to answer two questions. When did Murdock sleep? He had a habit of working long hours before I even rolled out of bed and yet somehow still had the ability to work past midnight. How did he manage to look freshly dressed? My clothes wrinkle if I think about wearing them. His shirt and pants always looked just pressed.

I opened the passenger door and removed a pizza box from the seat. I left it sitting prominently on a trash can in front of the hotel's revolving door. Then I fell into the seat, and he pulled out.

He glanced at me with amusement. "You smell like money."

"Yeah, I need a shower," I said.

Murdock skipped the turn onto Old Northern Avenue that leads to my street. We continued down to Summer Street and hung the left over the channel. "Where are you taking me?"

"The gang unit came through with an address for Moke. Thought we could shake his crib a little," he said.

"Could be fun. Speaking of trolls, I asked Cal to get us a line on where we can find C-Note. If I can get close to him, I can see if his essence matches anything I found at Kruge's office," I said.

Murdock drummed his fingers on the steering wheel. "You mean Kruge's office where Kruge was murdered, which is a case we are not working on? That Kruge's office?" He had a lazy smile on his face when he said it.

"Yeah, that Kruge's office," I said. He just shook his head slowly with the same smile.

When Murdock and I were at Yggy's last night, his essence had blazed around him unlike any human essence I had seen. In my natural, unfocused state, I'm aware of the essence around me like a type of peripheral vision. I sense stuff, but it's just sort of hanging there unattended. We leave essence everywhere we go, and the essence of where we go even lingers on us as well. Murdock's car, for instance, always has a residue of his essence because he spends so much time in it. Mine's there, too. It doesn't fade because it's constantly reinforced. The champagne flute I left at the reception has my essence on it, but that will fade because I've had only brief contact with it.

I focused my senses on him. Murdock's essence glowed next to me, not as brightly as at the bar, but more than it ever had before it changed. On our last big case together, he had taken a hit from a bolt of fey energy that almost killed him. Instead, it supercharged his body essence somehow. I can tell he doesn't understand what that means yet. If the fight at Yggy's was any indication, though, he's faster and stronger than he ever was. It's not easy for a human to knock out an elf, and he did it with one punch.

We approached the Reserve Channel, an inland water access that divided the southern edge of the Weird from South Boston. Summer Street crosses the channel and continues into Southie. In typically confusing Boston mapping, Summer Street also takes a right turn and runs along the channel. It makes giving directions interesting. Murdock took the right and pulled over.

Long, dark warehouses lined the street facing the channel. "What's the address?" I asked as we got out the car.

"It's more a location," he said and started walking down the embankment to the bridge.

This end of the channel had had a small inlet in it at one time. Over the years, as the neighborhood went downhill, the inlet had become a dumping ground until it was mostly filled in. You could have walked across it now. Right to the bridge. "You've got to be kidding," I said.

He glanced at me over his shoulder. "Hey, he's a troll."

We picked our way toward the bridge through sodden garbage. Out on the water, several boats in winter wrapping swayed at their moorings on a floating barge. Moke had a picturesque view as long as he didn't look down.

In the summer, the channel can be fragrant, and not in a good way. The cold weather kept the odor down, but the air still had the raw, flinty smell of dirt and dirty water. We went under the bridge. An amazing amount of trash lay scattered around—clothing, slumped cardboard boxes, a mangled shopping cart, split plastic bags of household garbage. Against the retaining wall stood a collection of major appliance boxes, packing crates, and skids woven together into a shantytown. Here and there, the homeless huddled around small fires. Murdock ignored them and made for a large heap of green corrugated roofing panels. A thick stench hit my nose, two days past fetid. Murdock banged on one of the panels.

"Moke. You have company," he said. The way he pushed back his coat, I knew he had unsnapped his holster. He banged again. "Moke! I don't need a warrant to come in there."

We could hear rummaging sounds and some actual growl-ing. Murdock stepped back as a double-height panel shifted opened.

"Awright, awright. Keep yer hat on," a deep voice said.

The panel swung out on a makeshift hinge. A troll shuf-fled out, his head bobbling on a long neck that protruded from a wide hunchback. His gray face held round black eyes, a number of yellow teeth protruding from between his lips, and one of the longest noses I've ever seen, misshapen and hooked downward. His hair consisted of several greasy strands that dangled straight down to his chin. He stank, of course. His patchwork suit looked so soiled that soap and water were clearly not part of the program.

He leaned forward onto his hands and squinted down at Murdock. "Hemph. Police. You tell that Ms. Beruthy I didn't take no cats. She got so many, she don't know if one's gone anyway. And they taste terrible, too."

"We're not here about cats. We're here about goats," said Murdock.

He narrowed his eyes at us. "Hemph. Stupid joke. Older than you."

"Are you Moke?" I said, just to confirm Murdock's infor-mation. There might not be many trolls in the city, but too often people assume there are fewer than there actually are. You just don't see them.

He nodded. I resisted the urge to hit him for destroying my blood evidence. But you don't hit a troll unless you want to break a hand.

"Word is you run the T-Rats," Murdock said.

His great head swayed between us. "Don't like T-Rats. Hide from them."

The hard part about interrogating a troll is that you can't intimidate him with size or strength. Grabbing him by the neck and trying to shove him against the wall would make a scene that we'd both laugh at.

"What about Dennis Farnsworth? You know him?" I said.

He stared at me and didn't speak. Trolls can stay incredibly still, so still it's not unusual for someone to walk right past their large shadowed presence without even noticing them. Murdock and I exchanged a glance. Unfortunately, it was one of those glances that said this is what Murdock submitted my consulting fee invoices for.

I looked up at Moke and decided to try and provoke him into talking. "Rumor has it the T-Rats are underpaid and easy pickings. C-Note will pay double their current cut if they ally with the TruKnights."

Nothing.

"So, Detective Murdock and I are spreading the word. Sounds like a good deal and would stop the fighting."

More nothing.

"Everyone knows the T-Rats are in it for the money. Not a loyal one in the bunch. I'll tell you this since you don't like them, but one of them led me to some evidence in the Farnsworth murder."

"That's a lie. Was a flit that did," said Moke.

Success. I smiled at him. Trolls don't trust anyone easily, so they value loyalty more than most. Murdock would make a good troll, but he bathes too much.

"And you set the building on fire," I said.

" 'Nother lie. Was TruKnights." Moke settled back on his haunches.

"I didn't see any TruKnights. I saw T-Rats."

"You was on my turf. Fire had elf-stench." Another little trick trolls have. While druids can sense the essence of people, trolls can sense who manipulated essence. All fey manipulate essence and, unless they use their own, they pull it from their surroundings. If I found a ward stone, it would have essence running in it, but I'd have no idea who put it there unless whoever did it had been near it recently. Trolls can sense what kind of fey did it long after they're gone. Sometimes even the exact person.

"Why would the TruKnights kill the kid?" said Murdock.

Moke rocked his head. "Not all runners run for joy."

Joy was the current street slang for drugs. "Are you say-ing the kid was delivering something else?" I said.

Moke's hunchback rolled in what I took to be a shrug.

"Who was he running for? Kruge?" I said.

Murdock glared at me. I have to admit it was an amateur mistake, but the guy annoyed me.

"Yeah. Kruge," said Moke. Of course he'd say that.

"All right, I'll play. About what?" I said.

Again with the hunchback. "Kruge not like a lot. Not a lot like Kruge."

"A name," said Murdock. I could sense his essence start to spark up. Not a good sign. "Give us a name, or I'll haul in half the T-Rats, and we'll see how long the rest of your crew survives against the TruKnights."

Moke growled and stretched his head toward Murdock, who had the good sense to step back. No telling what might come out of the troll's mouth, or what might end up in it. Mur-dock unholstered his gun. Moke cocked his head at it, proba-bly debating whether a bullet would itch or burn. It would take more than one to slow him down.

"Kruge hate C-Note most."

No surprise there. "So do you. What makes you think I believe that?"

He worked his tongue over his teeth. "Croda knew. Kruge told her C-Note was trouble. Needed help."

"What kind of help?" said Murdock.

Moke rolled his shoulders. "Maybe he had a goat needed eating."

I smirked. I couldn't help it. Not everyone gets to throw Murdock's sarcasm back at him. "Where's Croda?"

Moke shifted his eyes toward me. He made no other movement, but I could feel his disposition change, a sense of anger and fear enveloping him. Anger I was used to from trolls, but fear? Trolls feared little. They could take a bolt of essence to the face and keep coming. They had few adver-saries who could match them in a physical fight. And their own innate ability to manipulate essence was not inconsequential. A fearful troll is not a good thing.

"Why bother Moke? C-Note trouble, not Moke."

"We're bothering you because a kid is dead, and we're not happy," said Murdock.

He shrugged again. "Go bother C-Note. C-Note kills. Moke just make people happy."

"Sure, happy, and occasionally battered and bruised if they don't pay for their happiness," I said.

It was my turn to get the growl. Trolls love to growl. Between their odor, their looks, and their size, the growl makes the picture complete. My feeble little shields flared up around me like a warning system, only one that would not stop a troll bite. Unlike Murdock, who had a better sense of self-preservation, I stepped up on Moke. His face loomed over me, twice as wide as my own, a foul odor wafting out of his mouth. I clenched my jaw.

"Let me tell you something, Moke. I am going to go see C-Note, and I am going to bother him. But right now, I want to know where Croda is, or I will come back at noon and tear the door off your hidey-hole."

Never underestimate the speed of a troll. Moke's huge hands pinned my arms to my sides, and he roared as he lifted me off the ground.

"You dare!" he screamed, his voice reverberating against the underside of the bridge.

"Drop him!" Murdock yelled. He had his gun out, judiciously pointed at Moke's head. Moke roared again and swung me at Murdock. I slammed into Murdock, and pain shot through my shoulder. Not such a good idea after all. Murdock went tumbling into a heap of trash as Moke stalked across the debris-strewn ground and shoved me against a support column.

"You want to see me kill? I show you kill!" I bit my tongue as he shook me. I could feel every bone in my body rattle. My head banged against the column, my shields screaming as they tried to soften the blows. With a futile effort, I tried to tap my essence, tried to reach deep within myself and breach the wall that blocked my abilities. A knife blade of pain sliced in my brain, and blood shot out my nose into Moke's face. Not the counterattack I was hoping for.

He tossed me through the air, and I landed on a cardboard shanty. Something struggled beneath me and shoved me aside. A lance of pain pierced my shoulder as I rolled. An old man appeared from within the box and ran off without looking back. I dragged myself to my feet, holding my arm against my side to keep it from hurting. Murdock was searching the trash for his gun as he yelled into his radio for backup.

I backpedaled as Moke lumbered toward me. Turning to run, my ankles twisted, and I landed on my ass. I dug my heels into the dirt and tried to scramble away. No point. Moke was on me in seconds and grabbed me by the torso. Yeah, I screamed. I admit it. A troll lifts you and slams you against a retaining wall, damn, you scream. Black and red spots flashed in front of my eyes. Then I was in the air again. I plowed into a garbage heap. Stunned, I tried to will my body to move, but it wouldn't cooperate.

I heard a shot. Murdock had found his gun. I shook my head to clear it as I heard him fire again. When my vision cleared, an unexpected sight greeted me. A thin young girl with short blond hair, dressed in fatigues and pink ski jacket, stood with her back to me holding her hands up to the oncoming troll. Murdock fired again, but Moke only flinched.

"Stop! Stop! Moke! Stop!" she yelled.

He was almost upon her when Murdock fired again. "Stop!" the kid screamed.

Moke skidded to a halt. For a moment, no one moved, the only sound the ragged breath of the troll. Murdock came forward, gun extended in front of him.

"It's okay, Moke," said the girl.

Breath still heaving, he turned his head toward Murdock. "Tell him to stop shooting me," he growled.

Keeping one hand up toward Moke, she turned her other

palm toward Murdock. "Please! Stop! I don't want anyone to get hurt."

I stumbled to my feet. "You're a little late."

Murdock gestured with his gun. "Back off! Now!"

Moke did exactly that. He took two steps back toward his hovel, leaving a dozen feet between us.

The pain from my shoulder made me grimace as I walked toward the girl. She couldn't be more than fifteen or sixteen, cute and scared as hell. She started to drop her hand. "Keep the hands where I can see them, and no one will get shot. Who the hell are you?"

She ignored the question. "Please don't let him shoot again."

"I asked you your name."

She held her hands out in front of her again. "Crystal Finch."

Even if I hadn't been fighting a faint, I would have rocked back on my heels. The last place I expected to find Dennis Farnsworth's girlfriend was under a bridge forcing a rampaging troll to back down.

I flicked my head at Moke. "Do you really have him under control?"

She looked at Moke. "Are you all right, Moke? Can he put the gun down?"

Moke closed his eyes and stepped back against his makeshift door. "No gun. I stop. No gun."

Murdock had not taken his eyes off the troll, sighting down his arm as he held the gun at Moke. "Connor?" he said.

I looked at Crystal, and she nodded. "As long as he doesn't move, I'm cool with it," I said.

Murdock backed toward us and away from Moke. He swung the gun at Crystal. "Open your jacket," he said.

"I think she has a knife in her left front pocket, but otherwise she's unarmed," I said. All fey are sensitive to metal, mostly because it screws up how we use essence. I can feel it at close range if I let myself, and given the weak field projecting off Crystal, I knew she didn't have a gun. Murdock leaned forward and pulled a small pocketknife on a key chain out of her pocket and slipped it in his own. Then he stepped back and holstered his gun.

"If you leave Moke alone, I'll take you to Croda," Crystal said.

"I don't think you're in any position to bargain," I said.

"Neither are you," she said. I hate smart kids.

Moke and I tensed as Moke moved again. "You okay, Crystal?"

"Yeah, Moke. Thanks. I think I'll be all right with these guys," she called over her shoulder.

He stepped back more. "You call. I come."

"Thanks for everything," she said.

Murdock pointed a finger at Moke. "Wait a minute! You're not going anywhere. You're under arrest for assaulting a police officer."

Moke's face broke into a jagged-tooth smile. "Not tonight."

Everything around us began to vibrate. Dust rained down from the bridge, and the dirt in front of Moke erupted. A wall of rock rumbled out of the ground, rising in a massive heap. When it almost reached the undercarriage of the bridge, it crested like a wave and rolled down over Moke, sealing him in against the retaining wall. Murdock looked at me in utter disbelief.

I shrugged with my good shoulder. "It's a troll thing."

Murdock's radio squawked somewhere nearby. He looked one more time at the rock wall and went to retrieve the radio.

I turned to Crystal. "Where's Croda?"

"I need protection. Big-time," she said.

"You'll get it. Tell me where Croda is."

As Murdock returned with his radio, I heard him call off the backup. Not that they seemed to have made any rush to get down to this end of the Weird.

She turned to Murdock. "I heard you guys talking. Are you really trying to find out who killed Denny?"

"You don't answer questions very well," I said.

She glared at me. "I'm trying not to die. Are you the good guys or not?"

"Good guys. Bad guys would have beat the hell out of the troll," said Murdock.

Crystal zipped her jacket and looked around. Most of the homeless who had been there when I arrived had made themselves scarce. "I was safe here. You've got to hide me somewhere until you get Denny's killer, or I'm dead."

"Tell us where Croda is, and we'll take care of you," I said.

She crossed her arms. "I can't. I ran, so I don't know exactly where she is. We can go look tomorrow when it's light."

"Let's go now," I said.

She began to bounce on her feet against the cold. "Dude, look at me. Every snitch in the Tangle will sell me out the moment we hit the Avenue. I'll be dead before daylight. Hide me tonight, and I'll take you tomorrow. Otherwise, I'll call Moke back."

I hate to admit she had a point. Her platinum blond hair would stick out, to say nothing of the jacket. The only neon pink in the Tangle is in the bar lights.

"The only thing I can give you is a lockup cell tonight. I'm not waking up my boss for a safe house until I know you have something," said Murdock.

She shook her head firmly. "I won't be safe there in jail."

Murdock looked at me, and I shook my head. A sixteen-year-old girl was not going to spend the night in my apartment. Even if I thought it was okay, the gracious not–Mrs. Finch would probably claim I molested her daughter.

"I have an idea," I said. I pulled my cell phone out and walked out to the channel to get a better signal.

Meryl picked up on the second ring. She never picked up on the first. "Hey. It's late even for you."

I breathed a sigh of relief. She didn't sound angry anymore. "I need a favor."

"At this rate, when I call in all the favors you owe me, you'll be my slave for the rest of your life."

I smiled. "Really? You'd be into that?"

"Funny. What do you need?"

"Can I stash a sixteen-year-old girl at your place for the night?"

"You're joking."

"Not in the least."

"Is this a kooky French comedy involving a maid?"

"No. That was last week. This week it's a murder witness who has a troll at her beck and call."

"She can stay, but not the troll. I'm still finding maggots from last time."

"Funny. Can you meet me on Summer Street by the Reserve Channel?"

I heard a heavy sigh. "Which one?" I told her and disconnected.

I went back under the bridge. I could tell by their faces that Murdock and Crystal were not getting along. "I found a place for you. If you don't bring us to Croda tomorrow, Murdock puts you in a cell."

Crystal looked uncertain for a moment, then nodded.

Murdock pulled at my sleeve. We moved out of earshot. "What's the deal?" he said.

"Meryl will take her for the night."

He nodded toward Crystal. "She says she won't talk until daylight."

I glanced back at her. She looked tired and scared. A kid scared enough that she only felt safe with a troll under a bridge. "If she saw what happened to Kruge, I don't blame her."

Murdock turned to look at her again, assessing what he wanted to happen. "Think we can trust her?"

I shrugged. "She managed to keep a troll from killing me. Let's give her a shot."

My cell phone buzzed against my thigh. Meryl's number lit the screen. "Let's go. Ride's here," I called to Crystal.

We made our way up the embankment to find Meryl leaning against a black car smoking a clove cigarette. She wore a long leather coat with matching black gloves and her standard Doc Martens.

"Crystal, this is Meryl. She's going to take care of you," I said.

Meryl took a drag and eyed her up and down. "Just so we're clear, he doesn't mean that in a milk-and-cookies kind of way."

"Not a problem," Crystal said.

Meryl jerked her head back. "You look cold. Get in."

I waited until Crystal had settled herself inside the car. "You have a Mini Cooper. Very nice."

She smiled. "Astute."

"I didn't know you even had a car. I thought you'd come in a cab."

Meryl smiled at Murdock. "Don't you hate it when he wants to chitchat at two in the morning on a work night?"

He laughed. "I'm not touching that one."

She looked back at me. "Hmm. Blood all over you, and, if I'm not mistaken, something's wrong with your shoulder. Did the kid do that to you?"

I smiled. "She's pretty tough. Would you mind helping me out a little?"

She rolled her eyes. "More favors." She crushed out her clove and placed her hand on my shoulder. Even through the glove, a soft white light glowed. Warmth spread inside my shoulder, easing the pain. I could imagine the ligaments and muscles knitting back together. She released me, and I rolled the shoulder. It felt much better. By the time I woke up, I doubted I'd feel a thing wrong.

She turned to Murdock. "You're pretty banged up, too. Here, this is on the house."

She placed a hand on his chest and called up her essence again. Murdock closed his eyes and smiled. Meryl pulled her hand away and gave him a curious look. "Interesting essence you have there, Murdock."

"So people keep telling me," he said.

Meryl looked up at me. "So what's the deal with the kid?"

"We just need to keep her out of sight until tomorrow. I think we all need some sleep, so how about we pick her up late morning or so?"

"Okay." Meryl opened the car door and slid inside. She buckled up and rolled down the window. "I'll drop her off wherever you want. You don't get to know where I live."

I dropped my chin and mock-glared at her from under my eyebrows. "Fine."

She smiled. "Sleep well, boys!" She made a sharp U-turn from the curb and drove back up Summer Street.

Murdock shot me a sidelong glance.

"Do not say a word," I said as we walked back to his car.

"What? You mean the whole flirtatious thing? I wouldn't think of it."

"Shut up."

We jumped in his car. Murdock cut over to the Avenue, and we cruised toward Sleeper Street. At this time of night, few people walked the streets. Even the Weird settles down by dawn. You could find an after-hours party if you wanted, but it was a weeknight, and only the diehards and desperate were out.

"Another interesting evening with Connor Grey," Murdock said.

"Hey! Talking to Moke was your idea."

He chuckled and shook his head. "Yeah, but provoking him into using you as a bat and me as a ball was not my intention. What set him off like that?"

"The crack about ripping off his door at noon. Sunlight kills trolls. I guess he took it more personally than I intended," I said.

Murdock pulled up in front of my building. "I have a doctor's appointment in the morning. Pick you up around noon?"

"Sounds good." I got out of the car and didn't even watch him pull away.

Up in my apartment, I chewed through a few ibuprofen and seltzer. Meryl might have sped up my shoulder healing, but she couldn't touch what was in my head. It was pounding. I could feel the hazy black cloud in there squeezing whatever was left of my brain.

I stripped out of my clothes and crawled under the bed-covers. I lay on my back and stared at the ceiling. Dawn was just a few hours away. I would have to get up then and do my sun rituals. Sunrise was always too early for me. The thing I hated was that the nights when I wanted to sleep the most were when I needed to do the rituals the most. I had committed myself to doing what I needed to do to recover from my accident. The damned mass in my head never went away, but I felt stronger since I had gone back to the rituals. Hell, my shields hadn't collapsed even when Moke threw me the second time. They didn't work as well as they used to, but they had held.

Despite my curiosity as to how Crystal Finch ended up with Moke, I was too exhausted to care. Partying with a couple of fairies, brawling with a troll, and flirting with a druidess healer all in one night can take their toll. The sad part is, it felt like just a busy day at the office. That's what the Weird can do to you.

11

My internal alarm clock woke me just before dawn. Gray light filtered into my living room, the cold gray of late fall. The soft hiss of the radiator whispered to me to get out of my nice warm bed. I ached everywhere. Meryl's healing booster had focused on the shoulder, so every other muscle reminded me that, yes, I had been tossed through the air several times the previous night.

I eased out of bed feeling every vertebra trying to decide whether it wanted to be closer to its neighbor or farther apart. I didn't think about the headache. I always have a headache, so I only notice the pain if it's reaching incapacitating levels. I slipped off my T-shirt and boxers and stood naked at the window, eyes closed, arms upraised. All across the city, hundreds, maybe thousands, of fey stood in the exact same posture, naked and waiting for the sun. I suppose if someone had a good vantage point and decent binoculars, the landscape made for a voyeur's wet dream.

Being fey means being in tune with essence on a level that human normals cannot grasp. It means feeling a connection with the world, with nature, with other beings, through the essence that binds everything. Human normals don't know what that experience is. Some have a vague sense—the sensitive types who get flashes of precognitive warning, or second sight, or dreams that feel important. The reality of the Convergent World, the world I was born in, my reality, never reaches the essence that Faerie has. Had. Still has. No one knows if Faerie is still there, missing the people and places that ended up here. But the fey here remember it and yearn for it. And so, each morning thousands stand facing east, preparing themselves for a ritual that reminds them of their abilities and keeps them connected to lost Faerie. Me, I just want the headaches to stop so I can get back to work.

I knew the moment the disc of the sun met the horizon. A flush of warmth fluttered in the center of my forehead and in the socket of my shoulder. Meryl's healing spell continued its work, drawing a boost from the new day. I inhaled, my lungs expanding to their maximum, and I began to chant the ancient words of greeting. As the sun rose higher, I moved through the postures I had learned as a child, pose and voice and essence entwining to realign the pathways within my body that enhanced the ability to manipulate essence. As the sun rose, I moved faster, the chanting became more urgent, my intellectual mind receding as I became one with the flow. That is the core of being fey—the ability to lose oneself completely, to find one's place in conjunction with the being of all things. As the sun lifted off the horizon, full white blaze above the heaving ocean, I thrust my arms down, my head back, and exhaled in exhilaration.

The problem with doing the sun ritual after a night of little sleep, is you want to stay up and enjoy the endorphins no matter how tired you are. I hit the coffeemaker and went into the shower. One of the nice things about living in an old warehouse not originally meant for residential use is that the heat and hot water boilers tend to be huge. Everyone in the building can probably shower at the same time and not feel a shiver. I still ached from Moke's love tap, so I let the water massage my skin. Essence may improve my constitution, but it still didn't make the bruises go away unless a healer manipulated them.

I dressed in jeans and a black turtleneck, poured a cup of coffee, and settled back in bed to watch the news. Nothing startling, the usual chaos and mayhem of a big city. Two more gang fights overnight, one not far from my apartment. The news cycled again on the top of the hour, and a name caught my ear. Gerin Cuthbern stood in front of the Guildhouse, a distinct lack of any of the usual Guild public relations lackeys in attendance. Gerin wore an embarrassingly outdated white robe of druidic office, which told me right away whatever he was droning on about had to be good. I turned up the volume.

". . . in this tragic time," he said into several microphones thrust into his face. "We extend to Eorla Kruge our deepest condolences and our prayers. In what can only be a small gesture of gratitude for all the work Alvud Kruge did for this city, indeed the world, the Boston chapter of the Druidic College offers as a sorrowful gift a place of rest for Alvud's body. His wish to leave his corporeal remains on these shores speaks volumes about how much he cared for Boston and its people. We can only respond by donating the land in the Forest Hills Cemetery for an appropriate burial and mourning spot for his friends and family."

The video clip vanished and the perky blond anchorwoman popped back on the screen. I laughed and lowered the volume. Keeva, I'm sure, was blowing a fit somewhere. Given that she wasn't standing by Gerin's side for his announcement meant he had just thrown a big wrench into her funeral plans. The Guild had their media protocols, which Gerin well knew, and he had just done a great job of breaking them.

I had to give it to Gerin, though. He knew how to play politics. Staging his announcement in front of the Guildhouse certainly implied their endorsement, although those in the know would know better, and putting Eorla Kruge—a high-ranking Consortium member—in a position to reject a cooperative gesture from the High Druid of Boston was elegant. Neither the Guild nor the Consortium could criticize him without looking like they were using Kruge's funeral as an excuse to play politics themselves. He was also laying the groundwork to make Eorla look ungrateful if she contested a director's appointment. A brilliant move. The man knew how to play.

Getting an essence recharge at dawn is great, but it's all a wash if I exhaust my physical body. It didn't help that a dream had bothered me. Dreaming gives me a bit of anxiety these days. Last spring I realized my dreams had taken on a predictive bent, an ability I never had before my accident. After midsummer, the dreams stopped, and I thought they were just a fluke brought on by the possibility that I might die. Sort of a heads-up from the Wheel of World to keep me on my toes.

Prescient dreams are metaphorical, and since I have little experience with them, I'm not very good at parsing the metaphors. For that matter, I'm still not sure when I'm having a prescient dream or just sleeping on too full a stomach. My morning dream consisted of apples falling and a chain that moved like a snake. That segued into Moke swinging Meryl and me in his hands. I woke just as he was about to smash us together. Nothing that Freud wouldn't be able to explain, particularly since, I have to admit, I was aroused by how it ended. At the same time, I had a sense of danger that I couldn't articulate. The last time dreaming felt that way, I almost died.

I called Meryl. She mumbled something into the phone about death and mornings, but I think she agreed to drop Crystal Finch at my place by noon. Meryl actually hates mornings more than I do. She's a Daughter of the Moon and avoids sunrise salutations except on the high holidays. I left Murdock a message to meet us.

She showed up on the dot of noon and summoned me downstairs with her cell phone. The Mini was parked neatly by the door, engine running, with Meryl in her leather and Crystal in her pink. They made an odd couple but were in an animated conversation.

Meryl powered down the passenger window when she saw me. "Thanks, Meryl. Was she any trouble?"

"He-llooo. *She's* right here, dude," said Crystal. She even waved. I hate the word "dude" from sixteen-year-old tough girls. I'm not their dude. As soon as I thought that, I felt way old.

"*She* can go wait in the vestibule," I said.

Crystal glared at me, then turned to Meryl. "Thanks. Again. I really appreciate what you said." Damned, if the kid didn't tear up and hug Meryl. And damned if Meryl didn't hug her back. Without another word, she got out of the car, looked quickly up and down the street, and ran to the front door I had left ajar. She closed it behind her.

I slipped into the passenger seat to get out of the cold. "That was sweet."

Meryl shifted in her seat to look at me. "She's had it tough, Connor. Cut her some slack."

I stopped myself from making another sarcastic comment. Meryl was right. I had no reason to dislike the kid just because she had managed to put me on her schedule instead of mine. She had reason to be afraid.

"Did she tell you anything about Kruge?" I asked.

"No. We talked about Denny. He sounds like he was a nice guy. She didn't need me interrogating her last night."

I nodded. "Yeah, okay. I'm guessing a troll doesn't have a very good shoulder to cry on."

Meryl gave me a stern look. "She'll help you. Just make sure you protect her."

I slouched in the seat. "I'm not made of stone, Meryl. I got into this because a kid got killed. I'm not looking for it to happen to another one."

She nodded. "I meant her feelings, Connor. You get a little single-minded sometimes. Remember, you don't know what she's been through. She did try to tell me what happened but froze up every time. Today's not going to be easy for her."

I heard a car come up and looked out the rear window. Murdock pulled in behind us and parked. I leaned forward and brushed Meryl's nose with my finger. "Thanks. You're a regular Jiminy Cricket sometimes."

She smiled. "Do that again, and I will bite you."

I chuckled. "I'll call you later, crazy woman."

I got out of the car, and she drove off. When I banged on the vestibule door, Crystal opened it and peered out.

"Are you ready?" I said it nicely. She nodded and followed me to Murdock's car. I tossed a donut bag into the back and sat down. Crystal pushed away a pile of newspapers on the backseat and made herself comfortable.

"Good afternoon, everyone," Murdock said. He pulled away from the curb and almost looked in his side view mirror when he did it. He felt different—smooth, for lack of a better word, as if his essence were spread over him in an even layer. Human normals usually feel that way to me because their essence is so weak. The fey tend to have variable flow about them, the essence more intense about their heads and hearts. His *midach* must have done something to moderate the extreme fluctuations I had been sensing.

"Where to?" I asked Crystal.

"The Tangle," she said. Of course. Murdock had already turned onto the Avenue, so we just drove in silence through the main part of the Weird. He stopped the car at Harbor Street. We could see the yellow crime scene tape on the Unity storefront. A Guild security guard hovered into view at the far end of the street, then flew back up.

I twisted in my seat. "Okay, Crystal, first you have to tell us what happened at Unity," I said.

She looked out the window with a look I've seen before, a slack look of disbelief at what she had seen. "Mr. K asked Denny to make a run for him. I went with him for the pickup."

"Do you know what he was running?" I asked.

She shook her head. "It had something to do with Float. Denny bought some somewhere. I found it. I was pissed 'cause I'm clean now, and I didn't want any drugs around. Denny said he wasn't using. Mr. K asked him to buy it for him and that he had to bring it to Unity, then do a run."

"Did Kruge use kids from Unity for runs a lot?"

She shrugged. "Yeah. Regular errands type stuff, if that's what you mean."

I looked over at Murdock. He didn't say anything. At the end of the day, this was still his case. I let the moment hang to give him a chance to jump in, but he didn't.

"Okay, so you got here and then what?" I said.

She wrapped her arms tightly against her chest. "Mr. K was here with Croda. He asked me to wait in the printing room. I couldn't hear anything at first, but then there was shouting. I opened the door a crack to see what was going on, and there was this big ugly troll yelling at Mr. K . . ."

"Would you recognize him?" I interrupted.

"Huh? Yeah, sure. Croda's the only other troll I met until Moke. Anyway, the troll said something about Denny having something and grabbed him. Mr. K got mad and pushed the troll and told Denny to run. Denny started running toward me, and the troll threw a fey-bolt at him."

"Wait a minute, a troll threw a bolt of essence?" Crystal nodded. Trolls manipulated essence, but not offensively. They worked it within things, particularly stone, but I'd never heard they could send it through the air. Unless C-Note had figured out how to work around it. And the idea of a troll doing that was pretty scary.

"And then Denny . . . he . . . he . . ." She started to cry.

Even though I've seen enough manipulation-by-tears, Crystal's reminded me to take it easy on her like Meryl asked. "It's okay, Crystal. Tell us so we can figure out what to do."

She nodded and took a deep breath. "The bolt hit Denny, and he flew through the air right at me. He hit the door, and we both fell. He didn't move at all after that. I think . . . I think that's when he died." The last part came out in a whisper. She started to sob again.

"You're doing good, Crystal. Take a breath and tell me what happened next."

It took a few moments for her to calm down. Any annoyance I had for her from the previous night was gone. "The next thing I knew, Croda was in the room. I could hear fey-fire and screaming. Croda grabbed me and Denny and ran out the back door. She took us into the Tangle."

"Can you show us?"

She nodded. "Take a left into the next alley."

Murdock crossed over Harbor and took the left. We were in the alley across the Avenue from the Unity alley. So far, it made sense. It was the direction I had sensed troll essence trailing away when Murdock and I checked out the back door of Unity. We crept down the narrow lane, large warehouses looming up on each side of us. Sunlight fell in complex patterns on the ground as it filtered through the network of fire escapes above. Old wooden pallets, an array of boxes and bags and tossed papers littered the gutters. At the end of the alley, a rusted car sat to the left.

"Go to the end and take a right," Crystal said.

We made the turn onto a wider service road between more warehouses. Even though we were more exposed to the sky overhead, the light felt dimmer. We were starting to move into the Tangle.

"Go about three buildings down," she said.

Murdock guided the car around piles of rubble, trash, and masonry discarded with no fear that anyone would object. The warehouses down here were no longer active, most of them burnt-out and boarded up. It had been a long time since city services ran garbage trucks. Murdock stopped the car.

Crystal leaned forward and peered through the windshield, then out the side. She closed her eyes. "Wait here and take the left when the alley appears."

Murdock craned his neck to look up through the windshield. "There's no alley turn here."

"There will be," said Crystal.

I scanned the buildings for the telltale signs of a spell, but there was so much ambient essence, nothing stood out. "The Tangle's full of illusions, Murdock. People put them up all the time. Sometimes they forget them and leave them running," I said.

We sat for twenty minutes. "Are you sure this is the right place?" I asked.

She nodded. "Yes, it's about the right place. It didn't take this long that night. Maybe it's broken."

A few minutes later I was about to suggest Crystal rethink the location when the brick wall to our left shimmered and vanished. Without a word, Murdock backed up and turned into the alley that had been hidden. Crystal led us through two more similar illusions and an odd series of turns around buildings that seemed to have been built in the middle of the road.

"We have to get out here and walk," said Crystal. We were in a stretch of alley that managed to look dark even in the early afternoon.

"You want me to leave the car here?" Murdock said.

"It's not like it's a Rolls," I muttered and let myself out. For such a trash heap, he worried about it an awful lot. Murdock and I walked a few feet behind Crystal as she made tentative steps forward. Ahead, old Jersey barriers lay in a heap like a very large game of pick-up-sticks. Crystal turned to her left and faced a gaping hole torn through the brick wall of a building. She seemed frozen in place.

"Where next, Crystal?" I asked when she didn't move.

She looked up at me, then back at the hole. "We went through here."

She didn't move, so I stepped around her and peered inside. Not much to see, just a large empty room covered with the ruins of the collapsed ceiling. The far wall was just gone. Where we stood, the light felt dim. Out beyond the other side of the building, it looked stark and harsh. I could feel the buzz of essence, an old resonance slithering over my mind.

The darkness in my head didn't like it. Something had happened here, something wrong. There were places like it all over the Tangle. Throughout most of the Weird, people avoided using too much Power for fear of the backlash. But here in the Tangle, all bets were off. No one cared what happened to anyone here.

"You ran straight through," I said to confirm my thought with her.

"Yes," she said behind me, her voice small.

I think I knew what was out there. We were close to the end. "I'll go first," I said.

Murdock pulled his gun and covered us. I walked across the room, feeling pain whispers all around me. When I reached the far wall, I stopped with Murdock at my side. We faced a long narrow courtyard, more an oversize air shaft. Opposite, a storage shed had been built into the side of the adjoining warehouse. Not much remained, its left and right walls still standing, but its front and roof gone.

Between the crumbled walls, in the midst of raw debris, Croda stood. She was about eight feet tall, stout, and thick-limbed. Her right arm was thrust up above her head, and her back was arched. Her face was bulbous, a small round tusk sprouting from each side of her wide, flat nose. And her mouth—her mouth was stretched wide in terror, sharp teeth visible, thick tongue protruding. The sun shone hard and white on her dead, petrified face. Now I knew why I had made Moke so angry.

We walked across the broken stones until we stood next to her. Crystal stayed back, refusing to come any closer than the perimeter of the shed.

I cleared my throat. "What happened?"

"We hid in there. We thought no one saw us. There was a loud sound like a big wind, and Croda pushed me down behind her. The next thing I knew, everything was flying apart. Sunlight was coming in, and Croda was screaming. Something reached in and grabbed Denny. Croda stopped screaming, but I could hear fey-fire. I couldn't see very well, but it looked like two people were in the air fighting. I think one was a fairy dressed in black, and the other was the troll from Unity."

I looked over her and frowned. "A troll? In the air? In *daylight*?"

She nodded. "I don't get it either. The troll had Denny, then the guy in black grabbed him away and flew off. I waited until I didn't hear anything anymore. Croda told me if anything happened to her, I should find Moke and tell him what happened and that he would take care of me. So that's what I did. I've been there ever since."

Murdock was standing on the opposite side of Croda from me. He moved nothing but his eyes, examining the frozen figure. She looked like a statue with clothes on. I started doing my own exam. "She's petrified," I said for his benefit. "Literally. As best I know, trolls don't just turn to stone when exposed to sunlight. They're attuned to stone. They call it the bones of the earth. It's their fey ability. When they're exposed to sunlight, their bodies become hyperconductors and immediately begin absorbing minerals from everything nearby. The sun acts as catalyst for a petrification process that happens in minutes."

"Sounds painful," said Murdock.

I nodded. It had to be. Effectively, she had mineralized, every cell in her body turning solid with compounds of iron or carbon or silica or whatever other elements were in the soil. The land we were on was an old industrial area. All kinds of chemical waste were below us. She glittered dully in the afternoon light, like a dirty cut gemstone in muted shades of white, black, red, and blue. I couldn't help thinking she was sadly beautiful in death in a way she could never be in life.

". . . *run, Dennis. Get out of here* . . ." a male voice called out. Both Murdock and I jumped back. Crystal screamed and ran. The voice had come from Croda.

"What just happened?" Murdock said.

"Give me a minute," I said. I let my eyes roam over her,

trying to find something out of place. Squatting down, I looked behind her and found the source of the voice. In Croda's left hand, the one hidden behind her back, was a small obelisk that fit almost entirely in her palm.

Murdock came around to my side. I stood and looked at Croda. "She has a ward stone fused into her hand. It must be a recorder. Her whole body is a ward stone now."

Wards can be charged with essence and spelled for all kinds of things. The ones back at my apartment worked like alarms. Some can immobilize anyone that comes within their fields. And some can work like glow bees, only they can record a lot more. To listen to them, you just have to hit them with the right amount of essence. I must have touched Croda, and my body essence triggered the recording. I placed my hand on her arm. I could hear a faint whisper, but nowhere near the clarity of the first time.

"What's wrong?" said Murdock.

"I don't know. Who knows what her body structure is now. The connection must be intermittent." I looked at him. "I hate to say it, but we need a stronger fey to pull the data off the ward."

Murdock looked around the courtyard. "Where's Crystal?"

I didn't have to look. Her fear was so strong, I could sense her essence through the building passage. "I'm pretty sure she's hiding in the backseat of the car."

"At least the car is still there," he said.

I laughed and shook my head. We picked our way out of the shed and walked back to the shattered building. A glitter of light caught my eye, and I stepped to the side.

"You find something?" Murdock asked.

He joined me near the edge of the courtyard. Sitting on the ground, half-covered in dirt, was the round, reflective helmet of a Guild security guard. It must have been knocked off in the fight. "I think we know where Crystal's fairy in black was from anyway. Got any gloves on you?" I asked.

Murdock patted his coat pockets and came up with one. I slipped it on and picked up the helmet. Definitely Guild issue. There were no identifying marks on it, though. There didn't need to be. The inside of the helmet retained the essence of the wearer. I looked at Murdock. "We have a problem. Let's get out of here before we're seen."

I hurried into the building, with Murdock on my heels.

"What? What did you find?" he said, as we came out on the other side.

"Crystal?" I called out. She poked her head up inside the car. I turned to Murdock.

"You need to make that safe house call now. That kid's got a target on her a mile wide," I said.

"What the hell are you talking about, Connor? Whose helmet is that?"

I looked up and down the street but did not see anyone. That didn't mean there weren't ears to hear. "Not here."

We got in the car. "Don't back up. Take us out to Drydock Ave and loop around the Weird. I don't want anyone on Harbor Street to see us if we can avoid it. Crystal, keep your head down."

Murdock drove quickly up the service road. Unfortunately, it took us deeper into the Tangle. The buildings loomed in, soot-stained and ominous. Years of fey occupation had left their imprint. What had once been standard industrial buildings had taken on grotesque flourishes. Gargoyles hugged lintels and rooftops. Windows had become leering portals of twisted stone. An odor permeated the car, acrid and chemical, evidence of spellcasters. My head started ringing like it did whenever I was near a scrying. From the pain, several people must have been trying to read the future. I closed my eyes against it, but it didn't help. The pain was inside me. A few moments latter, it subsided and was gone. I opened my eyes. We were out of the Tangle.

"Take me home," I said.

We didn't speak the entire way. When Murdock pulled up in front of my building, I hopped out and went around to his side of the car. "Get Crystal into hiding, then call me. I'll fill you in."

"You're not going to tell me now?" he asked.

I made my eyes shift significantly to Crystal, and Murdock got the message. I wasn't about to get her more involved than she already was. "Call me later."

I leaned down to look at Crystal. She was clearly terrified. "You did good, Crystal. Just listen to Detective Murdock, and you'll be okay."

"Thanks, dude," she said softly.

I tapped the door. "Call me," I said to Murdock.

"Will do, 'dude.' " He gave me a quick nod and pulled away.

I looked down at the Guild helmet still in my hand. Something dangerous was going on that I didn't have a handle on. Odd people were crossing paths. It seemed too bizarre to be just about drug runners out of the Tangle anymore. Whatever was happening wasn't going to like seeing the light of day. And the one thing I knew was key to putting it into place, was figuring out why Ryan macGoren's essence was inside a Guild security helmet at a murder scene.

12

After doing the digging on macGoren's business, I decided to see if I could get the other side of his story. Kruge obviously wasn't going to talk, but I thought someone else might. I hoofed it up to the subway and rode it into Copley Square.

The Teutonic Consortium consulate looks completely out of place in the Back Bay neighborhood near the square. I don't doubt it's just the way the Consortium likes it. It's a Bauhaus concrete structure in the middle of Victorian townhouses on Commonwealth Avenue. Out front stands a two-story statue of a grim-looking Donor Elfenkonig, the Elven King, dressed in light battle armor, one hand holding a sword, the other a staff. The staff used to be a niding pole, which is essentially a cursing staff. A horse's skull sat on the top, not so subtly pointed at the Ward Guildhouse several blocks away. Because of the Guildhouse's own protections, it never had much effect, but it annoyed the hell out of a woman who lived directly across the street from the consulate. She sued and would have never have won in court, but she did in the media. The Consortium might be guilty of many things, but even it didn't want to appear to be cursing

a retired old lady. They removed the horse head to stop pro-
testers from hitting it with paintballs.

I walked into the lobby for the first time in years. Unlike
the Guildhouse, the consulate had been decorated to impress.
In contrast to the austere exterior, wooden panels carved with
intricate forest scenes lined the lobby walls. Depending on
your politics, you either thought they looked like dramatic
pastorals or jackboot Disney illustrations. The bunnies were
pretty tough looking. Overstuffed seating arrangements filled
the rest of the room, soft velvets and earth-toned brocades.
Near the inner door to the main offices, photographs of Consortium notables hung with grandiose descriptions of their
contributions to the world.

I stepped up to a reception desk behind which sat two
male elves and a dwarf, all dressed in the same style plain
gray tunics.

"*Guten Tag.* I would like to speak with someone to arrange
a meeting with the Marchgrafin Kruge, please." I knew better than to ask directly for the widow Kruge. That would
have shown a distinct lack of ignorance of her status.

All three looked at me sharply, and one of the elves
chanted under his breath. I could feel a protective shield
build between us. No surprise. The Consortium had pulled
Eorla Kruge from her estate for protection before I even left
her husband's murder scene.

"Name, please?" said the other elf.

"Guild Director Connor Grey." I pulled out the Guild ID,
which I still had from yesterday. I was definitely moving in
the wrong circles again.

The elf took the ID and muttered over it, checking for the
Guildhouse essence seal. He told the other two in German it
was authentic. "Please wait, sir," he said as he picked up the
phone.

And I did, a long hour before another elf arrived from
within the building. He was tall, dressed as security in red and
black, and had a billy club on his waist. "I am the Marchgrafin's assistant. How may I help you?"

I stood to face him. He didn't look like a keeper of business calendars. "I'd like to see the Marchgrafin."

"She is in mourning, sir, and not to be disturbed."

"I understand. I need a few minutes of her time on an urgent matter related to her husband."

"She has had many such requests," he said.

"From Guild directors?"

He didn't respond.

"You have my credentials. Perhaps you would prefer to call Guildmaster Eagan to confirm my mission further?"

His face made it clear that he didn't like the subtle threat to go over his head. He walked to the reception desk and consulted with the other two elves. They cast looks at me several times. A few moments later, they stopped talking as the security agent considered. I hoped he didn't call Eagan. The Guildmaster would back me up, but I hated having to get an adult's okay. The agent picked up the phone and dialed. He spoke for a bit, then hung up and ignored me. I overheard enough to understand he called a superior rather than Eagan. Another twenty minutes went by, and two more security guards arrived. The first came back over to me.

"Are you armed, sir?" He didn't call in two more agents because he thought I was defenseless.

"Of course," I said.

"We will extend your rank the courtesy of retaining your weapon, but you may not draw it or appear to do so. You will not be allowed within twenty feet of the Marchgrafin. If you hesitate to follow any directives issued by any of the Marchgrafin's assistants, the consequences shall be swift and severe. Is that amenable to you?"

I smirked. "Amenable's not the word I would have chosen, but sure, that works for me." I couldn't help myself. The Consortium is so damned officious. He led me through the inner doors, and the other two agents fell in behind us. My head began to ache as they chanted, little nosey cantrips testing my defenses. For once, my missing abilities worked in my favor. The lack of even minor defenses conveniently sent the message that they weren't worth my trouble and probably was giving them a minor anxiety attack.

We rode an elevator in silence to the third floor. When the door opened, another set of security guards guarded the floor lobby. They were not taking any chances with Eorla. We walked down a long, stately hallway of pilasters and landscape oils and several closed doors. They led me into a large receiving room, easily thirty feet long and half as wide, a library lined with books I'm sure no one ever read. A healthy fire kept the room a little too warm. A single chair faced me across the wide floor, but I was not offered one of my own. Two of the guards entered with me, and we all waited while the third disappeared without saying anything.

A door at the far end of the room opened, and I was surprised I did not have to wait long for the Marchgrafin. She swept into the room with the first security guard at her heels. There was no mistaking who was in charge. Here we were in her element. I could feel the resonance of Power before she even reached me, some of it from her rings, but her personal essence was considerable.

Apparently, she had not been given the dictate of twenty feet because she continued walking past the chair. The security guards behind me immediately stepped in front of me to block me from her.

I smiled at her. She did not change her expression, but stared at me for several moments.

"Leave us," she said without moving her gaze.

Behind her, the first security guard stepped forward to stand by her side. "We have orders, m'lady."

She merely shifted her eyes at him. It didn't take a genius to understand a sending argument was going on between them. The guard lowered his gaze and flushed. "As you wish, m'lady," he said with a curt bow. He spoke to the other two guards in Old Elvish, telling them to take up positions outside the door. I found it amusing that they assumed I spoke neither German nor their own language. Once they had vacated the room, Eorla nodded and turned away from me.

"Let's sit by the fire," she said in a firm voice that said she was used to directing.

As I took a side chair from along the wall, I realized she was pulling her own chair forward. "Here, let me," I said.

"I've moved more than enough chairs on my own." Not bitchy, just matter-of-factly. I liked that in a royal elf, though I hadn't expected that from Eorla.

We settled before the fire facing each other. She was quite beautiful, beautiful in that uncanny way a woman can be where you can't quite believe anyone can look that way. Her haughtiness enhanced her attractiveness, though she was clearly a woman who drew her strength from who she was, not what she looked like.

"I know you are here-born, as they call it, Connor Grey, yet I sense something ancient about you. You have an old weapon with you?" she asked.

Without hesitation, I pulled my dagger from my boot. It really was ancient, a gift from my mentor Briallen, and had already saved my life once. It had a worn and stained sheath, but the hilt shone like newly forged silver and gold, with a large ruby on the pommel. Without hesitation, I held it out to her. If I had anything to worry about from Eorla Kruge, the blade wouldn't help me.

When she reached for the dagger, a few runes on the old sheath glowed a light blue when the field of her essence came near. Her hand hovered over the pommel, then closed into a fist without touching it. "It has been many years since I held a blade. I do not think now is the time to start again. Can you turn it for me?"

Eorla leaned forward and examined the dagger as I displayed it from several angles for her. As I pulled the blade out slightly, she grabbed my arm. "Don't. I sense it has an edge that yearns for blood. It is an undaunted weapon. Draw it only with purpose. I have seen it once before, a long, long time ago, in a very sad time."

"I just thought you'd like to see some of the inner engraving."

She leaned back in her chair. "Thank you. Why do you claim to be a Guild director?"

I shrugged. "It was more a half-truth. Would they have called you otherwise?"

"If I knew you were here, yes. It's not every day one gets to meet the man who almost killed Bergin Vize."

I hesitated before responding. In Germany, many people considered Vize to be a hero. The guards might have been uncomfortable leaving Eorla alone with me, but now I felt uncertain being left alone with her. "He almost killed me, too."

She nodded. "I know. Why are you here?"

"A young human boy was murdered the same night as your husband, and I believe the deaths may be related."

The corners of her lips pulled down. "I was not told of this."

"The Guild thinks he's not worth the trouble. I was hoping you could tell me anything regarding your husband's murder that might help?"

A bitter line crossed her face. "This division between fey and human is exactly what Alvud fought against. The night he died, Alvud said he had a meeting with a troll. I know the Guild is focusing on a troll woman that worked at the Unity offices. They do not seem able to uncover any new information. Are you saying you have?"

"I found some blood evidence in my case that may have been your husband's."

Eorla frowned. "I can't tell you how odd it is to have someone say that to me."

"I'm sorry. Can you tell me who might have wanted the Marchgraf dead?"

"I told the Guild a drug dealer made threats against Alvud. He was quite concerned about it."

Keeva hadn't mentioned she was looking at drug dealers in addition to Croda. "Did you tell the Guild that?

"Of course."

I had two trolls working drugs. Moke wanted C-Note out of the way enough to pit his gang against him. Framing

C-Note for Kruge's murder certainly wasn't beyond belief in a drug lord dispute. C-Note wanted control of the Tangle enough to kill the head of the TruKnights.

"What about business associates?" I asked.

Eorla considered for a moment. "My husband had many businesses, Connor Grey. None of them seemed worth his life."

"Can you give me an example? What about real estate?"

She gave me a sly, knowing look. "I see. You are here about Ryan macGoren and Gerin Cuthbern. They have been trying to buy Alvud's properties in that neighborhood."

I kept my face impassive at the mention of Gerin Cuthbern's name. In my business, you always want to look like you already know everything, but this was news. Still, you used what you could on the fly. "I know why macGoren wanted the land. But I don't understand why Cuthbern was interested."

"Because macGoren wanted it. Alvud was short on cash, but he was concerned that macGoren would force people out of their homes if he sold the land. Gerin and Alvud were old friends. Gerin was just as suspicious of macGoren's motives. He offered to fund Alvud's project by buying the land and keeping it out of macGoren's hands."

"You'll pardon me, Marchgrafin, but how does someone of Alvud's stature need cash?"

She smiled grimly. "People often make that mistake about monarchies. Titles do not automatically mean money. Alvud spent a great deal on his causes. He saw wealth differently than some people."

I looked at the fine cut of her clothing, the quality of the material, and decided to push the line. "Differently than you?"

She gave me a low laugh. "Aren't you the brash one? Yes, I have money, but if my family caught wind of my giving it to Alvud's causes, the flow would stop instantly. They don't share our politics. That's as personal a question as I will answer. What else would you like to know?"

"Do you think macGoren wanted the land enough to kill?"

Eorla sighed and shook her head. "In another world, maybe. That's the way things used to be in Faerie. You fought for what you wanted. But here, in this place, I doubt it. In my life, I have seen people kill for a crust of bread. My husband wasn't killed. He was savaged. Only a madman would do this. I think Ryan macGoren is an aggressive businessman. I don't think he's a madman."

"What did the Marchgraf need the money for?"

"A drug rehab program. If you have a drug lord who was going to lose his territory and his client base, I believe you have your motive."

I tried to smile, but it was awkward. "I tend to agree with you. The Guild seems more at a loss than we do."

Eorla nodded in slow agreement. "It's always about territory, isn't it? Who owns it; who uses it; who wants it. Gerin has offered to buy the property from me and deal with macGoren. I may agree to that. That place was Alvud's interest, not mine. I would prefer to work through the Guild."

I smiled. "Gerin will work against you." It didn't feel like telling tales out of school. Eorla wasn't stupid.

"Precisely. He preferred Alvud over me because Alvud personally worked to solve problems. He liked to meet the people he was helping and left the politics to me. My skills have always lain in that direction."

"You must have made a formidable couple," I said.

A melancholy smile flickered on her face. "I shall miss him terribly."

"I truly am sorry for your loss."

She sighed and looked into the fire, then back at me. "My grief has not reached me yet. The idea that I shall never again hear my husband's voice in this world is beyond my comprehension. When the time comes, I will mourn him deeply. Now, though, I keep seeing his smiling face as he kissed me and left our last embrace."

I felt the sound of her voice in my chest. To have lived with someone for centuries spoke of a relationship I could not even begin to fathom. I reached out and squeezed her hand, amazed that I did. One doesn't touch an elven noble without permission. She didn't object, even placed her other hand on mine. Despite what she had said, she was grieving already and sharing it with me. The Consortium needed more people like her and her husband.

I stood. "I'm sorry to intrude."

She looked up at me, her eyes deep and glimmering. "Vize is a fool, Connor Grey. Dangerous, but a fool nonetheless. Do not let revenge consume you. Men like Vize make many enemies. Let the Wheel decide his fate."

Hearing that was a nice surprise. Other than her offense at Nigel's remark about Vize—which could have been playacting—I hadn't had a sense of how she felt about her radical countryman. "And if the Wheel includes me in his fate?"

"Then that is the Wheel of the World. If that is Its will, you do not need to seek It. It will seek you. Remember that."

"I will," I said with a bow.

"Good luck." She dismissed me by turning to the fire. Normally, that kind of treatment by a royal ticks me off. It fit Eorla, though. She would have been exactly who she was with or without the title.

I pulled my collar up around my neck as I stepped out of the consulate. The air had gone chilly, and the October sky had become a hard, white sheet. After the warmth of the receiving room, I felt even colder. I walked east toward downtown with my hands jammed in my pockets.

Manus ap Eagan was not worried about a real estate transaction. With macGoren's public promotion for the Seacorp development, Eagan already knew about it. He obviously suspected something more, or he wouldn't have asked me to look into it. I had to agree with Eorla Kruge, though. MacGoren had nothing to gain with Kruge dead unless he hoped to take advantage of a grieving widow. But if he knew Kruge, he must have met Eorla. She was not a woman you could take advantage of easily.

My cell phone began vibrating with saved messages as soon as I was a few buildings away. I had set the ring to vibrate, but it hadn't gone off inside. The consulate probably had signal jamming in the building. Three messages had come in with a Guildhouse number, so I called to pick them up.

"Connor, it's Keeva. We have a situation. Get yourself to a secure location and call me immediately."

That didn't sound good. The next message came up.

"Connor, call me, dammit." Keeva again. She actually sounded concerned.

The next message was from a different Guild number.

"Hey, it's me. Just checking if you were dead. If you aren't, call me. If you are, call me anyway." Okay, for Meryl to put in a check-in call, something definitely was up.

I was only a couple of blocks from the Guildhouse. At the end of Commonwealth Avenue, I entered the Public Garden, a turn-of-the-century Victorian walking park surrounded by intricate cast-iron railings. Even at the tired end of fall, it manages to look attractive. The formal paths wind through a strange collection of statuary as well as landscaped flower beds and specimen trees, all now dormant.

I decided to call Keeva first. As I hit dial, my shields sprang up with such force, I hunched forward in pain. Simultaneously, a bolt of essence grazed my shoulder, and I spun off my feet. I could feel heat across my back, but no direct pain, so I didn't think I was on fire. I rolled to my feet and ran for cover behind a tree as another bolt flew past me. I ducked down as tree bark splattered through the air.

I felt a cold pressure slam into my forehead, a forceful sending. *Where are you?* Keeva's voice reverberated in my head.

I couldn't send my thoughts back. One of the many things I couldn't do anymore, my mental sendings just went astray. A bolt hit the tree as I realized I'd dropped my phone when I got hit. It lay about ten feet away. Another bolt struck, and the tree groaned and crackled. It hit close enough for me to recognize what it was—elf-shot, the expression of essence that the elves used. I dove away in a tumbling roll and grabbed the phone. Essence struck around me from two directions now, and I scrambled on my back trying to find the source. I wedged myself between a statue and the fence encircling the park.

More fey-bolts shot around me, but the bane of the fey proved itself in my favor. Between the bronze in the statue in front of me and the iron in the fence at my back, the shots warped around me and went wild. I had landed in a safe zone between conductive metals. I called Keeva.

"Where the hell are you?" she said when she picked up.

"Under fire in the Public Garden."

"Give me your exact location."

"I'm behind the statue of . . ." I twisted to see whose statue I was under. A fey-bolt struck it in the neck, and the head toppled down next to me. The abolitionist senator Charles Sumner stared eyelessly at me. "I'm behind the headless statue."

"Security's on its way."

The bolts of essence intensified. Whoever was out there was getting closer. I recognized a new noise, the loud hum of Danann fairy wings. In moments, more fey-fire rained down, only this time scattering in a pattern around me. Bolts stopped striking near the statue. Something dark swept overhead. Seconds later, a Guild security agent landed next to me, his featureless helmet tilted down at me. Without a word, he grabbed me by my shoulders and hauled me up. He spun me around, wrapped his arms around my chest, and launched us into the air. Several more security agents above us laid down a covering fire of essence to block another attack. We rose above the park, but I lost sight of my defenders as we swept behind the line. Below, I could see several people running, mostly humans getting out of the way. Here and there, shots of essence raked through the park from figures dressed in black and red leather. TruKnights.

The security agent flew me away from the fight, over the

final block toward the Guildhouse. As we rose above a hotel roofline, I could see the area in front of the Guildhouse cordoned off and more security agents stationed both on the ground and in the air. The agent brought me in close, avoided the front, and landed us on a balcony of one of the highest turrets, the landing platform for the security division. Without a word, he took off again. I stepped into to a large room and found more security agents preparing for duty.

"Someone will be coming for you, sir," a young Danann said as passed me and ducked into an adjoining room. I went to the door and watched him lifting boxes from the floor. A line of lockers covered one wall with a gym-style bench in front of them. Above, a number of helmets sat on a long shelf.

"Are those helmets always there?" I asked.

The Danann straightened up. "You're not supposed to be in here."

"I'm not 'in here.' I'm at the door."

He moved toward me. "Well, step back. We've had some problems, and no one's allowed in without permission."

I nodded at the helmets. "One's missing, isn't it?"

He placed his hand on my chest, not threatening, but with enough pressure that told me to step back. He looked out the door. Apparently, after satisfying himself that no one was within earshot. "How do you know that?"

"When did it go missing?"

"Four days ago."

I nodded. The timing was right. "Do you know whose helmet is missing?"

He spoke without looking at me, checking on the room instead. "They're not assigned. People just grab them. The landing bay is shielded. The helmets register when they leave and when they return, so we don't have to keep a head count in an emergency. Someone took off from here four nights ago and didn't return. It was the middle of the night, not a regular shift change, and no record of a security call."

"How'd they get in?"

He shrugged. "The ready room door is warded, but any-one with the right security level is allowed in."

"And it's a pretty high level if I remember."

He nodded. "Look, I don't know how you found out, but we're keeping it internal for now. It's not going to look . . . *hey!*"

He shoved me and ran for the landing bay. About a hun-dred feet out from the bay, security agents jostled for space as they came in for a landing. One group in tight formation carried someone, and another swept in from above too quickly. A flurry of wings and bodies bumped and pushed together. Whoever was carrying the passenger lost his grip. I watched horrified as I recognized Nigel Martin falling through the air. Agents dove after him.

With my senses on hypersensitivity, I saw a plume of essence ripple the air around Nigel. His descent slowed as he spread his arms. Like a bad joke, the agents attempting a rescue shot right past him. Nigel righted himself and rose, levitating the remaining distance to the building. He stepped onto the platform like he had just stopped by for a cup of tea. Within moments, agents swarmed around him in concern.

Not realizing I was holding my breath, I exhaled in relief. I should have known Nigel would pull that trick. It takes enormous control and energy, but high-level druids can do it. I had managed to get myself only a couple of inches off the ground before my accident, but then, I was still young by druid standards. Nigel had age and ability.

Looking bemused, he pushed his way through the anxious crowd. "I'm fine, gentlemen," he said. He stopped short when he saw me, a curious expression on his face. "Connor, good to see they didn't drop you, too. I imagine your luck would not have extended to the spontaneous return of your abilities."

You could have heard a pin drop. The security guards pulled away from him. It took a moment for me to realize my mouth was hanging open, and I clamped my jaw shut.

"That was a horrid thing to say," Keeva said behind me. I turned. She stood at the door, wearing her signature black jumpsuit, her unglamoured wings fully open and shimmering with white and silver light. She stepped to my side. "Are you all right?"

I removed my coat and examined the scorch across the back. "Yeah. Could use a new coat, though. Thanks for the backup."

"Part of the job," she said and looked significantly at Nigel. "That goes for both of you."

"What the hell is going on?" I asked.

Keeva looked around her. Half of the people in the room still had their helmets on. I could surmise what she was thinking. No telling who was listening.

"Let's go to my office," she said and left the room. I fell in behind her, and Nigel followed us into the hall. Keeva had left some underling holding the elevator for her, and we stepped in.

Keeva punched a floor number on the panel, anger on her face. "We had simultaneous attacks on Guild directors. Gerin and Ryan are at Avalon Memorial."

The elevator doors opened. We cut across to the opposite side of the building, not speaking with any other people, and rode another elevator up to Community Liaison. Once in her office, Keeva strode around her desk and sat down, gesturing for us to sit.

"Gerin was meeting with Ryan when they were attacked by one of the human xenogangs. A flamethrower." She grimaced. "They had a flamethrower. Gerin has minor burns."

"How's Ryan?" I had to ask. I wanted to know for my own reasons, but Keeva didn't need to know that. Yet.

"He's in surgery." She paused for a moment. I had to hand it to her. She was demonstrating enormous control.

I looked at Nigel. "Where were you when this was happening?"

He arched an eyebrow. "I was with Manus ap Eagan."

With a heavy sigh, Keeva dropped her head back and looked at the ceiling. "There was an attempt to break through the gate at the Guildmaster's home. The last report we had on the dwarf director was that he had not left the Consortium consulate in days."

"Convenient for him," Nigel said.

"That's what I was thinking," Keeva said.

"Why would you think the Consortium is involved?" I asked.

Keeva and Nigel exchanged glances, but it was Nigel who spoke. "The dominant gang causing trouble in the city consists of elves, and it's run by a troll. Can't you put it together, Connor?"

"Are you saying the Consortium is behind this?" I asked.

Nigel nodded. "I've been monitoring their movements since the Fey Summit last spring. The Consortium is planning something. I think this is a trial run to test the will of Seelie Court."

I looked from one to the other. "Alvud Kruge is dead," I said.

"Your point?" Nigel asked.

"*Marchgraf* Alvud Kruge, Nigel. Do you really think the Consortium would kill one of its own people, married to a royal family member?"

"Kruge was hardly an ally of the Elven King. I don't put anything past the Consortium," he said.

I couldn't believe they were so obsessive about politics that they were missing the obvious. "He was killed by a drug dealer, guys. The gang that attacked me were TruKnights. They've been trying to take over the Weird."

"There's not a gang in the Weird delusional enough to take on the Guild," said Nigel.

"Apparently, this one is," I said.

Keeva looked at Nigel. "Let's assume you're right, Nigel. Given Connor's attackers and a few of the others, would the Consortium recruit out of the Weird?"

He nodded. "It would make excellent cover for them."

Keeva turned her screen back. "I agree. I'm putting security sweeps down there until after Kruge's funeral at least."

"You can't hold a neighborhood responsible for the actions of a rogue gang, Keeva," I said.

She didn't look up. "It's just a visible presence until we know more."

"Keeva, I know what you're really suggesting. You can't put an entire neighborhood under martial law without more reason."

"Caution is enough right now, Connor." She began typing.

I looked at Nigel in disbelief. "You can't condone this."

Nigel stood and went to the door. "I do. These are troubled times that call for strong measures. Despite agreeing to a cease-fire, the Consortium has not changed. They still seek the destruction of the Seelie Court. Do you need anything from me right now, Keeva? I have security plans to work out with Gerin. I think you should see them."

She shook her head without looking up. "Thanks. I'll send you and Manus updates."

Nigel hesitated. "Connor, Gerin will be calling a meeting of the Bosnemeton tonight. Remember the path you once sought." He bowed his head and left.

She ignored me as she read whatever she had typed, probably an email by her body language. She clicked the mouse, no doubt sending a squad of security agents to the Weird to hassle anyone who spelled funny.

"Something doesn't fit, Keeva."

She leaned forward on her desk and put her head in her hands. "I know. But I can't make sense of it."

I felt a twinge of sympathy. Keeva might be many things I don't like, but most times her heart is in the right place. When she remembers she has one. "How are you holding up?"

Stricken, she looked up. "I've got two royal delegations I'm trying to keep separated, a funeral with a change in venue, a murder investigation going nowhere, and the entire board of directors attacked. How do you think I feel?"

"I'll help any way I can."

She nodded vaguely. "I thought you were dead. Your apartment was broken into. Why the hell did it take you two hours to answer your phone or my sendings?"

"I was blocked. I was checking my messages when I was attacked."

"Nigel's right, you know. There are factions in the Consortium that would like nothing more than to see the Guild in chaos."

I shifted in my seat. My coat might have taken the most of the essence that hit me, but my shoulders were definitely tender. "That's a huge risk. They'd have to be pretty confident to pull it off. And now that he's out of the room, I have to point out your blind spot. You're assuming Manus and Nigel had nothing to do with this."

The look of surprise that came over her face made me feel embarrassed. "Wow. I knew you had trust issues, but that's pretty extreme even for you."

I shrugged. "I'm being an investigator. Manus is definitely sick—I saw that myself. But you heard Nigel. He has just as much motive to make the Consortium look bad as they do the Guild."

"Do you really think Nigel would resort to murder?"

"I'm not saying that. But I don't think he's above using this situation to push the Consortium into a corner."

She seemed to consider the idea. "Kruge is the key to this. We figure out who killed Kruge, then we figure the rest."

"It was a drug dealer named C-Note. Eorla Kruge thinks that even if you and Nigel don't."

"And why would you know her opinion?" Anger had returned to her face.

I rolled my eyes in answer. "Because I listened to her, Keeva, which apparently you haven't. She told you a drug dealer might be a suspect."

"Wouldn't that fit your cover plot? She would support your theory if she were trying to throw us off the Consortium."

"Keeva, her husband's dead. That's a level of political ambition even you can't imagine."

She laughed, a bit weakly for my taste, but she laughed. "That's why we're looking for Croda. She may have been the killer herself somehow, but we're also running down her drug associates."

I didn't say anything. Not without knowing why Ryan macGoren had been at Croda's murder. "You don't need to put an entire neighborhood under martial law. You need to go after C-Note. His gang attacked me. It's him, pure and simple."

She gave me a suspicious look. "You seem awfully confident. What evidence do you have?"

"Word is C-Note's muscling in. Dennis Farnsworth died on another troll's turf. His name is Moke. He says it was C-Note's people."

Keeva smiled. "Putting aside that Moke may be playing you, has it occurred to you that your attack was coincidence? You're not really a director, you know. Maybe this C-Note's gunning for you because of Farnsworth."

I pursed my lips. I hadn't considered that. Crystal placed Farnsworth and Kruge in the same room. And there was still the matter of Croda's recording ward. I didn't think that was a coincidence.

"It's not the Consortium, Keeva. I feel it in my gut."

Keeva stood and moved for the door. "I've got a major security situation to handle, Connor. Don't leave the building. I have enough people to worry about."

"Are you arresting me?"

She shrugged. "Call it what you want. Now go find someplace to sit. I have work to do."

I decided now was the time to push her. "I have a question before you go. Why did Ryan lie about being with you the night of Kruge's murder?"

Her glare snapped back instantly. "He didn't lie. He had his dates mixed up."

"So, where was he?"

"Here. At the Guildhouse. He was here the entire time."

"Do you trust him?"

She gave me a long look, and opened the door. "Yes. I'm not a fool, though, Connor. And as much as I hate to admit it, I checked the security log. He was here. I was checking a blind spot." She strode away.

I trailed after her and walked down the hall to my old office. I sat behind the desk, spun the chair around, and put my feet up on the windowsill. Outside, Guild security agents did aerial sweeps of the surrounding city blocks.

Given the right motivation, I could believe anyone was capable of anything—even murder. But as the list of players expanded, the list of motivations seemed to expand even more. Clearly a power struggle was in play, both down in the Tangle and in the Guildhouse boardroom. The only connection between them was Ryan macGoren, and his involvement made no sense. I wanted to tell Keeva about the helmet, but she played games, too. And so did Nigel. And Gerin. Any one of them could be in a position to protect macGoren or hang him. I couldn't decide who to trust, if any of them.

My issues with the Guild were turning into fears. If they could turn my home into a prison camp, I had no recourse than to keep my mouth shut until I could prove publicly what had happened. As I stared out the window, I felt more alone than I had in a long time. It's bad enough to watch your back with enemies. It's worse when you have to do it with allies.

13

I lifted the receiver from the office phone on my desk. It had a dial tone, so I punched in Meryl's internal extension. She picked up right away.

"Hello?" Her voice had an odd, guarded tone.

"Hi, it's me," I said. I swung back to the window to watch yet another squad of agents fly in the direction of the Consortium consulate. I'm sure Keeva was on the phone explaining to Consortium security that they weren't spies. I'm sure she wouldn't be believed.

"Grey?"

"Yeah. Why do you sound funny?"

"Because I'm looking at the caller ID on my phone and wondering if I've been sucked into the past somehow."

I chuckled. "You watch too many science fiction movies. I'm hiding in my old office. Care for a visitor?"

"Sure. You're not dead, right?"

Glancing to my left, I smiled. Virgil had moved his gargoyle self from his lower perch to the nook right outside my window.

"No. Minor scorching. I'll be down in a sec," I said and hung up.

A familiar cool flutter touched my mind. I had felt it before, like a sending, only more subtle and less identifiable. It was how gargoyles communicated.

A circle contains and excludes but defines itself, Virgil said.

That sounded like an abstract philosophical game. Gargoyles never make any sense when they speak. At least, I don't think so. They only make sense afterward, and then you kick yourself for not understanding. I've tried to figure out Virgil, but I only end up second-guessing myself. I think he's sincere in trying to help. Why, I don't know. I've known very few people that gargoyles have spoken to. As far as their conversations go, Virgil was downright chatty with me, but most of the time I had no idea what he was talking about.

You don't send your thoughts to a gargoyle like you do to other fey. You think loudly, and they appear to overhear. I've never had a conversation with Virgil unless we were near each other. It made me doubt gargoyles could actually do sendings, but no one knows much about what they can do. I relaxed my mind and thought, *Sometimes I feel my entire life is running in circles.*

Jested truth makes dangerous folly. The stroke of a sword injures the heart of the wielder and his foe.

I didn't like the sound of that. My dagger was a sword, after a fashion, but I didn't know how to make it turn into a sword. The one time I did it, it felt more like the sword was using me than the other way around. *No jokes, then, Virgil.*

When he didn't say anything, I thought he was finished speaking. It's really hard to know when the conversation is over when you're dealing with a talking stone that doesn't move.

Bones, he said.

I stared at him, pointlessly trying to read something, anything, into his words. Sometimes runes are carved on bones, which are thrown to read the future. Elves favored it, but I didn't know anyone who actually knew how to do it.

I don't understand. As usual, I thought, hoping it wasn't loud enough for Virgil to hear.

Bones, he said. The coolness floated away. Virgil was done speaking. I stared at his little naked body, wondering if he ever felt self-conscious with his goods hanging out for all to see. He moved somehow, though I had never seen it happen, and yet he never moved his hands from his knees to hide his groin. Maybe he felt no shame. Maybe he didn't understand it. I grinned as a thought occurred to me. Maybe it was because he had nothing to hide.

If possible, the Community Liaison offices were even emptier than the last time I was there. Everyone must have been running around outside dealing with the hysteria. I would have mobilized everyone if I were in charge. I would lock down the Guildhouse, sure, but I wouldn't try to take on the Consortium and an entire neighborhood simultaneously.

I took the elevator straight down to the subbasement. Meryl smiled for a fraction of a second when I walked into her office, then wrinkled her nose. "You smell like burnt cow."

"It's new." I turned to show her the scorch marks on my jacket.

She whistled appreciatively. "Nice miss."

"Yeah. It was fun."

She leaned back in her chair. "So, is it a fascist wet dream out there?"

I nodded. "Nigel thinks the Consortium is behind the attacks."

Meryl snickered. "Nigel thinks the Consortium is behind everything. I swear the man is itching for a war no one wants."

"He was never this single-minded before."

She gestured at me. "He's pissed at them. They took out his main man."

That took me by surprise. "Me? Are you talking about me? He's pissed because of my injury?"

She nodded. "Before you lost your abilities, the scuttle-butt was that you were being groomed in case hostilities broke out. You were one of the few here-born with major potential."

You could have knocked me flat with an eyeblink. Nigel wasn't one for compliments, but now that I looked back, I could see what Meryl meant. He was always pushing me to work harder, trying to get me to join the Druidic College, teaching me ways to use my abilities even when he wasn't happy that I had gone the Guild route. It made a sort of sense. "I never realized. No one ever said anything."

She grinned. "Ha! With your ego? Are you kidding me? No one in their right mind was going to give you more reason to strut around like a peacock."

I didn't say anything. Meryl wasn't the first person to comment on my arrogance, only the most vocal. I don't think I impressed her enough for her to be diplomatic.

"I've changed."

Her grin broadened. "No shit. Almost dying a couple of times has done good things for you."

She had a point. When your life hits bottom, you can't help reevaluating things. Losing my livelihood and being abandoned by people I thought were my friends made me understand what it's like to be on the other side of privilege.

"Look, I need to get out of here. There's a meeting of the Bosnemeton tonight, and I have to do something before that."

Her eyebrows went up and hid behind her bangs. "Do something?"

I nodded. "Yeah. Keeva's got the building locked down tight, and I don't want to be followed."

"And you're not going to tell me what it is?"

"Nope." We had a playful staring contest involving lots of smirking and grinning. At last, Meryl sighed.

"Okay. I'll show you a way. But I want details later."

"Deal," I said.

I stood as she got up from her desk. She started around it,

then walked right through the wall of her office. Impressed, I stared at the illusion. The space between an overflowing credenza and an old filing cabinet looked like a perfectly normal wall. It took a lot of ability to maintain, even more when you had to contend with the amount of essence and warding in the Guildhouse. And I hadn't sensed it there at all. Meryl was damned good at what she knew how to do.

"Coming?" Her voice sounded muffled coming through the illusion, as though she were calling out from a good distance.

I walked through the wall after her, feeling the spiderweb tingle of essence skim over my body as I went through it. Meryl waited on the other side with a small flashlight. We were in a narrow tunnel that looked much like the other subbasement hallways, only without the doors. Behind me, I could see Meryl's office as clear as day.

"You're full of surprises," I said.

"Did you really think I'd have an office with only one door?" she asked. She turned and led the way along the tunnel. The light dimmed the farther we went from her office, and she turned on her flashlight. "I found this tunnel by accident one day. Took me a while to create the opening in the office, but it was worth it."

I could feel warding along the walls. If I had to guess, I'd have said we were moving between Guildhouse storerooms, which were filled with all kinds of things that had essence to spare. As a chief archivist, Meryl kept it all in check, making sure nothing disappeared or reacted with something else or exploded. By the odd fluctuations in warding, I could tell there had to be more openings, but Meryl didn't seem inclined to give a tour.

We reached the bottom of a flight of stairs. Meryl paused and held up her hand. After a few murmurs, a small ball of blue light no bigger than a glow bee danced up from her palm. Still murmuring, she tapped my forehead with her free hand, cupped both her hands together, then tossed the light ball. It swirled up into the darkness.

"There. I've opened the warding for you at the top. No one will see you leave."

"You're a marvel," I said.

"I know. Just go straight up. Don't let me catch you using this without me."

"Thanks." I kissed the top of her head and started up the stairs before she had a chance to hit me. I've given her the top-of-the-head peck before, and she hates it. Or seems to.

As I went higher I heard a low hum that slowly grew louder. The stone steps vibrated beneath my feet.

"Don't get hit!" Meryl called up from the darkness.

I reached the top. Seeing nothing but blackness, I stepped forward into another warding. And almost got hit. A subway train hurtled past. I jumped back so fast, I almost fell back down the stairs. After surviving an attack by elves, it would be just my luck to get hit by a train. I could hear giggling down below. Shaking my head, I went through again and found myself on the tracks next to the Boylston Street T station platform. The train that that almost hit me was loading passengers. I ran a few feet along the track, slipped between a gap in some fencing, and jumped onto the nearest car before the doors closed.

I didn't bother sitting since I needed to change lines at the next station. Down the aisle from me, a well-dressed older woman dozed in her seat, her purse clutched in her lap. She wore a large felt hat with a long pheasant feather. I could just make out the tops of two familiar pink wings coming up the other side of her. Joe peered at me from over her hat and put his finger to his lips. Hovering above her, he bent the feather down and tickled her nose with it. She shifted in her seat without opening her eyes. He did it again, and she waved her hand up. As the train screeched on the curve into Park Street station, he knocked the hat off and vanished. The woman startled awake, looked down at her hat, and glared at me. I tried to maintain an air of innocence, but she looked convinced I had something to do with it.

The train pulled into the station. I hurried down a flight of stairs to the Red Line. I used to take cabs everywhere. I used to have a car service at work when I wanted it. Now I take the subway and hope I don't miss trains. It bothered me at first. But then I learned public transportation is what real people do. Only the fey thought they were too good for it. But sometimes I still missed the car service.

My next train came in, and this time I sat as close to the corner as possible. Right on cue, Joe appeared unobtrusively on the next seat, hiding between me and the wall of the car.

"That was naughty," I said.

He shrugged and smiled. "It was an ugly hat."

"I guess you do have a point."

He stretched out on the seat. "I heard you were attacked. Elves really don't like you, do they?"

"A lot of people don't."

He chuckled. "I have a message from Callin."

"I was hoping that's why you were here." Even though it had been only yesterday since I had called Callin about C-Note, the connections between C-Note and Kruge had become more firm. I really wanted to meet the troll.

He jabbed me with his toe. "Hey, I don't have to run messages, ya know. I'm not a glow bee."

"Sorry. I've had a long day already. What does Cal have to say?"

"He said C-Note works out of a club in the Tangle called Carnage. Cal said they're moving a large amount of some drug called Float tonight, so C-Note will probably be there."

I frowned. "And why does Cal know something like that?"

Stinkwort rolled his eyes. "You guys aren't happy unless you're suspicious of each other, are you? Did you ever stop to think maybe he doesn't like your friends either?"

"Does he like you?"

Stinkwort gave me his ear-to-ear smile. "Everybody likes Joe!"

I laughed as the train pulled into South Station. Joe winked out before anyone saw him. I rode the escalator, an old

wooden one with slats angled down that gave just enough trac-
tion to keep you from falling onto the person behind you, up
to the street.

Light was already fading as I walked along Summer
Street. Joe reappeared when I made the bridge, far enough
away from downtown so that people wouldn't gawk at a flit,
close enough to the Weird where he might be ignored. I
could see a Guild security squad flying an open surveillance
pattern above the Northern Avenue bridge.

"Feel like going for a walk?" I asked.

"Sure. Well, I'll watch you walk," he said as he fluttered
along beside me at shoulder level.

"How do you always manage to find me, Joe? People had
no idea where I was this afternoon, but you manage to show
up in a subway car."

He gave me a confused look. "I look for you."

"No, I mean *how* do you look for me? How do you know
where I am so you can show up?"

Joe pursed his lips. "I look for the nothing with the spot.
You're the only thing like that."

"Thing?" I asked pointedly.

He laughed and twirled around again. "Everything is a
thing. I look for the thing I want to know, and I find it and
then I go. You used to have a flavor, but now you have nothing with a spot in it."

"This is making my head hurt," I said. If I ever needed to
understand why people get so frustrated studying flits, this
would be Exhibit One. Flits have an inability to clarify anything they think is self-explanatory.

"Right! That's the spot!" he said.

The spot. Oddly enough, I think I understood what he
was trying to say. It's exactly how the doctors at Avalon
Memorial have described the thing in my brain from the
reactor accident: a dark smudgy spot that shows up on di-
agnostics but seems to have no mass. They have no idea
what it is. Its physical shape tends to change over time. But
it never goes away. The doctors, however inept I might

consider them, have always had the courtesy not to refer to the rest of me as nothing. But that's Joe. He doesn't mean anything by it. It's just his way of stating what, to him, is obvious.

I stayed on Summer Street, avoiding the Avenue since that's where Keeva's goons seemed to be focusing their attention. Occasionally, they would hover into view above us but drop back pretty quickly. We were basically walking a vague boundary line between neighborhoods, where people from the Weird and Southie stumble into each other, turn around, and go back to where they feel more comfortable. I made a point of keeping a steady pace and keeping to the open to avoid arousing suspicion.

Unfortunately, to get to where I wanted to be, I had to pass near the Kruge crime scene. There, the security agents had been keeping a constant post, watching everyone who walked by. And walk by we did. I felt a little ping as one of the guards tested my essence, but, given my physical condition, he must not have been impressed because no one followed us.

Turning off Summer Street, I strolled another few blocks, taking a roundabout path to bring me to the Tangle. It was getting near sunset and, as much as Joe made a damn fine bodyguard for his size, I didn't want any TruKnights to see me after my earlier encounter.

Joe's eyes gleamed with excitement. "Are we going to see this C-Note guy?"

"Not yet. Later, if you're interested. Right now, I need to preserve some evidence." We wound through alleys on the perimeter of the Tangle, damaged, sooty places glowing with essence in shades of blue-white and yellow and red. Joe seemed to think he was on a roller coaster as he rode their strange currents with a look of glee. My head had a constant buzz, annoying, but no more painful than my usual headache.

We finally came to the building where Crystal had hidden with Croda. Stinkwort became quiet, his face grim. Flits are sensitive to essence in ways no other fey are. They feel it more, and the nastiness that I felt in the old building probably only hinted at what he was feeling. We came out into the courtyard. Joe gasped when he saw Croda.

She was as we had left her, perhaps a little more menacing looking in the shadows of twilight. My senses picked up no new scents in the area, which gave me some assurance that the site hadn't been compromised.

Joe hovered up near her face. "How sad. I remember her."

"You knew her?"

He nodded with a melancholy air. "Yeah. She used to have a cave near Caerdydd in the old country. Loved baby rabbits. Used to eat them like popcorn."

One thing about being socialized in the Convergent world was hearing something like that and being startled and not startled. Stinkwort was from a time and place where horror was mundane. I knew these things intellectually, but the reality is still disconcerting.

I reached down and tugged at Croda's hand with the ward in it. It didn't budge. I tried pulling from various angles, but she had truly become stone. I think if I'd had a sledgehammer, I'd still have had a hard time. I stood back and looked at her, trying to figure another way.

"What, pray tell, are you trying to do?" Stinkwort asked.

"I need the ward in her hand. I need to know what's on it."

"Why don't you just play it?"

"My baseline essence isn't strong enough. I wanted to avoid calling up more if I could."

"Is that all? I'll do it." He landed on her hand and sat down. A subtle pink glow surrounded him as he let his essence flow. It spread down and wrapped the ward.

"*. . . you've gone too far, and I . . .*" crackled through the air. Shots of Stinkwort's essence glimmered all through Croda, grabbing at bits of the recording that seemed to have flowed out of the ward and into her body. Voices echoed from different angles of her body, sometimes faint, sometimes clear, too often indecipherable.

"... *C-Note. Float is more than you* ..." By the accent, I'd peg that as Kruge.

"... *telling you to stay out of it, Kruge, I'm warning* ... *if you'd only stopped following* ..." Rough, guttural, had to be C-note.

Kruge, again. "... *and you. That glamour doesn't fool me. I've seen enough to* ... *to see right through it* ... *worse than I* ... *I'm stunned you would* ..."

Then a vaguely female voice that must have been Croda. "... *it's him, sir, know it by the feel* ..."

Kruge: "... *macGoren. Manus will hear* ... *messenger. Leave him* ..."

C-Note: "... *too much. You leave me no choice* ..."

The sound of something falling, maybe a chair, then Kruge: "... *run, Dennis. Get out of here* ... *No!* ..."

A crackle of essence-fire, followed by a jumble of voices.

C-Note: "... *no witness. You've forced me* ..."

Kruge: "... *stop! stop!* ..." A substantial amount of hissing played out, the unmistakable sound of essence-fire, then an anguished shriek that had to have been Kruge. Another scream that I took to be Croda. Struggling sounds came next, and the discharge of more essence-fire.

Then Croda again, her breath ragged as she ran: "... *children, got you* ..."

A girl screaming. It had to be Crystal, her voice coming through hysterically. "... *Denny! Denny! Say something* ..."

"... *hush, hush. They'll hear* ... *Denny* ... *his spark is gone, child* ..."

More sobbing and the pounding of Croda's loud footsteps and heaving breath.

"... *in here. Hide and quiet 'til night. Hush, now, hush* ... *No! No! He's coming!* ... *he's found* ..."

The metallic screech of the roof coming off the storage shed. Screams from Crystal and Croda, the latter quickly drowning out the former as the troll died. A constant sobbing, very loud, as Crystal crouched right up to the ward stone behind Croda.

We could hear the essence fight Crystal described, the sound of static and bursting of stone, garbled voices, then one phrase at a distance in a new voice: *"I will have it."* Ryan macGoren. I recognized him clearly. Then the sound of wind and Crystal's sobs fading out.

Joe released his essence, and the glow faded back into him. He had a pale cast to his skin that could not have been from what was for him a minor expenditure of essence. "That was awful."

I nodded. The anguish in Croda's death cry had sent chills up my spine, and Crystal's sobs were gut-wrenching. I looked up at the troll's face, now twisted forever in pain. "We have to hide her, Joe. I'm betting C-Note didn't realize she had a recording ward or that Crystal was hiding with her. If he did, he wouldn't have left her here. I don't want anyone else stumbling in here."

I dragged pieces of the storage shed roof through the debris and leaned it against Croda. It felt rude to do, but at least it caused significantly less damage than what I had intended by breaking off her hand. I had no idea how trolls felt about their dead, but now I wouldn't have to find out if breaking her would have been some kind of sacred violation. Somewhere, Joe found an old tarp sizable enough to cover most of her. Between that and the roof sheeting, at a glance no one would notice she was there.

"Let's get out of here," I said. In silence, we made our way back. Night had fallen, and I felt it was worth the risk to go directly down the Avenue. I just wanted to be away from the courtyard as quickly as possible. Walking through the Weird, I could see angry faces glaring up at the hovering Guild agents. I could not believe how many Keeva had sent.

When we reached my building, an agent stood guard at the door. He stepped out from the building as soon as we turned the corner, but relaxed his posture as we drew near.

"Good evening, Director Grey. We've had no activity since this morning," he said.

"Thanks," I said, trying not to sound annoyed. He was

just following orders. Keeva and Nigel were to blame, not him. I went up the stairs, and another guard waited outside what was left of my door.

"Good evening, Director Grey. Your apartment is secure," he said.

"Yeah, I heard," I said. Joe flew in ahead of me and went directly to the kitchen cabinet where I kept cookies. I surveyed the shambles of my living room. Truth to tell, it was only slightly worse than usual. My apartment door lay to the side of the entrance, the hinges sprung and a big dent across the middle. I picked it up and turned to the agent.

"Nothing personal, but if you have to be here, I'd prefer you stood down the hall."

The agent looked down the hall, gave a curt nod, and walked away. I propped the door in the opening. Even before I went into my study, I knew what I was going to see. My computer was in considerably more parts than one would think possible. At least they hadn't destroyed my books. I slid my hand down the side of the filing cabinet and retrieved my laptop. I had backup files hidden in the kitchen. I'd had more than my share of destroyed computers, so I'd learned to plan for them. I'd have to reload my video games, but at least the data would be intact.

Joe sat on the edge of the counter eating Oreos. Before he even asked, I poured him a glass of milk. He refuses to touch my refrigerator, so I humor him.

"I'm hitting the shower," I said. Cheeks bulging, he nodded and waved.

Hot water soothed aching muscles. Between wrenching my shoulder and rolling around in the Public Garden, my body was not happy. I had just gotten over some major injuries in the past few months, and some of them throbbed with remembered pain. In the midst of my shampoo, I caught Gerin's sending about the Bosnemeton meeting. He certainly waited until the last minute. I'd barely have enough time to dress and get to Thomas Park in Southie before it started. I didn't particularly care for the sound of an old man's voice in my head when I was wet and naked either.

"I've got to go to the Bosnemeton," I said to Joe as I pulled on a black sweater and jeans. I had to rummage to find my druid meeting robe. It's bleached muslin, not my favorite color. I always feel silly wearing it, but as High Druid, Gerin insisted on traditional garb.

"I'll come, too," said Stinkwort.

"You know Gerin will have the place warded against everyone but druids."

He pouted. Flits can pretty much get in anywhere they want. The only exceptions I know are druid Grove meetings, the odd Unseelie Court warding they run into, and the first day of new security at the Guild. They break the latter pretty quickly. Some people thought that was a problem, but I didn't. As a species, flits were exceedingly loyal to the Seelie Court at Tara, and not one had ever been accused of being a spy. "Fine. I'll wait outside."

I moved the door and, once in the hall, replaced it. Pointless, but it made me feel better. Down on the Avenue, I hailed a cab. It was the only way to get to Southie in time, and though I wasn't rolling in cash, I had a little extra to spend this month. Joe entertained himself by squeezing in and out of the cash slot in the Plexiglas barrier between the front and backseat. The cab driver tried hard not to be fascinated.

I pulled out my cell and called Meryl.

"You're in a cab," she said.

"Do I want to ask?"

"They started tracking you a little over an hour ago on Old Northern. The security monitor says you just left your apartment, freshly bathed and got in a cab."

"It says I *bathed*?"

She giggled. "Naw. I threw that in as a guess. What's up?"

"I'm on my way to the Bosnemeton."

"You're late. Gerin's doing the 'we are separate, but one'

crap." I rolled my eyes. If I hated Guild politics, druid politics could be even worse. The roles of men and women were still being adjusted, and Gerin was an old conservative.

"How'd you like to go dancing later?"

"Sure. Who's asking?"

"Funny. Ever hear of Carnage?" It was a rhetorical question, I knew. I had given up trying to stump her with questions about anything and had almost reached the point of just assuming she knew everything about everything. It's a thought pattern, I am sure, she would like to encourage.

"*You* want to go to Carnage?"

"You know it? I have a little business to take care of there with Murdock, but it shouldn't take me that long. I thought you might enjoy going."

"Uh, yeah, I know it. I'll go."

"Good. It's a date."

"It's not a date. It's a field trip for me to be amused at the sight of you in a dance club."

"Ha-ha. I'll meet you after the meeting." We disconnected.

I called Murdock. "I've got a line on C-Note tonight. Do you want in?"

"Depends. Are we investigating the Kruge murder, which is not our case, or the Farnsworth murder, which is?" he said.

"Yes."

He chuckled. "True. I was just checking to make sure you were still on the case. I do have to justify your consultant fee, you know."

"Stickler. Swing by Thomas Park in an hour or so and pick me up."

"Will do." He disconnected.

I dropped my head against the seat, wondering if I had a security agent following in the air. Nigel had made no secret of the Bosnemeton meeting in front of Keeva, so I didn't quite see the point. Every member of the Grove in the city who could be there would be there. Gerin liked nothing more than to strut his stuff in a crisis, so this meeting would be the usual boring posturing. I would have skipped it if

Nigel hadn't taunted me. It felt a lot like reverse psychology, but I wasn't going to give him a point to score later by not showing up.

I had trusted Nigel with my life, and now I felt that trust misplaced. Was I really just a soldier to him? A pawn in his political games? Wasn't I more than that to him? I thought he cared. To think otherwise would be a blow. Not to my ego. My ego was still tougher than it should be. It hurt, though. And confirmed for me all the more to work the cases Murdock called me for. I had a pretty good idea now what it was like to be dismissed because of powerlessness. If I could ease that pain for someone else, like some poor kid who died in the Weird, maybe it would ease my own a bit. I thought a lot of people cared about me until my accident. Some did, including the little guy in front of me who was trying to fit the door lock in his mouth.

"Stop that. It's got germs all over it," I said to Stinkwort.

He made a sour face. "And you have no idea how it tastes."

14

The cab let me off near a side entrance to Thomas Park in Southie. I stood on the sidewalk pulling the robe over my head. I wasn't alone. Only the more conservative druids like to walk around in their robes, so almost every meeting of the Grove seems to begin with a dressing room on the sidewalk. I walked up the steps into the park with Joe by my side.

The Bosnemeton grows on one end of the park on a hill overlooking Boston and the harbor. During the American Revolution, the Continental Army fortified the hill and scared the British all the way to Canada. While a nice New Englandy tower went up to commemorate the event, no one realized at the time that druids had planted oak trees at the other end of the new park. Before anyone knew it, a sacred grove was born, and the first fey/human court battle began. Eventually the whole church and state tussle went away and an uneasy truce was called. So now the druids can hold meetings of the Grove as long as they don't annoy the neighbors, and the neighbors don't go into the Grove.

You never approach a druid Grove directly, but trail along a winding path. Once you start on the path, you must enter the Grove before turning back to the world. I started on the way, nodding to the warders who always took a post outside to keep tourists away.

My sensing abilities kicked in on their own as I neared the entrance. That happens sometimes. All the ambient druid essence in the air, not to mention the Grove itself, can enhance abilities. On the final approach, I could see a thin layer of an *airbe druad*. It's an essence barrier—literally a "druid hedge"—much like a body shield, only created by spells. Druids are particularly adept at making them. The skill used to come in handy during battles to protect fighters. The one on the Grove was mostly for privacy, and held a warding that prevented non-druids from entering. As I passed through it, Joe hovered outside, his eyes roving over the haze for a break in the spell. He never finds one, but he always tries.

Majestic white oaks encircle a single tree in the center of the Grove, a few curled leaves clinging to their stark limbs. The meeting had already begun. Gerin Cuthbern stood beneath the central tree wearing his long white robe and the double torc around his neck that symbolized his rank as High Druid. Senior druids who act as Elders of the Grove stood next to him including Nigel and Gillen Yor. Gillen makes me smile. He's a short, cantankerous sort, who looks like he dresses in whatever oddments might have been handy when he rolled out of bed. At meetings, his robe always looks like he gave up putting it on halfway through.

If I ever needed a reminder of how far I had fallen, the Bosnemeton provides a nice geographical representation. Ranked in a semicircle in front of the Elders were the members of the Grove, the more experienced druids in front, fanning out and back to those with the least control of their abilities in the rear. I took my place near the rear, with mostly teenagers behind me. Not far in front of me, Callin stood, eyes bloodshot and a bruise on his cheek. When he noticed me, he nodded, then turned his attention back to the front.

Gerin is a stickler for form. Which means I spend a lot of time going over my grocery list in my head while he warbles his way through the invocations. Nigel always looks patient, Gillen considerably less so. I've learned to catch naps on my feet, which has the added benefit of looking like I'm meditating. After an interminable time, Gerin called out *"Awen, the spirit is here!"*

On the stone table in front of Gerin lay his copper blade of office. On the other side of the tree, druidesses stood, their cup sitting on its own table in front of them. The women's white robes accentuated a pallor on all their faces. They didn't look happy, but they rarely did when only the High Druid led a meeting. Gerin liked to put up a thin barrier between the two sides of the Grove. He says it symbolizes the halves we each bring to the whole. The women think he's a chauvinist pig.

"My brothers and sisters, tonight we speak of the rule of law," Gerin intoned.

Someone snorted loudly behind me. I glanced over my shoulder. Most everyone had their hoods thrown back. The only people who pulled their hoods forward were either embarrassed by their position in the Grove or wished to remain solitary for the meeting. Or cold. After the warm season, Gerin usually charged the Grove's warding with heat, but tonight he hadn't bothered. Between the robe and my jacket, I was warm anyway. I finally decided the snorter was a short guy near the entrance with his hood pulled all the way down. Like all situations that lend themselves to pecking order, those in the back got away with commenting and laughing at the proceedings without fear of Gerin's anger.

"Will you get on with this," Gillen muttered loudly enough to hear.

"My brother, I am the voice of the Grove. Do you challenge it?" said Gerin

Gillen made a disgusted face. "Let's keep it moving. I've got work to do."

Gerin didn't react to him, but faced the crowd, or rather

the men. He kept his back to the women. "My brothers and sisters, we are under siege. I have been attacked in my own city." He waited while those few who hadn't heard what happened could be properly aghast, as though someone's attacking a druid never happened. It was rare for the High Druid to be attacked, but hardly shocking. "It pains me, brothers and sisters, that the respect for this Grove has fallen so low."

He began to ramble in his arch manner. Sometimes I think he's read too many ritual guides. I know he's written too many. While I let my mind drift, a swift pain in my head brought back my attention. It was just a spasm, but it felt like my brain had cramped.

Gerin held his staff across his body as he talked. Most druids no longer used them. They're big and bulky and have an aggravating tendency to get forgotten under restaurant tables. But then that's Gerin.

"And so I propose an opposition to the Guild for their failure to protect."

"What an odd thing to say, Gerin," Nigel said in a dry tone.

"I am High Druid of the Bosnemeton Circle, Brother Martin, in case you have forgotten how to address me."

Nigel placed his hand over his heart and gave a shallow bow from the waist. "My pardon, High Druid. But the fact remains, you are more representative of the Guild than anyone here."

"Save you, Brother Martin."

"Save me," Nigel said.

"And you have failed this Grove, Brother Martin. When the opportunity arose to bring strength to the ruling council of the Guildhouse, you passed it by. I would not stand here with burns if you had stood by me when we had the chance." From my angle, I couldn't see any burns. I wasn't going to be the one to ask him to lift his robe.

"Oh, please, Gerin—High Druid—it's not a ruling council. It's a board of directors. I'm not interested in Guild politics," Gillen snapped.

Surprisingly, an annoyed murmur ran through the crowd. Granted, Gillen did not have many admirers, but everyone usually respected him. Not that he cared either way.

"That's the point, Brother Yor. The Guild fails to rule where it must and fears to rule where it should. The Grove had an opportunity to change that, and we failed. You, Brother Martin, failed us, with the aid of Brother Grey."

There are times when I love being the center of attention. This was not one of them. Having several hundred men in ceremonial robes glance in your direction when you're blamed for something is not pleasant.

"Connor Grey merely sat in for Briallen, as you know. And if she were there, she would have pointed out the same flaw in your thinking as he did," said Nigel.

"Irrelevant," said Gerin. "The point is our unity. The Ward Guildhouse crumbles under years of Danann rule. It is the withered body of a dying man."

Murmurs of agreement rumbled through the crowd. Gerin knows how to work a crowd. My head twinged at the shots of essence flowing around me as people conferred through sendings.

Gerin was going into full chant mode, raising his staff, turning on the solemn voice. "It is the duty of a Grove—to guide the guideless, to teach the ignorant, to . . ."

"To rule both Grove and Guild? Is that what you're after, Gerin?" asked Gillen Yor.

"Why not? Why not the Grove?" he said.

"Gerin has led us well!" someone shouted. No doubt a plant. More murmurs went up from the gathering and more surges of essence. Using ability in the Grove was frowned on, but I doubted Gerin was going to complain tonight. The essence pulsed against my head, sharpening my senses painfully. I let my body shields come up, a fuzzy little barrier that brought some relief.

"The Grove should run the Guild!" Gerin shouted. More shouts went up.

"Emotion clouds your judgment, Brother Cuthbern," Nigel

said. Sweet little dig not using his full title, but not crossing the same line Gillen had. More boos than cheers.

"I could have been killed. We must stop them," Gerin said. Nice of him not to mention I almost got killed, too. People were getting caught up in the idea. Essence swirled around me in cascading waves. My senses were kicking into overdrive. I wanted to shout myself, but from the sharp knives of pain digging into my skull. I couldn't understand it. I had been bombarded by essence before, and it had made the black thing in my head recede. I had actually been able to use my abilities for a short time. But this was different. The thing in my head seemed to clamp down harder. Maybe it was because the source was druidic, too similar to my own. Whatever didn't allow me to tap essence, didn't like other druidic essence either. I decided Gerin's blustering wasn't worth the pain.

I pushed my way through the ring of men behind me, who were surging forward. They were all shouting Gerin's name. I wasn't the only one leaving. Just as I reached the entrance, Gillen Yor pushed past a knot of people and stomped through the druid hedge, grumbling under his breath. I stepped through the barrier and breathed a sigh of relief. The pressure abated immediately. Whatever games Gerin was playing, he played them inside the Bosnemeton.

I pulled my robe over my head as I walked down the stairs.

Joe popped in right in front of me. "What the hell is going on in there?"

"Gerin's on one of his power trips again." I rolled the robe up and tucked it under my arm.

Joe glanced back up the stairs. "He needs to relax more. Did you invite him to the club?"

I laughed. "Not likely. Have you seen Murdock?"

Joe cocked his head. He was doing whatever it is he does when he looks for someone before teleporting. "He should be here any minute."

I was about to comment that Murdock's the only person

who shows up late more often than I do, when I noticed a druid come stumbling down the stairs and stagger away. It was the little guy who had snorted loudly. He still had his hood up, but moved as if in pain. He put a hand out to steady himself against the stone wall surrounding the park. I went over to him.

"Are you all right?" I asked. He nodded and waved me away. Then the shoes beneath the robe caught my eye. I'd know those Doc Martens anywhere.

"How did you get on the men's side of the Grove?"

A hand went up to the hood and pulled it open slightly. Meryl glared at me. "Rat me out, and you die."

"Are you all right? You're pale as a ghost."

She nodded again. "Yeah, it's just my girl-nads. That time of the month's coming sooner than usual."

"You can feel those?" I asked.

She narrowed her eyes at me. "Oh, now I remember, you're a *man*. Of course I can feel them, you idiot." She took a few deep breaths. Her body shields shimmered around her, and she straightened up. "Ah, that's better."

"How the hell did you get through the hedge?" I said.

She grinned. "It wasn't easy."

Joe fluttered up. "Tell me! Tell me!"

"Sorry, Joe. Gerin would be annoyed if he knew I got in, never mind how angry he'd be if he caught me telling his secrets, even if I do think he's an idiot."

Murdock chose that moment to pull his car around the park. I opened the passenger door. "Do you want a ride or did you bring your car?" I asked Meryl.

She marched around the door and sat in the seat. She smiled. "I'm not taking my car into the Tangle." She gestured toward the backseat. "You get the compost heap. Hi, Murdock."

He smiled. "Compost? Is it something I drove?"

I opened the back and pushed some trash across the seat. It wasn't that bad. I'd seen it worse. Joe found it interesting enough to rummage around in it.

"Gerin turned the Bosnemeton into a boys' club, and someone's not happy," I told Murdock.

He looked at Meryl. "Don't you ladies have your own island somewhere?"

Meryl smirked. "Yeah, right. It's where we run around in star-spangled swimsuits."

I think the biggest mistake I had made in my social life recently was introducing Meryl and Murdock. They took to each other like sarcasm and snark. At first I was their main target, but they finally moved on to the rest of the world.

We wound our way through Southie while Meryl explained druid gender politics to Murdock. She made several good points. Convergence had not been kind to the old order. Gerin liked to cling to the notion that women didn't want to be involved in politics. Of course, he tends to forget that not a few druidessess have had more influence in Faerie than he apparently ever did.

We entered the Tangle. A blue haze crept along the streets, ghostly translucent in the dim streetlights. Small neon signs flickered here and there, subdued signposts for bars that didn't want to draw attention but didn't want to be overlooked either. No one moves quickly down here, especially at night, unless they're running. The quick step is the fear step and draws the curiously malicious. No loud talking, and especially not laughter. It's a place of hard coolness, the strut of confidence and threat.

Meryl made Murdock park on an empty side street. Pulling up near the club would attract minimal attention, but more than we wanted.

"Ditch the coat," she said to Murdock. He looked down at the camel-hair, one of his favorites. He took it off, folding it neatly on the driver's seat. Underneath it, he had worn black pants and a white button-down shirt. "Egads, Murdock, this is the Tangle, not Newbury Street." She turned to me. "Give him your sweater."

I shrugged out of the turtleneck without debate, happy that I had decided to wear the black T-shirt. Murdock took off his shirt with a bemused smile and pulled the sweater on. He's broader in the chest than I am, so it fit snugly, very sixties British spy movie. Meryl opened her robe and threw it in the car. Murdock and I stared. I'm not sure if our jaws dropped, but they should've. Meryl wore her red Doc Martens with white ankle socks, a red and white midthigh skirt in candy-cane stripes, and a strapless top in red-freakin'-vinyl that molded her curves from cleavage to waist. She flipped her magenta bangs and smiled. "Let's go, boys."

Murdock and I exchanged glances. "My dates never wear vinyl," he said.

"Not a date!" Meryl called back. We caught up with her at the corner and came out into one of Boston's amusing intersections called squares. Eight streets converged into a tight formation, buildings wedging in like slices of cake. No one in their right mind would try and drive through it without praying to whatever gods they held dear. As it was, a half dozen cars clung to the curbs, burnt-out husks of metal that had been there long enough to rust. One of them had a parking boot clamped to its tire, whether in tribute to the traffic department's efficiency or indifference was unknowable.

A cluster of people waited on a sidewalk on the far side of the square, some in outfits that made Meryl's look demure. And the women were even more scantily clad.

"Don't talk," Meryl said as we stepped up to the club. No sign over the door, but down in the Tangle, if you didn't know where you were going, you shouldn't be there. Following Meryl, we skirted around the waiting queue.

On one side of the entrance, a dwarf worked the line, while on the other, a tall, lanky fey surveyed the crowd. He was one of the solitary fairies who didn't have any prominent clan affiliation. Not with his yellow-barked skin and damaged, spiny growths like hair on his head. No high fairy clan would ever claim him as their own. He might even be Unseelie, one of the unwanted who banded together to protect themselves from the pretty fey with the nasty essence bolts. He turned unsettlingly white eyes toward Meryl, and his face cracked open in what passed for a smile. "Long time no see, M. What brings you down to party town?"

Meryl gave him a cool nod. "Hey, Zev. Just playing with some friends. Can you let us in?"

His white eyes glittered over us, lingering a moment on Murdock. "New policy. Fey only."

She smiled coyly and stroked the bent thing in the middle of his face that I hoped was his nose. "I don't see any humes, do you, Zev? You know me."

Zev looked down at Murdock, then at the dwarf. When he was sure the dwarf wasn't looking, he slipped a small stone in Murdock's hand. It was a ward stone, and I felt Zev's essence on it as Murdock put it in his pocket with a nonchalant move yet puzzled face. No one would mistake Murdock for an Unseelie with it, but it interacted with his essence enough to keep suspicion down that he was just a human normal. My senses were still hyped-up from the Bosnemeton, and I could see little flashes of purple light cascading around him.

Without a word, Zev gave us his back, unhooking the velvet rope as he did so. We walked through and entered the club. Inside, the hallway closed in tight with bodies, the walls glistening with some kind of phosphorescent life. The floor vibrated beneath our feet. We came around a corner to a blast of heavy bass, filktronica crushing out any chance of conversation.

The cavernous space of Carnage unfolded before us, four wide floors above ripped open to make more height. Crumbled concrete and jagged rebar hung over the main floor, where hundreds of fey danced in a pandemonium of light and sound. Old metal elevator cages enclosing a live band lined the edge of the second floor, five people with drums and electric lutes and harps. The singer groaned into a microphone, her voice adding a sensual growl to the rhythm of sound.

Meryl's arms shot into the air, and she sashayed into the

mix. I made a mental note to kill her for this later. I don't like dancing. Murdock dove right in, though, taking right to the music. Learn something new about people every day. Of course, all the drugs in the air probably helped. I could smell plenty of weed and a couple of fey concoctions. I did my usual simple shimmy-in-place and looked around.

Carnage was the current place for hot music and the seen scene. I recognized more than a few faces from the arts and leisure pages of the *Boston Globe*. The place was simply one in a long string of gathering places that placed a premium on edgy and illicit. I had been in more than a few despite Meryl's belief. They burst into existence with regularity, only to fade when the mainstream found them or the cops did. A new one would spring up before the lights went up on the last one.

All the menace was in the posturing. The most uncool thing to happen to you in the hottest club in town was to get thrown out of it. So, a strange mélange of people bumped and ground against each other who would never give each other the time of day otherwise. The Carnage crowd had a distinct Teutonic bent, with dwarves and elves from more clans than I had seen in a while. Not a few fairies swooped overhead, their eyes glazed with a feverish high. Squirreled away here and there were more solitaries, strange denizens who lingered in the shadows even here. You didn't see many of them in Boston. They kept to themselves, feared for their lives, and made do with the lot life had given them. Copperskinned men with overly long arms showed sharp teeth as they teased a skeletal woman, naked and pale, or an amphibious fey of indeterminate sex.

No flits, though. I realized Joe wasn't with us, nor were any of his brethren anywhere that I could see. I thought he'd wanted to come. Knowing him, though, he had found something fascinating under Murdock's car seats.

We spent the better part of an hour moving around the floor. What I couldn't see in the darkness, I could sense. Fey essence everywhere, some minor spells working, mostly on glamours to make the hot look hotter. A lot of action seemed to be going on in alcoves around the upper levels but nothing that shocked me. I left Murdock and Meryl on the floor to get some water. With everything else going on in the room giving me a headache, I didn't want to increase the head pain with alcohol.

I didn't want to think about the structural integrity of the building, but hoped the extra warding I was seeing and feeling was enough to hold it all together. Ripping the floors out to create the open space had weakened the structure, but someone who knew how to work stone materials, probably a dwarf or maybe C-Note himself, had used essence to strengthen what remained. Essence could be used to create tough barriers in and of itself. Bonding it to existing brick and mortar made it even stronger.

I leaned against the bar and caught sight of Callin. He stood across from me, a section of gyrating dancers between us. He talked with a motley crew of fey who looked like trouble. I was going to have a conversation with my brother sometime in the near future. It would end in anger, I'm sure, but I at least had to try to understand why he chose to put himself on the wrong side of things so often. He finally caught sight of me but didn't come over, making it clear he didn't want us seen together. After a few minutes, he caught my eye again and with an imperceptible nod indicated a wide set of closed doors visible on the third floor above.

C-Note is up there. Don't do anything stupid, he sent. The man was hanging out with drug dealers and gangs and was telling me not to do anything stupid. I couldn't complain too much at the moment, though. He had let me know that C-Note would be here tonight when I asked him to find out.

I shimmied my way back onto the dance floor to Meryl and her dancing fool partner. They couldn't hear me, but I got them to follow me through the flailing arms and legs and wings to the steel staircases that twisted up to the second and third levels. Once above the band, the sound diminished.

People milled about what was left of a floor that had become a balcony overlooking the dance floor.

"What's up here?" Meryl asked.

I nodded behind me toward the sheet-metal door. "That."

By the way Meryl's nostrils flared, I could tell she was sensing what I was. "Haven't you boys had enough of trolls lately?"

"I wish. Care to join us?"

She held up her hands in refusal. "I'm not a field agent."

I couldn't blame her. I was about to nail the connection between my murder case and Keeva's. Guild politics being what there were, Keeva would find ways to make Meryl miserable if she caught wind of her involvement.

Murdock took up a flanking position on my right as we walked to the door. In the short time we'd been working together, Murdock and I had fallen into comfortable patterns. All my other partnerships had an element of competition in them. Not Murdock and me. We worked well together because we had our own areas of expertise. In fey situations, he had no problem letting me take the lead. In human normal, I let him take it.

An elf shifted in front of the door, a TruKnight by the black and red jacket. He didn't say a word, just stared. Several others lurked nearby, pretending not to notice us.

"Tell C-Note I want to talk to him about Dennis Farnsworth," I said.

He didn't move. Murdock stepped in closer. I had an uncomfortable moment as I felt his essence charging up, but he looked calm. He didn't make any move for his gun, but from his stance I knew he'd have it in his hand before the elf knew it. "Open the door because you don't want to make me mad."

The elf smirked. Any fey would. Most elves are pretty good at sensing essence since they like to manipulate external sources rather than their own. Despite Zev's ward stone muddying Murdock's essence so it didn't feel human, the TruKnight clearly thought whatever Murdock was, he was no match for an elf. After seeing Murdock in action at

Yggy's, I almost wanted to watch him wipe the smirk off the guy's face. I felt a soft flutter in the air around us, which meant the elf was sending. Sure enough, he nodded a moment later and opened the door.

After we entered, he closed the door behind us, muffling the blasting music to a pulsing bass vibration. The room stretched long and cramped. The air was thick with smoke and incense that my head problem hated. Fey lounged on couches along the walls, elves and dwarves mostly, but with a few drugged-up fairies and brownies. The ones that bothered to notice us gave condescending smiles. The rest were either deeply involved with each other or stoned on something. At the far end sat a table, and behind the table sat C-Note.

As trolls go, he had been hit with the ugly stick more than most. His wide, pockmarked face was cut by a long, sinuous nose with nostrils a man could fit his fist in. He watched us with tight, round eyes nestled deeply at the bridge of that nose, long tendrils of eyebrows twisting up into a thick mane of greasy brown hair. Even seated, both Murdock and I had to tilt our heads up to look at him. By the expanse of his chest, I'd guess he hailed from the mountains. Most of the Teutonic trolls from there seem built from the raw bedrock.

C-Note rubbed a dull gem on a leather cord around his neck. As we approached, I could see a long, black staff of wood clenched like a royal scepter in his large, taloned hand. A leash wrapped around the other hand and trailed to a collar worn by a naked woman. She crouched on the floor beside him, silvery white skin laced with healing wounds and bruises. Her coarse hair hung to the floor, charcoal gray and matted. She looked at us with no emotion, eyes a deep brilliant green yet empty. Just the hint of saliva glistened at the corner of her parted lips.

"What can I do for you, Connor Grey?" C-Note asked. I recognized the growling sound from the ward stone Croda had.

"You know me. Good. This is Detective Murdock," I said.

He showed rows of sharp little teeth. "I know him, too. He's been hassling some of my friends."

"Your friends are thugs," Murdock said. Good for him, I thought. It paid not to show intimidation. Not that I had any doubts about Murdock.

"Who's your date?" I asked.

He looked down at the woman and jerked the chain. She shuffled closer but didn't change her expression. "Just a pet."

I clamped my jaw shut. I had no idea what she was about, if she chose to be where she was or not, but the situation made the hair on my neck stand up. The collar on her neck seemed to be constraining her body as well as her essence. I could feel an ache in my head. With all the drugs and essence flowing freely, the pressure in my head had decided to take the worst time to build.

"Where were you Sunday?" I asked.

He leaned back in his chair. "Why should I answer that?"

"Because we have evidence you were at a murder scene, and I'd like to know the tall tale you're going to tell about not being there," I said.

A wheezy rumble that I took to be chuckling came up from his chest. "You have nothing to threaten me with. The Guild would have sent someone. Thank you for amusing me, though. Now get out."

A dwarf with a black hoodie stepped closer. I looked down at him and smiled. "Banjo, right? I told Moke you guys work for the highest bidder."

"I work for myself. Get moving," he said. He didn't have to ask me twice. I wanted out of the room. There's no direct connection between physical size and essence, but trolls throw off a lot. Between C-Note and all the other fey in the room, my head was splitting with pain. Amused eyes watched from several corners as we left, the patronizing looks of superiority. It works wonders on the less self-assured.

The door opened with a burst of music and closed carefully behind us, too indifferent to give us a good slam. Not that I would have welcomed it. The essence situation was no better out on the balcony and came with a pounding bass line just in case they missed any of my aching synapses.

"Did you get a good sniff?" Murdock asked.

I nodded and tapped my nose. "Yeah. He's definitely the other troll I sensed in Kruge's office. We've got our murderer."

Murdock moved to the makeshift railing and looked down at the dancers. I joined him.

"It won't help us in court. It'll just be your word," Murdock said.

"It'll help with the Guild. We've got Crystal, the recording and essence confirmations from me, and Keeva's medical examiner." I ticked them off on my fingers. It was definitely enough evidence. "He just bought himself a murder conviction."

"That doesn't help our case," Murdock said.

I didn't respond. He was right. Taking down C-Note for Kruge's murder would work with the evidence we had but bring no justice for Dennis Farnsworth. Lots of fey crimes weren't considered crimes by human standards and vice versa. Murder overlapped, sure. But satisfaction in one court rarely meant satisfaction in another. But no human court would trust a fey ward stone as firm evidence or the word of a hooker's daughter as credible. The only satisfaction Dennis's mother would get was in the fey world, and that might not be enough for her. I still had to figure out macGoren's involvement. Maybe it wasn't just going to end up with C-Note.

We made our way downstairs and found Meryl dancing up a storm all by herself. She had attracted quite the crowd of onlookers, some of them basking in the glow of her natural essence, some of them turned on by a lone woman dancing with such confidence. Clouds of fog steamed onto the floor, laced with an herbal concoction I recognized as a euphoric. I glanced at Murdock, saw the glitter in his eye from the drug reaction. I followed his gaze to the vents above us. C-Note had come out of his office to check out the scene.

He leaned on his black staff as he watched the crowd.

Only his eyes moved, faint points of light buried deep. A Danann fairy soared up and hovered in front of him. Her wings undulated with the rhythm of the music as her head fell back in an ecstatic roll of pleasure. Her body swayed to the right and back. Another Danann joined her, and a third. The three of them began to move in unison, arcing backward to dive toward the dancers, only to loop away just above their heads. I felt a shiver as I realized they were mimicking the rhythm of C-Note's staff. He was playing with his compulsion drug. Then I realized, the dancers moved in a rhythmic shuffle, hands up and moving as if in a breeze. They wound in a coiling circle, lost in the music, yet nearly synchronized in their movements. Float apparently was fairly potent.

Flushed with exertion, Meryl appeared in front of us. "I see the Big Ugly is still on the loose. I'm thinking he didn't confess and beg for mercy."

I smiled down at her. "Something like that. You looked great out there."

She nodded at the dance floor. "It was fun until the fog. There's something in it I don't recognize. I'll take my own drugs, thank you."

"Float. It's what C-Note's been dealing."

Meryl cocked her head and narrowed her eyes. "Do you feel the essence? It's odd."

"What's odd?" asked Murdock.

"The essence," I said. "Most drugs are what you would expect—some kind of chemical-based reaction. They have essence like everything else, but this stuff has more essence infused in it. It gives me a headache, actually."

Meryl pursed her lips. "I have cramps again."

Murdock shot me a look that was all about what-the-hell-did-she-just-say.

"Thanks for sharing," I said.

I felt Meryl bring on her body shields. "Thought so. They're gone. I had cramps just like this at the Bosnemeton."

"Why are we having this conversation?" I said.

She poked me in the chest. "You just said Float gives you a headache, and you had one earlier at the Bosnemeton."

I looked up at C-Note, but he was gone. The headache had spiked again in his office. Meryl grabbed my arm and pushed out her body shield. A momentary coolness spread over me as it interacted with my own essence and the heat in the club. The pain in my head instantly became its usual dull background buzz. She released me, and it spiked again. Too bad I didn't have enough body shielding to pull that trick.

I could barely hear our conversation, so we moved into a hallway that led deeper into the building. I leaned in close to them. Probably one of the few places that doesn't look suspicious is a loud club. "Kruge seemed to be arguing with C-Note about Float getting out of control. If Meryl's right, it's already spread beyond the Weird."

"But what does it do?" Meryl said.

"Janey Likesmith says it has some sort of compulsion in it."

Murdock startled us by laughing. "I was wondering why I wanted to dance so much."

"At least you can dance, unlike *some* people," Meryl said, eyeing me.

"Focus, please. We need to find out what's in this stuff," I said.

Meryl raised an eyebrow. "We?"

"You don't want to help?"

She shook her head. "I told you, Grey, I'm not a field agent."

I gave her a slow smile. "Are you afraid of Keeva?"

She smiled back. "Hardly. I just want to make sure I steal enough office supplies before getting booted out of the Guild for getting involved in another one of your harebrained ideas. Besides, this is no outfit to play Nancy Drew in."

She had a point. The only women I knew who wore vinyl tube tops and miniskirts on secret missions were comic book superheroes. I can just imagine what Meryl would do to me if a supervillain looked up her skirt.

I shrugged. "Okay, I've got my cell phone in case I need the cavalry."

"Don't be too long. I'd kill for some Chinese food right now," she said.

I gave her a coy smile. "A kiss for luck?"

She pecked Murdock on the cheek and smirked at me. "Good luck."

Murdock looked surprised, then embarrassed, then cocky. I annoyed her by chuckling. "Thanks. Let's go."

As we walked away, a sending hit me like a slap at the back of my head. *Be careful.* I glanced back, but Meryl had moved over to the bar.

"What's the plan?" Murdock asked.

"Callin told Joe that a major shipment of Float was moving tonight. I'm guessing that fog on the dance floor was a quality check, and it's still here."

"So what if it is? We don't know if it's illegal yet."

I had considered that. Lots of fey drugs were technically legal, only because human courts had no real way of determining what the heck they did unless they were sampled. And no court yet had upheld a ruling based on the idea that someone in the DA's Office testified they got high.

"Because we need to know why it's important enough to C-Note to murder one of the most prominent people in Boston."

The sounds of the club receded as we took a dim side corridor grimed with the evidence of an old fire sooting the walls. The only essences I felt back here were the lingering trails of people consummating their desires, Murdock's strange billow of more-than-human colored by Zev's ward stone, and the thrumming of raw essence holding the stressed building up. We moved deeper into the darkness, the band whispering its bass line through the floor like a warning.

15

We picked our way through a collection of needles and con-doms and discarded clothes to a boarded-over door marked as an exit. With a few yanks, we made enough space to slip through into a stairwell. Dead buildings have a stink of their own, an organic smell that's a rank mélange of dampness, dirt, and unwashed bodies. We made our way up to the sec-ond floor and stopped on the landing.

Murdock leaned over the railing and looked up. "Big building. This is going to take a while."

I tapped the side of my head. "Maybe not. I can feel this crap. It's above us."

What I didn't say was that I could feel Float as pain, a constant pressure from the blockage in my head. I don't know if it hurt because my abilities wanted to reach out to the essence or because they wanted to avoid it. We moved up two more flights, the pressure increasing. As we turned on the landing to the next floor, I stopped. "Here. The pain less-ened when we came up here."

We moved back to the fourth floor and pushed against an access door. It gave grudgingly from long disuse. An

intersection of hallways faced us, shattered walls with gaping holes revealing empty rooms streaked with graffiti. A
green triangle with a futhark rune for "F" figured prominently, the sigil of the TruKnights. When you find yourself
on gang turf, it always feels like trespassing, no matter what
badge you may have in your pocket. Turf is turf, and you
know when you're on someone else's uninvited.

The floor vibrated from the dance floor directly below us.
Eerie lights flickered through chinks in the flooring, lighting
tendrils of smoke that trickled up from downstairs. Despite
the pain, I opened my mind a crack, letting my sense feel the
essences in the air. It hurt like hell, tight pinpoints stabbing
at my temples. I was going to have a hell of a residual headache the next day.

"Back here," I said. My voice felt louder than it was. I
could feel Float essence increasing as we wound our way
through a warren of rooms. It flared up suddenly, as if someone had opened a door. I stopped. Murdock had his gun out
of his waistband even before I had chance to say anything. I
nodded in front of us.

A wall hid our view, an open door to the left. I could feel
the distinct signature of a living being, the raw essence that I
used to identify people, but I couldn't quite place what was in
the next room. I sensed something else, a mix of energies and
smells that spoke of an herbal lab, like an unventilated version of the one back at the Guildhouse. Something squeezed
my brain like a claw, and shots of blackness dotted my vision. Not good. I had to pull back and tighten my range.

We edged toward the door, the silence broken by the
steady thump of the club music mixed with the softer
sounds of a working lab, things boiling and dripping, the
steady hum of a gas flame. I peered into the room. We were
on the short end of a long room, laboratory counters laid
down the middle to the opposite side. Glass and copper tub-
ing coiled from a series of glass vessels, a fantastical array
of decanting apparatus strung across the space. I could feel

a presence, rich and intoxicating, that pushed back against the ache in my head.

"Someone's in here," I whispered. I crouched and slunk into the room. The distillation gear pulsed with malevolence. Float. I could feel its essence battering at my mind.

On the far side of the room, a woman lay on a table. It took a long moment to realize she was bound and another to see that it was the woman C-Note had had leashed. Leather straps held her down, one across her head, torso, hips, and legs. Still naked, she looked even more tragic. An IV line ran from her arm to a bag hanging off the table, dark blood dripping with slow rhythm through the tube. She sensed my presence and shifted her eyes toward me, more aware now than when I had first seen her.

I stood and motioned Murdock in behind me. He moved in, gun out, and flanked me on the other side of the lab table. I crept down the room to the woman.

"Free me," she said, not so much an order, but stated in a way that said she expected me to help. There was no question as far as I was concerned. I started undoing the strap across her torso.

"What are they doing to you?" I asked.

"Stop," said Murdock.

Surprised, I looked over at him, then down at the woman. A wave of essence cascaded over me. It felt warm and pleasant, dulling the strange headache that Float gave me.

"Free me," she said with a bit more force this time.

My hand went back to the strap. Murdock stepped forward, a look of concern on his face. "Connor, what the hell are you doing?"

Confused, I looked up at him. "What gives, Murdock? She's in pain."

He kept scanning the windows and door behind him. "I'm just wondering why something as strong as a troll would feel the need to restrain a small woman."

He had a point. Of course, size meant little in the fey

world. I'd seen Joe take down a Danann fairy in a sword-fight. I dropped my hand.

"Why do you stop? What does this man say that makes you stop?" She sounded genuinely surprised and confused.

I felt it again, an essence surge surrounding me. Looking down, I realized I had put my hand on the strap again. I pulled it away. "Don't you understand him?"

Her eyes went to Murdock. His head flinched a moment, but he remained where he was. "I do not know this language," she said.

"What is she saying?" Murdock said.

I tilted my head at him. "You don't understand her either?"

He shook his head. "It's Greek to me."

"Free me," she said. I felt the compulsion to release her again. I forced myself to listen to her speak, heard rough rolling sounds through an auditory illusion of English. "How are we speaking?" I asked.

"You are druides. I am drys. By the wood, I beg you, free me, cousin."

My jaw dropped. As she said it, I knew it for truth. Many fey like to style themselves as higher beings, even gods and goddesses. But they're nothing more than different species. A drys, though, a drys is the real deal, essence incarnate, the heart of the oak. I didn't believe they really existed. I thought they were just mystic mumbo jumbo.

"Shit, Murdock. I think I just found religion," I said, loosening her restraints. "Trust me, Murdock, it's okay. We have to get her out of here."

He nodded, but didn't move to help. "Make it fast. I don't like this."

I pulled the needle out of her arm and helped her into a sitting position. Even seated, I could see she wasn't going to be able to walk out easily. She slid off the table to stand unsteadily. Searching the room, she pointed. "The staff. I will need it."

I followed her gesture to an oak staff leaning in the corner near a closed door. I took it in my hand, almost dropping it in surprise. A field surrounded the wood, thin, but strong. "The wood's alive. Why put a field on a staff to keep the wood alive?"

"It's all that's left. If it dies, I die. He needs me," said the drys.

"Yes, he does," a voice said. Murdock dropped behind the table, his gun sighted on a figure in the doorway. The drys stood between us, her overwhelming essence blotting out everything to my senses. I hadn't felt C-Note at all.

The drys lifted her hands and stepped toward him. "I would be free. You promised."

"You will be soon," he said.

She moved closer to him, her hands raising higher. "Please, I cannot wait. You will have to bury me if we wait any longer."

He lifted a clawed hand toward her, and she paused. "Get back on the table, Hala, or I shall not be happy. You know what happens when I am not happy."

She drifted away from him toward the table, a look of anguish on her face. He extended his hand toward me. "The staff, please."

I held it across my chest and stepped back. I could feel my mind straining to use the staff, lift it toward him and knock him back. It would hurt me, but I still wanted to do it. Hala's eyes bored into mine. I could feel her in my head willing me to act, demanding I comply with her desire. I lifted the staff even though I knew it was pointless. The mass in my head wouldn't let my ability through. I knew that, but she had control over me. This was the compulsion in the drug. It was the drys. C-Note had figured out how to use her blood to control it.

The troll took a step forward. "This is pointless. You cannot escape."

"Stand down," Murdock said.

The lock on my mind released as Hala turned her attention to Murdock.

C-Note turned toward him. "There are volatiles in here, Detective. Do not be foolish. You must know it's useless to use a gun against me."

Murdock chambered a round. "I'm not too bright."

Without hesitation, C-Note thrust his hand at Murdock. As he did, I was aware of every movement, every fraction of a second. Something about Hala augmented my senses. I could actually see the essence swirling out of his hand and wrapping itself into a spell of yellow fire. I couldn't stop it with ability, but I had the staff. I swung it into the path of the spell. The field on the staff sparked, and I felt a jolt. The spell veered over Murdock's head and hit the end of the lab table in a shower of sparks.

Murdock spun toward the explosion, dropping to the floor. With barely a shrug, C-Note flipped the table at him. In an instant, Murdock's essence blazed up around him. He caught the edge of the table as it fell toward him and tossed it away.

C-Note didn't move. I think he was shocked. I was. He recovered and lifted both hands, Power beginning to emanate between them. The drys took the moment to pick a side.

"No!" she screamed and lunged at him. She hit him in the back, and he staggered with arc lights of essence springing wildly from his hands. Murdock was right, she packed a wallop for such a small person. A cascade of lightning sprang to life throughout the room. The front of a cabinet burst open, its contents shattering on the floor. The shock of lightning hit it, and flames leaped up.

C-Note recovered his balance. Essence built up in his hands, a shimmer that would turn into visible light any moment. A swirl of more essence rolled from the drys and surrounded him. C-Note stiffened, and the power drained from his hands.

"Enough. Let us leave this place," she said.

He turned toward her, anger in his face. "Do not defy me. I will bring more pain on you than you can ever imagine."

"How the hell did you get control of a tree spirit?" I demanded.

C-Note's eyes flicked from the drys to me. "Once I found her, it was only a matter of time."

Hala's eyes went to the lab table with its menagerie of glass. "He twists the will of the wood with his mind. He spreads it like plague. He takes my Power and controls people's minds."

Billows of smoke rolled through the room, and I moved back to the windows. "Let's move this," said Murdock. "Something tells me this building's not up to code."

I glanced at the fire. "I want to know what you're doing, C-Note."

"Connor, the fire . . ." Murdock warned.

The smoke thickened along the ceiling. C-Note looked up at it, not too happy, either, but I wasn't letting him off the hook.

A surge of essence welled up from Hala. "Tell him."

He glared at her, setting his jaw. I could see him struggling to resist.

Impatient with him, Hala spoke. "The Guild. He strikes at the heart of the Guild. He seeks to rule. I have heard him swear to do it."

I could see C-Note's essence building. Almost effortlessly, he shrugged off Hala's spell. "And I keep my promises," C-Note said. A shock of white fire blasted from him, knocking us from our feet. More lab equipment toppled, glass breaking, liquids flying across the floor. My head screamed as my body shields came up. I felt pricks of glass deflecting off me. My vision blurred as I huddled on the floor. Hala's essence augmented my shields, but the mass in my head fought against her.

Flames shot up as something ignited. I scrambled back. Murdock stumbled toward the door. The fire leaped between us. I rocked to my knees. "Murdock! Get Meryl!" I shouted.

He stood indecisively, his gun sighted on C-Note. The troll threw a bolt of essence at him. It missed, hitting the wall behind him. The floor shook as the essence reinforcing the building absorbed the hit. Murdock ducked through the door.

C-Note tilted his head, and I felt a tremor run through the building. He was pulling any available essence into himself, drawing it from the spells holding the building together. As he pulled it into himself, the walls began to buckle as they lost the essence holding them up.

"I never imagined you would get this close. I am impressed," said C-Note.

"Murdock! You can't fight him. Go!" I shouted over the noise.

He didn't answer, but I felt his essence recede. I stood and leaned on the staff. It felt slick in my hands, vibrating with essence. Hala stood between me and C-Note, oblivious to the fire. Her eyes blazed with emerald light. C-Note stared back, his own eyes a feral yellow. I could feel pulsing waves of essence from both of them. The room trembled as they absorbed energy from their surroundings. C-Note pulled faster, though. He had the advantage. The building was mostly steel and concrete, of little use to a nature spirit like Hala, whose abilities tapped into organic matter like wood. C-Note stepped forward, and she backed away. The air vibrated with Power as he pulled more essence out of the building.

"I will die before I let you touch me again," Hala said, her voice resonating with Power.

"You will die when I say," said C-Note. He thrust his hands out, and she fell back with a groan. The staff shook in my hand. It was living wood, probably the only thing in the room from which Hala could draw essence. She didn't tap into it. Instead, I could feel her trying to absorb what she could from the building, the odd bits of wood essence trapped amid all the stone and metal.

I stood helpless. Hala's essence was augmenting my body shields, but they were only defensive in a fight. I couldn't use the staff itself, so I held it out to her. "Take it!"

Mistake. It seemed to break her attention, and her own shields wavered. "Keep it away from me!" she cried out.

I wasn't going to argue. I could see the fear in her eyes, but I didn't know why. My gaze roved the floor, looking through the scattered equipment. I edged toward the door.

Without taking his eyes from Hala, C-Note gestured toward the door Murdock had run through. The fire danced across the floor and blocked the exit. The floor began to undulate from the stress of the two of them drawing essence. Hala stepped back again, broken glass piercing her feet. I looked down at the glass. Sometimes essence works like electricity. Sometimes like light. It doesn't work well through glass.

I opened the window. Cold wind whipped my hair. No fire escape, but a wide ledge. It ran along the building to the corner, past the burning wall. We'd have a few seconds of protection.

"Hala, take my hand!" I held it out to her.

She looked at me, uncertain. It seemed to finally dawn on her that this was not a winning fight. Keeping her shield up, she grasped my hand and let me pull her out onto the ledge. The wind lashed her hair into a frenzy. She didn't even shiver.

"Hit him with everything you've got!" I yelled.

She let loose a burst of essence that bloomed like a star in the room. C-Note reeled under it and fell back. We ran. I pulled Hala behind me, her body spent of its Power. The windows rattled as C-Note recovered and tried to grab us with a binding spell. It passed harmlessly through the glass. As we reached the corner of the building, wind blasted at us around the corner. I steadied myself with the staff.

"Don't let it touch me," Hala said, her voice strained. If possible, she looked even more ill. We sidestepped around the corner. I breathed a sigh of relief when I saw the fire escape. The relief vanished instantly. The wrought-iron stairs ended two flights below. We had to go through a window or up to the roof. I decided to go up.

The tar roof rattled under our feet as I helped Hala over the parapet. At the back of the building, smoke roiled upward. "We have to keep moving," I said to Hala.

We ran for a stairwell penthouse near the front. A blast of essence hit us halfway to the door. I sprawled on my face, and the staff skittered away from me. I rolled over to see Hala lying facedown. Beyond her, C-Note was pushing his huge bulk through the penthouse at the back of the roof. He pointed at us, and let loose with another blast. It flew over our heads and shattered the front stairwell penthouse.

I rocked to my feet. With two quick steps, I grabbed the staff and hauled Hala up at the same time. I could feel her strain to gather essence from around us, but we were out of her element. I hustled us toward the front.

"He's not trying to kill us," I said. Hala didn't respond. He could have killed us twice over by now, but he'd let his shots go wide. He wanted Hala alive. We made it to the remains of the penthouse. C-Note shot another blast, sending bricks and wood timbers into the air. Without a thought, I hugged Hala to my chest and flung both of us into the exposed stairwell. She landed harder than I did.

"Come on. We can make it," I said. She pulled herself up, heavy with exhaustion. Holding her waist, I forced her to walk down the stairs. The essence holding them drained away and vanished. Gravity asserted itself, and the stairs sagged beneath us with a nauseating slowness. With a roar, the remains of the roof flew up, taking part of the stairs and walls with it. We fell, tumbling over each other, arms and legs tangling, and collapsed roughly on the floor.

A knife of pain stabbed into my forehead. I curled into a ball, retching. I cursed loudly. Of all times, someone was scrying. I shook off the pain and crawled to Hala. Her head lolled against my shoulder.

"Come on, come on. He's coming."

Her eyes fluttered. "Don't let him get the staff."

I had dropped the damned staff again. I searched frantically through the chaos of the hallway, feeling my way more with my ability-sensing than vision. Its essence flared against the dullness of the building. I grabbed it and rushed back to Hala, as plaster dust from the ceiling poured on our heads. With a thunderous sound, C-Note plunged through the ceiling in a rain of brick and mortar. As he landed awkwardly, I pushed Hala into an adjoining room.

The wall exploded behind us, and the building shuddered. The essence holding it together receded, coalescing up and out in the hall as C-Note pulled more into himself. Cracks appeared in the floor, and it canted sideways. We tumbled against the far wall. Smoke from the spreading fire poured in from the next room.

C-Note stood at the door. "Give me the staff."

I didn't bother answering. He wouldn't just let us go if I gave it to him. C-Note stepped into the room. Whether from his weight or from its own overloaded stress, the floor groaned loudly. With a screech of metal, it slumped and shattered into the club below. I could hear screams as the music stopped.

I clutched Hala to my chest as we perched on a small patch of floor still clinging to the wall. Fifty feet of open space yawned below us. People scattered from the dance floor. The rumble of an explosion shuddered up from below, and the lights went out.

In the surreal silence that followed, the fire surged into the remains of the room. With my back to the wall, I could feel the building swaying with a nauseating rhythm. Hala was lying next to me, unconscious.

"This isn't the way to die with a naked woman," I said. I stroked her hair. She either didn't hear me or didn't think it was funny.

Gusts of wind pushed the smoke back. On the opposite side of the cavernous hole in the floor, C-Note hung with his arm wrapped around an exposed beam. He stretched a clawed hand toward us. The staff moved, pulling away from me. I tightened my fist, but the field around it made it slick. I gripped it with both hands. C-Note flexed his hand, and the staff wrenched itself from my grasp. It sailed across the open space to the other side, flying directly into his out-stretched hand. As he closed his taloned fingers around it, the staff shimmered and morphed into the black staff he had had with him earlier.

Hala jerked her head up with a scream. C-Note pointed the staff, and she began to slide away from me. I grabbed her hands as she clawed frantically, her eyes wide with fear. We both slid toward to the edge. With a subtle flick, C-Note lifted the rod. Hala flew from my hands, her fingers raking my skin. She flailed backward through the air, screaming. She didn't fall but careened across the gap. C-Note held out the staff. Hala's body twisted into an ugly smear of flesh and bone. What was left of her hit the staff and she imploded, a burst of green essence that the rod sucked in.

C-Note swung himself into the exposed hallway and faced me. "You fight a pointless battle, Connor Grey. A new day dawns, and the old order passes away. I will bring order where there is only chaos."

He lifted the staff and pointed at me. The envelope of essence on it shimmered, and Teutonic runes blazed whitely along its length. An arc of yellow essence hissed through the air and hit my ledge. It jerked away from the wall, sliding off its support rods with an ear-piercing whine. It bent under my weight. I rolled to my stomach and clutched at whatever exposed beams I could reach. The wall began to slump like wet clay. The building shook violently, and the whole front of it fell into the street.

I slid to the edge, my feet swinging out into the open space. The concrete beneath me became pliant and mal-leable. It welled between my fingers, locking my hands in place. Something hit me in the back, thrusting my face against the remains of the floor. The air vibrated with so much essence, my vision blurred. The ledge sagged, drop-ping like soft wax. I dangled in the air as the last connection to the wall stretched thinner and thinner. The concrete be-came a thing alive, a viscous flow that filled my mouth and my nose. It oozed around me like wet clay. I felt one final wrenching jolt as my weight finally pulled the ledge free.

I fell. Smoke and flame swirled around me as I plummeted. I tumbled four stories through the remains of the building. Just before I hit the ground, I heard a scream.

16

I could hear the soft sound of a slack tide on the shore, and below that, the incessant pounding of my head. My body felt like deadweight. With an effort, I dragged my eyelids open and closed them immediately against the light. I tried again more slowly. My eyes burned and itched as I stared at a whitewashed, pitted cement wall. I wasn't outside. The air smelled of dry stone and bacon. Someone rustled papers nearby. Closing my eyes, I rolled onto my back. I heard the sound of newspaper being folded and dropped. I didn't move as I sensed a dwarf move toward me.

"I know you're awake. You snore on your back, you know. I've been rolling you over for hours." The voice sounded muffled. I opened my eyes. Banjo stood over me—well, barely—his thick arms crossed over his chest. He wore his characteristic black hoodie with the yellow bandana.

"You do wash those clothes, don't you?" I asked.

He snorted. "I smell better than you do." He turned and stepped out a door on the other side of the room. I sniffed. He had a point.

I curled up into a sitting position, every muscle in my

body protesting with ache. The saliva in my mouth felt thick and pasty. Something shifted in my throat, and I coughed. Something grainy came up. I spat out what looked like sand.

Wrapped in a tangled sheet, I was sitting on a wide couch. My clothes, obviously laundered, hung neatly over the back of a chair next to me. My torso was covered with streaks of black and gray grit. I brought my hand to my chin and mouth, rubbed a dry film I found there. I had apparently been puking up dust.

The large square room had no windows, a brightly lit space laid out for entertainment. Against the far wall, a large-screen TV played one of those mood DVDs of a long stretch of southern beach, all soft white sand and glittering ocean. Two leather recliners faced the TV, one huge, the other normal size. A pool table took up space on the other end of the room. A very expensive stereo system was racked on the wall next to the door. The oversize chairs made it clear enough what lived there, and my ability sensed an essence that confirmed the who. How the hell I fell to my death and landed in Moke's living room was probably an interesting tale.

Banjo returned with a tray and placed it on the coffee table. A water pitcher, two glasses—one with water, one with something foul—a bowl of what smelled like chicken soup and a chocolate bar. "Drink the water first," he said. I didn't need an invitation. I felt desiccated.

Banjo walked over to the normal-size recliner, picked up a newspaper from the floor, sat down, and leaned back. After a moment, he pulled out a pair of reading glasses. I drank the water, watching him ignore me as he read the paper. I could see the date, so unless he was behind on the news, I had fallen to my death the night before. I refilled the glass, drank it down, and refilled it. The room-temperature water tasted like the best damned thing I ever had.

I felt Moke before I saw him. He came into the room wearing the largest pair of jeans I had ever seen, a tailored button-down shirt, and an expensive cardigan sweater. His hair was washed and combed. He was still troll-ugly.

"I'm either hallucinating or in some bizarre version of hell," I said.

Moke smiled, his yellow teeth somehow not as offensive when he was cleaned up. "Naw, it's just our cave."

"If this is a cave, it's the nicest one you've ever had, Moke," Banjo said without looking up.

A deep laugh chortled up from Moke. "Heh, he gets to complaining about anything. He hates to stay under the bridge. Too cold, too cold, he says."

He stood over me, the smile still on his lips. Sitting naked except for the sheet, my head pounding like a drum set, I felt a little vulnerable. I stared up at him and sipped more water. He reached his massive hands out and cupped my head completely. I didn't move. I felt a short pulse of essence, an odd shifting in my head, followed by a loud pop. A trickle of sand poured out of my ears, and the sounds in the room became clearer.

Moke brushed his hands together and sat down. "How ya feel?"

"Like I fell four stories on my head."

He nodded. "You're fine. I worked the stone. Banjo, he gave the timing of it, he did. A good job that." The dwarf looked at me over the tops of his glass, smiled, and went back to reading.

"I thought C-Note was melting the stone to kill me," I said.

"Nah. He wanted the wood maid. Don't know why. Skinny little thing, not much meat." He gestured to the foul-smelling glass. "Drink that now. Ya need to drink."

I picked it up. "What is it?"

Moke rumbled a laugh. "A little this, a little that. Clean the good earth from yer gut."

"And how did the earth get into me?"

"Like I says, I worked the stone. Made ya a nice slurry to slow ya down, keep ya from crackin' yer head. Then I wrapped ya in earth and pulled ya down below. Spelled earth gets in all nooks and crannies. Ya gonna die if ya don't drink that."

"Maybe I should go to Avalon Memorial."

Moke shrugged and laughed again. "Ya could. They never get the sulfur right. Burn ya gut, they will. Burn for years."

I looked at the yellow-tinged liquid. If Moke were going to kill me, he would have by now. I took a deep breath and downed it. It felt hot going down, but not burning. I drank more water.

"Why did you save me?"

Moke grinned wider. "Banjo sees many times, many days to come. The ones ya die, not so good for me."

I looked over at the dwarf. Now I understood the sharp pains I had at Carnage. "He was scrying."

Moke smiled. "Banjo best far-seer scryer ya ever meet, I says. He picked time. I grabbed ya."

My chest tightened. He said building collapse. "How many died?"

Moke shrugged, a great shifting of the hunch on his back. "No one died that I know. Lots hurt, though. Yer gun cop friend screamed his head off that the building was on fire. Banjo started a fight, too, and everyone run like crazy. Stupid TruKnights. It was kinda funny to watch, though."

I breathed a sigh of relief. You take your chances in the Tangle, but the building would still be standing if I hadn't gone in. I looked at Banjo. "Thank you. Sorry I thought you were a traitor."

He didn't look up. "Cops aren't the only ones who work undercover, you know."

I pulled the sheet up around me and slid back against the wall surveying the room. Moke watched me. He cocked his head at the TV. "Pretty, no? The night is beauty, but light is, too. I like TV. Better life here."

I smiled. I bet he liked game shows. "You were right, Moke. C-Note's trouble."

Moke nodded. "C-Note thinks yer dead now. He's not very good troll. Didn't even know I was there."

"I need to get out of here," I said.

Moke stood. "Give it an hour. The bathroom's right out

that door. Ya can take a bath if you wanna. Banjo don't like smells, so's he keeps sweet stuff in there." He turned to Banjo. "I'm gonna go up and sleep, 'kay?"

"Do not bring any cats back." Banjo looked at him sternly.

Moke laughed again. "I said ya could cook them next time."

He went to the door. "Moke?" He turned. "I'm sorry about Croda."

A wistful expression came over his face, his long, twisted nose almost quivering. "I knowed Croda a long time. She was a fine-looking woman, that one. Ya know, us trolls and ogres and giants are all the same. People of the Berg. We's not like those crazy elveses and flittery kinds. The bones of the earth are all one. Croda was a strong woman." He sighed and pounded his chest with a nod. "I still feel her strength. Her heart's gone, but she died brave." He strode away.

"Wipe your feet when you come back," Banjo yelled. He settled back against the recliner and focused on his newspaper again, a pen poised in his hand. "What's a seven-letter word for 'mask'?"

The potion took that moment to demonstrate its effect. I ran for the bathroom. After a half hour, I could see why Moke recommended waiting. I finally showered, the water sluicing trails of grime off me and onto the glass tile floor. Reaching up to turn the shower faucet off made me smile at the strangeness of standing in an oversize shower room. When I dressed, I went back into the living room to find Banjo asleep in front of the TV.

I shook him. "Sorry, got to go."

He frowned and shifted himself out of the recliner. He led me past the bathroom where a long hall ran on for several dozen feet with a series of closed doors. I could smell Moke more strongly. Banjo didn't go any farther than the second door, which led to a stark utility tunnel.

"So, what likely potential future did you see me in?" I asked to the back and top of his head.

He didn't turn. "I get paid good money for answers like that."

"But it's good, right?"

He didn't answer right away. We turned a corner and began ascending a flight of stone stairs. Every so often another hallway would branch off, or the stairs would split in different directions. "I wasn't looking for your future. Moke asked me to do a little looky at C-Note. All I know is, with you dead, business didn't look good for us. With you not dead, it looked fifty-fifty."

Moke dealt drugs. He made money on other people's needs, sure, but that didn't always mean the same thing as trading on addictions. Whatever his dietary habits or his line of work, I wasn't going to complain that keeping me alive kept him in business. I was willing to cut him some slack. This time, at least.

The great oxymoron of scrying is its unpredictability. Dwarves were good at it, though druids would debate that. Seeing into the future had complications and ramifications. You never see exactly what *will* happen, but what *could* happen, based on certain circumstances. The most you could do with a particular vision was to make a choice to try to set it in motion. But the moment you made that choice, new permutations arose that did not necessarily lead where you'd hoped. For that reason, it was nearly impossible for the scryer to see his or her own future. "What did you see?"

He shrugged over his shoulder. "It wasn't about you. I only figured out you were the wild card at Carnage by what was going on around you. There was something odd about you in the visions. They slipped around you like they didn't know you were there. Never saw anything like that."

That gave me a cold feeling. Several months earlier, Briallen had done a scry and failed to see anything. A disaster almost occurred. Whatever was dancing around in my head liked to keep its secrets when it came to me and the future.

Banjo stopped on a wide landing and pointed up another long flight of stairs, dimly lit. "This is as far as I'm going. I

have to start dinner; otherwise, he's going to eat something
that's bad for him. Up there, through the door, and you're
out. It closes behind you. Make sure you're on the other side
when it does, 'cause I'm only priming it for one opening,
and if I have to come let you out again, I ain't gonna be
happy."

I nodded. Angry dwarves are almost as bad as angry
trolls. "Thanks. I don't plan on hanging around."

He tapped his forehead and bowed. "Nice working with
you."

I went up, and he went down. At the top of the flight, I
came to a standard wooden door that opened into a small
vestibule. I could feel a warding spell snap into place as soon
as the door closed behind me. I opened another door opposite the first and found myself standing under a flight of
brownstone stairs, daylight streaming in from the sides. I
stepped out from under the steps onto the sidewalk in front
of a boarded-up building.

A prickling sensation swept over me. I held up my hand
to see fine swirls of earth-toned particles radiating essence. I
rubbed the back of my hand, feeling a resistance layered
over the skin. I allowed my sensing abilities to open to check
it out. I didn't have much experience with stonework, but I
recognized silica and calcium embedded into my hands. I
pushed my body essence at it, and the layer moved. I pushed
harder, and a fine layer of dust rippled up on my hands.
Moke's spell had wrapped me in stone at Carnage, and I
could see how it worked now by attracting stone particles to
bond with my own essence.

I recognized Fargo Street, just south of the Tangle. It
wasn't a long walk from my apartment. As I started up the
street, Joe appeared so close to my face with his sword
drawn that I jumped. His fierce look quickly turned to relief.
"Where the hell were you?" he asked.

"I went underground. Literally."

He narrowed his eyes and hovered in close. "Are you
okay? You've got troll essence all over you."

I nodded. "It's a long story."

He looked up and down the street like he expected a horde of Visigoths to charge at him. Seeing none, he sheathed the sword.

Where are you? Burst into my mind so sharply I stumbled. "Tell Meryl I'm fine, Joe. Is she okay?"

He paused a moment. "She says you owe her a new pair of Doc Martens."

I smiled. Whether she realized it or not, I could tell she was concerned enough to be upset. "Tell her I said 'deal.' Where did you go last night, Joe?"

Joe looped and dipped around me as I walked. "I couldn't get in. They had awesome security on that place. Tell me what happened."

He circled around me as I gave him the rundown, peering at passersby with suspicion. His head whipped around to face me as I got to the end of the story. "You took a shower in a troll's bathroom?"

"Uh, Joe, did you miss what I said? I met a drys, almost died, and found out C-Note is going to attack the Guild."

He nodded. "No, I heard that. How bad did it smell?"

"What?"

"The bathroom."

I decided not to argue. "Actually, it didn't. It was very clean."

He nodded in puzzled consideration. "Really. I wouldn't've thought. Were there dead things?"

We turned onto D Street and made for Summer. "Not obvious, though I did smell something not very fresh as I was leaving."

Murdock cruised up on the left and stopped. I cocked an eyebrow at Joe. "Just how many people did you do a sending to?"

He smiled. "Just two. We thought you were dead, you know. Meryl saw you fall before the whole building went down. That woman should go into demolition. You should have seen her tear into the place looking for you."

I had a recollection of someone screaming when I fell. "She did?"

He nodded. "I had to force her to leave. I couldn't see you at all. I thought you were dead, but she didn't."

I opened the car door and tossed a paperback novel and some newspapers off the passenger seat and sat down next to Murdock. Joe fluttered into the backseat and began rummaging through the mess. "Hi," I said.

Murdock pulled away from the curb. "So you're not dead," he said.

"You either."

He smirked. "I run fast."

I smirked back. "I fall slow. What happened to you?"

"I ran to get Meryl, but we couldn't get back up because the whole back of the building was in flames. Then it started falling apart."

"Your essence got pretty strong in there," I said.

He turned onto Summer Street. "I don't feel any different."

"Murdock, think about the other night at Yggy's. Didn't you notice how fast you were moving? Hell, you laid out an elf with one punch."

He pursed his lips. "I guess I did. I still don't feel any different."

He might not feel anything, but I did. I had met very few fey whose essence oscillated in strength like Murdock's did. It cycled from slightly elevated human normal to wildly strong to, like now, somewhere in the middle. "What's the *midach* say?"

"Nothing. Meryl insisted I get checked out this morning. I was at AvMem when Joe called me. Where are we going?"

I considered a moment. "The Guildhouse. I need to talk to Keeva."

Murdock goosed the accelerator. "What happened after I took off?"

"He met a drys, almost died, and learned C-Note's evil plans," Joe's voice came from somewhere under a pile of papers.

"Oh, be quiet," I said.

He snickered. "I told you I was paying attention."

I gave Murdock a few more details than Joe had. A curious look came over his face. "Explain the drys."

"It's like I said last night. They're legends. The belief is that real entities are obligated to keep the flows of essence balanced. A drys is a keeper of the wood and is the source of Power that druids tap. When a druid asks for a blessing, he's asking the drys."

"A goddess," he concluded.

I stole a look at him, but couldn't tell if he was being sarcastic or not. Murdock's Roman Catholicism is one of the wonderful contradictions about our friendship. He is a believer who wants to understand the crazy pagans. "Not quite. More an extension of a goddess. *The* Goddess, if that's where your belief lies."

"Is that what you believe?"

I paused, not expecting the question. What did I believe? If he had asked me the day before, I would have talked a lot about energy and reason. I knew what I was supposed to believe as a druid, but my rational mind always resisted. Essence was just there. I could tap it like an energy source. Whether I believed it was the extension of some higher power seemed beside the point. And yet, standing in the Bosnemeton, in a grove of oak with my brothers, I did feel Something. Feeling the purity of essence that Hala generated when I had held her, I felt Something. I knew what I was supposed to believe, even wanted to believe it, but I still hovered on the edge of that precipice, suspicious of taking that leap of faith. Maybe that was the missing key to my problem. Maybe allowing the old beliefs to become real in my mind was the step I needed to take to heal the darkness in my head.

"Let's just say I hope all of this has a reason," I said finally.

He nodded. "Hope is the beginning of faith."

I laughed. "I thought I was the one who just had a near-death experience."

Murdock shrugged. "Trust me. When you have a building collapsing on your ass, you find time for faith." He leaned over and pulled a manila folder out of the glove compartment. "I had a busy day."

I flipped the file open to a sheaf of notes with a photocopy of a store receipt for orange Nike running shoes. "You traced the Nikes?"

He nodded. "They were brand-new. I'd never seen them before, so I figured it might be easy to track them down. Newbury Street, of all places."

I shook my head. A poor kid from the wrong side of Southie ends up dead while wearing shoes from the most expensive stretch of pavement in Boston.

"They were bought with a credit card, so I ran the number," he said.

I turned the page and froze. I looked at Murdock. "Is this a joke?"

He had a sly smile on his face. "You wanted a connection to Kruge. We just got another one."

I held the credit card report, staring at it, still wondering if it were a joke. "Why would Keeva buy Dennis Farnsworth running shoes?"

Murdock pulled his chin in and looked at me from under his brow. "Well, don't get your hopes up yet. We've had this kind of thing blow up in our faces before. No one at the store remembers who bought the shoes. I have someone running the surveillance tape. It could be a big fat coincidence."

I knew Keeva well enough to know something was up. "Orange shoes are a coincidence? You know Keeva. She wouldn't be caught dead with someone wearing orange running shoes."

"It might explain why nothing's happening with her investigation, though," he said.

I slouched in my seat. I was at a loss. Other than Guild work, I could not think of a single reason Keeva would be involved with Kruge. Eagan and Gerin put me onto mac-Goren, not her. But they clearly had their curiosities about her; otherwise, they would have asked her some direct questions about her new beau. As much as Keeva and I had our differences, I had a hard time picturing her in a murder plot.

We made our way through downtown streets and turned toward Park Square. The Guildhouse sat like a fort under siege. Pedestrian traffic threaded through a narrow barricaded path, while concrete Jersey barriers restricted traffic in front to a single lane. Security agents flew overhead, running their random patterns, while brownie foot security patrolled the perimeter of the building.

Murdock pulled over to let me out. Joe flew nonchalantly around me, pretending he wasn't pulling bodyguard duty.

"You need to get the force on high alert," I said.

He nodded. "It's already done. You don't have to go in there, Connor."

"Yes, I do."

"We know C-Note did the Farnsworth murder. I sent Keeva the report this morning. You're done. Let the Guild handle the rest. If they convict, maybe the city court will hear the case, too."

"The Guild is tangled in its own politics. They're focused on the wrong thing, and I can't sit back and watch it fall apart."

"Why not?"

I shrugged. "Because shit happens no matter what. That doesn't mean I have to let it. I'm not giving up no matter what Nigel Martin thinks."

Murdock leaned back in his seat and smiled. "They made a mistake when they kicked you out."

He eased the car back into traffic and drove off. I joined the crowd of people on the sidewalk, trying not to push anyone as I made my way toward the front of the Guildhouse. Joe remembered his innate shyness and hung on to the collar of my jacket. He hadn't latched on to me like that since I was kid, only back then he was making sure I didn't run off into traffic.

"Move along!" one of the brownie patrols ordered as I

stepped around the barricade. I flashed him my Guild badge, looking worn from wear. He examined it suspiciously before stepping back and letting me through.

I felt a tug at my neck. "Ow!" said Joe.

He hovered a few feet behind me. His eyes twitched in all directions, his hands spread with a slight glow. "What's wrong, Joe?"

"Security barrier. It's not letting me in. They're doing something new."

I opened myself to the barrier, felt its invisible presence. It had the feel of the Grove about it, but different, a modification I hadn't seen before. Gerin's work layered over the usual Guildhouse barrier. I could feel the difference, the way it would let certain people through and not others. Flits had a higher ratio of essence to their mass than other species. Given everyone's fear that they would spy, they were usually the first species to be guarded against.

"Let him in," I said to the patrol.

The brownie seemed about to object, so I held up my badge again to remind him who he was talking to. I cringed inwardly. In less than a week with a piece of laminated paper in my hand, I had managed to get very comfortable pulling rank. I felt a tingle as the brownie opened a small space for Joe. He flew in and clutched my collar again, looking back at the brownie with a tough face.

When I pushed through the main doors, the central lobby appeared startlingly empty to me. The usual receptionists were gone, replaced by yet more brownie security. I had no problem inside getting through the checkpoint and took an elevator up. The Community Liaison floor hummed with activity. Up and down the halls, people either rushed in and out of offices or clustered in small groups. Dressed in their most formal attire, diplomatic envoys from both Seelie Court and the Teutonic Consortium kept pointedly apart, whispering among themselves while casting wary glances at each other. I turned the corner toward Keeva's office, only to be stopped by two security guards.

One held up his hand. "Appointments only, sir."

"I need to see Keeva macNeve," I said.

"Director macNeve is busy, sir. Please make an appointment with the desk," one of them said. The other let some essence trickle obviously into his hands until they glowed. He didn't move, just stood in my path as a warning.

I held up my board meeting pass without speaking.

"I'm sorry, Director Grey. We have orders from the Guildmaster."

"I don't have time for this. I have important information she needs to hear now."

I didn't push forward. I had worked with these guys enough to know that would end with me knocked on my ass. Glow bees zipped back and forth above our heads. I didn't have any on me.

The guard held a hand palm up and gestured back the way I had come. "Please, sir."

Joe flew up to the guard and poked his finger at the faceshield. "Let us through or I will peel that helmet off your head and shove it up . . ."

"Joe!" I said.

He looked at me. I pointedly tilted my head toward the glow bees, and his gaze followed. He looked back down to my face, somehow managing to make all his features look like flat lines of annoyance. "I am not a gl—"

I cut him off before the security guards could hear him. "Tell her you've breached the Guildhouse security, and if she doesn't see me immediately, you will have every flit you know swarming the place in five minutes."

He crossed his arms. "You better pick up the tab next time."

That was a recipe for poverty. I smiled my best I'm-lying-through-my-teeth smile. "Promise."

He blinked out. The guards didn't flinch. Moments dragged by. I glanced behind me at the various courtiers. Most of them seemed happy for the distraction from whatever political games they were plotting. The first security guard cocked his head and stepped aside. "Director mac-Neve will see you now."

I strode past him, just as Keeva sent me my own sending. *This better be good.* She practically threw it at me, it hit so hard. A swarm of glow bees hovered outside Keeva's door, Joe in the midst of them. "She's cranky," he said.

I entered the office. Keeva was already dressed for the funeral in a green wool coat that matched her pants. She wore a black blouse intricately embroidered with apple blossoms. "You look lovely," I said.

She pointed at Joe. "Lives are at stake, Connor. I want to know how he breached security, and I want to know now."

I twisted my head to see Joe. "Did you tell her that?"

Joe shook his head in exasperation and threw his hands in the air. "I'm just a glow bee. I say what I'm told."

I faced Keeva. "He didn't breach. I signed him in."

She lifted a cup of tea and leaned back, sipping. "You have two minutes. Make them good."

"A troll named C-Note is behind these attacks. He wants to take down the Guild. Good enough?"

Keeva arched an eyebrow. "You've been busy. What proof do you have?"

"A witness in protective custody and a ward stone recording. Murdock heard the threat to the Guild. C-Note controls the gangs with a compulsion drug called Float. It's spreading beyond the Weird. I know it's infected the druid Grove. It's made from the essence of a drys."

Her jaw dropped, and she laughed. "A drys? You expect me to believe that?"

"Murdock saw her."

She pulled her lower lip in. "Connor, no one's seen a drys in decades. Murdock is not credible on fey and, frankly, with your conspiracy theory habits, neither are you. The Guild is convinced the Consortium is behind this."

"The Guild or Nigel?"

"Both." She looked down at her desk, shifted her eyes to the computer monitor and back to me. I could practically feel her running scenarios in her head, trying to figure what she needed to do to get the job done while figuring out how to present herself in the best light. I've seen it before. It's how she works. "We have security at the funeral. Gerin's shielding Forest Hills Cemetery for the ceremony. Nigel's coordinating with Manus and the diplomatic envoys. I'm not worried about the funeral. I'm worried about the Weird. I'm trying to seal it down so no one can move in or out without my knowing about it."

"I did."

She glared at me. "Connor, bring me your proof, and maybe then I will contradict Gerin Cuthbern and Nigel Martin. Until then, I run things my way."

I decided it was time to shake Keeva's cage a little. "You haven't made any progress in your Kruge investigation."

She looked honestly startled. Looks aren't everything. "What the hell are you talking about? I've been looking for Croda. You know trolls are difficult to trace."

"Dennis had distinctive new running shoes on. Easy to trace. Your credit card bought a pair."

She leaned over her desk toward me. "What are you talking about?"

I stared her down. "Ryan macGoren has known where Croda is from the night of the murder. You bought Dennis's running shoes. I don't think it's me and Murdock with the credibility problem."

She jumped to her feet and pointed at the door. "Out."

I'd definitely struck a nerve, but it was time to go. I stood, but before I left, I gave her a last warning. "If the Guild is using Kruge's murder to provoke a confrontation with the Consortium, I'll expose you."

She was angry enough now that a little fey light glowed in her eyes. She pointed at the door. "I said 'out.'"

I moved to the hallway. "Keeva, if you don't increase security, you won't have to worry about finding a troll. One's going to find you."

17

The Guild had replaced my apartment door. The security agent remained posted outside at the end of the hall, though. While they had done a great job on the door, even fixing an old squeak, unfortunately they hadn't brought a housekeeper with them. My place looked like a gang of elves and fairies had run amok. Which, of course, was exactly what had happened.

I pulled two bottles of Guinness out of the fridge, popped one, and left the other on the counter to warm. The bottled stuff is nowhere near as good as tap, but it's better than the can. Or nothing.

I slunk into my desk chair and called Meryl. She picked up on the first ring, and I smiled. Someone was worried. "I saw you buried by a pile a rubble." The genuine concern in her voice felt oddly pleasurable.

"Believe it or not, Moke saved me. Are you okay?"

"Tired, but fine. What happened?"

I took a swig of beer and booted up the laptop. "Long story. I have to be at the funeral. Want to be my date?"

"Ooooo, a funeral. Sounds fun," she said.

"The service starts at sunset. Can you drive?"

She sighed. "Fine."

"Oh, and wear green. It's the elven color for mourning."

"Gee, thanks, I didn't know that," she said sarcastically.
"Oh, and Grey?"

"Yeah?"

"It's not a date." And she hung up.

Joe busied himself with cookies while I changed. I had
very little to work with but stumbled on a dark green shirt I'd
forgotten I owned. Even given the formality of an elven funeral, I wasn't about to wear green pants. As I pulled on my
boots, I could hear Joe laughing in my study.

"Now I get it," he said, his voice oddly hollow.

"Get what?" I called back.

The Guild security helmet I had retrieved from Croda's
murder scene came floating into the room. Two bare feet
dangled out of it. "How the Guild is keeping flits out lately.
They're letting in only essence they expect, not blocking
what they don't want."

I stopped myself from commenting. That's an old druid
trick, a modification of the shield on a grove. Gerin and
Nigel must have adapted it for the Guildhouse. As much as
I'd trusted Joe, he had a tendency to talk before he thought,
and who knows who would hear him. "Tricky," I said.

He circled around the living room, landed on the coffee
table, and rolled the helmet off. "Not really. I can think of
ten ways to get through now."

Downstairs, Meryl sent, and I startled. When most people do a sending, a subtle warning happens in your head that
one's coming. The person you're sending may be anywhere,
so the sending itself tends to travel in a thin envelope of
essence. The envelope is part of the searching and touches
your mind moments before the actual message. Not Meryl's.
Her sendings are incredibly focused to the point where they
find you and arrive instantaneously. It's like someone jumping out of a closet and saying "boo!"

"Are you coming?" I asked Joe.

He swung his legs back and forth from the edge of the coffee table. "Maybe later. I've got some business."

I smiled. "Be careful." I'm sure Joe's business entailed testing his new ideas at the Guildhouse. If there's one thing a flit despises, it is being told to keep out.

I passed three security agents on my way out. I jumped in the immaculate passenger seat of Meryl's Mini Cooper, reveling in the refreshing change of pace from Murdock's car.

"We look like catalog models for the goth professional," she said.

She wore a body-hugging leather jumpsuit and knee-high leather combat boots with lots of heel and buckles. Not a bit of it was green. In fact, the only green about her was her hair. She slipped on a pair of fingerless calfskin gloves and put the car in gear.

"*My* hair's not dyed," I said.

She flipped her hand through her hair. "Do you like it? I have it on good authority it was Alvud Kruge's favorite shade."

"It's perfect. For you." I smiled to keep it amusing.

She zipped around the block and coasted over the Old Northern Avenue bridge. "We've got a tail. Want me to lose them?"

I peered up through the structural beams of the bridge. Two security agents followed. "Nah. They'd be stupid not to know where we're going. Can we make a pit stop?"

"Sure, I'll keep the meter running," she said.

"I need to go to Avalon Memorial."

She looked askance at me. "Anything wrong?"

"No. Just need to visit a sick friend," I said.

Rather than deal with the street restrictions in place downtown, Meryl scooted up on the highway to loop around to Storrow Drive along the river. "You know you have troll essence all over you?"

I nodded. "It's a residual effect from Moke pulling me through stone. He said it has to clear through my system. Look at this." I held up my left hand, letting the light pick up a tracery of faint patterns across the back. "That's stone. I keep picking up ambient dust, and it bonds with my skin."

Meryl glanced back and forth from the road to my hand. "Does it hurt?"

I shook my head. "No. It uses my body as an anchor, pulling stuff to me like a body shield. Can't even feel it unless I focus on it. Now watch this." I mentally visualized the essence coursing over my body, sensed the difference between my own essence and the ambient troll essence, felt for the bonded stone, and pushed. It separated from my skin and slid off my hand like fine dust.

"You're getting my car dirty," Meryl said.

I wiped my hand on my pants. "Sorry."

She pulled up in front of Avalon Memorial. Guild security guards hovered in the air, with more brownie security on the street. They must have recognized Meryl because they let her park without a word.

"I shouldn't be long," I said.

"Don't be. I only have one CD in the car," she said.

I found macGoren lying on his side in his room surrounding by ward stone amplifiers. Two bowls of infusions sat at the end of the bed. My nose twitched on the betony and a hint of basil. MacGoren's left wing fluttered with a rippled texture and a few jagged holes. Danann wings didn't have the physical property of skin. They didn't have true nerves for that matter, so pain registered very differently. Regardless, the damage looked painful. The ward stones generated a field that amplified macGoren's own essence as well as the simply pure air essence that Danann fairies had a natural affinity to. The herbals soothed the spirit with a protective spell working against infection.

MacGoren overall looked hardly worse for wear. He languished on the bed in his blue silk pajamas reading a magazine. When he saw me, he tossed aside the magazine and stretched onto his stomach. "Ah, good. Company. Gillen Yor says I can't have my cell phone because it will disrupt the wards. I think he's just saying that to irritate me."

"You look like you're recovering well," I said.

He smirked with amusement. "I'm just here because I'll heal faster. I assume this isn't a social call."

"And why's that?"

He grinned. "No flowers. No candy."

"Why were you fighting a troll in the Tangle the night of Kruge's murder?"

He gave me a long measured look. "You found the helmet."

I nodded. "I found the helmet."

MacGoren shrugged. "You know I wanted a piece of land Kruge owned. He didn't want to sell. I thought I'd get on his good side by helping with the drug problem down there. A nightclub was the epicenter. It burned down last night as a matter of fact."

"Yeah, I heard about it," I said dryly.

MacGoren nodded. "This drug Float was the problem. I analyzed it and found druid essence. I brought it to Kruge."

"For which he was extremely grateful," I said.

MacGoren shrugged again. "Actually, he didn't believe me. But he was worried if that were true, then Gerin Cuthbern would try to cover it up to protect the Grove. Then he was afraid if he told Manus ap Eagan, Eagan would think he was maneuvering against Cuthbern and use it against him politically. So, he asked me to help, figuring since both the Guildmaster and I are Danann, Manus naturally wouldn't think anything suspicious of my motives."

It was my turn to smirk. "Naturally."

MacGoren ignored the dig. "Anyway, Kruge came up with the idea of recording the drug analysis and sending a sample to Manus via courier. I was supposed to meet the courier on Summer Street and take the evidence to the Guildhouse."

A piece of the puzzle fell into place. Fairies, in general, were good weather workers. Some Dananns specialized in it. "He was supposed to meet you up on Summer Street. You pulled the weather trick to drive away any witnesses and give Dennis Farnsworth safe passage through three gang territories."

MacGoren nodded. "Correct. When the courier didn't show up, and Kruge didn't answer my sendings, I went looking. I found Kruge. I don't know how the troll found out, but that wasn't part of the plan that I knew."

I could see what Keeva found attractive about him. She liked a good schemer. MacGoren paused, and the superior tone finally left his voice. "Then I saw something incredible, Grey. I saw a troll, in broad daylight, *flying*. Scared the living hell out of me. He had the courier, so I went after him."

"That was brave."

The idea clearly surprised him. "Yes, I guess you could look at it that way. I didn't find the ward stone at Kruge's, so I figured the kid had it. I took the troll by surprise. I lost the helmet in the tussle but managed to get the kid. The troll chased me almost to Summer Street. I felt a compulsion to drop the boy. It was like I had no choice."

"Why didn't you tell someone?"

He shrugged again. "With Kruge dead, I didn't have the evidence. If that troll could kill Alvud Kruge, he could kill me. I thought if I kept quiet, he would leave me alone. I didn't see any percentage in coming forward. Didn't seem to help in the end, though."

I shook my head. "People died, and you didn't see a percentage in coming forward?"

MacGoren frowned with a condescending look. "Please, Grey. Don't be naïve. If it wasn't this, it would have been something else."

"*Naïve?* You helped start a gang war. Maybe worse now."

He sighed as if bored. "It's all the same, Grey. They're all gangs. Xeno and elf thugs. The fey and humans. Seelie Court and the Consortium. They look for any excuse to play their games. I didn't cause anything they wouldn't have found a way to cause themselves."

"And you make a buck in the process," I said.

He nodded. "I always look for the percentage."

I didn't say anything. Despite what macGoren thought, I wasn't naïve. I knew there were people like him, people who single-mindedly pursue a goal and damn the consequences. I knew them. I knew myself. In another life, I was well on the way down that road. I don't know if I would have gone as far as macGoren. The fact that I didn't know, couldn't emphatically deny it, gave me a sour feeling in the pit of my stomach.

"Keeva's been looking for the troll that died. Why didn't you tell her where she was?"

"Because I would have had a lot of things to explain that I wasn't interested in explaining. Keeva's good at what she does. She'll find the troll."

"I know she will," I said.

"So, am I being charged with something?" he asked.

"I'll have to think about it. I know you're only talking because you know I'll have a hard time finding something to stick. For now, I'll keep thinking about it."

A shrewd look came over him. "Hold it over my head, eh? A Guild director for less than a week, and already you're playing games."

I didn't show how much he hit the target with that. "You could say that, macGoren. Remember one thing, though: I don't play by anyone else's rules."

I strode out of the room before he had a chance to respond. As I walked out of the hospital, I felt a dull depression settle over me. Everything that had happened in the past few days could have been avoided if macGoren had just opened his mouth. But he hadn't. Why bother when the only people hurt were the outcast and the shunned? Why bother when it would just make more headlines supporting his development project? Turf, land, territory. The hood. Whatever you called, Eorla Kruge was right. It was all about who had what piece of it and how they used it. It was always about control and power and greed.

I opened the passenger door to Meryl's Mini and let out a roar of rock music. She lowered the volume as I dropped into the seat.

I could tell by the look on her face that Meryl knew I wasn't happy. "Everything all right?"

"Yeah, I just confirmed Ryan macGoren is an ass."

She laughed as she started up the car. "I could have told you that, ya big silly."

I didn't say anything as we pulled back onto the riverside drive. Bone white trees stood guard over the thin strip of park. It was beautiful and empty. I stared and watched it go by.

"So you really met a drys?" Meryl asked, nudging me out of my brooding.

"Yeah, I did," I said. "She was . . . I don't know. Beautiful seems like such a lame word. I could feel the purity of essence in her. It was like the stories they told us when we were kids. She's what we strive to be, Meryl."

She nodded. "I've met a couple a long time ago. I don't think we can ever be that. They're more than human, Grey. We're just flawed vessels for essence. They *are* essence."

"That's why I'm going to the funeral. C-Note's tampering with essence on a fundamental level. He's torturing that drys. If he shows up, we have to get that staff away from him."

She sighed. "He said 'we.'"

A small flush of anger swept over me. "You have a problem with that?"

She shrugged and cut someone off. "No. You just assume I'm jumping on this bandwagon."

Sometimes Meryl's flipness grated on me. "Is anything important to you?"

She frowned. "You know, when people say that, what they really mean is why isn't what's important to me important to you? Yeah, Grey, things are important to me. I hate to break it to you, but I get to decide what those things are."

"That's not what I meant."

She cut the wheel hard to make the off-ramp. "Sure it is. Pick me up here. Get me this. Hide this chick. Help me get out of here. I live by the moon, Grey. That doesn't make me your satellite."

I clenched my jaw and didn't respond. A drys was the female aspect of the oak. As a druidess, she should be the one fired up over what C-Note had done even more than I was. "It's a *drys*, Meryl."

"I know that. That's why I'm driving to the cemetery. But it's my choice, Grey, not yours. I decide for myself whether I help or not. You don't get to judge that. You haven't earned it."

I dropped my head back and closed my eyes. Counted to ten. Shooed arrogant and controlling personality traits back into the closet. Smiled. "You're right. I did it again. I'm sorry."

"Thank you," she said, and pulled into a line of cars waiting to get into the cemetery.

I gave her a big-eyed smile. "That was our first fight."

She rolled her eyes. "No. Our first fight was about five years ago when you forgot to do some research and tried to cover your ass by telling people I lost the request form."

I patted her hand on the stick shift. "No. I meant as a couple."

She turned and looked at me, keeping her face completely blank. "If you don't move your hand, I will gnaw my own off at the wrist."

I did move it. "You will succumb to my charms eventually."

She smirked. "Let me know when you have some."

"I will never have the last word, will I?"

She parked the car and smiled. "Not my style."

18

The street swarmed with activity. A high-profile fey dying, never mind murdered, simply did not happen often. Everyone from street kids to ranking politicos roamed about, checking out the crowd and trying to get in the background of the live-TV camera shots. Meryl and I skirted around the rubberneckers and walked up the driveway to the cemetery.

Forest Hills Cemetery covers almost three hundred acres in the city of Boston. If there's one thing the old Brahmins did well, it was die in style. Fine landscaping, rolling hills, public art, and even a lake with an island. The trust that ran the place even encouraged the public to use the grounds as long as the graves were respected. I liked the attitude of life and death coexisting.

We went through the first security checkpoint at the main gate. I didn't know what Keeva's criteria were for access, but Guild members and guests were all allowed through with no questions. Once inside, the volume of curiosity seekers went down considerably. At a turn off the main path, the Boston P.D. had its own checkpoint for humans. Murdock strolled out from behind a van.

"I have some seats for us," he said as he fell into step with us.

"You're not on duty?" I asked.

He smiled. "I'm always on duty. They're only letting bodyguards into the main site. I said I was yours."

"Who's going to protect you from him?" Meryl asked.

He grinned at her. "I thought that's why you came."

"Don't go there," I said. Meryl jabbed me in the side.

He checked his watch. "Almost dark. The ceremony's going to start soon."

We walked briskly along the tidy lanes as dusk fell. Monuments stared at us with solemn gravity, growing luminous in the fading light. The essence of a cemetery is a strange thing. It's tinged with melancholy, of course, but also an unsettling amount of want and even rage. Not everyone goes gentle into the good night, and they leave a resonance behind them. I couldn't sense individual essence like Joe apparently did. It's more like a stew of emotion, each new voice adding to it, changing it, inflecting it. Ultimately, getting lost in it. Because that's how we end. Lost in the mix.

The mix ramped up as we came around a curve in the path and walked through an essence barrier. Murdock didn't feel it. From our brief passing, I could tell it had a sensory ability, registering the essence of everyone who passed through. Whoever was monitoring the shield must have been puzzled by a high-powered druidess, a human normal who felt fey, and a druid who reeked of troll traveling together.

The path rose between two oaks. With all the members of the Grove wandering through, the trees gave off a low hum, their essence glowing with the Power of the wood. I looked up at a majestic white oak, its many limbs branching and tangling, its thick roots gnarling into the ground, and thought of Hala, trapped in the last living bit of a tree, confined to nothing more than a sliver of a memory.

The crowd thickened over the rise. All manner of fey had come to pay homage to Kruge, a fitting final tribute to a man who had advocated unity. If anything summed up the difference between Seelie Court and the Teutonic Consortium, their approach to death did. Fairies dimmed their wings and walked, eyes downcast, as if acknowledging that even in their immortality, death was always hovering in the shadows. The elves, though, they strode forward, heads up, singing dirges, honoring life and defying death. Brownies and dwarves were not as dramatic as their more powerful cousins, but brought their own drama to the party.

A surprising assortment of solitary fey haunted the edges the crowd. Usually they avoid being noticed, fearing the domination games that go on among them. In the gathering shadows beneath the trees, I could see them furtively moving, their limbs glistening silver or red or green. Most solitaries make people uncomfortable. To human eyes, they resemble the stuff of nightmares, long-snouted faces and horned heads, hairy coats instead of skin or oddly jointed arms and legs that spoke of birds or lizards. Some wore smiles that sent chills and others held such sadness that no comfort could touch. Their eyes glittered in the dark, streaks of red and yellow as they moved among the graves, clawed fingers leaving white lines on tombstones.

Human normals make the mistake of thinking all solitaries are Unseelie, standing in opposition to High Queen Maeve. It's more complicated than just that. The Unseelie Court exists, but it shifted alliances more often than the weather, with solitaries moving in and out as the wind blew. Only when they all stood together did they form a true Court, and when they did, wars broke out. Of all the fey, they enjoyed Convergence most, if only because Seelie and the Consortium were too involved with each other to bother them. Kruge's unity message had to have rung deeply with them.

Torches lined the final path to the burial site, their flames edged in white and blue. Not ordinary fire, but druid-fire. They enhanced the ambient light and gave off a comforting heat as night fell, no small feat on a cool October evening.

People stood to the sides of the lane watching us pass with odd resentment. We shuffled behind others as one by one they passed two druids, one on each side of the path. Beyond them, I sensed an enormous shield barrier, extending up and to either side. Murdock passed through without stopping. As Meryl followed, one of the druids held up a hand. "The High Druid mandates the ladies of the Grove join a reinforcement circle outside the *airbe druad*."

Meryl peered at the man's hand as if it were a dead bird and not one she wanted. She looked back at the druid's face. "Tell Gerin that Meryl Dian said she's no lady."

His mouth dropped in surprise, as she swept by him. "Oh. It let her through. I guess that's okay then," he said.

He eyed me suspiciously as I approached and held up his hand. "I'm sorry. There's something not right about you."

"You don't know the half of it," Meryl called back.

I ignored her and took out my Guild badge. He held it for a moment, testing the essence on it, then looked at me. "You feel right, but have you had any encounters with trolls lately? We're supposed to look for troll essence."

"Yeah, I did. It's hard to get the smell off."

He nodded sagely. "Yes, I've heard that." He handed the badge back. "Don't be surprised if someone else gives you trouble."

"I never am," I said.

The mass in my head spasmed as I moved through the barrier. Essence shields don't usually bother my head. They either let me in or they don't. Curious, I opened my sensing ability and found a web of essence forming an intricate net. From the inside, I could see that it formed an enormous dome laced with druid essence, a sparkling white of lines against the deepening violet sky. It was the largest hedge I'd ever seen.

"That thing has to be covering a hundred acres," I said.

Meryl, of course, could see it, too. "It's huge. Gerin must have dozens of people powering it."

Murdock looked up. "I don't see it. We were told it was like the one druids use on the Grove. No one can get in without permission."

Meryl caught my eye. "Yeah, good luck with that."

We came to a wide shallow bowl ringed with ancient oak trees. Among them, fire pits had been dug and filled with more druid-fire. Down in the center of the clearing, an earthen ramp led into a freshly dug pit. Chairs fanned out like an amphitheater around the grave, most already filled with Consortium and Seelie Court representatives. A small section reserved for state and local human politicians sat near the edge of the field. Murdock led us to seats in an upper row that gave a view of the proceedings.

Down near the pit, Keeva paced. She kept tapping the side of her head in a way that told me she was wearing an earpiece. I could imagine she was sending just as much as listening to the earpiece. She probably had a multitasking nightmare on her hands. Not far from her, Gerin Cuthbern stood in a cluster of druids, but his eyes were more interested in the gathering crowd than anyone near him.

"Anyone see Nigel?" I asked.

"He's at the Guildhouse. He and Gerin were concerned that the entire Guild leadership in one place was a security risk." How Murdock manages to find out these details, I'll never know.

Farther along the section of seats where Gerin stood, I could see several high-level Guild administrators, but not the Guildmaster. "What about Manus?"

Murdock came through again. "Too ill to travel. Gerin's going to do the tribute for the Guild."

Among the human normals, ranking politicians ranged around the state governor and Boston's mayor like moths. A few men who were obviously police out of uniform, but not many. "Why so few Boston P.D.?"

"Will you relax? I've seen the plans. This place is locked down tight." Murdock was a helluva lot more confident than I was.

I cocked an eyebrow at him. "What could possibly go wrong, right?"

He smiled and shook his head.

At full dark, music began playing, a mournful dirge filtering down from beyond the druid-fires, Celtic pipes weaving in and out of the sad strings of dulcimers. People took their seats to watch the royal dignitaries from both sides of the fey world process in a wave of green mourning finery. High Queen Maeve's envoy stepped delicately along the main aisle, a ridiculous fop wearing an ornate brocade tunic over green leathers, his hair and wings fluttering around him like a peacock fan. His melodramatic expression of sorrow was priceless. A long line of courtiers followed him, intently aware of their spectators, as they moved with mincing steps behind the envoy. Next to the envoy, the Elven King's ambassadors strode, a male and a female, both dressed in battle armor painted green. They trooped in formation ahead of a company of archers and infantry. The male ambassador held a broken spear, while the woman walked with an unstrung bow and empty quiver. The two contingents separated as they reached the center of the clearing, winding their way into seats that faced each other across the open grave.

Horns blew and everyone stood. A solemn drumroll began as four elves in dark green livery pulled a cart along the ridge of the bowl. They turned onto the earthen ramp and eased the cart down into the pit. As they came even with us, I could see Kruge's remains, a linen-wrapped form wearing ceremonial battle armor. Someone had had the dubious honor of putting his body back together. His arms were crossed on his chest, and a ceremonial sword lay grasped in his hands, blade down. The cart bristled with weapons, an accumulation of years, part of the ritual burial of a warrior. The liverymen marched out of the pit and stationed themselves at the top of the ramp. More attendants appeared and placed a small wooden bench at the top of the pit ramp.

Eorla Kruge approached from the ridge, resplendent in her widow's weeds, a long tunic coat embedded with small gems that flickered in the light of the druid-fire. She wore a small diadem of gold and a long sheer veil draped over her head, a gossamer net of faint green that trailed across the ground behind her. In her hands, she held another diadem, plain and large. With careful steps she entered the pit, placed the large diadem on Kruge's chest. She removed one of her rings and tucked it into his hands. Everyone watched respectfully as she stood solemnly, her hands on his in final good-bye. She returned up the ramp. When she reached the wooden bench, she turned to face the grave and sat. The drumroll stopped.

A woman cloaked in dark blue stepped up to the opposite side of the pit from Eorla. With no introduction, she began to sing the Teutonic death ritual. Sitting between Murdock and me, Meryl groaned. "Wake me when she's done."

I suppressed a laugh. Teutonic priestesses had put more than one person to sleep with their songs. True to form, this one launched into a mind-numbing aria on life in High Elven German. Meryl squirmed. As the priestess sang, servants brought a vat of mead before her, and she blessed it with her song. The servants ladled the drink and passed the cups into the crowd.

Murdock's hand went to his ear. He leaned across Meryl. "Fighting at the outer perimeter. I have to go."

As Murdock hustled his way out of the aisle, I watched security agents, both elf and fairy, reposition themselves along the ridge. Keeva leaned toward Gerin Cuthbern to speak to him. Gerin rose from his seat, bowed to Eorla, and walked up the ramp.

The ceremony continued uninterrupted. Word of the fighting outside must have filtered through the crowd because I could feel body shields activating around me. The calling of so much essence in such a confined area made my head ache. I could see it, my own body activating my sensing abilities instead of its almost useless body shield. Essence of all colors glowed around me like small lanterns of light.

The mead reached the last row of seating and made its way toward us. Distracted by more security, I took the cup from my neighbor and began to sip.

Meryl's hand came up suddenly and grabbed my arm. "Wait!"

I looked at her curiously, and she took the cup from my hand. She peered inside, consternation on her face as she swirled the dregs. She inhaled and blanched, her body shields coming up so quickly she shuddered.

"It's Float," she hissed under her breath.

As soon as she said it, I caught another wave of essence rolling over the gathering. It tickled into my nose, laden with the spell I had felt at Carnage. I tried to shake my head to clear it, but only felt dizzy. My vision blurred suddenly, then my sensing abilities went into overdrive. All around me, essence crystallized sharply in my vision, a disconcerting overlay of color outlining everything. I could see the spells working in the druid-fires, the glamours that people wore, their innate body essence marking them by strength and species. And marking everyone was a malevolent green essence that matched the glow coming from the vat of mead.

It was just like when I held the drys, her essence boosting my ability to its greatest potential, but twisted by the compulsion spell C-Note had put on it. As essence materialized more distinctly around me, I realized why.

"I can feel the drys. C-Note is here, Meryl."

A collective gasp went up from the crowd. Heads that had been nodding with boredom shot to attention. At the top of the low ridge, C-Note leaned on his black staff. Keeva leaped to her feet before anyone else and moved into the aisle. Brownie and druid security materialized from the crowd and surrounded C-Note in moments. Eorla angrily rose from her seat as Consortium agents closed ranks around her.

"So much for security," Meryl muttered.

C-Note raised his staff. "Look at you, facing each other across the corpse of unity. You speak to unity, but you still plot against each other. Even now, some among you seek revenge for age-old grievances."

Surprised murmurs rippled through the audience as more people got to their feet. Keeva made her way up the ramp toward C-Note. He waved the staff, and she froze in place. Not a good sign. More people stood to watch the confrontation. The Teutonic ambassadors began to push their way up the ramp. Not to be outdone, the Seelie envoy led his own security closer.

"How the hell did he get through," I muttered.

Around us, the druid-fires flickered and smoked. My head buzzed with surging essence. Keeva should have been backing the crowd out. Trolls are tough to move physically, but she didn't even seem to be trying to break the spell on her. A few feet in front of her, the druids and brownies had an essence shield around C-Note, a nice piece of joined spell-working meant to hold him in place, presumably until the bigger guns showed up to cart him off.

C-Note was still talking, but the noise of the spectators drowned him out. Angry, rapt faces surged forward. The Guild security guards should have been down on the ground by now. They responded directly to Keeva via sendings, and she had to be calling them. Instead, they remained hovering along the periphery, white blazes of essence ringed above us. Something wasn't right.

I searched the crowd, but could see nothing other than people boosting their body shields. I paused as my eye slid over a trough of druid-fire near me. I could see the essence that powered it, but behind the normal flame, it seemed to be drawing essence from the trees around us instead of being powered by people. Anger swept over me. That wasn't how you worked a Grove shield. You didn't draw directly from the oak It was an insult to the spirits of the trees to use them for such a utilitarian purpose.

My head ached as I watched lines of essence from the druid-fires crawl across the gravesite. So much essence was in the air, it actually fed into my ability, amplifying it beyond what I normally could sense. The dark mass in my head seemed to ripple in my mind, pushing the bands of Power away from it like it did when I tried to call essence on my own.

Color cascaded in my sight, tangles of light like a multi-colored ball of fraying yarn. I could see links had formed among all the druid-fires around the clearing. The lines entwined, forming a dense spiral of Power that began to funnel down toward Kruge's grave. The spiral pulsed and grew as the heart essence of the oaks fed it. The druid-fires pulsed brighter as they fed more essence into the spiral. A huge pulse rolled along the lines, swirling along the spiral as it tightened into a nexus. Not at the grave. At C-Note's feet. He planted the staff on its very center and a shimmering barrier flowed up to meet the pulse. It was a hedge spell. C-Note was sealing off the entire clearing.

I grabbed Meryl's arm in alarm. This couldn't be good. "Get everybody out! Get them to run! Do it now, Meryl!"

I had to give her credit. Having just slammed me for telling her what to do, Meryl responded with trust. Without hesitation, she shouted a spell that sent a burst of primal fear into the crowd. Terrified without knowing why, people who had been gathering around C-Note suddenly spun away and ran up the slope. The few who didn't run, hardened their body shields in battle mode and reached for weapons.

The pulse reached C-Note. He absorbed the energy into his staff and slammed it on the ground. Bolts of yellow fire shot out and enveloped the brownies and druids around him. In unison, they turned away from him and started firing essence into the crowd. Keeva sailed up into the night sky in a radiant halo of white fire, a look of ecstasy on her face.

As the exchange of fire heated up, I pulled Meryl behind a large burial monument. We could see the whole of the clearing below us as a confusion of people turned on each other with weapons and essence-fire.

The Seelie Court ambassador took a blast of druid-fire full in the chest. Blood sprayed from his back as he soared through the air with the force of the blow. Chairs scattered as his body tumbled roughly through them. When his body finally came to rest, his essence wavered and vanished. At the same moment, the Guild agents above began firing at the Consortium ambassadors.

With a guttural moan, Meryl lurched forward, grabbing her waist. I sank to my knees as pain screamed through my head. Essence ricocheted around me, blinding my vision with red pain. I could feel myself losing consciousness, the pain increasing until I thought my mind would burst under the strain. Just when I thought I couldn't take it anymore, I felt a cool static flow over me, blocking it. I opened my eyes with a relieved gasp, realizing Meryl held my arm, her body shield forming an envelope of protection around the both of us.

Meryl was breathing heavily. "The essence is tainted. I can't touch it without his spell grabbing me."

I lifted my head, shaking off the subsiding pain. I couldn't believe that in the space of a few moments, fighting had broken out in all directions. Essence-fire sparked from their hands and chests as they struggled, groups scattering into the cemetery, taking their fights with them. Shouts and screams surrounded us as essence meant to kill tore through the air.

Down near the grave, bodies lay prone everywhere, with no visible essence emanating from them. Dead. Dozens dead from both Seelie Court and the Consortium. In the center of it all stood C-Note, using his staff to draw more essence from the Power spiral he was creating.

One lone figure remained before him, tall and defiant. Eorla Kruge's torn veil rippled in the wind as she held her head high. She had an enormous body shield around her. "What the hell is she doing?" I started to get up, but Meryl pulled me to the ground.

"I can't protect you down there, Grey. We have to get out of here."

Eorla thrust one hand into the air. "Enough," she commanded.

C-Note peered down at her and grinned. "You're too late. I've lit the spark. I control the flame."

A wave of light spilled from Eorla as she shouted again. The light rolled off her and hit C-Note full on. He staggered back as her essence struck. C-Note held his black staff out, absorbing the blow. The image of an oaken staff flickered into view for a moment before resuming its black appearance. It had done the same thing at Carnage when it flew from my hands to his.

Eorla's eyes blazed with emerald light. "You're no troll."

He laughed with bitter scorn. "Nothing is ever as it appears to be, Eorla."

She drew a ball of essence from the air and threw it at him. It shattered on C-Note, grappling with his body shield. Impressively, it broke through. The level of Power I had sensed in her when we first met was not mistaken. C-Note's body shimmered, became a blur of color, and the glamour he wore slipped away.

Gerin Cuthbern leaned on the oak staff, staring at Eorla with a malevolent white light in his eyes.

19

"If you expect me to be surprised you did that, Eorla, you will be disappointed. I have never underestimated your Power," Gerin said.

She raised a hand glowing green with light. "You killed my husband."

Gerin nodded. "Which is regrettable. He was forcing my hand before I was ready, but his death became quite useful."

Eorla drew her hand up to cast her spell. Gerin smiled. "I killed your husband, Eorla. Nigel and Manus are dead now, too. I will kill you, too, if necessary. You were right about one thing: The fey need to be unified. The only way to do that is take away their Power."

Her hand wavered, whether in fear or consideration, I couldn't tell. "This is madness, Gerin," she said.

"Mad? You mean like Maeve and Donor, locked in their ancient grievances? You mean like you and Manus, bickering over a directorship? You think I am mad? Faerie is gone, Eorla. The old ways are all gone. Seelie Court and the Consortium play word games with each other, while the humans plan to destroy us. Do you not see it coming? To ignore that, *that* is madness."

Eorla did not say anything for a long moment. Incredibly, she dropped her hand. She turned a troubled face to the carnage around her. "You're killing people, Gerin."

He shook his head. "They're killing each other. I'm just pushing them to do what they want." He raised the staff. It glowed with white light. Teutonic runes floated in the essence. "Essence is mine to give or take now. The spell I have created is pulling it all to me. I will only allow those who share my goal to use it."

She turned back to him with a start. "That's not possible. No one has that ability."

"No? Look around you. Tell me it's not possible."

He was right. Essence revolved around him like a vortex, feeding into the staff. He held it with his body like a wild animal on a leash.

She balled her hands into fists. "You are starting a war you can't win."

"You can only fight me with essence, and if you use essence, you will be mine. Your choice is simple: Fade and die or bow to my will."

Eorla turned and looked down into the grave pit.

Gerin leaned forward on the staff. "Stand beside me, Eorla. Together we can remake this world. We can take the Power that the Seelie Court and the Consortium squander. You were born to rule. You know that. Be who you are. Be my queen, Eorla."

Eorla dropped her hand and crossed her arms.

"I don't believe this. She's considering it. Can you do anything, Meryl?" I started to move forward, uncertain how I could convince Eorla she had to resist.

Meryl grabbed my sleeve and held me back. "This is too big for me to handle alone, Grey. Every time I drop my shield to tap more essence, I get nauseated. We need to get help."

Eorla turned back to Gerin. "I cannot."

He smiled. "You will. I will have you by my side."

"I will not do it," she said. She raised her arms.

He shook his head. He thrust the staff forward. A shock of light burst out. Eorla threw out her arms, but she was too late. The light spun around her in a web of white-tinged green. I could feel Hala in that light, the direct Power of her essence binding Eorla with its strands. Living light swirled around her, and she became locked in a cage of essence.

"Watch, Eorla. See my Power. You will change your mind." Gerin smiled and dropped his head back, and the essence of the spiral pulsed into the staff and from the staff to him. A shimmering barrier of white light began to grow around him.

A blast of essence exploded in front of me. Instinctively, I held Meryl to the ground behind the monument, as another bolt landed near us. On the other end of the gravesite, two elves aimed bows loaded with elf-shot at us.

I smiled apologetically down at her. "I'm thinking run."

Meryl batted her eyes at me. "My hero."

Another shot chipped the stone in front of us. I grabbed Meryl's hand, and we dodged between stones to the top of the ridge. The elves kept shooting, but the essence spiral that Gerin had created was warping their aim. We dove through a yew hedge and landed in a circle of small mausoleums.

Meryl pointed vaguely west. "Gate's that way."

We ran among the graves, avoiding the lanes. All around us, we could hear the constant concussion of essence striking and the sounds of screams. Halfway to the gate, Guild security flew overhead. Keeva must have called in more airborne. We stumbled through yet another set of bushes and into the middle of a group of druids and brownies. They spun toward us, eyes glowing with essence, then relaxed when they apparently sensed that we were druid.

Meryl and I backed slowly in the opposite direction.

"Where are you going?" someone called. They all stared at us, waiting for an answer. Meryl and I exchanged looks. She shrugged, and we joined them in the lane. A brownie walked with us, her eyes glowing an unnatural yellow.

"I'm, like, so bad with directions. Is this the way to the gate?" said Meryl in fair imitation of an airhead.

A brownie looked at her with narrowed eyes. "Don't you hear it? He's calling us back."

Meryl scrunched up her shoulders and stuck her fingers in her ears. "An elf hit me in the head. I can't hear a thing."

The brownie stared at her, then spoke to a druid next to her. They glanced at us repeatedly as we followed along behind them.

I poked Meryl in the ribs. "We're trying to blend here."

She wrinkled her nose. "What do you want me to do, a zombie shuffle?"

Elves swept suddenly down the slope to the left. They moved in a fluid unison, chanting great bursts of essence at us. The druids and brownies ran for cover, returning fire. Meryl and I backpedaled and took the opportunity to make for the gate again. We turned a corner, and another group of elves blocked the path. We backed away as they moved forward.

"I hate when this happens," said Meryl.

"Can you take them out?"

She nodded. "But then I'll be worthless until I recover. I only have my own body essence to work with, remember? You'll have to leave me."

I shook my head. "Not an option."

The elves began to work a binding spell.

"I'm going to do it," Meryl said.

"No."

We backed against an oak. Meryl lifted her arms and began to chant. I felt a surge of essence behind me and something grabbed my head. An arm slithered around and grabbed Meryl's face. The oak tree became pliant, its bark slipping roughly over us as something yanked us inside it. My vision went gray. I felt dizzy with a strange twisting in my stomach and head. Then I was coughing on the cold ground beside Meryl. Off in the distance, I could hear fighting. We were in another part of the cemetery.

I got to my feet and helped Meryl up.

"We're dying," a voice said.

I turned to face the oak tree. Molded into the surface of the bark was a small woman, pale ivory skin, long silvery hair covering most of her nude body. "Hala?"

She ignored me, looking at Meryl instead. "I do not have much time. The druid is distracted. He strikes at the heart of the oak. He devours my sisters. We have nowhere to hide, little one. You are called."

"What do you want me to do?" Meryl asked.

"You are the only pure vessel left. We call on you for help," said Hala.

"What are you talking about?" I asked.

Meryl waved me off. "Shhh. This is girl talk." She turned back to the oak. "I'm only one person."

"You are strong. Remember your vow," Hala said in that same matter-of-fact tone she had used with me back at Carnage. It's hard to resist, even if she isn't pushing a little essence on you when she does it.

Meryl stared down at the ground.

"Meryl? What is she talking about?"

She looked at me, her face set grimly. "Looks like I'm it." Her eyes were haunted, resigned as someone on death row. It was a look I'd seen a few times, one I didn't like seeing on someone who was beginning to mean something to me.

I grabbed her shoulders, a little afraid of what she was saying. "What do you mean?"

She shrugged out of my hands and stepped away from me. "Get out, Grey. Find someone who can help."

"Dammit, Meryl, you're freaking me out. What are you going to do?"

She looked at me, still resolved, but with a touch of fear in her eyes. "I have a duty. I need to save the drys." She looked off toward the glow of Kruge's grave, and her voice became low. "Whatever's left of them."

I stepped closer to her again. "How?"

She held up her hands and backed away shaking her head. "No time, Grey. You can't do this with me."

"Meryl, talk to me! I don't like the sound of whatever it is you're about to do," I said.

She bowed her head, then looked at me. "Stay safe," she said. With a blinding flash of essence, she dove at the oak tree.

"Meryl! No!" I reached after her, but she was too fast. Black spots danced in front of my eyes, and she was gone. Hala had vanished, too. Desperate, I spun in place, but they were nowhere to be seen. Meryl had disappeared into the oak.

I pounded on the tree. "Meryl!"

This sound came out of me, a strangled outburst of frustration. She didn't answer. I had no idea what she had just done, but it scared me somehow.

The sensation of a new essence nearby brought me back to the immediate situation. My skin prickled as something moved in the darkness around me. *"Alone,"* it whispered. Dim yellow eyes gleamed around me. Another whisper, sibilant and menacing. *"Taste."* I turned again. More eyes. Something darted out of the shadows, small and dark. It snapped at my hand and fled back. A dark shape dropped out of the tree from above me. It clung to my back and clawed at my head. I threw myself to the ground and rolled. It screeched and jumped away. Taller figures moved forward. Solitaries. Dozens of them gathered around me.

"Bright, bright." A raspy chant.

I crouched, placing my hand on the ground. I could feel a wrongness there, felt the effect Gerin was having on essence. Even if I wanted to fight the pain of drawing it, he would have me. I slipped my dagger out of my boot. It burned in my hand with an almost unbearable heat. I tried to imagine it growing, lengthening into a sword. I had seen it do that once, but I didn't know how to make it happen. Even as a dagger, though, it was still a blade with a sharp edge. I launched myself off the ground, slashing at the nearest solitary, a tall bark-skinned thing with sharp teeth. It howled in pain, and I knocked it back. I charged forward, small hairy-faced figures scrambling out of my way. I ran.

A howl went up. The sound of bare feet slapping pavement and tearing at the earth followed me. My heart pounded as I ran. I leaped over tombstones, the wild shouts of the solitaries filling the air.

"Run! Run!" a high-pitched voice taunted.

I ran like hell. Some came right beside me, strange brittle fingers pinching and poking, then falling back with laughter. Adrenaline surged through me as I dodged among the sleeping dead. I began to pull ahead of them, but they kept coming, screaming and laughing behind me. I came out of a line of trees to a wide lake. I knew where I was now, the center of the cemetery. As I pounded along the path, more solitaries joined the pursuit, forcing me away from the path to the gate. Herding me back to Gerin.

A spiraling tower of essence glowed ahead, marking Kruge's gravesite like a beacon. I topped the hill and kept running down into the bowl. Still trapped in the chrysalis of essence, Eorla stood transfixed before Gerin. In the midst of the white tower of light, Gerin held his staff, its base planted firmly in the spiral of essence, drawing more and more power into himself. A drys revolved around him screaming. She spun faster and faster, funneling in toward Gerin. In a last surge of speed, the staff sucked her in. Another drys came sailing out of the trees, screaming as the essence spiral caught her in its vortex.

The shouts of the solitaries became louder, and I spun back toward the slope. They had reached the crest of the ridge, poised to descend on me, when the entire horde hesitated. They seemed confused. I could feel something coming with them, something huge. And it felt angry. A blaze of crimson essence seeped into the sky. The solitaries backed away from it, as the essence built behind them. They turned and swept down the slope toward me, madness in their eyes.

A cold feeling gripped my gut. I couldn't hold them off, not all of them. I brought the dagger up as the first of them reached me. If I was going to be trampled, I was taking a few of them with me. I slashed at the first of them, just as a chilling scream rent the air. A spiderlike solitary spun limply through the air as a blaze of blood red essence crested the hill. Then another solitary went flying, and another, tossed like leaves in the wind. The horde became a tangled knot of panic as they chittered and screamed, scattering from the gravesite. As the path up the slope cleared, my jaw dropped in disbelief.

Murdock strode toward me in an enormous cloud of crimson essence, the strength of it blotting everything around him. By some trick of the light, the essence amplified his size, and his skin literally rippled with Power. His eyes glowed with a feral glow as he closed in on me, glaring like he didn't know me. He stopped abruptly, his breath ragged. Recognition slowly came into his face, and he smiled. "I thought I'd find you in the middle of everything."

Amazed, it took a moment for me to speak. "What the hell happened to you, Murdock?"

He just shook his head. "I brought an old friend of yours."

Nigel Martin stepped from behind him, strolling out of Murdock's essence as if he were just coming back from a walk.

Relief swept over me. "Nigel! Gerin said you were dead."

Nigel tilted his head at me as if I had just explained the obvious. "I think it should come as no surprise to you today that Gerin is wrong about many things." Typical Nigel. He stepped around me and approached Eorla. I could see the power of a spell wind out of his hands as he held them up to the essence surrounding Eorla. He nodded. Turning to Murdock, he reached out a hand. "You seem to have clean essence in abundance, Detective. May I?"

Murdock shrugged and held out his hand. Nigel gripped it

hard, then plunged his free hand into the cocoon surrounding Eorla. He convulsed with the shock of contact. Murdock gasped as essence flowed down his arm. Nigel pushed the stream of essence into Eorla. The illusion of Murdock's massive frame slowly shrank until he was the man I knew. The cocoon around Eorla flared brightly and went out.

Dazed, she swayed on her feet. Nigel held her arm to steady her. She shivered violently and looked up with clear eyes. "You live," she said, her voice soft but not surprised.

"As do you, Eorla," he said.

She gazed up at the towering cone of light. Still holding her arm, Nigel guided her forward as though leading her onto a dance floor. As they neared the light hiding Gerin, Nigel spoke intently into Eorla's ear. She shook her head once. He kept speaking. She looked him in the face then, her eyes glittering. At last, she nodded and faced Gerin.

Nigel looked back at me and smiled. "Learn to heal yourself, Connor. If this doesn't work, the world will need all the help it can find."

He clasped Eorla's hand. The air shimmered in front of them as they approached. Eorla began to sing as Nigel held out his hand. They glowed with essence and stepped through the shimmering air. For a moment, we could see the three of them. Then a flare pulsed outward, wrapping them in a dome of white light.

"Connor, I think we have another problem," Murdock said quietly.

I looked up. Several hundred fey ranged around the ridge of the bowl. To one side, elves waited in chant phalanxes, wedges focusing power to the point. Their bows were drawn with the green blaze of elf-shot. Druids and brownies spanned the opposite ridge, essence blazing yellow and white in their eyes, Danann fairies in Guild security uniforms hovering above them. In a mixture of confused alliance, solitaries scattered throughout both sides. High overhead, Keeva hovered, her red hair and wings flaming against the night sky.

I nodded in agreement at Murdock's mastery of understatement. "We're fucked."

The green trail of a single elf-bolt streamed overhead. All hell broke loose. I grabbed Murdock's arm and threw us into Kruge's grave. We landed hard beside the cart as a storm of essence raged over our heads. Murdock rolled to his feet and drew his gun. I reached into the cart and lifted a longsword from Kruge's cache.

"How many bullets do you have?" I asked.

Murdock glanced down at his gun. "Fifteen."

I smiled. "Good. For a moment there, I thought we were in trouble."

He chuckled under his breath, keeping his eye on the battle. I took up position with my back to him. Murdock's essence might be spiking like crazy, but he had no true ability. Neither did I. The only defense I could think of was not to get noticed.

That plan lasted five minutes before an elf jumped down in the pit. I don't think we were his target. He seemed genuinely surprised to see us. Before he had a chance to move, I hit him hard in the face with the sword pommel, stepping back with the blade pointed at his throat. He fell dazed against the side of the pit.

"We have no quarrel, but I will kill you before you breathe a word," I said. It was a gamble. The elf probably could sense I was a druid, but he had no way of knowing I had no ability. I tried to look so confident I could take him with the sword that I didn't even need to bother with essence. With the back of his hand, he wiped the blood from his nose. Without a word, he flipped himself backward out of the pit.

"I believed you," said Murdock.

"I wasn't bluffing," I said. I would have killed him. It's what you do when you have no other option.

War cries and death screams filled the air. High above, Guild security agents kept firing at the Consortium side of the fight. Gerin must have been working on Keeva a long time for her to go along with this.

Something dark fluttered overheard, then dove at us screeching. Murdock reacted instantly and fired his gun. The bullet tore through a leathery wing, and the thing pinwheeled away.

"Nice restraint," I said.

"I was trying to kill it," he said without taking his eyes away from the sky.

Pink light flashed between us. Murdock aimed his gun at it, and I swung my sword up. A shocked Joe blanched and held up his hands. "Whoa! I brought help!"

"Sorry, Joe. Things are a little touchy," I said.

Murdock turned back to the fight. "It's your brother," he said.

"Are you kidding me?" I peered over the edge of the grave. Trying to cut a path at the top of the bowl, Callin fought like a man possessed. A second after I saw him, I felt a new welling of essence behind him, wild and unrestrained. The Cluries poured out of the trees, manipulating the warped essence around them. The Clure himself stood back-to-back with Cal, a ridiculous smile on his face.

"Not bad," said Murdock.

"They're in their element in this mess," I said. As chaos-casters, they knew how to use the unpredictable. It's why they function so well when they're drunk.

Guild agents swept down at them, shooting streaks of essence that bounced wildly in all directions. They didn't touch the Cluries, but it kept them pinned at the tree line. As Keeva moved into view overhead, the guards increased their attacks.

"Joe, Keeva's controlling the guards. Can you take her out?" I asked.

He looked up at her and sighed. "Oh, great, she already doesn't like me."

I looked at him from under my brow. "Joe, please."

He pulled his sword and winked out. A moment later, I saw a flash of pink near Keeva. She shot a bolt of white lightning at him. He vanished and reappeared behind her, hitting her with a blast from his sword. As she turned to face him, he vanished again, repeating his attack strategy over and over. The Guild security guards hovered in confusion as she focused her attention on Joe. He vanished again, longer this time, as Keeva whirled in place looking for him. It would have been amusing under different circumstance. A brilliant flash of pink appeared above Keeva. Joe dove with his sword point down and plunged it into her head. I felt the blow in my stomach.

Keeva tumbled senselessly through the air as Guards raced up. They caught her before she hit and rushed away with her body. Joe popped in next to me.

He reappeared right in my face. "She said hi."

"Dammit, Joe, I think you killed her," I snapped.

"Oh, calm down. I didn't use the blade. I gave her a head shock. She'll wake up in a week or two," he said.

It worked, though. Without Keeva, the Guild agents seemed to come to their senses. They moved up higher and began deflecting essence instead of firing it. It wasn't enough, though. The agents and the Cluries were too outnumbered to stand their ground against everyone else.

The malignant green veining of Gerin's spell contaminated the essence around me, radiating from the dome. It infected everything—the ground, the trees, and each and every fighter. Gerin hadn't lied. No one could tap essence without becoming thrall to his spell.

A deep rumbling built around us as the ground vibrated.

"Now what," I muttered.

The trees shook in a frenzy as a gale wind came up. The tremor increased. Dirt cascaded into the pit as Murdock and I scrambled up the ramp. Trees toppled as the earth heaved upward. The fighting slowed as people felt the effects. The shaking became more severe, and I lost my balance. I grabbed at a tombstone to steady myself. My sensing ability kicked in as a wave of essence flowed over me. A misty halo rose above the ridge, pure essence flickering in a viridian arc across the sky. I could hear a voice raised in song, chanting words I didn't recognize, a deep language resonant with the Power of the wild oak

The light above the ridge grew brighter and a spray of rock and earth shot into the air as more trees fell. Everything stopped. The wind. The tremoring. Everything but the song of Power. Dust hung in the eerie gray light, outlining a diminutive shape.

On an upthrusting of bedrock, Meryl glowed with preternatural light. My chest ached at the sight of her, her face taut, her eyes roiling with light. She was still alive. I couldn't believe how beautiful she looked. And terrifying.

A silence fell, a thick heavy pause as though for breath, while the light around Meryl grew even brighter. She threw back her head and screamed. Wind roared as essence cycloned out of her, tearing up everything in its path. A thick, rushing wave of it tore through the fighters, knocking them away like specks of insignificance.

Bolts of essence leaped from her hands, raking across the ground, while above her it fanned into a blaze of flaming emerald. With methodical precision, the lines of Power sought out the taint from Gerin's spell. Incandescent flashes burst out everywhere as Meryl's attack burned through the green veining. It gave way before her, retreating into the glowing dome of light. And then she stopped, her voice cutting off abruptly.

In the unnerving quiet of the aftermath, Meryl stood alone facing us from the top of the slope, a fierce white light still glowing in her eyes. My chest ached with astonishment at what she had done. Wherever her essence wave touched, it purged Gerin's spell until the entire clearing was devoid of his Power.

As I got to my feet, the sword felt awkward in my hand. Granite from the tombstone had flowed over my skin. I could see the troll residue clearly now, an azure haze over my body. With pain stabbing in my head, I forced my essence to push the stone off me. It crumbled into dust.

Murdock stood next to me, his gun clenched in his hand, breathing heavily. He didn't say a word but nodded at me.

Behind us, the dome rumbled and groaned. In a tumult of color, it expanded with a deep shudder. A wave of dizziness came over me as I felt a pull at my chest. Essence flowed under my feet like the undertow of surf. It streamed into the dome, leaving nothing but dead earth behind it. Truly dead, without a spark of life or essence in it. The dome pulsed and bulged, lightning crackling on its surface. We backed up the slope away from it.

"A harrowing," Joe said, his voice thick with horror.

I didn't realize he was still with us. He hovered behind me, his face white with fear. For a moment, I thought a trick of the light made him appear transparent. Then I realized it was no trick. Joe was fading.

"Get out, Joe. Get out before it kills you!" I shouted. He brought his hands in front of his face. I could see through them, saw his eyes widen. The dome was pulling his essence out of him, sucking up his life force with frightening speed. Without another word, he winked out.

Essence coursed past us in ribbons of color. Murdock and I backed away as the dome ground closer. A new wind came up, and we pressed against it to the top of the ridge. Meryl stood alone now, still glowing with enormous Power. Everyone else had fled.

"What the hell is a harrowing?" he asked.

"An essence storm." It was Meryl's voice, but unlike the way I had ever heard her. She had came down from the spire of rock and stood next to us. "It sucks up everything in its path. I've never heard of one getting this big. I could only force back Gerin's spell, but he's unleashed more Power than I can stop. It's over. We've lost."

Before I could say anything to her, Murdock gasped and staggered away from me. He grabbed his chest and crumpled to the ground. I crouched by him. He was unconscious, his essence caught in the flow of the harrowing. It leached off him in rivulets, merging with the streams rushing down into the dome.

Meryl looked over at us, her face uncomfortably calm with the power of the drys still within her. "Lay him on stone. It will protect him for a brief time." As quickly as I could, I dragged Murdock past her and lifted him onto the stone vault of an exposed grave. Above the vault, its monument read AS THE BONES OF MAN JOIN THE BONES OF EARTH, THE CIRCLE IS COMPLETE.

I hoped Murdock wouldn't take it as a bad omen when he woke up. If he woke up. Standing on the granite soothed the pain in my head. My own essence was trying to release, but the mass in my head kept it in check. For once I was grateful for it.

I looked over my shoulder to Meryl, who was facing away from me. "Are you okay, Meryl?"

She didn't look at me. When she spoke, she sounded almost like herself again, only with a note of despair that tore at me. "I tried to save the drys, Grey, but we'll never get out of here in time. There's no anchor to the harrowing. It's out of control."

"The drys are inside you, aren't they? That's what Hala meant by vessel."

She just nodded, staring into the dome. Except for the dome, darkness surrounded us. From my vantage point, I could see off into the cemetery toward the city, everything dead and devoid of essence. The darkness spread as I watched, an ugly black stain moving faster and faster as more essence drained into the harrowing.

A discharge went off like thunder. The dome moved closer, covering several acres now. It pulled at my essence, but the mass of darkness in my head resisted, not letting any leave my body. Just like it did when I tried to use essence, it resisted and pulled it back. I started to laugh. I'd been wishing the darkness in my head would go away, and now it was the one thing saving what little ability I had left.

"It's going to explode. I can feel it," Meryl said.

We didn't speak, watching it all end. A cold sensation came up my legs. The granite from the tomb was trying to bond with the troll essence on me. Standing next to Meryl was enhancing it. I shook the stone off. As I did, I felt the pull of the harrowing even more strongly. The granite flowed up again. I was about to shake it off, but paused as my eye caught the epitaph again.

I looked down at it for a long moment, then back at the glowing heart of the dome. Stone acted as an anchor for essence. It's what made ward stones do what they do. The thing in my head resisted the dome. It fought the pull of the harrowing.

I looked at the epitaph again and thought of Virgil's cryptic comments about bones and circles. "Dammit, Virgil, I hope like hell you didn't mean hide inside a tomb," I muttered under my breath.

I stopped fighting against the troll essence. The remains of Moke's spell still clung to me. All the ambient essence seemed to have stabilized it instead of letting it dissipate like Moke said it would. As soon as I relaxed my body shield, the spell began to bond with my body essence. It catalyzed the spell even more, drawing the stone around me like it had done at Carnage. The granite softened under my feet, then flowed like water, sliding over my body. It ran up my legs, spreading up my back. I shuddered at the cold sensation of stone oozing around my chest, encasing my torso, seeping over my groin. Tendrils crept up my neck, curled over the back of my head and down over my face. I could feel it even in my eyes. I held my hands up as the last of my skin vanished beneath the stone.

I was completely encased now. "Meryl?"

She looked back at me and gaped, the color draining from her face. "What the hell have you done, Grey?"

"I think I can stop it," I said.

She made as if to touch my arm but then drew her hand back. "How?"

I smiled, feeling the oddness of the stone forming the familiar expression. "Turn myself into a living ward stone. I'm going to try and anchor it."

She looked doubtful. "It'll suck the essence out of you before you even reach the barrier. You saw what was happening to Joe."

I shrugged. "I have to try. We're going to die anyway. You can give me some breathing space, though. Charge me with everything you've got."

Her face set with resistance. "That could kill you."

I shook my head. "I'm hoping not. Not with this thing inside my head. It won't let me tap my own essence, but it's not bothering with the troll essence. I just need a boost to get me through the barrier."

Anguish crossed her face as she tried to decide. At least she had an advantage over me when she took the drys inside herself. She probably knew it wouldn't kill her. We both knew we had no idea whether my idea would work.

"I'm asking, Meryl. You don't have to do it. Either way, I'm going," I said.

She breathed heavily as she held back emotion. Tears welled up in her eyes. "Damn the Wheel," she said, her voice sharp with a bitterness that surprised me.

The Power of the oak surged within her, and her eyes turned a pure white. Stepping up to me, she pulled my head down to her face. Instead of letting her essence flow through her hands, she pressed her lips against mine, holding me tightly. I wrapped my arms around her as essence flooded over me. The Power of the drys rushed into me, my body humming as the granite absorbed it. Still Meryl held on, refusing to end the kiss. At last, she slumped against my chest unconscious. I caught her in my arms and lowered her gently next to Murdock.

The dome trembled closer. I debated whether to wait, but decided the inevitable was inevitable. I felt the harrowing pull at me while the mass in my head pulled in the opposite direction. I took a deep breath and stepped up to the dome.

The essence from Meryl's charge clawed at it with razor shards of lightning. The last of the drys essence tore a jagged opening in the barrier. I stepped into the light.

Everything

went

white

20

White.

Sound stopped. The howling wind. The groaning oaks. Gone.

Whiteness filled my vision. I paused for several long moments, but nothing changed. The white remained, all encompassing. I looked behind me expecting to see Meryl and Murdock lying like the dead on the tomb, but I saw only more white.

Above me. Around me. Below. White simply was. A mass of dense essence that emanated purity. I had the impression of solid ground beneath me, yet my feet did not rest on anything. With nothing to orient myself in the space, a sensation of weightlessness made me dizzy.

The essence had a current. I could feel it flowing around me but not through me. The stone protected me. The thing in my head held me together. Radiant waves streamed over me with a magnetic-like pull. It all flowed in the same direction, and I followed. I put one foot in front of the other but could not perceive any forward motion. I began to doubt I was even moving. The more I walked, nothing changed, but I pushed forward anyway.

A humming pricked at my ears, a low bass tone. Once I noticed it, I realized I had been hearing it for some time, growing louder, vibrating in my chest. In my groin. In my head. It came from the direction the essence was flowing.

A core of white light, whiter against the white, towered ahead. I couldn't tell if I were seeing it with my eyes or sensing it with my druidic ability. The dark mass in my head shifted, a literal, physical movement of wrenching pain worse than anything I had ever experienced.

I hunched forward, nausea ripping through my gut. A shock of white essence burst from my eyes, a sensation I hadn't had in a long, long time. It hurt. It felt good. But it wasn't me. I didn't do it, and I had no control over it. It was just the thing in my head, adjusting to wherever I was, releasing essence like a pressure valve as it realigned itself in my head. The mass clenched again, and the essence stopped flowing out of me.

I staggered in confusion as a darkness flickered across my mind, like a lid had come down and shut out all thought, then lifted off again. Like a blink inside my head.

I looked around. Everything was white. Something tugged at my memory. I had been here before. I remember being angry and running and falling into a bright white light of essence. I turned slowly in place, trying to remember why, trying to remember what this place was.

My mind blinked again.

I jerked my head up, feeling like I had passed out. People surrounded me, staring at me. Some I recognized, and some I didn't. Their faces held a multitude of expressions—fear and horror and sadness. Then the screams began.

My mind blinked.

Everything around me was white. I lay on my back staring into a nothingness of white. I was here again. This place. Above me, I could see two vast shadow shapes. Powerful shapes speaking with words I couldn't understand. They moved closer.

My mind blinked.
My mind blinked.
My mind blinked.

I didn't know where I was. Everything around me was white. Facing me, a core of white essence burned like a star. I moved toward it. Near its base, the white seemed—darker—not as brilliant. I kept moving toward it. The darker white faded to gray, then the first hints of color. The color began to resolve into three figures standing around the column. I remembered them. I remembered why I walked here. I remembered who these people were.

Nigel, Eorla, and Gerin faced each other in a loose circle. They all reached toward the center, gripping Gerin's staff of oak. None of them moved. I could see their faces now, their expressions frozen in a rictus of agony, their eyes white in their sockets. Gerin held the staff with both hands, his head thrown back. White essence smoked from his eyes and open mouth.

The staff hummed with power. Teutonic runes spiraled around it, incandescent green glows against the shining white essence of the wood. I could feel the drys trapped inside it. I could feel Hala there. She had hidden in Meryl and then me. Then I used her to break through the dome. The spell had pulled her back in. More drys were with her. I could feel them, too, their Power caught in Gerin's spell. I could feel Nigel and Eorla, their focus on the staff, forcing themselves against what was left of Gerin's mind. They had come close, pushing his will back, stopping his control. They had achieved only a kind of equilibrium. But they had only stopped Gerin, not the spell. I could feel nothing from the High Druid. He had lost control of the spell and had lost the fight with Nigel and Eorla. His mind had dissipated. He had lost his mind. Literally. Into the white.

I saw what Nigel and Eorla had tried. They had joined their essences, joined their knowledge, into a counterspell. They had wrenched control away from Gerin but did not gain it for themselves. Like Gerin, they could not both fight their adversary and the spell. In achieving the stalemate, the spell had broken loose, guideless, mindless. They did not have the Power to contain the essence and reverse its course. I could feel the spell's hunger, a massive maw sucking in essence. Running free, it had no equilibrium to achieve, nothing to anchor or contain it. It would just continue to feed itself, devouring more and more essence until it exploded, exploding with an energy never seen before, obliterating everything in its path. Maybe never stopping. Maybe exploding forever. Maybe.

I looked down at my hands. They were stone, sheathed in granite. I remembered this happening, remembered doing this to myself. I looked up at the essence running free. It had no anchor. I remembered someone saying something about an anchor. Something about a harrowing needing an anchor. Something to ground its energies and interrupt the spell. Stone. It needed a ward stone. I remembered why I had come here. I reached out my hand.

My mind blinked.

I was surrounded by white. One moment I was running, and the next there was white. I turned. Bergin Vize had been standing behind me, a look of fevered hope on his face. His youth surprised me, his almost black hair worn long for an elf, fanning out as though filled with static. I had thought him older. He held his hands out in front him about a foot apart. A gold ring hovered between them, pulsing with essence, revolving around a shaft of light.

Vize's eyes locked with me, and he smiled. "One door opens; another closes," he said.

I reached for the ring.

My mind blinked.

My hand was extended toward the staff. My hand wore stone. My body wore it. Like a ward stone. I was a living ward stone. The dark mass in my head held me back for a moment. But only a moment. Pain cut through my mind as I reached forward and closed my hand around the staff. A hot, searing jolt coursed through me. I screamed as the thing in my head tore open and

everything

went

white

21

The odor of scorched earth tickled my nose. I opened my eyes and stared at the night sky. The air felt cool on my skin, but the ground felt warm. Pinprick sensations danced all over my body. I sat up slowly, every muscle aching.

A crater surrounded me, charred and deep. Nigel and Eorla lay nearby, still and pale. I winced as I opened my senses. Their essences glowed feebly. They were alive, but barely. I pulled myself painfully to my feet, staring around me in confusion.

At the center of the crater stretched a blackened body. I breathed through my mouth to avoid the rank odor of burnt flesh as I stood over the corpse. Gerin Cuthbern was unrecognizable, but I knew it was him. Even in death, he clutched the oaken staff in his gnarled hands. Ash shivered and flaked off the staff in the light breeze. No essence emanated from it. Without the last vestige of her tree, Hala had dissipated—died, I guess. The realization made me ache inside, knowing that I had come so close to something so sacred. I touched the staff, and it crumbled away from my fingers. After everything that had happened, that made a lump form in my throat.

"That was a fine party," someone said.

I turned to see the Clure sitting on the edge of the crater, his feet planted in the dirt, elbows propped on his knees. He toasted me with a flask and took a deep drink. Someone was lying next to him and, as I mounted the slope, I realized it was my brother. He looked beaten and worn. But he lived. I could see he lived.

"Is he all right?" I asked when I reached the rim.

The Clure looked down as if surprised to see someone lying next to him. He patted Cal on the chest. "Cal? He's just fine. More knocks to the head than usual, is all." He held out the flask. "You look like you could use a drink."

I took a slug. Smooth, amber whiskey. I smiled. "How'd you know I like Jameson's?"

The Clure looked at me in shock. "People don't?"

I laughed as I looked around me. Kruge's gravesite was gone, replaced by the crater. Dark lines of char spiraled down to the center where Gerin lay. Guild security agents flew over and down to Nigel and Eorla. Across the way, I could see two bodies lying on a grave.

"Tell Cal I said 'thank you,' Clure," I said.

"Will do." He nodded, sipping from the flask.

I made my way around the crater as more security descended to help. By their essence, I knew the bodies were Meryl and Murdock before I reached them. They lay side by side as if asleep. Alive, though. Thankfully alive. Relieved, I eased myself down beside Meryl and watched as Nigel and Eorla were flown out of the pit on litters.

Meryl sat up. She rubbed her face, looking down at Murdock first, then over at me.

I held my hand out to her. "Are you all right?"

She nodded groggily as she took my hand and swung her feet around to sit next to me. "Yeah. I was just trying to remember the last time I woke up in a graveyard with two guys."

"What happened?" I asked.

Disbelief etched itself across her face. "You don't know?"

I cocked my head sideways to try to read her face better. "Did I do something?"

Confused emotions played across her face, as she searched for an answer. "Uh, yeah, you did."

I looked down at Gerin. "The last thing I remember is you showing up."

If possible, her eyebrows rose higher. "That's it?"

"That's it."

She gave me a strange look. "You don't remember anything after I stopped the fighting?"

I shook my head. A sick, frustrated feeling crawled into my chest. How was I going to deal with the frustration of not remembering again? "Dammit, Meryl, why can't I remember?"

Meryl gave my arm a squeeze. "Don't worry about it now. You will."

"What if I don't?"

She looked up at me with a small smile. "Then we'll never know why you're bald."

I ran my hand over my head and discovered why the air felt so cold. Smooth skin met my touch. Even my eyebrows had vanished. I pursed my lips. "I guess I missed more than a few things."

Meryl hopped off the vault. She stooped and picked up something. Her face became still, then stricken. She turned away abruptly, and I realized she was crying. I slid off the vault and wrapped my arms around her. She actually let me. I kissed the top of her head. "What is it?" I asked.

She leaned her head against my chest. "I couldn't save the drys. I made a choice, and they died because of it."

I knew Hala was gone, but now I realized that I only felt Meryl's own essence inside her, not all the drys she had held within when she purged Gerin's spell. I didn't know how many there had been. I couldn't even begin to fathom the loss. "What choice?" I said.

She wiped her nose with the sleeve. "It doesn't matter. It had to be done."

She held her hand out to show me a small silvered acorn resting in her palm. "Seed of an oak."

"The promise of the Grove," I added. Even without touching it, I could feel that spark of essence within it, the potential for new life.

Meryl let it fall from her hand into the crater. It rolled down into the barren remains of what had happened there, a hope awaiting the right moment to become something more. We didn't say anything for the longest time.

Meryl looked up at me. "Want a lift?"

I grinned. "I didn't want to ask."

We wound our way through the gathering police and Guild agents and slipped in among the trees. As we walked into the silence of the graveyard, Meryl slipped her arm through mine. "Just so you know, Connor, this date totally kicked ass."

"Not a date," I said. She jabbed me in the ribs.

As I dozed listening to the steady rhythm of the heart monitor, I scratched my head for the umpteenth time. A week's worth of growth made a good stubble, but it itched like hell under a knit cap. At least I had some eyebrows back.

"Where's Ryan?"

I lifted my head and smiled. "He'll be here soon. I told him I would wait."

Keeva looked at me from her hospital bed, eyes dim, face pale. "Gerin?"

"Dead."

"Good," she said. She pushed herself up into a sitting position. "How long have I been out?"

"About a week. You took a nasty hit to the head," I said. Joe had made me promise not to stell her. He hated when someone didn't like him.

"I can't believe what I did," she said.

I stretched in the chair. "You weren't yourself. Gerin was apparently poisoning you for weeks. We found Float all over your office."

She stared at the ceiling. "This puts the Guild in a shambles, which probably makes you happy."

"Don't blame me. I just pointed out the cracks. You guys didn't bother to fill them," I said.

"How's Manus?" she asked.

"Fine. His house was attacked, but they managed to fight it off." I was glad Tibbet considered me a friend. I had never seen her go boggart. The reports I had read said it was not pretty when she was done.

"Nigel?" Keeva asked.

I nodded. "Recovering."

"You're awake," Ryan macGoren said as he came through the door with the kind of flower bouquet hotel lobbies used. He set it on the nightstand and leaned down to kiss Keeva. She smiled up at him. I considered how frightening it was that the two of them had found each other.

I stood. "I'm going to go. Get better, Keeva. You've got a Guild to rebuild."

Keeva sighed, then grimaced at some pain. "Thanks."

I paused at the door. "Oh, and macGoren? Call the Office of the City Medical Examiner and speak to Janey Likesmith. Donate any equipment she asks for."

He arched an eyebrow. "Is that my penance for being bad?"

I smiled as coldly as I knew how. "It's just a start."

I found Nigel's room two flights up. He lay in a stone crèche that was highly charged with essence. He smiled when he saw me. "I wondered if you'd stop in."

"Thought I'd return the favor." I couldn't resist the dig.

He nodded, the smile slipping. "I deserved that, I guess. Gillen Yor tells me you remember nothing."

"Again," I said. I leaned against the wall just outside the field generated by the crèche.

He nodded. "Bad habit, that."

"What about you?" I asked.

"I remember Eorla and me entering the field of Gerin's spell. He was already lost. Eorla and I stabilized it, but we couldn't control it."

"How did you convince Eorla to help?"

He rubbed the edge of the sheet that lay across him. "I appealed to her nature and her desire. Eorla and I have the same goals. We're just on opposite sides of the debate," he said.

I frowned. "In other words, you made a deal."

He quirked his lips with a cagey smile. "Compromise, Connor. That's how we get things done."

I didn't want to get into that particular conversation. "You'll need all the compromising you can get. Gerin set back Seelie/Consortium relations fifty years."

Nigel nodded. "Maybe not a bad thing. The Consortium needed a slap down."

"So did the Guild," I said.

It was his turn to frown. "I wish you wouldn't take what happened between you and the Guild so personally, Connor. It's shortsighted."

I laughed. "Really? You guys didn't seem to be very long-viewed when you were attacking each other."

"There are matters of weight you know nothing about, Connor. Truly important matters that are more than just one man's problem." He used that superior tone he has when he's lecturing the ignorant. I'd heard it often during my training. It didn't intimidate me anymore.

Exasperated, I shook my head. "I've been thinking about what to say to you for a week, Nigel. Sometimes I thought I'd let it go, and sometimes I thought I was being petty. But you know what? I can't let it go.

"Look at you. And the Guild. And the Consortium. Some of the most powerful fey in the world, who think they know better than anyone else, and one man was able to bring it all crashing down."

I ticked off the list with my hands. "Gerin knew just how

to manipulate each and every one of you. He waited until Briallen was away because he knew she would have sensed the drys in his staff. He turned Keeva into the good soldier because he knew her ambitions. He played Manus's fear of competition to distract him. And you, Nigel, he laid little crumbs that led to the Consortium, because he knew your obsession with beating them. And you know what? A dead human boy and a druid with no ability wrecked everything for him. Not the ones with so-called ability."

He shifted uncomfortably in the crèche. "That's simplifying things a bit."

"Is it? You've said to me on more than one occasion that I've left the path. Let me give you a bit of wisdom, Nigel. When you pick one path and never reconsider, you never know when you're lost. That's what's happened to the fey."

He pursed his lips. "If that's what makes you feel better over the loss of your abilities, Connor, then you really are lost."

I shook my head and smiled. "Here's something else I'm starting to learn, Nigel. Ability isn't just what you can do with essence. You've let your fey ability define you and your world. Without it, you're the one who's lost. Ability is a state of mind, too. If you consider nothing else, consider this: Somehow I succeeded against Gerin where you failed."

One side of his mouth dipped down in anger. "Happenstance."

I shrugged. "Call it what you like. Luck. Fate. Whatever. The Wheel of the World turns as it will, Nigel. You don't turn It. One of these days you'll figure that out. And when you do? That's when you'll really start learning."

And then I just left. Didn't wait for him to respond. Didn't wait for his permission to leave. I just left. As I passed through the door, I felt oddly elated. I meant every word I said. Better yet, I believed every word I said. Life gave me things, then took them away. It gave me a chance to reconsider everything. Luck or not, I was on a new path, one I didn't hate so much anymore. Not after finally understanding where and how I learned my arrogance and what it could do to twist you.

Guild security agents were hovering high overhead, still on high alert, as I left the hospital. Down in Back Bay, their Consortium counterparts patrolled the streets. Both the Guildhouse and the Consortium consulate were armed camps until who killed whom and why got sorted out, if it ever did. Even the Boston mayor had gotten into the act, declaring wide swathes of the city as no-fey zones to ease the human fears that it wasn't safe to be around the fey. Temporary, he says. We'll see.

No one would rest easy for a while. Gerin's spell had damaged essence, twisting it here, erasing it there, and weakening it everywhere. Uncertain tomorrows weighed on the minds of the great and the small. Deep-seated desires for power and control cluttered everything. The Consortium feared Seelie Court. Seelie Court feared the Consortium. They nursed angry grievances over Convergence and blamed each other for it happening. Humans fear the fey, and the fey fear the humans. And every night, everywhere, they all go to bed, fearing the dawn, tossing restlessly as they plot or worry about the new day, their sleep disrupted by unquiet dreams of power and hope and fear. Not a one of them knows what will happen. Some people look forward to that. Some dread it.

Joe flashed into the air next to me. "You okay?" he asked.

"Yeah. You?"

He put on quite the show of considering the answer. "Actually, I'm feeling a little faint."

He somersaulted in the air, screaming with laughter. We had been doing this routine all week.

"You know, Joe, you're obviously hiding your fear of death with jokes."

He stopped and looked at me doe-eyed. "Am I that transparent?"

I smiled. "I can see right through you, buddy."

He squealed and did loops. I glanced up at Avalon

Memorial, grateful that for once I wasn't lying inside. As we turned in the direction of the Weird, I shook my head at the turns my life had taken. Things change. The Wheel of the World turns the way It will. I had to get up in the morning, had to face the day and hope for the best. That's just the way it is. One door closes; another opens. A shiver went through me.

about the author

Mark Del Franco lives with his partner, Jack, in Boston, Massachusetts, where the orchids tremble in fear since Mark killed Jack's palm plants. Please visit his website at www.markdelfranco.com for more information about the Convergent World.